GATE CRASHERS

GATE CRASHERS

PATRICK S. **TOMLINSON**

A TOM DOHERTY ASSOCIATES BOOK
NEW YORK

This is a work of fiction. All of the characters, organizations, and events portrayed in this novel are either products of the author's imagination or are used fictitiously.

GATE CRASHERS

A Tor Book
Published by Tom Doherty Associates
175 Fifth Avenue
New York, NY 10010

www.tor-forge.com

The Library of Congress Cataloging-in-Publication Data is available upon request.

ISBN 978-0-7653-9864-2 (trade paperback)
ISBN 978-0-7653-9865-9 (ebook)

First Edition: June 2018

Printed in the United States of America

0 9 8 7 6 5 4 3 2 1

This book is dedicated to George Carlin, who taught me who to question and how to curse.

Magellan 1700m

Cargo Bays (6)

Reactor Cooling Fins

Reactor Cooling System Lines

Beamed Energy Receiver

Transfer Sail housing (Retracted)

Reactor Bulb

Exposed Gravity Well Projectors

Reactor Cone

Totally not Nuclear missiles

Just normal navigational Lasers. honest.

Beamed Energy Receiver

Transfer Sail Housing (Retracted)

He3 Tanks

Decoy/Probe Launchers

Small Craft Bay

Gravity Well Projectors/Hyperspace Window Generators Hidden inside

Bucephalus 900m

CHAPTER 1

It was a cold, dark night in deep space. Of course, that's the sort of night experienced spacers preferred. A hot, bright night meant you'd flown into an uncharted star. Such nights were known for their brevity.

The American/European Union Starship *Magellan* streaked through the vacuum at a sliver under half light speed. When christened sixty-two years ago, *Magellan* was heralded by reporters, tech writers, and industry mouthpieces as a marvel of engineering, which she was.

They also described her using words like *graceful*, *elegant*, and *sleek*, which she most certainly was not. The sight of *Magellan* brought to mind a seventeen-hundred-meter-long mechanical jellyfish with an inverted bell made of a giant dinner plate, drainage pipes, and an entire box of novelty bendy straws.

Buried beneath a jacket of water built into the ship's hull to shield them from cosmic radiation eager to redecorate their DNA, the crew chilled through the dull bits of their journey in cryogenic pods set at less than a tenth of a degree above freezing. Hearts beat once every other minute. Blood flowed with the speed of buttercream frosting. Dreams played at a pace that would make a Galápagos tortoise glance at its watch.

The year was 2345, and *Magellan*'s 157 peoplecicles were just a sliver over thirty light-years from Earth. As they slept, *Magellan* was hard at work. She balanced the deuterium flow to the beach-ball-sized star in her stern, which was the source of her power, extrapolated the trajectories of thousands of bits of stellar dust no bigger than a flake of crushed pepper, and then used her battery of navigational lasers to vaporize those flakes on intercept courses.

One would usually attribute the quaint human tendency to anthropomorphize machines as the reason the pronoun *she* was applied to a starship. However, *Magellan* herself had decided long ago that any entity that selflessly nurtured so many helpless children must be female.

As she pondered her myriad duties, one of her ranging lasers blinked, beeped, and generally made a nuisance of itself. *Magellan* gave it the cold shoulder for several nanoseconds before she caved to its persistence and queried its data packet to see what was so important it couldn't wait a millisecond.

What she found caused her only the second moment of confusion in her sixty-two years of operation. The first happened many years ago when her chief engineer had tried to explain the appeal of chewing tobacco, with little success.

This time was worse. The laser revealed an object, sixteen meters long, less than two light-hours ahead of her. After a few milliseconds of data streamed in, *Magellan* determined, while abnormally large for space dust, the object did not pose a direct threat, as it was not on an intercept course. Curiously, it was not on any course at all.

Out of tens of millions of particles *Magellan* had spotted, projected, and vaporized, she'd never observed one that wasn't moving. You didn't end up in the void between stars without inertia; it just wasn't possible. Because she was an exploration vessel, her software possessed a certain baseline curiosity, and the paradox of the object ate at her processors. However, her ability to make command-level decisions was deliberately limited to the protection of her crew while they were incapacitated. Since the object didn't pose a danger to crew safety, her programming didn't permit a course alteration. If she wanted more than the meager data she could acquire in a two-hundred-million-kilometer flyby, she'd need to wake the captain.

Safely waking from cryosleep was a two-hour ordeal. As the body slowly warmed, neurons fired with the vigor of an asthmatic 4×400 relay team. Imagine the pricking-needles sensation felt when an arm falls asleep and map it over one's entire body. If that weren't enough, the sluggish metabolism of cryo caused a buildup of the same toxins that result from a three-day bender.

This marked Allison Ridgeway's sixty-second cycle. As her consciousness stirred, Allison drew on the considerable experience she'd acquired in college to deal with the worst hangover imaginable. She kept her eyes closed until they stopped lying to her, placed one foot on the ground to anchor her sense of balance, then grabbed the pod's hydration tube and sucked down as much fluid as she could stomach. After an eternity, Allison sat up and pondered how to use her feet.

Something was missing.

"*Maggie?*"

"Yes, Captain Ridgeway?" answered a soothing voice that sounded suspiciously like her mother.

"Why don't I have a soul-crushing headache?"

"I don't know, Captain, but I can probably synthesize a compound to approximate the effects."

Allison smiled. It was tough knowing if *Maggie*, as she liked to call the ship, was still naïve or if she had developed a dry sense of humor. She suspected the latter.

"How long have I been out?"

"Three weeks, two days, seven—"

"Three weeks?" she asked. Crews woke for one week per year to keep their minds fresh. They'd gone through the cycle less than a month ago. "We just crossed the thirty. We won't reach Solonis B for eight months."

"That's correct, Captain. However, I require your judgment."

"You mean you require my authorization to indulge *your* judgment."

The *Magellan* reflected on this for a moment, and decided there was no reason to lie. "Yes, Captain. Please join me on the bridge."

"I'm not dressed."

"You're the only person awake."

"I'm freezing and covered in cryo snot, *Maggie*."

"Yes, of course. I await your arrival on the bridge once you're more comfortable."

"It's all right. You're in a hurry, I get it."

Allison staggered along the wall toward the showers. The hot water rinsed away the cold, viscous fluid clinging to her body, which felt and smelled like used fryer oil. She was glad not to wake with the headache for once.

Allison put her hair in a towel and walked to her locker. She retrieved a plush, embarrassingly expensive pink bathrobe with matching kitten slippers. It was a small luxury she afforded herself, and she sank into the depths of its soft warmth.

She moved to the RepliCaterer and finished her waking/hangover routine with an order of hot coffee with double cream, two sugars, and a grape popsicle, which it produced in seconds. The RepliCaterer was an amazing device. Half waste-recycling plant, half food processor. It was best for morale to ignore which half the food came from. Crews had long ago named it the DAQM—Don't Ask Questions Machine. Feeling vaguely human, the fuzzy pink captain made her way to the transit tube.

The bridge was awash with the gymnastic light of holograms and the dry breeze of air processors. It had the sterile yet lived-in look of a small-town doctor's lounge. Allison dropped into her chair and spilled the remains of her coffee into her lap.

She grabbed the towel from her head to rescue her bathrobe from the brown stain. "One of those mornings."

"Actually, Captain, it's 1537."

"The worst mornings usually start in the middle of the afternoon, *Maggie*. So what's important enough to wake me eight months early?"

A cloud of pitch black expanded in the air in front of Allison's chair as an intense holographic field persuaded the ambient light to saunter off somewhere else. A faint, blue, 3-D grid materialized. A small icon representing the *Magellan* appeared at the center, with course and velocity information in red.

There was a green circle far in the simulated distance with nothing but a single pinprick of white at its center. It, too, had course and velocity data displayed in red, but they both read *zero*.

"Magnify, please." A small box opened next to the green circle. The image inside was just a larger smudge. Allison grimaced, then glanced at the radar returns and spectrographic data. "Right, then. Our object is sixteen meters long with a high metal content. Great, we've discovered an iron meteor."

"Captain," *Magellan* purred, "is there anything else about this object you find interesting?"

Allison knew she was being patronized, but studied the numbers. With a flash of realization, her finger launched toward the ceiling, then pointed at the blurry image. "It's not moving. How does a rock get into deep space without momentum?"

"I arrived at the same conclusion; hence my decision to wake you."

"Good work, *Maggie*. What's our time to flyby?"

"Forty-seven minutes, six seconds from now."

"How close will we be able to get if we alter course?"

"At our current velocity, we will pass within ten light-minutes of the object."

"That's still more than an AU. If we start a full deceleration right now, how much of that can we cut?"

"Another four and a half million kilometers."

"Not nearly enough." Allison churned through a dozen other possibilities, but they were all worse.

Even with *Magellan*'s powerful eyes and ears, a flyby from such distance wouldn't improve on the smudge by much.

Allison fixed on her decision. "Well, nothing for it. *Maggie*, begin a full decel and plot a spiral course toward the object. We should be close enough by the third pass to get decent readings. Once we've satisfied your curiosity, we'll resume previous course and speed."

"Immediately, Captain."

"Why do I get the sense of playing a bit part in Kabuki theater?"

"I'm sure I don't know what you mean, Captain."

"Uh-huh." Allison felt a sudden kinship with harps.

Maggie poured a flood of deuterium into the nuclear furnace at her stern. A torrent of enraged electrons charged through the scaffolding of superconducting conduits connecting the reactor to the engines at the bow.

The engines were front-mounted because gravity propelled *Magellan*, at least that's what space was led to believe. In fact, protected behind the concave shield that formed her bow, bulky generators created and focused gravitons into a point ahead of the ship, duping the surrounding space-time into perceiving a large mass. Fooled by this theatrical bit of three-card monte, space obligingly curved itself into a well and pulled the ship forward. This was the origin of the slang term *yank*, as opposed to the more colorful etymologies proposed by several limericks popular among dockyard workers.

Allison felt the almost imperceptible lurch as the internal gravity adjusted to compensate for the appearance of a new gravity well a few degrees off their heading. Turn sharper than that, *Magellan*'s keel would break under the stress. With little to maneuver around in deep space, this wasn't usually an issue. Seconds flew by as Allison tried to stay on top of the riot of raw data the various sensors returned.

"Are there any other crew members you'd like me to wake?" *Magellan* asked.

"So I can get blamed for putting them through two hours of amateur acupuncture and vertigo just to see an asteroid? No, none of them have done anything to deserve that kind of treatment for at least twenty years. Then again, there was that spittoon incident . . ."

"Chief Engineer Billings threw his supply of chew into a waste receptacle after that unfortunate event, Captain," the ship added in defense of her personal physician.

"Really? He went cold turkey?"

"I don't believe he switched to turkey, Captain."

"No, it's a . . . never mind. So he quit?"

"Yes, for three days. Then he started growing a tobacco plant in hydroponics."

"It's the thought that counts, I suppose."

Crimson numbers on Allison's display trickled down as the range fell. Telescopes slowly resolved the smudge into a slightly more coherent blur, which wasn't much help. The spectrograph was another matter. It reported that the object was comprised primarily of titanium, with traces of several other metals, which was as likely to occur naturally as a petrified tree made of Portland cement. Allison was excited, and more than a little anxious.

Magellan broke the silence. "Captain, I'm detecting a signal coming from the object."

"Why are you only detecting it now?"

"The signal is weak. I mistook it for background static, but after correlating the last several hours of data, a pattern emerged."

Allison realized she was sweating. She felt torn between the hope of hearing a completely benign radio echo and the excitement and danger of discovering something more interesting. "Let's hear it, then," she said at last.

What came through the speakers had a musical quality. Specifically, the sound of a pipe organ being fed through an industrial shredder, complete with an organist in a mad dash to finish a concerto before the hammers reached his seat. Yet as alien as it was, she knew instinctively the sound wasn't static. There were patterns and rhythm in the noise. Allison Ridgeway, captain of the AEUS *Magellan*, successfully beat back the impulse to hide under her chair.

She took a moment not to vomit. "*Maggie*, forget the spiral course.

Bring us to a zero-zero intercept, five clicks from the object. Wake everyone. I want that thing in *my*—I mean, *your*—shuttle bay yesterday. And get the QER online. I need to talk to Earth."

"Immediately, Captain Ridgeway." *Magellan* tried not to let any smug vindication creep into her tone.

Without success.

CHAPTER 2

A moment should be devoted to explain the groundbreaking technology referred to as the QER. The Quantum Entanglement Radio is one of the great accomplishments of mankind, although it had so far failed to supplant sliced bread for the top spot in popular colloquialism. The QER operated through the principle of quantum entanglement. At the core of each set of devices sat a pair of neutrons. Once entangled, these neutrons precisely imitated each other's behavior instantly and over any distance as if by magic—which, if you're honest, is all quantum mechanics is, minus the hats, rabbits, and bisected lovely assistants, but only because these things don't exist at subatomic scales.

The rest of the device was comprised of an impossibly small gravitational manipulator that controlled the spin direction and speed of the particle, and very sensitive Heisenberg detectors to record the reply. These functioned by surreptitiously observing the entangled particle from behind a nanoscale newspaper and dark sunglasses, so as not to arouse suspicion. With this device, it was possible to send messages any distance instantly and with complete security, as there is no signal to intercept, jam, or modify.

It used to be believed that any outside force acting on one of the particles would break the entanglement, but as it turns out, that chap forgot to carry a one in his calculations, leading to his departure from the physics community and the complete unraveling of the Grand Unified Theory of Everything, since sarcastically known as the Grand Cock-Up.

There were drawbacks to QER communications, however. First, bandwidth was minimal. And second, only two neutrons could entangle, so there could only be direct communication between two points—wherever the paired machines happened to be. Typically, each colony world had a QER for its immediate neighbors and one back to Earth, and each yank ship had a pair connected directly to Fleet Communications. One primary, the other backup.

It was such a machine aboard *Magellan* that kept her in contact with Earth. It was this machine's twin deep in a basement outside Washington, D.C., that disturbed the slumber of Professor Eugene Graham.

Professor Graham was busy sawing a pile of logs that could jam up the Missouri River when an alarm woke him with a start.

Eventually, he gained control of his body and picked up the offending phone from the nightstand. A weak holographic field traced a ghostly image of his assistant, annoyingly well groomed for the middle of the night. At this hour, one should look as if they'd just been mugged.

"God, Jeffery, what? It's ten past two."

"I'm sorry to wake you, Professor, but you're needed in the Fleet Com QER Center right away."

The title *professor* was a remnant from Graham's previous life as the dean of Cornell University. Eugene's life took a rather drastic turn a few years ago when, against all odds, one of his former students, Danielle Fenton, achieved a stable political orbit and was actually elected. The newly minted member of the American/European Union Parliament submitted Professor Graham's name for consideration to lead the American/European Space Administration. The president offered him the post soon after. In an uncharacteristic fit of ambition, Eugene had accepted.

Eugene held the faint hope that he wouldn't have to get out of bed. He certainly didn't hold with the concept of being on call. In his measured opinion, being on call should be reserved for lines of work of a critical nature. Like delivering babies, or Chinese food.

"Can you forward the message?"

"Ah, no, Professor. Trust me."

Eugene sighed. "Naturally. Give me an hour. And tousle your hair. You look much too presentable for this time of night. People will get suspicious." He cut the connection, gave his young wife a peck on the neck, swung his legs to the floor, and made his way to the wardrobe.

While he dressed, he remembered his aircar was in for maintenance, so he keyed the automated valet to fetch his wife's and headed for the garage. His wife's small, sporty aircar waited patiently in the rooftop garage a minute later, gull-wing door open. He half stooped, half crawled in and reclined his ample girth into the seat.

"Good morning, Professor. Where would you like to go today?" asked the bright blue car.

"Well, I would like to go to Havana for a week, but I guess I'll have to settle for the Stack."

"Very good. Estimated flight time is twenty-three minutes. Door closing." The car's wispy wings unfurled from the fuselage like cigar wrappers. Thousands of tiny turbines whined to life. The aircar gently rose out of the central atrium of the garage, then accelerated into the cool night on the sound of an orchestra of mosquitoes.

The situation was probably bad. Disastrous, more likely. Jeffery was much too eager to please to be rude, so both the hour of his call and the fact he wouldn't discuss whatever the QER had to say were very troubling indeed.

Scenarios washed over the professor's mind like waves at high tide. Space exploration had always been a risky business. Disasters were constantly just a few degrees, centimeters, or a tiny course error away. Many ships had simply lost communication with home a dozen light-years away, passing into history as another mystery among dozens. Others radioed home that they'd been hit by a radiation spike and would succumb within hours. One infamous incident ended after a faulty operating system upgrade caused the ship's computer to mistake the crew for poultry, with tragic results when they failed to produce eggs. It took a special kind of personality to accept such a way of life. Eugene assumed it was testosterone poisoning, but that didn't explain the women . . .

The lights of Washington, D.C., glowed on the horizon. Whereas most major cities had a skyline of buildings that resembled a bell curve in their height, D.C. was inverted. The closer to the center one was, the shorter and older the buildings were. The blue aircar glided gracefully around the monuments and museums. It abruptly warped its wings to skirt the edges of the no-fly zone that surrounded the historic seat of the nation's power, painted bright white in an affront to purity. A roof-mounted battery of surface-to-air missiles tracked him as he passed with the feigned interest of a bored sentinel. The contents of Eugene's stomach made a pitched effort to storm the gates of his esophagus until the turn had completed.

The Stack was soon in sight. It was an immense, five-sided tower that had started life four hundred years earlier as the Pentagon building. The original structure had become the ground-floor levels of the tower as new layers were added year by year.

It was not the home of AESA headquarters, which was Berlin, but for purposes of global security, it was the permanent location of Fleet Com. It was widely agreed upon that no one was more paranoid than Americans. It only made sense that the securest location for AESA's network of QERs would be in the center of America's securest building.

Eugene's aircar was challenged by the building's automated air traffic control. Codes were exchanged, clearance was certified, and towers of disappointed weapons ringing the facility like fence posts stood down. The car nestled into an available slot and wrapped its wings around itself like a sleeping bat. With considerable effort and groaning, Eugene exited the tiny sports car and made his way to the entrance at a brisk pace. He arrived at the first of many checkpoints, each with identification and verification procedures that became more uncomfortably personal as they went.

"Good evening, gents." Eugene presented his hand to the door guards for his blood vessel scan.

The larger of the two guards looked up from his display after he read the name, stood to attention, and threw a crisp salute. He was as dark as five to midnight and appeared to be made of recycled warship keels.

"Professor Graham?"

"Yes, indeed."

"I'm your escort, sir," replied the guard in a flat tone.

"Well, I certainly wouldn't want to get between you and your duty. By all means, lead the way."

The two men walked down an endless series of halls and elevators. They formed a walking contradiction; the pasty middle-aged academic with no clearly defined waist, and the dark young marine with no clearly defined neck. The exception was in the eyes, which betrayed a fierce competence in both of them. They passed the expected series of security checkpoints and were waved through without challenge. They passed the door for the Fleet Com conference room, yet still they walked.

Eugene grew uncomfortable with the silence and unfamiliar surroundings. So he decided to attempt conversation. "So have you been assigned here long"—he snuck a look at the guard's nameplate—"Corporal Harris?"

"I'm not allowed to say, sir."

"Oh, well, then, how long have you been in the service?"

"I'm not allowed to say."

"Ah." Eugene felt flummoxed. "Are you from D.C.?"

"Not allowed to say that either, sir."

"Oh, come now, surely there's some nail we can hang a friendly conversation on."

"Of course there is," the corporal said. "We aren't just mindless automatons, you know."

"Well, no, I didn't mean to suggest . . ." Eugene was suddenly treading water.

"Heck, there's a whole list of topics that are authorized for use in everyday conversation with civilians."

"Okay, perfect. So what's the first item on the list?" asked Eugene as he grasped at the opportunity to get back on track.

The corporal looked sheepish. "I'm not allowed to talk about the list, sir."

"Right." Somehow the professor was unsurprised. "Well, how about I take a guess at a few topics and you can let me know if they're permitted?"

"That should be fine."

"Excellent. All right, can you talk about your family?"

"Absolutely not, sir. Gotta keep them safe from kidnapping or blackmail."

"Of course. That was silly of me. Football?"

"Not since some of the boys got into trouble with gambling debts."

"Weather?" ventured Eugene.

"Off limits since the development of the lightning gun and the tornado bomb."

"There's a tornado *bomb*?"

"Can't talk about the—"

Eugene waved an irritated hand. "Yes, yes. How about pets?"

"Pets? Sure, pets are fine."

"Excellent. So, Corporal, do you keep any pets?"

"No. I have allergies."

Eugene sighed. "Should have seen that coming. How much farther do we have to go, and don't tell me you can't talk about it."

"We're nearly there, sir."

"Excellent. Not that this hasn't been lovely, you understand."

After one last elevator ride, they reached the QER center proper, which took up an entire subbasement level. The doors opened to a stark white hallway. The end of the hallway was occupied by a very serious-looking metal blast door and an even more serious-looking marine Mk VI urban battle android. You could tell it was an urban model because it was only two meters tall and its weapons could *only* punch through several human bodies, but not the reinforced concrete wall behind them. Eugene didn't bother trying to strike up a conversation with it.

"Don't worry about him. He's activated only if things go south," said the corporal. "He's offline right now. They're remotely piloted by a marine operator anyway."

Eugene waved a hand in front of what he assumed were the machine's eyes. He mulled over the similarities between the battle android and Harris standing at attention.

"What gives it away?" he asked the young marine.

"They have a slight electric whine when they're active." Harris unlocked the blast door with a quick handprint and voice recognition.

The heavy door slid open with a pneumatic hiss. As the corporal turned to squeeze his shoulders through the entrance, Eugene reflected that young Harris could make a passable door in a pinch. The corporal stopped and opened one of several small drawers built into the wall.

"Please place your phone and any other electronic devices in here. You'll also need to power down any cybernetic implants as long as you're inside."

Eugene handed over his mobile phone. "All I have in my head is an eAssistant. It doesn't have a wireless connection."

Harris shook his head as he took the phone and placed it in the drawer. "Wireless isn't the issue. It's electromagnetic radiation."

"Ah. Finicky little devils."

While the battle android was certainly there for security purposes, the thirty-centimeter-thick door was not intended solely to discourage interlopers. The thickness of the walls and doors also isolated the entangled particles from any outside interference. The sensitivity of the QERs housed inside the next room put even the skills of a pea-detecting princess to shame.

Harris stood as far to the side as his size would allow. "I'll wait just outside to escort you back once you're finished."

"You're not coming in?"

"No, I don't have the clearance. Besides, between us, I have a feeling if anyone heard whatever message you were brought down here to see, they'd be changing assignments before they could even pack."

As Eugene stepped into the room for the first time, he felt the cool, dry air and low hum that betrayed the presence of superconductors. Humidity was kept very low to keep moisture's close friend corrosion from crashing the party. Bright display screens marked rows of machines. The hushed voices of a handful of techs in white coats were the only sounds to be heard above the din of electronics. Eugene's mind latched onto the memory of a monastery he had visited in his youth.

"What are you doing in here?"

The sharp voice from behind startled the professor out of contemplation. He turned to see a short man with wild silver hair whose eyes bored into him like corkscrews, which was quite a trick from behind his nuclear-rated safety glasses. He wore the same white coat as the others, but carried an old-fashioned clipboard and pen. An abacus hung from his neck.

With a sharpened tongue, he spoke again. "I asked you a question, sir. What is your purpose here?"

Eugene fumbled, "Who are you?"

"Who am I?" His voice rose. "Who am I, asks the impertinent stranger. I'm the QER Keeper, that's who. And anyone who has any business being here would know that already. So once more, who are you?"

"I, sir, am Professor Eugene Graham, administrator of the American/European Space Agency. I also happen to be the person who sets your department's budget and personnel allotments. I am here by the request of my personal assistant, whom I expect to be led to presently." Eugene leaned over the smaller man as he spoke, crushing him with the weight of his position.

The man relented and his voice changed. "Ol'right, no need for bruised feelin's. Me and my mates was just havin' a bit o' fun. It's pretty dull down here most o' the time." He motioned to the closest tech. "Hey, Marvin, go get that Jeffery fellow. There's a good lad."

"Er, thank you." Unsure of exactly which of the Keeper's façades was the act, Eugene was uneasy. "I suppose you don't get many visitors."

"Not a daily happenin', if ya follow." He looked at his clipboard for a moment. "But neither is a packet like this li'l bugga. Normally, we just write a daily report and send it on up. Sometimes, we see somethin' sensitive come in and we use our discretion on how much crypto to use. But we didn' even want to let this one through the Net." The Keeper let his glasses slip down his nose and looked Eugene directly in the eye. "We called your office, sir, but the only person still around was young Jeffery. He said he'd fetch you for us. This is the definitive need-to-know kinda packet, mind."

Eugene's thoughts sprinted. He'd never been called directly to the QER center before. He'd been to briefings at Fleet Com's office frequently, but that was many levels up. The topics of those meetings had been dark; lost ships, a plague ravaging the Tau Ceti colony. In the past, bad news was limited to merely traveling fast. Now, it could arrive instantly. Even in the parched air, Eugene was sweating.

"Here's your man now," said the Keeper.

The lightly muscled frame that carried Jeffery around lagged about a second behind him. He always seemed to be several steps ahead of everyone, including himself. It made for a very good, if a bit awkward, assistant. Eugene noticed that Jeffery's hair remained resolute.

"Good morning, Professor."

"Morning comes with the sun, Jeffery," said Eugene. "This is still evening."

"Um, yes. Sorry about that. I see you've already met Dr. Kiefer."

Jeffery cocked an eyebrow and glanced in the direction of the retreating Keeper, who busied himself sliding beads back and forth. "He's very . . . dedicated."

"*Committed* might be the word I'd pick." Eugene looked back to his assistant. "So what's this message, and how bad is it?"

"Well, it's not exactly . . . it's probably better if you just look for yourself. The *Magellan*'s machine is this way."

"Ridgeway's ship? It just reported in a few weeks ago to confirm they'd crossed the thirty-yard line. What happened to them?"

"Come see for yourself. It's just over there." Jeffery started walking before Eugene could respond.

As they passed unit after unit, the professor noticed the machines becoming progressively bulkier. The displays were more primitive. Fonts retreated backward through time. It felt like walking through an industrial museum. He passed one with a physical keyboard with a tiny logo of an apple with a bite missing. Since they only worked as paired units, QERs had to be replaced simultaneously, which might not happen for decades between trips. The oldest machines down here had run incessantly for almost a century.

The two men neared the back of the room, where Jeffery slid to a stop in front of two machines labeled AEUS *Magellan* A and B. He pulled up a message log on the first machine and highlighted the most recent entry.

"Well, here it is." Jeffery stepped out of the way to allow the professor closer. Eugene leaned in to read the message.

FROM: CAPTAIN ALLISON RIDGEWAY, CO, AEUS *MAGELLAN*

TO: ADMINISTRATOR, AESA

MESSAGE TEXT:

FOUND ARTIFACT SIXTEEN METERS LONG FLOATING IN DEEP SPACE THREE DAYS AGO. RECOVERED. CURRENTLY RESIDING IN SHUTTLE BAY TWO. PRELIMINARY EXAM TO FOLLOW.

STRONGLY SUSPECT NONHUMAN ORIGINS. PLEASE ADVISE.

END

Eugene sat for several seconds in stunned silence. His brain had read the last line of the message, but it just wasn't connecting the dots. He didn't know Allison Ridgeway personally, due to the fact that when *Magellan* launched, he was still trying to master the intricacies of two-legged locomotion. He was very familiar with her file, though. She was imminently qualified for her position as head of the expedition. Her mission reports were always thorough and punctual. She didn't seem like the sort disposed to histrionic overreaction.

"Professor?" Jeffery looked anxious, which ran counter to his usual grating state of wide-eyed excitement. "What are we going to do?"

"Do you remember what Montezuma II did when he mistook Cortés for Quetzalcoatl?"

"Yeah?"

"Hopefully not that."

"Okay . . ." Jeffery paused. "I was thinking in more immediate terms."

"Right, sorry." Eugene felt the weight of the future piling on top of him. "This is a little above our pay grade, Jeffery. We need a meeting with the president's team first thing in the morning."

"That's a pretty tall order, Professor. They don't move around the president's schedule on a whim, you know. What should I tell them?"

"The truth. That should suffice, for once. We have to get a game plan together before this hits the holos tomorrow."

"But we're the only people who know, aside from Dr. Kiefer and his men."

"That's more than enough vectors. Something will slip. It always does." Eugene turned toward the door. "Now then, I'm going home so that I can lose sleep somewhere more comfortable. Call me once you have the meeting arranged."

"What should we tell Ridgeway?"

Eugene slapped his forehead. "Of course, this is why I need you, Jeffery." He walked back to the QER interface, typed out a reply, and hit Send. They both headed back toward the door while the device worked its magic over the light-years. Eugene stopped near Dr. Kiefer and waved the man over.

"Now, Doctor. I scarcely need to explain the gravity of our situation. It is absolutely critical that we keep this under wraps until the government has time to prepare a plan of action and an official statement. If this isn't handled properly, it could lead to a public panic that would make the African Food Riots look like an ice cream social."

"Right you are, sir. We'll keep the ol' lips tight, no worries."

"Excellent. I know I can count on you."

The wild-haired man walked back to speak with his subordinates.

Eugene leaned over to whisper to Jeffery. "I give it until noon." He stepped to the door and looked back as it opened. "Once you have the meeting set, go home and get some sleep. I have a feeling we're both going to run low in the coming weeks."

With that, Eugene stepped through the door and nodded to Corporal Harris, who'd taken up position next to the android. Eugene took a moment to center himself and collect his thoughts.

"I'm ready to go home, Corporal."

"Very good, sir."

The door hissed open again, and Jeffery walked into the hall with something in his hand. He passed the two battle androids and held his hand out to the professor.

"You forgot your phone, sir."

"Oh, thank you, Jeffery. I'm obviously running on empty."

"Yes, sir, just go home and have a nightcap. Try not to think about the alien artifact." Jeffery heard someone behind him clear their throat. He turned around to realize in a moment of mortal terror that one of the androids was actually an enormous marine.

"I suppose you didn't see me here," Harris said with a tool-hardened edge to his voice.

"No, I thought you were a . . . oh no . . ." Jeffery looked at the man in much the same way a cornstalk views an approaching combine.

"It's all right, Jeffery. It's too late to change now," Eugene said gently. "It wouldn't have happened had I remembered my phone."

Corporal Harris let out a resigned sigh and looked the smaller man in the eye. "It's all right. It could have happened to anyone this late." He turned to address the professor. "I don't suppose *artifact* means broken pottery or flint arrowheads?"

"Not unless they were deer hunting in the vacuum of space," confirmed Eugene. "I'm sorry, Corporal Harris, but it looks like you're going to need to do that rapid packing we spoke about."

CHAPTER 3

Two hundred and eighty-five trillion kilometers away, someone else's night had stretched to infinity. Three days had passed since Allison ordered *Magellan* to a standstill. The entire crew was assembled in Shuttle Bay Two to hear their captain say something inspiring and historic. She was having enough trouble focusing on the next few minutes, much less coming generations. Her crew divided themselves into the usual peer groups of officers, academics, and technical specialists. It wasn't that different from your average junior prom, only their names had letters before or after them, usually ending in *D*.

The bay was optimized to launch and recover *Magellan*'s atmospheric shuttles. It was not optimized for sweeping oratories. As a result, the echoes of 157 people packed into a room already full of shuttles and mysterious artifacts had reached concert levels.

"Everyone, if I could please have your attention. Quiet down, please." Allison's voice didn't pass the first row, beaten back by waves of noise. "Excuse me. I'd like to get started . . ."

A whistle pierced the air like an arrow. "*Stow it!*" shouted Commander Marcel Gruber, Allison's executive officer. The order was obeyed involuntarily as every set of teeth in the room had gritted against the whistle. "*Better!*" He motioned to Allison. "Your floor, ma'am."

Allison nodded thanks. Ignoring the tiny tuning fork lodged in her right ear, she stepped up to the podium—well, a tool locker the size and shape of a podium. "As you're all aware, we haven't arrived at Solonis B. It's been only three and a half weeks since the beginning of our last sleep cycle. *Magellan* woke me three days ago when she spotted something . . . out of place."

Every eye in the bay glanced toward the artifact. About the length of an airbus, it was a seamless, polished silver, speckled with tiny micro-meteor craters. It looked like an hourglass stretched in a taffy puller. A block of unintelligible characters scribed into one of the metal lobes taunted them.

"At this point, we know nothing more about it than what can be seen with naked eyes. But that is going to change, people. Through luck or providence, we've been entrusted with this discovery. Ours are the only hands and tools that will handle it for decades. We all signed up to explore and push back the horizon. Well, the horizon of human knowledge sits right over there"—she threw a finger at the artifact without breaking eye contact with her crew—"and we're going to push until we find the *edge*."

Allison really put some Tabasco sauce on the last word, but she was rewarded by only a handful of harrumphs and a smattering of claps. Most of the crew continued looking anxiously over their shoulders. The murmur started again.

A voice managed to struggle to the surface. "We don't even know what it is. What if it's a mine or something?" The speaker was too short to see above the crowd.

"Well, one telltale sign of mines is the way they explode when they get near a ship. Seeing how it's already inside . . ." This outburst of common sense came from Ensign Wheeler, Allison's helmsman.

"What about the runes?" It was one of the engineers.

"Maybe they're warning labels!" shouted one of the environmental techs. "Like, 'Danger. Radioactive. Keep your balls at least one kilometer away!' "

The deep Southern drawl of Chief Engineer Billings came to life.

"If y'all think I brung that thing on board without passin' it by a Geiger counter first, y'all're duller than a field of sun-dried cow chips."

Some of the wind spilled from the sails of discontent, if only to permit the crew to ponder the nature of *cow chips*, which were not, as some of them assumed, thin slices of dried beef.

Content, the engineer looked back to his captain. "Ma'am, you wus sayin'?"

"Thank you, Chief." Allison raised her hands, palms out. "I expect once Earth has time to form a plan, we'll be ordered to come about and bring the artifact home." She let that settle in for a moment.

"I know we all have questions, serious questions. So we're going to work around the clock to find the answers." She held her breath for a moment and then took the plunge. "I intend to set up research teams to work rotating shifts while the rest of the crew sleeps."

Shouting exploded through the bay. Then Gruber's dreaded whistle hit them like an artillery volley. "This expedition may not be military, but this isn't a town council meeting either! The lady is in charge. Don't like it, you all know where the exit is." The XO pointed toward the clamshell doors that led outside. There was a small welcome mat on the floor, right next to the dachshund shoe brush.

The captain's gentle voice nudged aside the heavy curtain of embarrassed silence to resume her speech. "I don't think the choices need to be quite that extreme. We will start the rotations on a volunteer basis. If that proves insufficient, we will draw lots. No one will be excluded, not even command staff." She paused. "However, since we all volunteered to be here in the first place, I don't expect that will be necessary." Allison looked around the room, lingering on the eyes of a select, vocal few, until she was confident that she wouldn't need to go looking for straws to draw.

"We have a unique opportunity, people. Right there sits the proof of intelligent life beyond Earth that we've searched out for ten thousand generations. It simply doesn't get bigger than this. The chance to find that proof is the reason most of us gave up more than a century to be here.

"When I first realized what we had found, I was reminded of an ancient Chinese curse: 'May you live in interesting times.' I'm here to tell you, our times are going to be very interesting. AESA is assembling a crack team on Earth to handle the data and convert what we've discovered into usable science for our industries back home. We're going to be their eyes and ears. Literally everyone back home will be waiting with bated breath for every terabyte of data we can give them. So let's all do our part to ensure the ship runs smoothly and that we get good, accurate analysis of the artifact back to Earth as fast as the QER can relay it." She stepped back from the podium and crossed her hands behind her back. "Dismissed!"

A surge of cheers went around the bay. Even the few hecklers seemed to join in the exuberance.

Allison and Gruber walked away from the podium when Dorsett, the flight ops officer, approached them. Flight ops was a natural fit for Jacqueline. She appeared perpetually ready to take flight herself.

"Yes, Jackie, what is it?" Allison asked.

"Um, hello, Captain. I really liked your speech. I, ah, I have something I'd like you to see . . . I mean, have."

"Oh, wonderful, may I see it?"

"Um, yes, it's, ah . . ." Jacqueline reached into her cavernous backpack until it looked like she might fall in. Her arm returned with a yellow-and-black book. Not a page-reader screen, an actual paper-and-ink book.

Allison took the offered gift and read the title aloud: "*First Contact for Dummies: The Complete Idiot's Guide to the Most Important Moment in History.*" Allison choked on a giggle and let out a little cough instead. She looked at Marcel. "It's nice to know the crew has so much confidence in their captain."

"Oh, no, ma'am, I didn't mean—that is, I don't think . . ." Jacqueline's eyes went wide.

"Jackie, it's all right." She put her hand on the younger woman's shoulder. "I was only kidding. It's a lovely gift. Where did you find it?"

"It was my mum's, ma'am. She was with SETI. She bought it as an antique and always kept it near her desk, just in case. When I was accepted for *Magellan*'s crew, she gave it to me. She said, 'You'll be closer to the action than I'll ever get.' But if anyone here is going to be the first, it's going to be you, Captain. So I thought you could use it more than I could."

"I love it, Jackie. Tell your mother that I will read it, cover to cover."

"I wish I could, ma'am. She died eight years ago. Real years, that is." The young woman's eyes began to mist over.

Einstein said time was relative, but he never went through cryogenic sleep, skipping through the years one week at a time. For the universe at large, her mother had departed nearly a decade ago. For Jacqueline, it had been two months.

Allison realized she didn't hold a book but a Dorsett family heirloom. She held it to her chest and squeezed.

"Thank you, Jackie. I mean it. We're going to do your mom proud. Okay?"

"Okay." Her voice cracked, just a little, before she clamped down on it.

Allison switched to her captain setting. "You've got to get my shuttle refueled and repacked, yes?"

Dorsett nodded.

"Well, then, round up your people and get to it. You never know what we'll need it for next, right?"

"Yes, ma'am."

Jacqueline disappeared behind the shuttle.

Allison gave herself a little shake. "Sometimes I forget what everyone gave up to be here," she said to her XO.

"It's the life, ma'am; we all know what's coming when we get in the cryopod."

Allison shook her head. "I thought I knew what was coming before my preflight physical. I was wrong then, too."

CHAPTER 4

Felix Fletcher was on edge. This was not unusual, but his current anxiety was several standard deviations above the norm. Several factors were responsible.

First, he was on a collision course with the largest man-made object ever built. Second was the situation that had hurtled Felix away from Earth in the middle of dinner. A yank inbound from a two-decade-long resupply trip to Proxima Centauri had blown two of its gravity projectors spooling up to decelerate. Slowing it down was going to be, well . . . an optimist would say interesting, challenging, exciting, even. But since Felix's nerves resembled a loose bundle of stripped, live wires, he had a different set of adjectives.

Born in New Detroit, Luna, Felix spent his childhood in the moon's half-hearted gravity. Among Lunies, he was average height and solidly built, which meant among children of Earth, he was tall, gangly, and an unhealthy pallid color. Nature had boosted his mental-lifting capacity attempting to compensate. However, as any owner of a high-performance noggin could tell you, it just added another layer of social awkwardness.

Despite these setbacks, Felix had not turned into a basement-dwelling recluse. His talents for mathematics and constant tinkering had landed him in an exceptional graduate engineering program, and he was considered something of a prodigy inside the gravity propulsion community. Today, his abilities would be put to the test, as he'd been asked to troubleshoot the stricken yank while it hurtled through the Sol system at 40 percent light speed.

Directly ahead, and growing ominously in his field of vision, was the Unicycle, a circular particle accelerator five thousand kilometers in circumference. It was built in orbit at the L1 Lagrange point, one of the points in space where the game of tug-of-war between sun and Earth played to a draw. The sunward side was a ring of solar panels five kilometers across, powering the station and providing shade to keep the superconducting electromagnetic coils at a crisp and efficient three degrees above zero. Not the balmy zero on Earth, where thermometers are given a minus range so Northerners can puff out their chests about how tough the winters are. The real, absolute zero, which doesn't have negatives because there's nowhere else to go.

The array had a surface area of 24,920 square kilometers. With solar energy density at L1 of two kilowatts per square meter and 65 percent panel conversion efficiency, the Unicycle had 32.4 *terawatts* of electricity on tap. Or, if you like, the combined power output of forty-five billion horses, without the grain requirements or stables to muck.

It was a successor to the *Really* Large Hadron Collider in response to the failure of the Second (We Think That's Got it) Theory of Everything. The few physicists brave and/or delusional enough to tackle the Third (Fine, You Do it, Then) Theory of Everything ran their experiments inside. The array could also beam power to yanks on their way out of the system, and again on the way back in, greatly reducing the reactor mass they needed to carry.

It was built by a French consortium whose institutional experience spanned centuries, all the way back to the original LHC. The drawbacks to the French team were that the Unicycle only worked thirty hours per week and frequently started smoking.

"Excuse me, but are we going to start decelerating soon?" Felix squeaked to the pilot.

"We don't start our reverse for another fifteen minutes, Mr. Fletcher," the pilot responded curtly.

"Oh, okay. It's just that it looks awfully big. You have a lovely shuttle here. Very posh. I'd hate to see anything happen to it, or any of the passengers. Or crew, mind you."

"Yes, sir, but it looks big because, frankly, it *is* big."

"Right, then. I'll just, um, leave you to avoiding collisions, and other important piloting duties." He returned to his seat and his fidgeting. It wasn't that he disliked space travel. The empty space wasn't the part of the trip that worried him.

Felix glanced up from his duty-free catalog and saw the "Fasten Harness" light flick on overhead, accompanied by a three-minute countdown. This wasn't the gentle suggestion it would be on a terrestrial airline flight, mainly because the crew didn't want to clean up the mess if one of their passengers hit a bulkhead at five g's of deceleration. Nor was the harness a simple lap belt, but a web of thick straps and industrial-strength buckles strong enough to tie down a shipping container. At least they didn't waste time dithering about with safety lectures. Few people held illusions about the survival prospects of a space accident.

He got himself situated with thirty seconds to spare; just enough time to finish his drink before the shuttle flipped like a coin and the pilot pushed the throttle through the windshield. He let out a chirp as the harness did its best to squeeze his internal organs out through his nose. While the other passengers suffered under five times Earth gravity, he was subjected to *thirty* times moon gravity.

The beating continued for almost ten minutes before the pilot returned the throttles to neutral and Felix returned to weightlessness. By that time, the portals were totally filled by the Unicycle.

They drifted close enough to make out a few of the thin spokes that gave the facility its informal name. These spokes contained transfer tubes and power relays and connected to the docking hub and control center located in the center of the ring. Retro rockets fired. Once the shuttle had a solid lock with the Unicycle, Felix poured himself into the aisle and sloshed his way to the exit door, pretty sure he'd broken a rib or six.

After many flights into space, he'd learned not to check a bag. Anything security didn't confiscate became subject to a sorting system seemingly governed by a roulette wheel. Some statisticians claimed just randomly grabbing a bag from a different flight increased your odds of getting the right set of luggage.

Felix made his way to the check-in desk. Within an hour, he sat with over a dozen scientists and engineers doing their level best to make the crowded conference room look like an unsupervised day care. Data pads and holos displaying diagnostic results and course projections lay strewn about like discarded toys. Shouts and hand gestures from several continents permeated the air while the countdown clock wound its way toward zero.

Felix pecked away on a tablet and sat quietly in a forgotten corner, cross-checking his own projections against the simulations being run by the facility's Space Traffic Control computer. Math was his marble; tangents, cosigns, and vectors were his chisels and hammers. While the rest of the room argued over why their plans wouldn't work, he tried to find one that would.

Eventually, there was a lull in the battle while the parties regrouped and retrenched. Felix used the pause to spring his surprise attack.

"I think I have a solution," he proclaimed, rather meekly.

The announcement struck the collected scientists like a falling leaf. One of the older men broke away from the maelstrom and gave Felix a sideways glance.

"Did you say something, my boy?" Felix recognized him as Dr. Shuler of Cambridge.

"I said, I think I've hit on a solution."

Shuler chuckled. "Well, son, it's one thing to hit on a solution, but quite another to take it home."

Felix's eyes narrowed, and he tried to stare daggers at the man. He managed butter knives. "I'm cooking it breakfast."

The rest of the heads in the room turned to evaluate the new challenger. Several of them licked their lips.

"All right, then. Step right up, my boy, and let's hear all about this well-fed solution." Dr. Shuler swept his hand wide in a mocking invitation to the table.

Felix stepped up and linked his tablet to the holo-projector at the center of the table. Numbers and schematics danced in the air before him.

"Now, as we all know, the *Conestoga*'s down two gravity generators, cause unknown. Normally, we'd shut down the modules opposing the failed units to bring the system back into balance, but because the crew ran their diagnostic tests late, the failure was caught late. So now we can't afford to lose two more modules if we want to stop the ship in time."

This was a heavily censored version of what the rest of the room had yelled back and forth for the last hour.

"Since we can't shut down any additional modules, I've worked out a program that will redistribute power, reducing it to the modules opposing the burned-out ones, while increasing it to the adjoining ones to compensate."

"That's great, but you'll end up with the same power levels as if you were missing four units." The objection came from a thin, hawkish-looking, middle-aged man.

"Not really, because my program bypasses the safety limiters and gooses three of the modules to 135 percent."

This was met by three gasps, two chuckles, and one blank stare.

The hawk swooped in to pounce. "That's crazy, kid. You're begging for them to fuse just like the others. Engineers don't pick a spot to call 100 percent capacity out of a hat, you know!"

Felix absorbed the man's patronizing tone and let it fuel him. This was his territory, and he was going to defend it. He looked straight at him, hard enough for the man to avert his gaze.

"Yes, that's true. As it turns out, I do know a thing or two about engineering. I spent two days in a shuttle getting here, which left me with time to read the technical literature of the Mk 7a Gravity Projector Module. All of it." He paused. "In military applications, it has been rated for 125 percent emergency output for up to sixteen hours."

"That's the military version; this is a civilian transport," interrupted another scientist with an air of finality. "Those ratings don't apply to our modules."

"The only significant difference between the military and civilian models is the amount of shielding on the outer casings. The internal components are virtually identical. The ratings remain valid." Felix rolled right over the objection and pressed forward.

"So we're only going past their proven capacity by another 10 percent, and I think we can mitigate the risk of failure further if we divert the coolant flow from the fused units to the ones we're running harder. It should be a simple matter for the ship's engineers to reroute the plumbing."

A sturdy-looking man with rough hands stood to face him. "That's easy to say when you're not the one trying to hold a pipe wrench through a vac suit glove."

"If you can think of a way to get me out there in time, I'll do it myself." Felix held his ground.

The mechanic didn't relent. "Just who the hell do you think you—"

A throat cleared. The assembled scientists, engineers, and administrators turned to face the sound, which had come from a small woman with silver-streaked auburn hair sitting at the head of the table. Where the director sat.

"I think we all agree that M'sieur Fletcher's proposal is crazy, *oui*?" asked Renée Lemieux.

She was met with nods and a guffaw from around the room. They began to resume their bickering.

"Quiet." Her tone changed from light to reproachful. "For the last hour, you've all argued over very safe plans that can't work. M'sieur Fletcher has proposed a very risky plan that might." She let the words echo in their heads for a moment. "So if a better idea hasn't presented itself in ten minutes, we move on Fletcher's plan."

The advantage of having no reputation is you can bet it all and still not be out much if things go badly. The wager worked out for Felix.

Felix watched from the huge bay windows of the Unicycle's Space Traffic Control module with several other people from the conference room. The *Conestoga* was still light-hours away. The only things to see were pinpricks of light, the last surviving photons of the long march from their parent stars.

Felix reflected on the millennia-long odyssey those ancient rays of light had undergone just to bounce off the back of a naked ape's eye. It hardly seemed worth the investment in time and energy, but it was the only reason humans knew anything about their cosmos. Light speed was the great-grandmother of all speed limits. It stood on the side of the road connecting every star. It loomed over all matter and energy and demanded absolute compliance. To Felix's mind, a just universe would contain a way around Einstein's tyranny.

A siren derailed Felix's train of thought, and he was back in the STC module. Technicians swarmed about, preparing to warm up the Unicycle's particle accelerator and point it downrange. If one knew where to look, one could see tiny ripples in the starlight, like looking through an old center-spun window where gravitational lenses projected into space from the facility's own generators would focus and aim the indescribably powerful particle beam the Unicycle was about to produce.

After decades in space, the *Conestoga* had burned through almost all of its deuterium fuel. Like all interstellar yanks, a receiving dish was fitted to its aft designed to catch energy beamed by the Unicycle, which served as the ship's power source inside the solar system. If everything went to plan, the *Conestoga*'s crew was already busy playing plumber with the ship's coolant system. The beam would fire in a few minutes. The crew had just enough time to finish the modifications for the beam's arrival . . . in thirteen hours.

The clock reached zero. Behind Felix, Ms. Lemieux pressed a holographic toggle in the shape of a huge red button outlined in yellow and black stripes. The lights overhead flickered and dimmed for a brief time.

That was it. There was no deafening *BZZZZZZZZZZZZZZ*. No retina-melting light poured through the view ports. The only evidence anything happened at all was a very slight shimmer around the edges of the gravitational lenses as a few rogue particles were kicked clear of the stream. They looked like tiny aurora borealis. Boreali? Considering he was witnessing the most powerful machine ever built, Felix felt the whole experience was anticlimactic.

"Penny for your thoughts?" Director Lemieux asked, taking position next to him.

"I'm sorry. A what?" Felix could hardly be blamed for this naïveté. The penny had been dropped from U.S. currency more than two centuries ago. But they kept turning up.

"Of course, you are too young. It means, what are you thinking about?"

"Oh, right. Um, I guess I'm thinking about anything except what's going to happen in thirteen hours, if I'm honest."

"Ahh. Nervous about your plan, *oui*?"

"No. About the crew." Felix ran his fingers through his hair. "The mechanic in our meeting was right about one thing. It is easy when you're not the one taking the risks. Right now, they're hanging off of a bit of scaffolding with wrenches and plasma cutters, because they believe my plan will save their lives."

There was silence for several long seconds. Lemieux spoke again.

"You are wrong, M'sieur Fletcher, at least twice." Her tone was gentle. "First, they are hanging out there because I recommended it to M'sieur Graham, who, as head of the AESA, ordered them to do so. And, second, you have also taken a risk, maybe a big one, no?"

"I don't see how." Felix shrugged.

"You risk your plan will not work and people will die."

"Yes, but they would also die if we did nothing. All our other yanks are light-years away from here. We wouldn't be able to catch them before they ran out of power entirely."

"Granted, but that's not how headlines are written. Instead, they say things like, RESCUE PLAN FAILS, WITH FATAL RESULTS. It's not fair, but it's true." The Frenchwoman made a sympathetic gesture with upturned palms. "But maybe the even bigger risk is for your plan to work."

This wasn't what Felix had expected. He looked positively incredulous. "How's that now?"

"I mean to you personally, of course. Do you really think you were the only one in the room to consider running the modules hot?" Lemieux stared straight into the younger man. "No, I'm sure it had occurred to at least three, maybe four of the others."

Felix looked like a raccoon in headlights. "Well, then, why didn't they speak up? The rest of the plans were garbage. It was the only thing that had any chance of working."

"Ah, but the rest of the plans were safe."

"Safe for who?"

"For them, of course. No one else spoke up because they didn't want to take on the responsibility. They have interests to protect, some political, others professional. They don't want to risk damaging their careers."

"I don't care about that; I just want to do the job and give the *Conestoga* the best odds possible."

"I know. You have that luxury because you don't have any position to defend. That's why I asked for you to come out here. The rest of them are pigeonholed by success. So you see, if your plan succeeds, you risk revealing them to be cowards. Even if you're right, you will probably make enemies today."

She still spoke gently, staring deeply into the abyss on the other side of the glass. "Not to worry, I will not be among them."

"Well, that's a relief," Felix said sarcastically.

"I take it these factors did not weigh on your mind when you decided to speak up?"

"I didn't even know they *were* factors. I thought professionals valued results."

"Of course they value results, so long as they can take credit for them." Her face was contorted as bitterness and humor fought for supremacy. Renée looked at Felix again. "Let me ask you something. If we'd had this talk before the meeting, would you have acted differently?"

"No." Felix didn't hesitate. "I guess I have different priorities."

Renée gave Felix a knowing smile. "I thought not. But don't be so quick to judge them. You may find your priorities drifting when you have the big office and a dozen subordinates clawing to drag you from it. You would be surprised how many of history's great men can thank petty rivalries and office politics for their success." She turned back toward the room and patted Felix on the shoulder. "But don't be too concerned yet. You could still get lucky. After all, your plan might fail."

"Gee, thanks."

With that, the Frenchwoman walked away. Felix felt as though he'd survived a rather convivial scolding. He was left with the competing desires to either speed up or indefinitely delay the next thirteen hours. But time was busy keeping everything from happening all at once, and took no notice. His eyes drifted back to the stars.

Some twenty hours later, while the *Conestoga* and her crew bled off velocity like accumulated pounds before a class reunion, Renée Lemieux snuck away from the Space Traffic Control center and headed down to the Unicycle's QER room.

Renée switched on a holographic keyboard, entered Professor Eugene Graham's private email address, and typed a short message in the air.

He's the one you want.

The director hit Send, smiled to herself, and turned off the machine.

CHAPTER 5

Deep inside the Stack, Felix sat in a comfortable chair at a solid wood table, utterly perplexed about why he was there. The room was large, yet sparse. It had the feel of rented space, never serving a defined purpose. The head of AESA, Professor Eugene Graham, had broken into Felix's apartment the night before as he returned from the Unicycle and offered him a job. The details of which he'd been less than forthcoming about. Not that Felix would remember anyway, on account of how many little rum bottles he'd indulged in on the flight home.

Felix was joined by Graham's assistant, Jeffery, and a horse of a man named Harris. Also present was a quirky Englishman with hair like exploded cotton, who couldn't stop playing with an abacus slung around his neck, while a pair of lackeys to his right watched with reverent attention. Felix questioned why he'd gotten out of bed at all.

Graham's chest expanded like a bellows before he spoke. "Good afternoon, everyone. I've asked you here because we've added another member to the team." All eyes turned toward Felix. "This is Mr. Fletcher. Today is his first day, and this meeting will serve as his introduction to our little project. Please keep in mind that he may need a little patience and extra explanation. To that end, let's recap." He keyed the table and the room's lights dimmed.

The center of the table opened like an iris to reveal the built-in holo-projector. The air above it coalesced into a shape like two silver bullets joined at the tips.

"Twenty-five days ago, the AEUS *Magellan* wrote home to announce an artifact of unknown origin recovered in deep space. Spectrographic analysis determined its shell is comprised of a titanium and palladium alloy we've never seen before. Further isotopic tests show the metal was not mined on Earth or any of our colonies. Further, *Magellan* discovered this signal keeping the neighbors awake . . ." Eugene tapped another key. The room filled with a bizarre yet fascinating noise. The result one might expect if Salvador Dalí had taken up composition.

"The object was found motionless four light-months away from the nearest star, yet the signal is too weak to reach it. That's about as far as we've gotten."

With some reluctance, Eugene looked toward the cotton ball to his right. "Dr. Kiefer, how are we doing on the communication bottleneck?"

"Well, we've fired up the *Magellan*'s reserve QER, so that doubled our bandwidth. And Marvin 'ere"—he slapped the closest lackey on the shoulder—" 'e's workin' on some new data compression programs. That should speed things up another 20, maybe 25 percent."

"Excellent. Keep working on that, Marvin. We'll need to be able to shift huge amounts of data once they crack the artifact open and the research really gets going. The fewer delays the better." Eugene looked to his assistant. "Jeffery, how goes the unwanted publicity front?"

"Better than expected. We feared word of the artifact would leak immediately."

"Can't imagine who might leak mission-critical information accidentally," said now *Sergeant* Tom Harris.

"Look, Thomas, I said I was sorry. Besides, you got a promotion out of it." Jeffery found his track again. "Anyway, we decided to head it off and leak it ourselves to a few of the most fringe, sensationalist, and disreputable independent news sites. They've been running strong on the 'Government / Alien Cover-Up' angle ever since."

Harris spoke up again. "Okay, I'll bite. How is that 'better than expected'?"

Jeffery grinned. "Once we selectively leaked the story, it found itself in a wilderness of other conspiracy theories, false-flag accusations, Antichrist sightings, the usual noise." Jeffery smiled broadly. "It's currently fighting for its life against the nutters who still believe the planet is some sort of flat discworld. Our story is almost completely lost in the noise."

"That's brilliant," said Felix. "I've had to deal with some of these people. There are still folks out there who insist the moon landings were faked."

"But you're from the moon," Eugene said.

Felix shrugged. "It doesn't faze them. When I told one of them I was from New Detroit, he insisted I was a government hologram and started trying to wave his hand through me. They're impenetrable."

"Maybe our yanks could use them as meteor shielding," Harris added.

"Well, just this once we can be thankful for the sad state of education," Eugene said. His gaze passed over the young Lunie. "You seem to be taking this well, Felix."

"Ah, yeah, I'm fine. Just curious how I fit into all this."

"A perfectly natural question. None of us here has an engineering background. Dr. Kiefer and his men are educated in particle physics and quantum theory, but their technical training is limited to the QERs they maintain. You're sort of the reverse. Your experience is light on theoretical physics, but heavy on real-world applications. You know how things work. Therefore, where you fit in will be to take what we learn from the artifact and put it to practical uses."

Felix put his hands on the table. "Just so I'm clear, last month, a ship stumbled onto an alien thingamajig, so you've recruited me, a twenty-four-year-old college student, to remotely watch a crew thirty light-years away tear it apart and build stuff from what I see on the screen?"

"That about sums it up," Eugene said.

"Oh. All right, then." Learning about the job didn't have the reassuring effect Felix had hoped for. "Who does our little project answer to?"

"Well, that's a good question, one that hasn't really been answered yet. At this point it's more an issue of who we ask for money and how much we tell them about how we spend it."

"So we're like teenagers?" asked Felix.

"Yes, now that you mention it. Liberating, isn't it?" The rest of the room chuckled. "Look, Felix, people way above my pay grade are in the decision loop here, so don't worry. The cops won't burst through your door in the middle of the night."

"Why should I worry about cops? My boss handles the residential break-ins."

"Touché," said Eugene. "What do you think you'll need to do the job?"

"I don't know exactly. I've never built a reverse-engineering department from scratch before. But for starters, I'll need work space, a quantum computer loaded with dynamic modeling software, access to theoretical physicists, and a molecular printer for rapid prototyping. Most importantly, I'll need something to copy."

Eugene looked to Jeffery, who consulted his data pad. "There's work space open here. The computer and the mol printer will be simple to acquire. We can probably bring in any physicists on the AESA payroll you want to consult, so long as they can pass security checks, so give us a list of people that need to be cleared." Jeffery looked up from his pad. "But as far as source material, that's up to *Magellan*."

CHAPTER 6

The rows of lights whipped past as Allison pushed herself through the hallways. Sleep came sparingly over the last month, so she tired herself with longer runs. Despite the low humidity on board, her sweat flowed freely.

The cause of her insomnia sat strapped in a cradle as she passed Shuttle Bay Two. Flickering lights danced across the artifact in the observation gallery windows. Despite being 0120 hours, a solitary figure remained hard at work.

Allison paused. Years of training and habit compelled her to glance at the pressure door's status screen, where a silhouette of a man stood against a green background, indicating a good seal and full atmosphere in the bay. She transitioned through the airlock, then walked briskly across the floor toward the artifact and the workman.

"That you, ma'am?" called Chief Engineer Billings's unmistakable drawl from behind a welding mask.

"Yes, Chief, it is. What are you doing up so late?"

Billings opened his mask. "The lady begs her own question."

"I suppose that's true. Couldn't sleep. Running to wear myself out. I saw someone was still here, so I stopped in."

He nodded. "Know what you mean. I couldn't sleep, neither. Decided to go one more round with the probe here." He looked back at the silver form and rapped it with his knuckles. "She is one tough filly to break."

"Why call it a probe?"

"Don't rightly know, ma'am. I'm guessin' since we been sendin' out probes fer what, four hundred years now? It sure ain't one of ours, but it makes sense it'd be one of *theirs*. What else could it be this deep in the black?"

"Names and labels have power, Steven." Allison pitched her voice toward the "tender and supportive" end of the spectrum. "Maybe it is a probe, but I don't want you to pigeonhole your thoughts. We need open minds."

Billings considered this for a long moment. "Well, I'm sure yer right, ma'am. People's complicated, they let their heads git hog-tied over the littlest things. I wouldn't want yer job, ma'am. You have to keep dozens of us runnin' smoothly. I just have to worry about *Mags*. And now this li'l devil, I suppose."

An intimidating and expensive array of broken tools surrounded Billings. Drills with bits snapped off, a circular saw with the blade worn down to the sharpness of a Frisbee, empty acetylene and oxygen canisters, a hydraulic shear with a bent piston. A serious-looking backpack caught her eye. A cylinder shaped like a cheese wheel filled its base. It had shoulder straps and a length of conduit connecting to some sort of handgrips and what looked like a hose nozzle. Allison's hand moved to touch it, but Billings grabbed her by the wrist.

"Ah, not that one, ma'am. No offense, but it's not for beginners."

"Is it dangerous?"

Billings blushed. "It's my own design. And it might conceivably be in violation of a handful of workplace safety regs and maybe an old nuclear arms control treaty."

"And it's on *my* ship?"

"It gets the job done. Usually . . ."

Allison backed away respectfully from the backpack and looked again at the broken tools, then back to Billings. He was holding a plasma cutter.

"You know, we can't requisition replacements for this stuff," she said.

"Yes, ma'am, I explained that to the pr . . . artifact here. But she's not in a listenin' mood. So far, everythin' I've used to try to open her's been about as effective as giving a frog a haircut with a harmonica."

The chief had taped off the hull section where he'd tried to penetrate, and he labeled the effect of each tool with a marker. Some light scuffing was the worst damage he'd managed to inflict. The metal wasn't even discolored.

"What about access panels?" Allison asked.

"Don't have none. She's totally seamless." He reached for an opaque cylinder. It had bright yellow warning labels in the shape of tobacco leaves on the side. He had obviously taken steps to prevent a replay of the spittoon incident.

"Still trying to put a hole in your lip?" Allison admonished.

"Won't have to open my mouth to spit. Think of the time I'll save."

She stuck out her tongue in disgust. "Blech. That's awful, Steven. At least tell me you use mint chew."

"No, ma'am. Real men chew Copenhagen because it tastes like topsoil, or Kodiak because they say it's got asbestos in it."

Allison felt she was right on the verge of an important insight into the male mind, but pulled back. Some mysteries were better left unsolved. Her eyes gravitated toward the inscriptions on the artifact's skin. Aside from these and the tiny pockmarks of stellar dust collisions, the surface was flawless. No rivets, bolts, weld lines, or any other visible clues to the method of its manufacture.

"In all seriousness, Steven, can you open it?"

"Oh, I can open it, all right, ma'am. It ain't indestructible. Them micro-meteor craters tell me that much. Gimme a rail gun and I'll have it open fer you right quick. The trouble is findin' a way to open it without blowin' all the fiddly bits inside to kingdom come."

"I see your point."

Just then, *Magellan*'s voice interrupted their conversation. "Captain Ridgeway?"

"Yes, *Maggie*? What is it?"

"Forgive the intrusion, but a QER burst just came addressed to you."

"Thank you, *Maggie*. I'll take it on the bridge in a few minutes." Allison looked back to her chief engineer. "Keep at it, Steven."

"Don't worry, ma'am. I'm not movin' from this spot till I git my peep show."

"Well, it seems we've stumbled into the most complicated bra strap in history. Good luck."

Allison left the bay and resumed her jog toward the bridge. She arrived a few minutes later, wicking sweat from her forehead. The navigational plot sat in frozen stillness, as it had for nearly a month. Her navigator and communications officer sat at their stations with looks of determined boredom.

They'd been in contact with Earth almost daily. There'd been a flurry of activity in the beginning while they set up the research lab around the artifact, tied the primary and backup QERs together to increase their data transmission rate, and sorted out the crew duty shifts.

Then, things quieted down. Aside from software updates, news feeds, and personal messages, the last three weeks had included no new orders. After more than half a century spent at half light speed, they weren't moving. Her crew was feeling the doldrums, like sailors waiting on a favorable wind.

Allison reached her chair and looked to her communications officer. "All right, Prescott. Bring up the message."

"Immediately, Captain."

The screen on Allison's armrest went white with black text.

FROM: EUGENE GRAHAM, ADMINISTRATOR, AESA

TO: CAPTAIN ALLISON RIDGEWAY, CO, AEUS *MAGELLAN*

MESSAGE TEXT:

HURRY HOME.

END.

Allison's jaw clenched hard enough her teeth ground against each other like continents. "That's all of it? Are they getting charged by the letter or something?"

"Maybe they're trying to be succinct," Prescott offered. "Besides, wasn't this the order you anticipated?"

"Yeah . . . three weeks ago," Allison fumed. "Still, it doesn't matter now. We have our marching orders. *Maggie*, warm up your reactor. Let's pull up stakes."

"Yes, Captain." *Magellan* decided not to ask why the situation called for meat.

"Wheeler, plot a best-time course for Earth. Spare no deuterium. We'll have to stop and fill up anyway."

"Aye-aye, ma'am."

The ship's navigator was a bit of a redundancy. *Magellan* could, and usually did, plot her own courses with much greater precision than any human could manage. But in space, it was always wise to have redundancies, and skills needed to be practiced to maintain their polish. Still, *Magellan* checked the ensign's math and suggested a couple of tweaks.

After a few minutes, Ensign Wheeler was ready. "Course plotted and uploaded, ma'am."

"Thank you, Ensign," Allison said. "*Maggie*, let's get started. If we're quick enough, we should be back in time for the 2406 Olympics."

"Coming about, Captain," *Magellan* said.

The deck swayed subtly as thrusters fired and the ship pivoted around her center of mass to line up with a distant Earth.

"Patch me into ship-wide," Allison said.

Prescott touched a pair of holographic keys in the air above her station. "You're live, ma'am."

"Attention, crew. We've received our recall order. We're coming about to begin our trip home. Please return your tray tables to their original upright position and observe the No Smoking signs. Thank you."

Outside, the space ahead of *Magellan* stretched into an invisible pit. The ship lurched forward as it fell into the artificial hole. Allison sat in her chair for several satisfied minutes as she watched their speed build. Content that everything was in good order, Allison stood.

"Ensign Wheeler, you have the bridge until Commander Gruber relieves you. I'll be in my quarters catching up on sleep."

She almost reached the hatch before it all came apart.

Magellan cried out, "Captain, I'm detec—"

She was cut off by the deafening sound of a runaway airtanker crashing into a gong. The noise echoed throughout her corridors and hallways, resonating through her very bones. Everyone on the bridge froze solid as the blood retreated from their faces. Even before the sound faded, sirens replaced it. Warning lights blazed and flashed. Allison sprang back to her chair.

"*Maggie*, talk to me! Did we have a collision?"

"I'm trying to discern the problem, Captain." Conflicting data poured in from *Magellan*'s peripheral sensors. Some registered an impact, others insisted it was an internal explosion, while still others said they didn't really want to take sides. The ship was confused and frustrated.

"Com! Call out to the section chiefs and get me damage reports. There's no way we didn't break something." Allison paused. "And get the XO up here."

The com officer confirmed the orders and got to work.

"Captain," Wheeler broke in, "we're listing off course. Losing acceleration!"

Allison immediately feared a projector imbalance. Even a small failure in the projectors while they were at full power would lead to shearing forces that could break *Maggie*'s spine.

"How bad is it?"

"Minor, but detectable."

"Cut the drive."

"Aye-aye." The ensign slid the virtual throttles down to zero.

"Hull breach!" Prescott shouted. "We're venting air from Shuttle Bay Two."

"Alert the damage control team. Is it a rupture, or did the main doors pop open?" asked Allison.

"Outer doors report secure, Captain," said *Magellan*.

"Cameras, let me see the inside of the bay." There was a brief pause.

"Internal cameras are offline in that section. There appears to be a short somewhere in the wiring trunk," reported *Magellan*.

"Perfect. Com, route me to Chief Billings. He was in Bay Two the last I saw him.

"Connected, ma'am."

"Steven, are you still in Bay Two? What can you see?"

She was met with static.

"Steven? Steven, respond."

"Chief Billings's vital signs are spiking, Captain. His heart rate is over 150, and his breathing is erratic." *Magellan*'s voice had a palpable edge of worry to it. "He appears to be unconscious."

"Alert sick bay for incoming, and get me through to Gruber!" Allison snapped.

Commander Gruber's voice jumped out through the speakers. "What's going on, Skipper?"

"Working on it, Marcel. Where are you?"

"Coming up the tube toward the bridge now."

"Turn around. I need eyes in Shuttle Bay Two. Billings is down, and we're venting air through a breach. I need you to oversee rescue and recovery. Pull whoever you need."

"Aye-aye. I'll check back when I get there."

"Ma'am," Wheeler interrupted, "I've brought our throttle to zero, but we're still listing, and now we're decelerating. Something is causing drag."

"How? We're in open space!"

"The ensign is correct, Captain," said *Magellan*. "I am losing velocity at a rate of 0.7 meters per second."

Allison's mind jumped back a handful of seconds. "*Maggie*, just before the explosion, or whatever, you were about to tell me something. What was it?"

"I had detected a gravitational anomaly, localized just starboard of amidships."

"That's near the shuttle bay. Is it still there?"

"Yes, Captain. It is holding relative position."

"It's following us?" Allison dismissed the idea. "No, it can't be outside. It must have an internal source; malfunctioning g-deck plating?"

"I cannot confirm that hypothesis, Captain. Several short circuits have blinded my internal sensors in Shuttle Bay Two and surrounding sections."

"Prescott, is anyone on scene yet?"

"Lieutenant Dorsett just arrived."

"Put me through." Allison had control over her voice again. The initial adrenaline spike had leveled off. "Jackie, can you hear me?"

CHAPTER 7

Orange strobe lights blazed all around Jaqueline Dorsett, casting perverse, elongated shadow puppets onto the corridor. She ignored them.

"Jackie." Allison's voice burst into Jackie's mind through her internal com.

"Ahhh, yes. I'm here, ma'am." Apprehension resonated from the young woman's voice like a plucked violin string. "I'm standing outside Shuttle Bay Two. It's a complete mess."

"Stay calm, Jackie. I need you right now. Chief Billings is in there somewhere, but he's unresponsive. What can you see?"

"Okay." Jackie took a deep breath and exhaled through her nostrils. "I'm by the gallery windows. The artifact is pressed up against the aft bulkhead. I can see fog forming in the air around it. I think that's the hull breach."

"Good, Jackie. Keep going. Do you see Steven?"

Jacqueline scanned the room for her crewmate. She tried to fight back the fear of finding Billings wounded, or worse. He had a famously short temper for faulty equipment, and the man had an aficionado's flair for stringing together obscure curses. But Billings had always been kind and patient with her. Jacqueline looked up to him like an older, stronger brother. She feared losing him, too. She forced her eyes back to the task at hand.

"I don't see the chief. The entire center of the bay is clear. Shuttle A2 has been shoved all the way to the forward bulkhead. So have all of the tables that we set up around the artifact, and, um, tools, maybe?"

"Cleared by an explosion?" Allison inquired.

"I don't think so. There are no scorch marks or smoke."

Something crumpled caught her eye. It took a moment to click, because the orientation wasn't what she had been looking for.

"I see the chief!" Jacqueline was relieved. "He's fine. He's leaning against the back of the shuttle."

"That's great, Jackie. Can you get his attention?"

"No, he's facing away from me."

"That's all right. Can you open the door?"

Something about the chief nagged at her brain. His posture? It could wait.

"Just a second." Jacqueline reached over to the control pad and keyed the door. It flashed a red screen with the outline of a man being forcibly inverted. "No. The door's locked down from the breach. The fail-safe won't let me through."

"Don't worry, we'll override it from here."

As Allison spoke, a hand appeared on Jacqueline's shoulder. She jumped and let out a startled scream.

"It's just me, Dorsett," said the sturdy baritone of the XO. "Captain, I've reached Shuttle Bay Two. Lieutenant Dorsett is here with me."

Jacqueline looked on while the conversation continued in Commander Gruber's ear. She stole a look back to Chief Billings. He was still upright, but leaning very awkwardly. His knees were bent, and he held his arms at odd angles against the side of the shuttle. Furthermore, he didn't seem to be moving. Something was very wrong. Gruber's voice brought her to attention.

"Dorsett?"

"Sir."

"We need to get the chief. Where is he?"

Jacqueline pointed.

Gruber followed her finger until he, too, spotted the engineer. "Good. The airlock is being overridden right now. Captain says there's at least one radiation hazard in there with him, so keep an eye on the rad alarm on the wall."

"Yes, sir."

"Follow me through."

The inner door to the airlock opened remotely. Gruber stepped into the chamber. Jacqueline followed. The door closed and air cycled to equalize the pressure.

Gruber consulted the door display. "Looks like the breach is pretty slow. There's still over 70 percent pressure in there, but we need to be quick. Your ears will pop, and you might get light-headed, so watch for blackout."

"Okay." Jacqueline's anxiety rose rapidly. She hadn't had time to get into a vacuum suit, nor had the XO. Stepping into a room open to deep space in your pajamas didn't make many top-ten lists.

The outer door opened. Her ears were buffeted by the intense whistling of atmosphere as it raced through the tear in the hull. The center of the room looked swept clean. Everything was piled against the far wall. Not the smallest washer or nut lay in the middle. Everything except the artifact, which had fit itself neatly into an artifact-shaped dent in the far wall.

Something was terribly wrong. Jacqueline's mind struggled at the answer. "Wait a minute."

"No time, Lieutenant," replied Gruber. "Come help me with Billings." He started walking toward the chief.

Jacqueline's perception shifted. The scene reoriented in front of her. Everything fell into place.

"Marcel, *freeze*!"

The XO's muscles obeyed the order without consulting him. Jacqueline's voice unwittingly carried a maternal quality selected by evolution to reach into the brain stems of young boys and shut down their motor control.

Jacqueline took a tentative step forward and pulled an eight-millimeter wrench out of her pocket and lobbed it into the air. It sailed in the expected parabola for a bit, then it took a sharp turn in midair and rocketed straight and level toward the far wall at an impressive speed. It hit the bulkhead and stuck like well-cooked pasta.

"What the hell?" Gruber shouted against the whistling.

"Look," said Jacqueline. "The chief isn't *leaning* against the shuttle, he's *lying on top of it*. The far wall is the floor, and everything fell onto it. If you had taken another couple of steps . . ."

Comprehension dawned on Gruber. "I would have fallen sideways. How, though? There's no g-deck plating on the wall. And why is that over there?" He pointed to the artifact pressed into the other wall. Jacqueline could only shrug.

Gruber spoke into his com. "Captain, we have a big problem." He responded to the unheard question. "It's like the forward wall is producing gravity. Everything, including Chief Billings, has fallen onto it. The effect seems to begin about a meter away from where we're standing."

"I think it's the artifact," Jacqueline said absently. "It's pushing against the rest of the bay somehow. That's why it's the only thing on the aft wall."

"Like a kind of propulsion?"

"Yeah, like our gravity drive, except"—she paused to take a heavy breath—"repulsive instead of attractive."

"Lieutenant Dorsett believes it's coming from the artifact, some sort of antigrav engine. I concur."

He listened to the captain's reply. "I don't know if we can do anything in time, ma'am. The effect seems to be several g's. Even if we could climb down there, we wouldn't be strong enough to climb up again, much less pull Billings out." He, too, began to feel his lungs pull hard for air.

As the two of them pondered their dwindling options, all the tools that were stuck to the wall shifted and crashed to the floor like a box of cymbals tipped off a table. Billings slumped to the floor in a pile.

Across the room, the artifact fell to the deck with a thunderclap. The tear in the aft bulkhead that had been covered by the artifact now lay exposed. The remaining air escaped with a deafening sucking sound.

"*We gotta move!*" Gruber charged across the deck and skidded to a stop at Billings's feet.

Hyperventilating, Jaqueline struggled to keep pace. Stars burst forth in her eyes, then whole constellations. She took a knee to avoid falling flat. Through blurred vision, she saw Gruber start to drag Billings by his shoes.

The room spun, and her ears popped painfully. Jacqueline could see Gruber stagger badly, so she called up what little reserves she had and grabbed one of Billings's legs. The temperature plunged, and a thick fog rolled in from nowhere. They heaved back toward the door. Gruber's nose bled freely. Jacqueline's field of vision shrank to a tunnel with the airlock at its center. Just a few more steps.

Then, all sound simply died. Jacqueline opened her mouth to scream, but the vacuum ripped the air out of her lungs. She could see through squinted eyes that they were at the threshold of the airlock. Before she could hit the key, her vision faded to black . . .

. . . then, back into light. Jacqueline lay with her legs in the airlock and torso in the hallway outside. The outer door leading to the bay was sealed. Her skull felt like a road crew were repaving the inside of it.

Gruber and Billings lay next to her. Both looked as bad as she felt, but they were breathing. Breathing had taken on new importance for her. She swore to spend more time in the pool practicing holding her breath. Jacqueline could hear shouting and footsteps coming down the hall from both directions.

"Marcel?" She prodded him. "Marcel, are you awake?"

After a moan, a weak voice from somewhere far in the past replied, "I can't go to school today, Mom. I have a fever . . ."

She smirked and rolled her eyes, which hurt. "All right, you'd better stay in bed then."

Gruber's inner child grinned victoriously.

Jacqueline looked toward the gallery windows and into the shuttle bay that had almost taken her life.

Thick beads of water had formed on the glass and obstructed the view. They grew until two linked up, merged, and attracted the attention of gravity. As the drops slowly rolled down, they cannibalized the drops ahead and gained momentum, until they sprinted for the floor, leaving a clear streak in their path.

Jacqueline rolled toward the glass, her chest still heaving painfully, and wiped off a wide arch with her hand. The pane was frigid. The condensation distorted her view, but she could still see the artifact lying on the deck by itself.

As she listened to the sounds of people shouting and running, movement in the bay lassoed her focus. On the silver skin of the artifact, one set of engravings began to flash blue. Immediately next to it, a line of white light traced a circle in the skin. Once the circle was complete, the lights faded. The circle moved outward a few centimeters, then pivoted down, and revealed a hole in the hull.

She stared at it in rapt fascination. Lights glided through the interior, pulsing and flowing. It was like looking into a transparent, bioluminescent fish. A chuckle broke her attention before deteriorating into a raspy cough. She turned and saw Chief Billings propped up on an elbow. He smiled and winced simultaneously through a swollen face.

"Ta-da!" Billings said quietly. "And now, fer my next trick . . ."

CHAPTER 8

Allison ran a gloved hand over the tear in the hull and peeked through for a view of faraway stars. "Would someone tell the Houston Houdini to warn us before the encore?"

"Well, you did ask him to open it, Captain," chided *Magellan* through the com in Allison's helmet.

"Yes, but not quite so theatrically." Allison turned to view the artifact, which now lay diagonally across the floor. The circular hatch lay to the side. "But we're in. Now we can get down to the real work."

"And all it cost us was twelve thousand cubic meters of life-giving air," said Nelson, the engineering department's second in line. Chief Billings's injuries would keep him on the disabled list for at least a week. Gruber would be nursing a concussion for a few days. Jacqueline actually came out the best; she suffered superficial bruising to a good portion of her epidermis from vacuum exposure.

"How long to fix the hull?" Allison asked.

"That's simple. We can epoxy the fissure and restore airtightness within the hour. Then we can pressurize the bay and weld in a permanent patch. Call it 1700 hours."

"How about internal sensors and cameras?"

"That's going to take a while. Anytime you have to troubleshoot shorts and severed cables, there's bound to be time wasted on dead ends."

"Understood. Still, be as quick as you can. I'd also like you to set up a couple of temporary remote cameras to keep an eye on your people and our guest here in case there's another crisis." She thumbed at the artifact. "And let's fabricate a good, strong cradle in case it tries to bolt again."

"How big are its muscles?"

"Huh?"

"If I'm going to build a cage, I don't want to build one strong enough for a man only to find out it's going to hold a bear."

"I see your point. *Maggie*, how strong was that gravity anomaly at its peak?"

"Three point six standard gravities, Captain."

"Thank you, *Maggie*."

Nelson nodded. "We'll plan for seven g's and get started."

"Hull breach first. Page me when the patch is welded in. I'm heading for the bridge."

A short tube ride later and Allison walked onto the bridge and found a relieved Ensign Wheeler.

"Ensign, you're relieved," said Allison.

"Thank you, ma'am. I'm starving."

"You should've said something sooner."

"I figured you were busy with more important things," Wheeler replied.

"So did I miss anything up here?"

The navigator looked over his shoulder at Prescott's com station. "You could say that."

Allison turned her head to look at the tall, freckled ensign to her right.

"Out with it then, Com," Allison said.

"Well." Ensign Prescott called up the necessary files. "As you know, the artifact was broadcasting this signal when we discovered it." She tapped a key in the air and the now familiar, if still unsettling, sound filled the bridge. She let it play for a few seconds, and then interrupted. "Now, however, the signal has changed to this." Prescott pressed another key.

Allison strained to listen. Her ears knew it wasn't quite the same, but she was having trouble spotting the differences. It was like trying to figure out exactly which Christmas song was being butchered by grade-school carolers on your front porch.

A very upsetting thought occurred to Allison. "When did the signal change?"

"As soon as the artifact shut down its drive."

"I was afraid you would say that."

It didn't take a Holmesian leap of deduction to assume that the new signal was something like, "Help, I'm being stolen," or, "Over here! They took the bait!" The growing tiger pit in Allison's stomach convinced her the best place to be was a very long way away.

"Can we mask it?" Allison asked.

"I'm not sure how. We aren't carrying any jamming equipment," said Prescott.

Allison knew she was right. The average exploration vessel was far more interested in trying to detect mysterious signals than in hiding them.

Allison rubbed her forehead and concentrated. "What about our radio telescope's frequency filters? We use them to screen out wide-frequency background noise from pulsars and such. Couldn't we use them in reverse to block this one frequency?"

"Ought to," said Prescott. "I'll get to work on it right away, ma'am."

"Good." Allison felt like she deserved the big chair for the first time in a while. "But first, put me through to Engineer's Mate Nelson."

Prescott sorted through a few screens in the air in front of her and finally clicked on Nelson's picture. "You're connected, ma'am."

A translucent image of the young man hung in the air in front of Allison. "Hello, Nelson. I don't want to rush you, but the cradle just got shoved to the top of your priority list. Put as many people on it as you can until you start to trip over each other."

"We'll have to put repair of the internal sensors and cameras on hold, ma'am."

"It can't be helped. We need to get moving again, and we can't do that until the artifact is secured."

"Understood. We'll have it done by the end of the shift, Captain."

"Good man." She cut the link and turned back to Prescott. "As soon as you have a plan of action to mute our guest, let me know. Use whoever you need, provided they aren't working on the cradle. That includes anyone in cryo."

"Yes, ma'am."

Allison turned to look at her navigator. "Wheeler, you have a few more hours in that chair in you?"

"As long as you don't mind if I order a burrito from the galley."

"Knock yourself out. I'm getting some rack time."

"Understood, ma'am. Sweet dreams."

Allison arrived in her cabin a few minutes later and collapsed on the bed. The collar of her uniform had been rubbing at her neck for the last few hours, so she unfastened it and let the lapels hang open.

She caught a glimpse of herself in the full-length mirror. The sight wasn't pretty. It reminded her of the disheveled look she carried through most of college, which she had spent in alternating states of insomnia, inebriation, and mortal panic. Except now she didn't have the excuse of wine to account for her appearance.

"Who are you? And what did you do with my regular body?" she asked the reflection. It stared back at her expectantly. She shook her head. Allison tried to prop up the shopping bag under her left eye. She decided a hot shower before bed would do the trick. And considering that one of the perks of being captain was a private bathroom complete with shower, she was in luck.

She locked her cabin door, then disrobed and put the uniform into the acoustic washing machine. It was a water-conserving device that cleaned clothing using ultrasonic waves to vibrate away dirt and skin cells. A similar system had been used in earlier yanks for all types of cleaning, including acoustic showers. These were unpopular with crews, mainly because it felt like being screamed at by a million angry fleas. They were quickly phased out.

The water from the showerhead was just below what most would consider scalding, exactly how she liked it. Thin rivers snaked their way down the hills and valleys of her body. She could feel Gordian knots of muscles unwind under the rhythmic pulses of water. It had been a long day, a long month.

Allison began the ritual of second-guessing the day's decisions, an ancient rite indulged in by almost anyone in a position of authority. First, she regretted not ordering construction of a cradle for the artifact as soon as it was brought aboard. That was shortsighted.

Then she regretted ordering Gruber and Dorsett into the shuttle bay before they had donned vac suits. The leak had started out small and stable. Quick number crunching had determined there was plenty of time for them to grab the chief and exit before the pressure dropped to dangerous levels. Of course, with the cameras knocked out, no one could have known that the leak was only small because the artifact was covering most of the breach, or that the artifact was about to fall back to the floor.

But that was the mistake. She'd assumed the leak would remain small and steady without knowing what had caused it in the first place. It was a stupid assumption to make, one that nearly ended the lives of three of her best people.

Allison filed away the misjudgments in her "Learning Curve" vault, but she'd never been this close to losing people before. It was enough to take a big chip out of the self-confidence that was the foundation of her command.

"Allison, may I ask you a question?" said *Magellan*'s familiar voice.

"Huh?" Allison jumped and almost slipped. "*Maggie*, did you just call me Allison?"

"Yes. I've noticed that you often refer to other crewmembers by their first names when you are discussing matters of a personal nature." *Magellan* paused. "Was it inappropriate of me to do so?"

"No, *Maggie*, it's fine. It was just different." Allison turned off the shower and quickly slipped into her pink, fuzzy bathrobe. "What did you want to ask me?"

"Are you bothered by your backside?"

Allison stiffened and tried to look at her posterior. "Well, I haven't really given it much thought," she lied. "Why, is there something wrong with my 'backside'?"

"Yes, from a design standpoint. You can't see it. It is a blind spot. Doesn't that bother you?"

Allison got the impression she had missed something and tried to back up. "I can see it in a mirror when I need to." A flash of insight hit. "This is about your cameras and sensors in the shuttle bay, isn't it?"

"Yes. There is a whole section of myself that I can't see, possibly the most important section at the moment. It is very . . . I believe the word is *disconcerting*."

"And you wonder how we humans live with a giant blind spot behind us all the time," ventured Allison.

"Yes. It seems that it would leave you feeling constantly vulnerable."

"Well, I was born with it. It's not something that I just lost, so it's normal for me. For a human, it would be really strange to see in every direction at once as you do. I don't know if I could cope with it."

"I think I understand."

"Besides, you have blind spots, too. I know for a fact you don't have any cameras in the showers or sleeping quarters."

"That's true, but those locations are not mission critical. Nothing important happens there."

Allison smiled devilishly. "I can think of a few couples who would disagree strenuously with that. Just give it some time, *Maggie*. I'm sorry I have to delay your repairs. I can tell it's bothering you, but I have to weigh the risks of sticking around here for too long. There's just too much we don't know right now."

"I understand, Captain."

"Good. I'm glad."

"Thank you, Allison. Good night."

"Good night, *Maggie*."

Allison spent several long seconds considering the oddity of acting as emotional support for her own ship. Of course, crews had been talking to their ships since the first bundle of reeds were floated across a lake. But ships didn't traditionally *start* those conversations.

She shook off the thought and slipped out of her bathrobe, then reclined on the narrow bed to write a badly needed report back to the research team on Earth. Once that task was complete, she ran it through to Prescott's com station to be placed in the QER queue, then shut off the lights in her cabin and fell into her pillow.

Moments later, she was asleep.

CHAPTER 9

Felix sat at his desk and read Ridgeway's report for the fourth time.

Magellan was damaged and several crewmembers injured when the artifact tried to make a break for it. Captain Ridgeway believed the artifact had reacted to the chief engineer's attempts to gain access to its interior. The explanation didn't sit well with Felix, and he hadn't been bashful about it in their morning strategy meeting. The trouble was he had no better explanation.

That was the bad news. The good news was an access panel had popped open and they could begin surveying the interior. To Felix, that begged the question, why would the artifact pop its lid if it were trying to escape? He shooed the nagging thought. His eyes wandered the room. Professor Graham had been true to his word. Felix's office would cause jealousy-induced apoplexy in any number of university physics departments. At his fingertips, he had a networked bank of quantum computers, the latest U-Make-It molecular printer, a pressure chamber with zero- to one-hundred-g gravity generation, a miniature fusion reactor linked to a Möbius strip particle accelerator, secure holo-links to two dozen different AESA research centers, and a device in the corner that he couldn't quite remember the purpose of.

Eugene had been honest about the compensation as well. Felix's first payday had been an eye-opening experience, not that he had any idea of how to spend it. People accustomed to lean times generally reacted in one of two ways to a sudden cash windfall. Either they take great care to ensure that it lasts, or they spend it as quickly as possible to get back to more familiar financial territory.

Considering his fondness for numbers, Felix intended to be the former. Still, he was glad to leave the old college apartment behind. He splurged on a new, larger two-bedroom closer to the Stack, after clearing out his college loans and printing out the discharge papers just so he could piss on them.

He'd fallen into a surreal routine after a few days. Scanned and searched on his way into work every morning, he ate lunch in a cafeteria filled with scientists, bureaucrats, soldiers, politicians, and spies, and frequently conversed with people many trillions of kilometers away.

Felix was tired. It had been a nonstop sort of day. The words of Ridgeway's report weren't going to change by themselves, and there would be no new information until a cradle was finished for their ill-behaved artifact. He shut down his display and locked the system.

He made his way out of the building and said good night to the door guard. Exiting security was always so much easier than entering. Felix had almost reached his car when he spotted Jeffery.

"Still here, Jeff?"

"Just called it a day. How about you?"

"Same story."

"Say, Felix. I'm meeting Thomas for a drink. Want to join us?"

Felix pondered this for a moment. "Eh, why not? Where are we going?"

"Some place downtown called Captain's Mast. We can take my car."

They arrived a little past nine to a scene already in full swing. The overall theme was nautical, with anchors, chains, and netting throughout the décor. At the bor's center was an impressive gray steel mast, on which were mounted a variety of radio and radar antennas, some of which spun. The clientele consisted mainly of young service members and young people hoping to service members.

At the bar was a choir of Royal Navy sailors drinking grog and loudly singing lewd sea shanties. Sitting quietly next to them was Sergeant Harris. Jeffery and Felix slid in next to him.

"Hi, Jeff. I see you brought Felix!" Harris shouted over the din. "Glad you're here!"

How long is your yardarm . . .

Felix pressed his mouth next to Harris's ear. "You, too, Tom. So what are you having?"

How thick is your barrel . . .

"Leinenkugel's. Let me buy you one."

How much brass in your bells . . .

"All right. Thanks!" shouted Felix.

How deep is her harbor . . .

"Just one rule: no office talk, okay?"

And can she stay for a spell!

"No problem. I came out to escape, after all."

The bartender delivered Felix's beer, and Harris thumb-scanned it onto his tab. By then, the Royal Navy sailors had broken into a moving rendition of "Is That Rust on Your Foghorn?"

The well-lubricated crowd cheered, danced, and sang. People shouted at a blown baseball call, argued politics, and performed the sort of unintelligibly complex mating rituals that gave anthropologists fits. Then the entrance's double doors burst open, and the din died down as every head pivoted to investigate. A man in a striking white, perfectly tailored and pressed AEU Navy dress uniform stood astride the doorway. He lingered a moment, feeding off the crowd's gaze.

Physically, there wasn't much to distinguish him from the average sailor. He certainly didn't possess Harris's stature, who was once afforded a respectful distance by a bull rhinoceros in musk, but the newcomer's *presence* was another matter entirely. As he looked around the quieted room, he seemed to take ownership of it. Once satisfied that everyone had seen him, he strode toward the bar.

"Who's that?" Felix asked in a hushed voice.

"You've gotta watch the vids more," Harris said. "That's Commander Maximus Tiberius. He drives a subcarrier. Got two unit citations for valor already."

Commander Tiberius arrived at the bar and reverently put one hand in the air, the other over his heart. "Ladies, the next round is on me. Sorry, gents, but I'm not here for you."

This was met with a chorus of exited cheers and disappointed groans.

Felix wrinkled his nose. "Seems a bit of a manicured caveman to me."

"Don't be jealous, Felix," Harris said. "That caveman saved a lot of marines' lives last year in Indonesia."

Instead of arguing, Felix occupied his mouth with a pull from his beer.

There are only two ways a child saddled with a name like Maximus Tiberius turns out. He either becomes confidence personified, or he ends up trapped inside the name like a cruel irony. This child, who already had a beer in each hand and a girl under each arm, had settled on the first option early in life.

Maximus looked down the bar and took stock of Harris. Experienced bar patrons make it a point to become fast friends with the bouncers and the biggest guy in the room. It wasn't Maximus's first time in a licensed establishment, so he pushed past the girls ensnared in his personality orbit to introduce himself.

"Evening, Sergeant." He pointed to Harris's beer. "The leathernecks I drink with usually handle heavier stuff than that."

"We're just unwinding from a long shift, sir. Besides, I don't see anything stronger in your hands."

"Well, there's a fix for that. Barkeep, scotch! Leave the bottle."

Several hours and a precarious pyramid of empty shot glasses later, Felix, Jeffery, and Harris sat in a large booth being regaled with tales of Maximus's recent South American exploits. A group of onlookers clung barnacle-fashion to his every word. Much to Felix's surprise, Jeffery had leaned over to rest his head on Harris's shoulder, who did not object. Were they on a date? Felix hadn't picked up on any signs of a budding romance at work. Then again, with his abysmal romantic record, he probably wouldn't have known if he had.

"And by the time he came to, he was stark naked save for his belt, covered in seaweed, and tangled up in a rusty old buoy."

The crowd roared with laughter.

Jeffery leaned over to Felix. "What's a buoy?" he asked quietly.

"An anchored float used to mark territorial boundaries, shipping lanes, and navigational hazards in the days before integrated GPS piloting." Felix spotted a bulbous white-and-orange contraption among the collection of navigational paraphernalia suspended from the ceiling and pointed to it. "That's one there."

Maximus, who'd paused his monologue to allow the Brits to begin a new set, followed Felix's index finger but picked out the wrong target.

"Well, go ask her to dance," Maximus prodded.

"The buoy?" asked Felix.

"What? No, the girl."

Felix looked down from the ceiling and spotted her. She sat patiently while her friend was chatted up. She was striking, yet unconventional.

"Oh, no. I wouldn't want to embarrass her. I'm not much of a dancer."

"Then you need another shot. Everyone can dance with enough liquor."

"I . . . wouldn't know what to say," Felix objected weakly.

"What does that have to do with anything?" asked Maximus. "Just talking to them is the point; it doesn't matter what you say. Here, watch . . ."

Maximus stood up from his seat and pushed past the throng. He walked up to the young woman and leaned over to speak into her ear.

As he spoke, her eyes went wide. She slapped him smartly across the face.

Spectators love a good crash-and-burn, regardless of the context. The crowd burst into applause as Maximus took a small bow and walked back to the table.

"What did you say to her?" asked Felix when Maximus returned.

"I said, 'Are you a french fry? Because your starch stiffens my collar,'" he said through a smile and a rapidly reddening cheek. "It's easy. See?"

"See what?" replied Felix. "You were shot down. And assaulted, I might add."

"It's the rule of twenty-three, kid. Provided you aren't catastrophically ugly or disfigured in some humorous way, you only need to talk to an average of twenty-three women before you find a taker. It's all in the numbers."

"And get slapped a dozen times in the process?"

"That's what the alcohol is for. It makes you brave enough to do it, and it numbs the sting of rejection."

"What if they throw their drinks at you?"

"Open your mouth and catch as much as you can," Maximus said with a grin. "Now if you'll excuse me, there're at least sixty ladies still in here. I can get a three-way together before bar-close if I'm quick enough."

With that, he grabbed his drink and dove back into the gyrating mass of people. Felix watched him go and shook his head.

"Unbelievable. He's like a chauvinist parody. A hack wouldn't write that dialogue."

"He's just comfortable in his own skin," Harris said as he absently twirled a finger through Jeffery's hair.

"He's even more comfortable with other people's skin," Jeffery quipped as they watched Maximus approach his next quarry, apparently with more success. When this didn't elicit a response, Jeffery nudged Felix. "Hey, you okay?"

"Hmm? Yeah, fine. I was just thinking about buoys."

"Oh." Jeffery smiled. "I had no idea. That's great, Felix. I know just the guy to set you up with."

Felix rolled his eyes. "Not *boys*. *Buoys*, with a *u*. You know, that thing you asked me about like five seconds ago?"

"Right! What about them?"

"Not sure, but something about them is bugging me. Almost like déjà vu, except backward."

"You mean you have a strange feeling you've *never* seen one before?" asked Harris. "That's what us non-geniuses call not knowing something. I can see how that could be confusing for you."

"Funny man, Thomas. It's not that. More like . . . like I'm going to have seen one before, but I haven't yet. Does that make any sense?"

"How many have you had?" asked Jeffery.

"I guess not," said Felix. "It's not the alcohol."

"Right, because scientists always experience vague feelings of causality-violating temporal paradoxes when they're sober," said Jeffery.

Felix continued, "Anyway, no. I've only had the two shots and this beer."

"You're still on the same beer?" asked Harris.

"Yeah."

"Should I hire a babysitter for it?"

"Fine. You know what?" Felix grabbed the bottle of Leinenkugel's and pulled down the remainder. Then he stood up and marched straight as a yardstick toward the bar.

"What's he doing?" asked Jeffery.

"I think he's just getting another drink," answered Harris.

"No, he's . . . oh no. He's talking to that girl who smacked Tiberius."

"Hmm, didn't think he had it in him. Not enough of it at least."

Jeffery looked away. "I can't watch. What's happening?"

"Well, she hasn't leveled him yet, so that's an improvement." Harris paused. "In fact, they seem to be heading for the dance floor."

"Really?" Jeffery turned to see for himself. "I thought he said he couldn't dance."

They both watched Felix with rapt attention for a few moments until the song hit its stride and the pair started to move.

"Well, at least he's honest," said Harris.

To be fair, it wasn't that Felix lacked coordination or rhythm. The problem was that his body had been calibrated for lunar gravity and hadn't really adjusted to Earth, despite the last three years. What they witnessed didn't resemble dancing so much as an arthritic flamingo in combat boots *trying* to dance.

There are different ways to be the center of attention. One tends to inspire envy; the other tends to generate sympathy. Felix charged ahead heedlessly until his partner could bear it no longer. She stopped him, gave him a peck on the cheek, whispered something to him, and then walked back to rejoin her friend. Felix returned to the booth and sat down.

"Well," Jeffery said, "what did she say?"

"Her name is Chianti. She said I was very sweet and should come back and find her again when I have a matching set of feet."

"It beats a sharp stick in the eye," said Harris.

"Or a slap in the face, for that matter," Jeffery added. "Are you going to be all right in here, Thomas? I should run Felix home."

"No, you guys have fun. I can get a cab."

"Are you kidding?" Harris said. "Go get some rack time. These are my people. I'll have more friends in here by the end of the night than you can count."

"All right. See you at the office tomorrow." Jeffery stood up and realized he was a little worse for wear. "I think we'll let the car drive home."

Felix walked out into the beautiful autumn evening while Jeffery used him as a portable lean-to.

"So, you and Thomas are a . . . thing?" Felix ventured cautiously.

"I wouldn't say that, yet. We're enjoying each other's company. But please keep it private. The office doesn't need to know."

"I understand. I'm happy for you."

For those inclined to see them, the stars above put on a dazzling show to rival the city's skyline. As frequently happened, Felix found himself lulled by their spell. They were little islands of heat and light in an incomprehensibly vast, frozen ocean of darkness. Anchors of hope.

Then he had another thought.

"That's it!"

"Sure is," Jeffery said with inebriated gusto. "What are we talking about?"

"It's a buoy. The artifact isn't a probe. It's a buoy. That's what was bugging me."

Jeffery experienced the sudden jolt back to sobriety usually caused by red-and-blue lights in the rearview mirror. He straightened up.

"How do you figure?"

"Think about it," Felix said. "*Magellan* found it just sitting in the middle of nowhere. The only thing it was doing was broadcasting a signal to empty space. It wasn't running away from the chief engineer's attempts to open it; he'd already thrown everything in the book at it without as much as a scuff mark. It only acted when *Magellan* moved away from where they found it. That must have been its assigned anchor point. It thought it was drifting. It wasn't running, it was trying to maintain its position."

"All right. Sounds good so far. Then why did it stop and open itself up for them?" asked Jeffery.

Felix wrestled with the question for a few steps, but then the answer fell into place. "Because it broke."

"Broke? It's been sitting out there for who knows how long already, and it's impervious to a determined redneck wielding a plasma cutter, yet it picked that exact moment to break?" He shook his head. "Too convenient."

"Not necessarily. Maybe something knocked loose when it hit the bulkhead. Maybe it burned out its drive. A space buoy would only need the equivalent of station-keeping thrusters. Maybe it was overwhelmed by how fast the *Magellan* accelerated and shut down."

"If that's true, it would also explain why the message changed," said Jeffery. "It's probably squawking to the aliens who put it there that they need to come and fix it."

"Which is why the hatch opened, in preparation for the maintenance crew it's expecting," Felix concluded. "I'll wager a week's salary that the hatch leads directly to a gravity drive system and that it's burned out."

"No dice. I know a bad bet when I hear one."

They were almost to Jeffery's car by then. He squared to look at Felix.

"Now comes the scary question," Jeffery said. "If it's a buoy, was it put there to warn ships about some unseen danger, or to mark territory?"

"I'm not sure. It could even be a bread crumb to mark a trail. We don't know enough yet to cross anything off the list." Felix stopped for a moment. "We've got to get a message out to Ridgeway regardless. She needs to know that somebody may come looking for that thing."

"Agreed. Looks like we weren't finished at the office, after all."

They climbed into Jeffery's waiting Volkswagen Swift, which smelled the alcohol molecules wafting off of them and promptly locked the manual controls.

"Sorry, sir," said a sultry feminine voice, "but I am too young and pretty for the scrapyard."

"If you'd waited a moment, I would've asked you to drive," Jeffery said.

"Where would you like me to take you?"

"The Stack, please."

"You just had to spring for the 'edgy attitude' upgrade," said Felix with a snort.

"Just shut your door."

With that, wings deployed, turbines spooled, and the Swift sped away from the parking hangar into the sky.

"We're finished here, Captain," Nelson said. "The artifact's all strapped in."

"Good man," said Allison. "Helm, resume course. Get us the hell out of here."

"Resuming acceleration along present course, Captain."

"Com, how are we coming with jamming the signal?"

"We should be ready to test it within the hour, ma'am."

"Well done. Let's just hope it works."

Magellan's reactor surged, gravity projectors tricked the space ahead, and both ship and crew pulled away deeper into the black abyss.

As the white hull of *Magellan* piled nine hundred meters per second onto her speed, a wrinkle in the darkness accelerated to keep pace. It appeared no more substantial than the flicker of heat above a stretch of highway in summer. An impressive array of recording devices and passive sensors switched on and started taking notes.

CHAPTER 10

The twin suns of the Baylisee system gleamed off the silver hull of the small cutter and filled the command cave with light. The system's primary was an enormous blue Galfor-range star that had already consumed most of its fuel.

In the timescale of the cosmos, it would soon swell to many times its present size as a prelude to its ultimate destruction in a titanic explosion, vaporizing itself completely. Too big even to leave behind an infinite well.

The benefactor of this cataclysm would be its neighbor: a relatively small, red Dipier-range star. Unlike its hard-living fraternal twin, this small sun would last for many ages more, and the debris from the larger star's death would seed its orbit with precious heavy elements. It would be enough mineral wealth to form a system of planets, and with some luck, maybe even a new generation of life.

The cutter's pilot looked on, contemplating the future of the system. Each star had a duty to perform—the enormous blue smelting furnace and the tiny red factory. He tried to appreciate the irony of their relationship. The giant sun burned so brightly that its neighbor could barely be seen. It overpowered it in mass, luminosity, heat, pressure, even the range of materials it could produce. But it was merely a flash, a set-builder for a grand play. The glory and adoration would eventually go to its tiny companion, which would still be around to oversee a civilization emerge on one of its future worlds. The inhabitants would worship their meek little sun as a god, without ever knowing of the contributions of its giant blue kin.

D'armic tried to appreciate the irony, but he hadn't taken his pills. He continued to look on because without them, he couldn't grow bored either.

The slender creature had mottled gray skin and soft features arranged in an outwardly humanoid body. He wore no clothes because unassisted, he didn't feel shame. He and his ship were of Lividite origin.

If one were not a student of xenoanthropology, the Lividites would appear to be the most erroneously named species in the long history of arbitrary labels. They were not an angry race. In fact, they were devoid of *naturally* occurring emotions of any sort.

They were dependent on artificial mood-altering chemicals to experience any response beyond their baseline stoicism. Emotions could be had in pills, patches, injections, nasal sprays, syrups, slow-release gel tabs, and suppositories for when they needed to feel like someone was a pain in the . . . well, you know the rest.

The average Lividite packed a small container with drugs to induce friendliness, annoyance, excitement, frustration, and satisfaction before leaving for work. They planned their day around when to take the drugs so that the emotions would appear at the appropriate times. It was a time-honored prank among schoolchildren to mislabel the drugs of their classmates with hilarious results, so long as everyone had taken their Humoric.

It's only with study of Lividite history that the name's origin comes into focus. Many tens of thousands of years ago, the Lividites were the single most destructive, genocidal, xenophobic, and all around prickly race in known space. They were so irrationally violent that their neighbor races (after a ruinous multigenerational war triggered by a careless embassy valet) staged an intervention for the entire planet and sponsored the population through ten generations of anger management counseling.

After this episode, Lividite society bred for emotional stability and fair-mindedness. However, after many hundreds of generations, this guided-breeding program had selected the emotions right out of the population.

Hearing of the situation, an off-world pharmaceutical company specializing in psychoactive drugs recognized the unprecedented business potential and quickly set up R&D centers, retail outlets, and an enormous marketing apparatus to chemically supply the blasé species with all their emotional needs.

As it happened, this particular Lividite resented his drug dependency mightily, at least while he was taking his Resentitol. The rest of the time, he tried to keep the *memory* of resentment fresh in his mind. D'armic was part of a small but growing group that extolled the virtues of drug-free living. It wasn't that they wanted to abandon emotions. Quite the opposite. They wished to experience the full, subtle palette of genuine emotions in real time. Not the delayed, monochromatic effects of ingested chemicals.

However, the vestiges of natural emotions that remained in the Lividite genome were faint indeed. But they were real, and to D'armic and those like him, quality counted far more than quantity.

Frontier managers spent tours lasting many years out in wild, undeveloped areas of space, a role for which Lividites were ideally suited. Without specific drugs, they couldn't grow lonely or homesick. D'armic had picked his career path because the travel central to the job allowed him to pursue experiences that he surmised would have the most emotional impact.

In his time as a Bureau of Frontier Resources officer, D'armic had gone solar-sailing around the shattered moon of Xemji, rode an untamed four-winged Telerack through the center of a storm vortex on Oerm, and watched the famous Korge of Datron perform his wildly popular stand-up routine in the ten-millennia-old Vilaj Amphitheater, where he made such impolitic observations as, "Why is it illegal to pay someone to rotate your obigon, when it's perfectly legal to do it for free?" and "Do androids think oxidation is an embarrassing skin condition?"

His pursuit of the drug-free emotional life is what caused D'armic to detour to the Baylisec system in the first place. He'd estimated the immensity of the blue primary star and the undertones of destruction and creation the pair represented might stir unexplored feelings of awe, inspiration, irony, or even insignificance.

But the result of this experiment had been no different from the others. No matter how intense the experience, a tiny trickle of feeling was all he could conjure. He just hadn't found the right levels of danger, absurdity, beauty, or accomplishment to clear a channel for the wellspring of emotions he believed was trapped below the surface.

D'armic took a moment to soak in the view outside his windows, then turned back to the cutter's navigational panel. He had spent enough time here already, and his duties called elsewhere.

An alert popped up in his field of vision. One of the buoys in the Earth network, #4258743-E, to be precise, had thrown an error code and requested maintenance. It wasn't alone; at least three others had logged errors in the last two cycles. D'armic made a note of it and resolved to bump the health of the buoy network further up his priority list. But for the moment, it would have to wait. There was the trimming of sun-weeds in Okim and the burgeron migration in the Tekis Nebula to worry about.

There was always more for a frontier manager to do, and many larims to go before he could sleep.

CHAPTER 11

After events in the shuttle bay landed three of their shipmates in sick bay, the crews' feelings toward the artifact were understandably ambiguous. So it should come as no surprise that the first crewman to go through the hatch was assigned through a highly technical process of elimination, guaranteed to select the most qualified candidate.

A rock-paper-scissors tournament.

After "winning" six consecutive games, one of Dorsett's team, Specialist Mitchell, had been picked. He would hold the camera and other sensors as they recorded the proceedings. Chief Billings and his team would analyze these recordings locally, and the AESA experts back on Earth would handle them in turn.

Mitchell was buttoned up in a bright yellow hazmat suit, along with the extra precautions of oven mitts, pilot's helmet, and a baseball umpire's chest pad someone had brought along. Allison supervised the beehive of activity on the deck and conversed with the translucent hologram of her chief engineer. In theory, Billings was still recuperating in his quarters, but couldn't quite bring himself to stay out of things.

"So, Steven, what do you think of that Poindexter they have back on Earth, Mr. Fletcher? Does his buoy theory hold water?" asked Allison.

"Too early to tell," Billings replied. "It makes sense on some levels, but it doesn't explain everything. Fer instance, if it was s'pposed to just sit in space at three degrees Kelvin, why have such a powerful heat dissipation system on the hull? Makes as much sense as air-conditioning on a snowmobile."

"It does seem a bit out of place for the duty," Allison concurred. "I've been thinking, too, if it were a buoy, what's its job? Marking territory doesn't make sense, because even a relatively small border, say a sphere a couple of dozen light-years in diameter, would require billions of these things. Even if it were possible to manufacture that many, it seems like an awful waste of resources. An advanced race must have a better way to draw a line in space."

"What about a lighthouse, warnin' us of danger?"

"I don't buy that either. Hazards to navigation in space aren't like sandbars or coral reefs hiding beneath the waves. Black holes, magnetars, and supernovas do a pretty good job of announcing themselves. So what could it be marking?"

"Don't know, ma'am. That's what's got me worried."

"I never pegged you as one to fear the unknown."

"A healthy fear of the unknown has kept mankind intact for a very long time. I see no reason to abandon it now."

"The unknown is what we're out here for, Steven. Ah, it looks like Mr. Mitchell is about to take the plunge."

Specialist Mitchell was perched atop the improvised gantry ladder that led up to the artifact. He resembled a nervous kid in water wings on a ten-meter diving board as he peered over the threshold festooned in protective equipment.

"Ma'am?" said the image of Billings.

"Yes, Steven?"

"Could you turn my camera so's I can see what's happenin'?"

In an age of holograms, it could be difficult for the subconscious to remember who was actually present and who was a mirage.

"Oh, right. Sorry." Allison repositioned the camera that fed images back to the chief's quarters.

Fluorescent blue and purple lights from inside the artifact shone off the plastic visor of Mitchell's helmet. With a deep breath, he committed to the task and eased himself inside. Nelson handed the camera and sensor packet down to him.

"How are you doing, Mr. Mitchell?" asked Allison.

"I'm all right, ma'am, but there's not a lot of crawl space."

"What do you see?"

"It's bright as Fremont Street in Vegas in here, Cap." He turned on the camera and its wireless feed.

The assembled officers, scientists, and technicians turned to the holo-projection that appeared on the deck in front of the artifact's cradle. Ribbons of light moved in waves through the interior, flowing over and past the organic shapes that formed the artifact's internal components.

As they looked down the cylindrical space toward one end, the light pulses swirled around one component in particular. It was iridescent and shaped like a nautilus shell in cross section.

The chief's image pointed a finger toward it. "Can I git a better look at that, ma'am?"

"Mr. Mitchell, would you move in toward that spiral component, please?"

"No problem, Cap." Mitchell inched forward and brought the part into better focus. "Is this better?"

"Yes, that fine. Just hold it steady for a moment." Allison turned to Billings's holo-avatar. "What are you thinking, Steven?"

His brow furrowed in contemplation. "It's tiny, but it does bear a resemblance to one of our gravity projectors, at least the amplifier."

"But what are the odds that alien technology would parallel our own that closely?"

"Pretty good, actually. Math, physics, and chemistry are universal. Stands to reason that any engineerin' based on them's gonna have similarities, no matter who's tightenin' the bolts."

Allison regarded her chief engineer with approval. It would be easy to hear the drawl and fall into centuries-old assumptions about his mental horsepower. She, however, had learned better over the course of their voyage. Allison would put her redneck up against other people's whiz kids anytime, anywhere.

"Look here, ma'am." Billings's ghostly finger pointed at the center of the floating image of the part.

Allison toggled a control in the air and zoomed in on the area. The ripples of light that pulsed through the interior of the artifact converged off-center on the spiral, surrounding an area of discoloration.

"You think that's a short circuit?" Allison asked.

"Seems like an obvious assumption. Them lights are pretty insistent about drawin' attention to that spot. Probably their way of idiot-proofin' repairs."

"So Mr. Fletcher was right."

"It's gittin' hard to dispute." His voice was a mix of disappointment and admiration.

Mitchell interjected, "Should I continue the survey, Cap?"

Allison looked at Billings, who gave a small nod. "Yes, go ahead and finish up the initial scan. Once we've had a look, we can go back to the areas that interest us the most."

"Aye-aye, ma'am." He pressed on, recording as he went.

Much later that day, Allison sat in one of *Magellan*'s conference rooms surrounded by the department heads she'd thawed out for this shift.

Things progressed so rapidly that her small crew began to stumble over one another. She wanted to get them all on the same page, or at least the same book.

"All right, everyone. Simmer down," Allison began. "We're all here now, so I think we can get started. As you're all aware, we only have another couple of weeks before this shift ends and the next group takes over. We have to get as much done as possible while keeping impeccable records so that they can pick up where we leave off, with as little confusion as possible. The last thing we want is for our replacements to waste time backtracking what we've already done." She waited until she received nods of agreement from around the table. "That being said, let's go around the room and get a status summary from everybody. We'll start with you, Nelson. How is your team faring with the internal sensor repairs?"

"We have good news there, I think. We're almost certain we've identified all of the shorts and blown relays. Now all that's left is pulling up the deck plates to get at the bad wiring."

"Good work. How much more time do you need?" asked Allison.

"Another shift. Two at the most."

"Excellent. Did you hear that, *Maggie*?"

"Yes, Captain. I am . . . glad to hear that." *Magellan* had a fairly good understanding of human emotion; however, she had little experience expressing her own. It was the difference between listening to a symphony and playing the cello.

Truth be told, Allison wasn't even certain *Magellan* had genuine feelings or if some quirk of her software merely imitated what she saw in her crew.

"Thank you, Engineer's Mate Nelson," *Magellan* said.

"Hear that, Todd?" said Billings's holo. "Not many of us wrench monkeys get to toil away on machines that actually show their appreciation." Billings looked at him for a long moment. "Todd?"

"Hmm?"

"Aren't you forgetting something?"

"Oh, sorry. You're welcome, *Maggie*."

"Much better."

Allison nodded. "Wheeler, how goes navigation?"

"We're already up to almost 40 percent light speed. Another couple of hours of accel and we'll be at max. Reactor mass is dropping quick, though. Our margins are going to be thin."

"Any signs of pursuit?" asked Gruber.

"Scopes are clear, except for some localized fuzziness from one of the aft sensors. It came out clean after diagnostics, so I'm pretty sure it's interference from one of the shorts that Nelson is working on, given the cluster's proximity to Shuttle Bay Two."

Allison's face scrunched with concern. "Define 'fuzziness.'"

"The readings just don't add up quite right," Ensign Wheeler said. "They aren't showing anything there—no mass or energy readings, for instance. It's almost like the sensor is looking at the same chunk of space as all the others, just through smudged glasses."

"Sounds like the sort of echo you git with a bit of gravity projector leak," added Billings.

"What do you mean?" asked Allison.

"Well, if the projectors ain't synchronized exactly right, some gravitons can scatter away from the main projection and cause unfocused echoes. They ain't near intense enough to form a real gravity well, so they just make the space-time near them look a little weird to most types of sensors."

"When was the last time they were tuned?"

"Oh, I recon about sixty-five years ago when they wus bein' installed. That's not usually what wears out on the projectors. The crash might've thrown one out of alignment, I s'ppose."

"If it is an imbalance, how much will it degrade our drive capacity?"

"Trivially, like a slow drip off the bottom of a fire hose. Addin' the mass of the artifact probably had greater effect. That's one of the reasons the synchros ain't a real high maintenance priority, the other bein' that they're a real pain in the neck to git at."

"All right, fair enough. Ensign Wheeler, if it persists after Mr. Nelson is done with his repairs, I'd like to know."

"Yes, ma'am," said Wheeler.

"And provided it's still there, Steven, I'd like you to run whatever tests are needed to confirm your guess once you're up and about."

"Anything fer you, ma'am."

"Next, Prescott. Are we making any headway deciphering the artifact's signals and runes?"

Prescott leaned forward in her chair. "No, ma'am. We've not made any progress on translation. I'm sure now the signal contains multiple distinct layers. It's probably some kind of data compression, but we're having a devil of a time isolating them."

"Well, don't let yourselves get discouraged," said Allison. "It's not like you're translating Spanish." She turned away and looked again at the translucent image of Billings. "Now for the main course. Steven, you've completed the preliminary survey of the artifact?"

"Yes, indeed. And we're even further from understandin' it than we wuz this mornin'."

"That doesn't sound encouraging. What have you learned?"

Billings's image leaned back in his chair and folded his arms over his chest. "Well, the first thing we stumbled on is—"

CHAPTER 12

"—it has no power source." Felix was breathless. He waved a frantic finger at a rough schematic of the artifact's layout. It was standing room only in Felix's lab as members of the Artifact Research Team, or ARTists, as they'd taken to calling themselves, listened to Fletcher's preliminary findings on the raw data the *Magellan*'s crew had sent.

"Whoa. Slow down, Felix," Eugene said. "What's powering the transmitter, then?"

"No, that's not the problem," replied Felix. "It has power, plenty of it, in fact, but it's not coming from anywhere. Here . . ."

He pulled the schematic from his tablet and transferred it to his lab's holo-projector. A crude diagram of the artifact's inside materialized two meters off the floor. He pointed toward the central shaft that bridged the two lobes of the artifact.

"Right there is where the power is coming from, then it travels down these conduits to the different nodes"—a spiderweb of power lines fluoresced—"but there's nothing connecting back to the generator. There's no fuel tank, no reactor mass, nothing that I can find actually being converted into electricity."

"That's weird," Eugene said. "A battery maybe?"

"No way. There's almost forty megawatts coming out of that thing, and that's just at idle. I've estimated that it must have peaked at almost a full gigawatt when it had its gravity drive running. It's just not physically possible to achieve that kind of energy storage density."

"An ol'-fashioned fission plant?" Dr. Kiefer asked while absently arranging beads on his abacus.

"Nope. Geiger's flat. There's limited waste heat, but no radiation means no fission." Felix shook with excitement. "Energy just flows out while apparently nothing flows in. But it gets even better."

"Or worse, depending on how much you value maintaining a comfortable little bubble of preconceptions about the universe," Jeffery said.

"Anyway. From mysterious free energy to inexplicable inefficiency." Felix was moving too fast to pay attention to Jeffery's wit. If Felix's mind were a hamster, the wheel could have powered a house. "*Magellan*'s crew has also identified the transmitter. It's located on the other side of the buoy in the opposite lobe." Felix threw his hands in the air in exasperation. "Here's the problem. The transmitter's using a majority of the forty megawatts that mystery 'generator' is cranking out. For that amount of power, the signal should be exponentially more powerful. Apparently, energy comes from nowhere, flows into the other lobe, just to fall into a bottomless pit. It doesn't make any sense!"

Felix was becoming visibly upset. The whole situation offended his finely honed sense of reason and logic. Space-based engineering was all about efficiency and getting the most out of every kilogram. For all he could tell, the buoy ran counter to this fundamental ethic. Using a transmitter so huge in both size and power consumption relative to its observed output was as wasteful as burning stacks of first-edition books so you could read the paper.

"Calm down, my lad," said Eugene's round face. "Not everything makes sense at first glance. Now, have you found anything that we can learn from? Something to build off of?"

Felix willed his arms back down to his sides and took a deep breath. "Yes, I've had a close look at the scans of the antigrav device."

He moved to the other side of the suspended hologram and enlarged the spiraling component.

Several of the physicists leaned in hungrily.

"It is very compact, maybe small enough to build into a large aircar, and there are a number of ingenious design shortcuts that contribute to its small size that we could take advantage of immediately." He circled the hub at the center of the spiral. "Look here. The graviton pathway in the amplifier grows in diameter relative to the intensity of the beam. Ours are a constant diameter, which means they're actually too big for most of their length. That's a big waste of both size and thermal efficiency. I'm already growing a prototype."

"What about how it's producing antigrav? That would be nice to learn," Harris said.

"I don't know yet. The design is recognizable as a gravity projector immediately. But there are a number of noticeable differences in the layout. Any or all of them may explain how it makes antigrav."

"Can't you just reverse the polarity or something?" asked Harris.

Felix grinned. "Can you reverse the polarity to make a bullet jump back into the gun? I really wish it were that simple, but that sort of thing only works in the vids."

To his credit, Harris didn't seem the least bit flustered. He was smart enough to not be embarrassed by two things: the limits of his knowledge and the questions he needed to ask to expand them. "One more miracle for the pile, then."

"Don't start talking like that," Eugene said, "otherwise some crazy cult will spring up to worship this thing. They're like weeds waiting for a good rain."

"Speaking of weeds and the sorts of things that crawl through them, I'm fairly sure I picked up a tail last night," Harris interjected.

"Well, good on ya, boyo, but I don't sees what your bedroom conquests gots to do with our work here," Dr. Kiefer said impatiently.

Harris looked at the wild-haired physicist with amused disbelief. "Not *tail*, *a* tail. What I meant was, I'm almost certain someone tried to follow me home last night. It could be nothing, or it could mean someone is trying to gather information about our little extra-credit project," Harris continued. "We've all got to be especially careful about our operational integrity. We need to guard against unintentional leaks and be very careful to whom we speak and where. Always be aware of your surroundings and the possibility of eavesdropping. Under no circumstances is anyone to discuss the project over an unsecured phone line, and not at all over the Web."

Dr. Kiefer stirred. "That all sounds prudent, but we farm out loads of number crunchin' to the dispersed AESA hypercomputer network. That 'as to go through the 'net."

"I'm talking more about the public Net, hologs, AR virals, that sort of thing," Harris explained. "But still, from now on, everything sent around the AESA *internal* network needs to be sent with a minimum of Q4 encryption." The *Q* stood for unbreakable quantum encryption. The *4* indicated the fourth generation, because hackers had broken the first three.

Eugene put a hand on Harris's shoulder and looked at the rest of the crowd. "All right. I think we all understand the importance of discretion, and I've asked Sergeant Harris to keep a very close eye on that aspect of our operation. He's officially head of security as of this morning. So everyone please defer to his expertise on security issues."

Eugene patted the marine. "However, we can't lose sight of our main goal. We need to be cautious, but wringing maximum knowledge from the artifact is our job. Toward that end, I want everyone to break up into their research groups and start working on the issues we've identified today. That's all for now."

The room emptied quickly as the group scattered to the four winds. Only the nucleus of Eugene, Jeffery, Harris, and Felix remained. They looked at one another for several long moments with equal parts consternation and satisfaction.

Jeffery broke the silence first. "Quite the little production we're running here," he said, "and the real work has only just started."

"And the vultures are already circling," added Harris.

"Were you serious about being followed, Tom, or was that a line?" asked Eugene.

"Oh, no, I was serious. I spotted a tail while doing some grocery shopping."

"Wow, that's really surprising," said Jeffery.

"The tail?" asked Harris.

"No, the grocery shopping. I just figured you plugged into a wall at night."

Harris rolled his eyes. "You know I don't. Anyway, when I realized what was going on, I ducked into the employee lounge and waited for him to go by, then I started to trail him. Oldest trick in the book. It was total amateur hour. Got a look at him, too."

"Did you get a clean memory flash?" asked Felix.

"Only of the back of his head," answered Harris.

"Can you think of anyone who'd want to tail you personally, Tom? For reasons outside of our work here, I mean," Eugene said.

"My stalkers are usually of the feminine persuasion," Harris added with bravado.

Jeffery snorted.

"All right, Casanova. Very good," said Eugene. "Jeffery and Tom will try to ID our mystery guest, and I'm sure Felix here will be too busy trying to strangle answers out of the artifact to get into any real trouble." He looked at Felix, who'd already stopped paying attention in favor of frenetically scribbling notes on his tablet. Eugene shook his head. "Meanwhile, I have appearances to maintain. There's an AESA strategy conference in Berlin tomorrow, and the administrator can't really be absent without raising suspicions. So while my heart will remain here, my ass needs to go home and pack."

Felix looked up from his display. "Should we keep you updated on any breakthroughs while you're gone?"

"Ever the optimist, hmm?" said Eugene as he stroked his beard. "You'd better not. I'm going to be inundated with mission plans and budget proposals most of the time I'm away. Besides, that's just another message someone could intercept. The technical work is largely your responsibility, Felix. I rely on your judgment to guide the direction of everyone's work." Eugene checked the time. "Oh my. We've run quite long. I must bid you all adieu."

"Tom and I should get cracking on the interloper. Need anything, Felix? Coffee?" Jeffery asked.

"Nope, I'm good. Good luck with the search."

"Same to you," Harris said.

As his coworkers and friends left, silence once again blanketed Felix's lab. All that remained was the low hum of the holo-projector. Felix turned his head toward the suspended image of the artifact, laced his fingers, and cracked his knuckles.

"All right, sweetheart," he said. "You and I are going to have a little fun."

CHAPTER 13

"Our fuzzy patch is still there, ma'am," Ensign Wheeler said.

"Blast," Allison said. "Nelson, are you sure all the bugs are worked out of the internal sensors?"

"I triple-checked the connections, Captain," the engineer's mate said. "If there's a fault somewhere, it's buried deeper than I can find."

"My own diagnostics show no evidence of irregularities in Mr. Nelson's repairs, Captain," *Magellan* added.

"Great." Allison sighed and her unease raised a notch. "Oh, it's not you, Nelson. I was just hoping your efforts would clear up this little mystery. Tell your people they did well and then take the next two shifts off."

"Thank you, Captain." His image disappeared as the link was cut.

"Where's Chief Billings?" Allison asked.

Prescott searched for the engineer. "PT in the pool."

"All right. Leave him be for now. Just drop him a note to see me when he's free." She stood up from her chair at the center of the bridge. "Ensign Wheeler, you have the bridge. I'm headed for Bay Two."

"Aye, ma'am. I have the bridge."

Allison stepped into the transfer tube and keyed her destination. As the tram snaked its way through *Magellan*'s bones, Allison found herself brooding. Nelson's repair work had hit a few unexpected snags, meaning his team had spent an extra day crawling around on the floor ripping up deck plating. Meanwhile, Jacqueline had learned the shuttle was more damaged than her initial estimate once they really dug into it. Work continued.

Compounding her concerns, the fuzzy anomaly wasn't just a side effect of the damage to the internal sensors as Wheeler had guessed. That still left the projector imbalance Billings had suggested, but it was another unknown. When it came to her ship, Allison found unknowns as comforting as a wool sweater on fresh sunburn.

The tram doors opened. Allison turned right in the direction of the shuttle bays. As always, she was grateful for the tall ceilings her builders had afforded *Maggie*. Designers of interstellar ships made runway models look positively nonchalant about weight. Every single gram that could be cut meant less fuel to carry, greater range, higher speed, or more available payload. As a result, weight-saving holes were cut into everything from frame members to fork handles. Floors were not solid but grated. Ceilings went uncovered, leaving plumbing, ductwork, and electrical lines exposed. Most interstellars looked as though their skin had been picked clean by mechanical vultures, leaving their innards exposed. The dimensions of everything from hallways to living quarters trended toward claustrophobic. It had taken forcing a team of prominent designers into a six-month tour on board one of their creations before concessions were made for secondary concerns like preservation of the crew's sanity.

As a result, a person two meters tall could stride confidently through *Magellan*'s corridors without bashing his or her head on a gray water return pipe. Two people could pass each other in the same hallway without turning sideways and rubbing their reproductive organs together, although some did anyway.

Allison neared Shuttle Bay Two. Progress, of a sort, was being made on their study of the artifact. One of the engineering rankings had somehow tripped two more maintenance panels, making direct access and observation of the interior much easier. They'd mapped the major components and had a good idea of the function of many of them, although the physics of the power plant continued to elude them.

Unfortunately, they'd gotten nowhere with the translation. In some respects, that was to be expected. Deciphering an alien language, with its arbitrary sounds, symbols, and opaque cultural context, was necessarily more challenging than determining the purpose of a bit of machinery, but without the language, the intent of the artifact's builders would remain a mystery.

Allison found herself spending more and more time staring at the runes and listening to loops of the two messages. They were stuck in her head like an annoying jingle. She knew she was not alone; she'd heard Prescott humming a familiar . . . *melody* wasn't the right word.

She arrived at the airlock and keyed it open. The inner door closed behind her and the air cycled a bit, then the outer door opened. The bay echoed with the sounds of a dozen conversations, clanging tools, shuffling feet, and the occasional curse word. To her right was the artifact. Techs, with probes and cameras in hand, swarmed over it like ants on a piece of candy carelessly dropped by the gods.

To her left was the damaged shuttle, its maintenance panels strewn about the floor. Allison saw a short set of legs, which she was fairly confident belonged to Lieutenant Dorsett, sticking from one of the openings. She walked over to the shuttle.

Jacqueline was nose-to-purge-valve with an attitude control thruster inside the shuttle. Her small stature and delicate hands made her a perfect fit for the sort of tight spaces mechanics were always getting into.

"Mitchell, hand me an eight-millimeter torx-head socket, will you?" echoed Jacqueline's voice from the hole.

Allison looked around, but Mitchell was not in sight. Allison looked at the worktable next to Jacqueline's feet and tried to locate the requested tool. Finding a strip of hexagonal sockets, she quickly found the one marked eight millimeters and offered it to Dorsett's waiting hand.

"I said torx-head, Mitchell. C'mon, do I need to use my teeth?"

"Sorry, I haven't had much wrench time," Allison said, amused.

There was a sound of inrushing air and a metallic clang.

"Oww!" shouted Jacqueline.

"Are you all right, Jackie?"

"Um, yeah. Sorry, Captain, I didn't know you were there."

"That's all right," Allison said evenly. "Explain to me what you need."

"It's an eight-mil socket, except it's a six-pointed star. On the left side of the top of the cabinet."

Allison picked up the tree in question and found the correct attachment. She handed it to Jacqueline.

"Okay, that's it. Thank you."

"You're welcome. How much longer before it'll fly again?"

"Five hours, tops."

Allison looked at the parts, panels, and wires surrounding her feet. "Are you sure? There seems to be a lot left to do."

"It always looks worse than it really is. Is Mitchell out there with you?"

Allison scanned the bay for wayward specialists. "He appears to be flirting with the cuter of the two xenobiologists."

"What? Excuse me for a moment." Jacqueline shimmied out from the hole and marched across the deck to her subordinate.

Allison smirked as Jacqueline passed. She looked away as Jacqueline explained to Mitchell several important distinctions between a duty shift and recreational time.

Allison looked back at the worktable and its myriad of tools when something caught her eye—a maintenance manual. It was printed on a stack of actual paper almost six centimeters thick, sandwiched inside a grease-stained three-ring binder. Digital page readers had replaced most printed technical manuals almost three centuries earlier because of the ease with which they could be updated. Jacqueline must have printed the pages out and assembled them herself.

It was a strange duality, Allison thought. Jacqueline spent her entire career working with technology, studying it, repairing it. Yet this manual and the book she had gifted to Allison some weeks earlier were from a bygone era.

Allison flipped through the pages. The manual was printed in English, German, Spanish, French, Russian, Mandarin, and 13375p33k. For ease of use, AESA communications had to be sent in all the official languages of its member countries. This reduced the potential for miscommunication.

With a page reader, however, messages were automatically displayed in whatever language had been set by the user. There must have been some software glitch in the printer when Jacqueline—

From the recesses of Allison's brain, an idea pounced on her so suddenly that she nearly dropped the manual. She gasped with excitement and ran toward the artifact, manual in hand. She shoved her way past Jacqueline and Mitchell, pushed aside the red-faced xenobiologist, and circumvented one of the out-of-shape researchers.

Allison stood in front of the set of runes near the center of the artifact. She ran a finger down the etchings. She looked at them with fresh eyes, a key preconception eradicated. Everyone had been trying to translate the runes as one complete message. That was the reason no progress had been made.

She looked at each character individually, then contrasted the characters against their neighbors. The symbols were definitely alien compared to any Earth language, but the styles of the symbols were also subtly different from each other. The more she stared at them, the more she felt like she was looking at Latin, Cyrillic, Greek, and Arabic. One seemed to be completely separate, like someone threw hieroglyphs into the mix.

It wasn't one message. It was the same message repeated six times, the same word repeated six times in six different languages before moving on to the second word, and so on.

Then Allison remembered what Prescott had said about the signals in their briefing several days ago.

"I gotta go!" Allison said. "I'll be on the bridge." She ran toward the airlock.

"Captain!" shouted Jacqueline.

"What, Jackie?"

"I still need that." She pointed at the maintenance manual still in Allison's hands.

"Oh, right. I'm sorry." Allison hurried back and handed the book off to Jacqueline, who regarded her with suspicious eyes.

"You are going to tell us what this is about, right, ma'am?"

"Yes, later. For now, just get my shuttle moving."

"Yes, ma'am." Jacqueline saluted smartly.

With that, Allison made her way back to the bridge. Ensign Wheeler heard the doors behind him slide open and turned his head just as Allison strode through.

"Well, that was quick," he said.

"Prescott!" Allison found her seat. "You said there were different layers of data in the signals, right?"

"Yes, ma'am."

"Would that be *six* layers, by any chance?"

"That's right, Captain. How did you know?"

"Because starship captains are omniscient."

"Oh."

"If my guess is right, the six layers aren't data compression; they're the same signal being broadcast in six different languages," Allison said. "Look here." She brought up one of the holo-images of the runes. "We kept thinking it was one message, but it isn't. Each word is repeated six times using a different alphabet before moving on. We've got them all jumbled together."

Transfixed, Prescott leaned closer to the display and inspected the columns with a fresh perspective. The symbols seemed to mutate before her eyes.

"Impressive, Captain. I've been staring at these things for days without catching that. So have the people back on Earth."

"It was just a bit of serendipity, but still it looks like we've found our Rosetta stone."

"Let's not jump ahead of ourselves," said Prescott. "People could read Greek when the Rosetta stone was discovered. Since we don't know any of these, all we've really learned is that we have half a dozen alien languages that need translation instead of one."

"True, but now you can cross-reference them. That should help, especially now that you have both written and spoken versions of each."

"It might speed things up, at the very least," Prescott observed. "By the way, ma'am, Chief Billings called up here only a moment after you left. He asked you to call when you got back."

"Okay, put me through," Allison replied.

Prescott flicked through the first handful of crew icons until reaching the one for Billings, Steven Oscar, and keyed the intercom.

A one-quarter-sized holo appeared of a fit man, naked from the waist up, soaking wet from a shower, sporting a mat of chest hair and a Texas A&M tattoo over his left pectoral muscle. "Hello, ma'am. Thanks fer returnin' my call."

"Steven, could you please tip your camera up about twenty degrees, for the children?" Allison motioned to Wheeler and Prescott.

"Of course. Wouldn't want anyone left feelin' inadequate." Billings smirked.

Wheeler snorted in mock indignation. Billings reached out, and the holo recentered on his head.

"Thank you," said Allison. "What's up?"

"Well, I'm sure our fuzzy spot ain't a projector imbalance."

"How do you know that? I thought you said it would take a long time to get to the synchronizers to check them."

"Yup, at least two full days."

"So how did you check them so fast?"

"I didn't."

Allison stared at him blankly for a moment. "Well, that's certainly a time-saver, but then how do you know the projectors aren't responsible?"

"Because we turned 'em off yesterday once we were done acceleratin'."

"Should have thought of that," Allison said sheepishly. She caught a glimpse of Prescott starting to snicker. "Not a peep out of you."

"Wouldn't dream of it, Your Magnificence," Prescott answered innocently.

"Well, since it's not the projectors, could it be faulty g-deck plating?" Allison asked.

"No, ma'am," answered Billings. "G-deck plating is a localized effect; the gravitons scatter randomly after the first couple of meters. The projectors are what actually *focus* the gravitons. It's like shining light through an optical lens. Most of the light falls into one point, but spots can appear if the glass ain't just perfect."

Allison pondered for a few moments. "But it still doesn't seem like there's anything actually there. Is there any record of a natural phenomenon causing this effect?"

"Yeah, but not one that tracks perfectly alongside a ship movin' at one-half c. I don't know. Maybe it's anchored onto us somehow, gravitationally, or magnetically. Beats me at this point. Alls I know is what it ain't, and it ain't comin' from nothin' wrong with *Mags*."

Everyone on the bridge looked at one another uneasily, not quite sure what to do or say next.

Magellan stepped into the silence. "Captain, if I may make a suggestion?"

"Of course, *Maggie*. What's on your mind?"

"We can conduct an experiment to determine if the anomaly is natural or artificial. If my course is adjusted, even minutely, we can observe the anomaly's reaction. If it also changes course to match mine in unison, that would be strong evidence that it's bound to us in some way. However, if there is any delay in its course change, or if it fails to change course, then that would confirm that it is piloted and therefore artificial."

"Simple. Straight to the point. I like it," Allison said. "Navigation, alter course one arc minute starboard for thirty seconds, then bring us back to our original heading."

"Yes, ma'am," said Wheeler. He quickly keyed in a few commands. "Beginning our turn . . . now."

Magellan slid gently sideways as the bridge crew anxiously monitored her sensor readouts. An all-too-familiar ranging sensor reported back to *Magellan* with an attitude that had grown to border on overconfidence. The fuzzy anomaly had changed course to very precisely match *Magellan*'s.

But more important, there had been a delay of three seconds before it made the adjustment. They were being followed. The seconds ticked down to zero, and Wheeler altered their course again to point them back to Earth. Again, there was a delay in the reaction of the anomaly, although it was noticeably shorter the second time. Not only were they being followed, their unseen pursuer was a quick learner.

If *Magellan* had any hair on her neck, or a neck, for that matter, it would have stood on end. Allison, on the other hand, had both. The hair on her neck was straight and stiff as cactus spines. Allison brought up all of *Magellan*'s different sensor feeds and linked them to the bridge's main display, but the void jealously guarded its secrets.

Uncertain of what to do next, but certain that doing nothing wasn't right either, Allison reached down into a storage compartment beside her chair and pulled out the yellow-and-black book with the irreverent, condescending title. She surveyed the eyes of her fellows, daring one of them to make a wisecrack.

When none of them took up the gauntlet, she opened the book to the rear to get her bearings. Jacqueline had previously instructed her in the use of the index, as Allison had never read a book without a search feature before. She found the proper page reference and flipped to it . . .

SECTION 4: ENCOUNTERING E.T. IN SPACE

Congratulations! You've discovered another space-faring race. Now, don't panic. The fact you're reading this means you haven't been vaporized. This is good evidence the aliens aren't mindlessly violent.

That said, there are some steps you should take to mitigate the chances of catastrophe.

STEP 1: Immediately purge any macho fantasies of outgunning or outrunning the alien vessel. Odds are that any aliens you find in deep space are many hundreds or thousands of years more advanced than mankind. So fighting them using any primitive weapons you have will probably be as fruitful as throwing rocks at a nuclear aircraft carrier. Likewise, running from them could make you look scared or guilty of something. Just act cool, like you belong there, which you don't.

STEP 2: Maintain the status quo. Do not take any actions that could be misinterpreted as hostile. Such actions include charging lasers, aiming missiles, opening weapons ports, using active sensors, deploying drones, launching fighters, or anything else that might give them an excuse to reduce your ship to its constituent molecules.

STEP 3: In case things do go wrong at some point, it would be awfully nice to let Earth know what's going on. That way if they don't hear from you, they'll have some idea what happened, giving humanity time to prepare for the invasion caused by whatever you did to offend the alien techno gods.

While unlikely, it's possible that a unidirectional signal, such as a laser, could be intercepted and used to establish Earth's heading, leading hostile aliens to mankind's doorstep. Instead of risking the entirety of the human race, use an omnidirectional signaling device, such as a radio.

"How about a signal that doesn't actually go in *any* direction?" said Allison aloud, addressing the long-dead author.

"Ma'am?" asked Prescott.

"Nothing. I need you to cut the research data feed from one of the QERs so we can send a message to Earth."

"Right away, Captain." She set to work, grateful for the distraction. "The QER is ready and linked to your station, ma'am."

"Thank you." Allison brought up a virtual keyboard and typed out a short message. She sent it. "All right, resume the data feed."

"Yes, Captain."

Allison turned back to the book. Below step three was a light gray box with an icon of a person waving a finger. The individual resembled a slice of pepperoni pizza. It said:

> Tip: Further measures to protect Earth should include preparations to wipe your computer's memory in case of a hostile boarding. If you're thinking about fending off the alien boarding parties, refer back to Step 1. Don't overlook dispersed forms of memory, such as data tablets, laptops, external hard drives, or separate mainframes on shuttles, probes, escape pods, and so on. If there isn't time, refer to "Self-Destruct" in the index.

Allison decided to skip the "Self-Destruct" section for the moment, but she could appreciate the logic behind taking a few simple precautions, even if the logic was born of a comical level of paranoia.

"Helm, I want you to alter course for the moment. Move us four arc minutes off our present heading and hold that course until I tell you to resume."

"Aye-aye, ma'am," responded Wheeler. An uneven tone betrayed his confusion, but he discharged her instructions without question or further comment.

Allison smirked with satisfaction. "*Maggie*, I want you to create a temporary folder and move any files pertaining to Earth's location, our colonies, astronomical references, and our navigational logs into it. Be ready to permanently delete the folder on my command."

"Yes, Captain; however, without that data, I cannot plot a bearing to Earth."

"That's right, and neither can anyone or anything else," said Allison.

The rest of the bridge nodded in understanding.

Allison could see her own anxiety reflected in the expressions of those around her. Yet despite the weight of their trepidation, or perhaps because of it, Allison's people weren't balking under the pressure. Just the opposite. They were as cool and collected as she'd ever seen them.

"The folder has been created and filled as you requested, Captain."

"Thank you, *Maggie*." Allison turned her eyes back to the book that had, against all probability, survived to become her impromptu checklist.

She considered the odds against a book finding its way through three hundred years into the hands of the singular human being that would actually benefit from it. Allison saw the invisible hand of providence in the improbable circumstance, right until she remembered the author had obviously written the whole thing on a lark. Perhaps the fates were bored and in need of a laugh. She proceeded anyway.

> STEP 4: Now comes the hard part: striking up a conversation. Unless you've been whisked to some faraway galaxy through a wormhole or something, you're probably still relatively close to Earth, at least in astronomical terms.
>
> Provided this is the case, you will still be inside the sphere of radio and TV signals we've been squawking out for decades to anyone who'll listen like a bunch of overconfident idiots. Therefore, if the aliens have any notion of your origins, they will be expecting you to attempt communication using old-fashioned radio waves, and there is a fair chance they have studied one or more human languages.

> Do not use laser or any other directed-energy type of communications first, as this could be misinterpreted as an active scan or weapons range-finding.

"Com," Allison said, "how's our RF transmitter?"

"Practically new. Hasn't been used since it was tested sixty years ago."

"Excellent. Dust it off and hail the anomaly."

Magellan's radio was only a backup device. Within a star system, com lasers carried the mail because of the impressive bandwidth they could handle. Farther out, QERs did the work once the light speed delay made lasers impractical. Radios were reserved for distress signals, because you didn't have to point them, and you never knew where help might come from.

Prescott dug through command screens until she unearthed the link to the long-disused radio.

"What frequency should I use?" asked Prescott.

Allison paused. She hadn't thought about that. "All of them. Cycle through the entire spectrum."

"Ready, ma'am." She pressed a key in the air. "Hail sent."

CHAPTER 14

If anyone on board *Magellan* could see it, the unknown ship trailing them would've resembled the most malicious, violent, nightmarish predator dredged from the coldest depths of the darkest ocean. The sort of seemingly impossible carnivore that's all teeth and jaws, with a body thrown in as an afterthought.

But they couldn't see it.

The reason they couldn't see it was because the ship was so evil and menacing in appearance that if a photon of light approached the ship on a sidewalk, it would cross the street, just to be safe.

It took a few microseconds for *Magellan*'s hail to travel out on the right frequency across the twenty-seven kilometers of space that separated the vessels. But once it did, a very different crewman on a very different bridge picked up the signal. The being gazed at the sensor display through metallic eyes. A tiny muscular motor in the glowing red iris whirred as he leaned closer.

"Vel Noric, apologies," the creature hissed. "The human vessel is signaling us."

"Impossible," answered the ship's commander. "We're sheathed; they can't know we're observing them."

"Of course, Vel. I hadn't considered that. Forgive my incompetence," said the sensor operator.

Noric hadn't bothered to learn this one's name yet.

Even among his crew, the Vel was an imposing figure. That was saying something for a species that resembled the end result of a drunken hookup between a Gila monster and a hyena.

Noric stood nearly an entire crest above anyone else on board, and out-massed his closest competitor by 20 percent. This was not pure chance. Noric had cultivated many favors among the hierarchy tasked with personnel assignments. They were gracious enough to see that his first crew was on the small side.

Noric figured it was a good survival strategy for an untested Vel in the Turemok military, and it had proven true. There had been one Pal'kuar dominance rite since he'd been appointed Vel, only one. The . . . finality of the outcome served as insurance that there would not be another on this tour.

"Vel, would it please you to judge an observation?" asked his Hedfer-Vel, J'quol.

Noric hesitated. He'd picked the youth as his Hedfer-Vel because he was deferential, lacked ambition, and was too slight of build to act on his ambition should he inadvertently come across any. These were time-honored criteria for picking one's subordinate in a system that had little need of retirement benefits for former commanders, on account of all of them being dead.

But several things had planted the seeds of doubt in Vel Noric's mind about his Hedfer-Vel. He was different from the others. J'quol was not quick to anger, but neither was he quick to cower. He could be very methodical, thinking things through from many directions. He always stood by his ideas, even if he phrased objections in a properly subservient manner. And he could be manipulative, exploiting weaknesses or disagreements among the crew to further the Vel's orders.

Noric realized J'quol's eyes were still looking at him, while new eyes had turned to investigate.

"What was that you said, Hedfer-Vel? I was . . . contemplating something."

"I apologize for intruding on your thoughts, Vel. I asked would it please you to judge an observation?"

"Proceed."

"Only moments before sensor interpreter Kotal detected the . . . emissions from the human vessel, it had made a series of small course alterations."

"Yes." Noric exuded boredom. "Probably dodging pebbles too big for their excuses for energy weapons to destroy."

"That was my initial conclusion as well, Vel. However, by chance, I had been looking at our navigational sensor readings at the same time. There was no such debris for them to avoid."

This was obviously a fiction, as the two different data sets were not displayed simultaneously. He couldn't have been viewing them both "by chance." He would have needed to call them up separately and deliberately. J'quol was taking care to present his argument in a way that wouldn't make the Vel look stupid in front of the rest of the command crew.

Normally, this would be a very good quality in a subordinate. In this case, however, Noric wasn't so sure. He couldn't shake the feeling that J'quol was putting on a performance. There was something entirely too calm about J'quol. Almost . . . Lividite.

Noric grew impatient. "Come to the tip of the tooth, Hedfer-Vel."

"With haste, Vel. I believe the human commander suspected our presence, perhaps a faint sensor reading, but had reason to doubt his conclusion. So he altered course to see if we followed in unison. Any delay in our course adjustment would prove that we were not a trick of his sensors."

"Continue," Noric said, interested.

"Almost immediately after the course alteration, their commander sent out the signal we detected. I believe the human vessel has detected us faintly and is attempting to initiate communication."

Vel Noric rolled back on his heels and leaned on a handrail. His synthetic irises shrank to pinpoints as he mulled over the theory.

They'd been shadowing the human thieves since intercepting the buoy's requisition for repair. As best as his crew could deduce, the humans had stumbled onto the buoy purely by luck. In accordance to their foul nature, the first thing they did was hope no one was looking, tuck the buoy under their coats, and run for home.

Normally, that would've been justification enough for Vel Noric to capture or destroy the vessel on charges of piracy. Unfortunately, after reporting the matter, the Assembly of Sentient Species, in its unassailable wisdom, had ordered Noric and his ship to remain hidden and report on the Earth vessel's actions. Apparently, hijacking wasn't a sufficient crime to perturb the centuries-old noninterference policy regarding humanity and similar lower species.

The Vel wondered precisely what it would take for the Assembly to take the threat of Earth's rapid advancement seriously. Would the humans need to invade a member world? Collapse a star perhaps?

He reached a decision. "Your observation is sound, Hedfer-Vel. That . . . complicates things." He found his chair and sat down. "For reasons beyond my understanding, the noninterference dictum remains in place. We were to remain hidden and observe. Somehow, they have seen through our sheath. By itself, that has compromised our assignment. Now I must decide how to salvage the situation."

"You have ideas on that facing, Vel?" asked J'quol.

"Yes, what we should have done from the beginning: destroy the vessel. If they do not get back to Earth, they cannot alert them of their discovery or deliver the technology in that buoy to their scientists. The last thing we need is their engineers digging around inside of it and leaping forward a century."

"Would that not violate noninterference?"

"That was already violated when they detected us. It's just a matter of degree."

"True. Would it please you to judge another—"

"Just throw it out, Hedfer-Vel," Noric said testily.

"Yes, Vel. Analysis of the buoy will confirm for them that it was not built by other humans. So detecting our vessel would not be their first evidence of another sentient species. The humans have a saying—'That dog is already out of the sack.'" J'quol folded his arms. "Besides, destroying the vessel may be seen as an overreaction. You know how . . . squeamish the Assembly can be about such things."

That was certainly true. Noric could hear the objections coming from the review members now. "They were unarmed and defenseless," they would say, completely missing the point that that's when you *want* to attack the enemy. The clawless cowards certainly didn't voice such qualms millennia ago when the Turemok military was the only thing preventing the Lividite war machine from overwhelming the entire sector.

The Assembly's idea of long-term military strategy seemed to be to allow every planet full of savages to frolic about space giddily until they were technologically advanced enough to pose a real threat. It made as much sense as hand-rearing Gomeltic hatchlings until they were big enough to eat you.

But that was someone else's problem. If Noric ordered the human ship destroyed and the Assembly disapproved, that would be *his* problem.

"Your observation is persuasive, Hedfer-Vel. Tiller, open a portal and move us to one-third Dar-Penyog from the human vessel. That should put us well outside their sensors. Once in position, continue observation until we receive updated orders. And find out what went wrong with our sheath to cause this mess in the first place!"

Without delay, the (nearly) invisible ship came about, flexed its muscles as if to pounce, and then leaped headlong into a hole in space.

"They've disappeared, ma'am!" Wheeler shouted from his nav station, bewildered.

"They left?" asked Allison.

"No, well, yes. Sort of. They didn't leave, exactly. There was a strange energy spike. Now they aren't appearing on our scopes."

Allison queried the last ten seconds of sensor data and watched the playback. It was exactly as Wheeler described. A bizarre blip, then the fuzzy anomaly simply vanished.

"What the hell was that all about?" she asked no one in particular.

"I don't know," replied Prescott, "but I'll feel a bit better with one less mystery hanging over our heads."

"Amen to that." Allison sank into her chair. Whatever it had been, Allison was relieved it had decided to bug out instead of start shooting.

"Helm, resume course for Earth."

"Aye, ma'am."

CHAPTER 15

As the months piled on, Eugene found the accumulated pressure of work took progressively longer to leak back out again. His "retirement" from teaching had proven more strenuous than even the worst parts of his old life. There were times he found himself wishing to return to the days of grading an entire lecture hall's worth of doctoral theses, just for the rest it would represent compared to the last year.

Wrestling with politicians added greatly to his frustration. Eugene had taught political science for two decades before moving on to AESA. He thought he had a pretty good handle on the political environment and the dangerous species that inhabited it, but detached study was far different from direct interaction. Like the difference between watching lions prowl in the zoo and listening to them prowling outside your tent in the dead of night.

In spite of this, Eugene was not immune to the infectious enthusiasm permeating his group of brilliant shut-ins. He found he possessed more energy than he'd had in years. He came home exhausted, but slept deeply and awoke rejuvenated, often with enough exuberance to give his wife a proper rise-and-shine before going back to work.

Most important, progress was being made. Felix's reverse-engineering team had yielded tangible results. They'd already developed an advanced gravity projector both smaller and more efficient than traditional designs. Simulations estimated a vessel fitted with them could reach 0.55 c, a 10 percent increase, which would cut months or even years off round-trip journeys to the colony worlds, and time equaled money.

The ARTists had set up a shell corporation to hang the new patents in. Venture capital flowed into the company accounts, supplementing the project's AESA black budget and swelling their ranks further still. There was a real risk to such maneuverings. Anyone nosy enough to take interest could see the shell for its true nature, and they still hadn't identified Harris's secret admirer from nearly a year ago.

But neither had there been any repeats of that performance. Harris must've scared whoever it was off the trail. Still, curiosity tended to trump fear over the long run, and there were always others to take up the torch.

Eugene glanced at his watch. It was an antique mechanical piece, a gift from the university upon the end of his tenure, and quite valuable to the right collector. Feeling a little ancient himself, he wore the anachronism proudly, even though it had taken over a year to get used to reading the hands. He still couldn't do it at a glance, which forced him to look a second time: 7:48 P.M.

That was enough for one day. The rest of what people continued to call paperwork, despite not containing any paper, would still be there in the morning. In fact, if past experience was any guide, it would find a way to fornicate and multiply.

Eugene locked down his computer terminal and placed his tablet in his coded briefcase, genetically tagged to him. It acted as a sort of reverse fire safe. Should anyone else attempt to open it, the contents would be thoroughly incinerated, without damage to anything outside the case. The flammable mixture contained its own oxidizers, allowing it to work underwater and even in a vacuum. Eugene felt this was overkill, as, if he found himself floating in space, document destruction wouldn't be his most pressing issue.

Eugene was about to extricate himself from his disarmingly comfortable chair when he saw shadows lurking through the frosted glass of his office door. He tensed for a moment, until he recognized the squirrelly tenor of Mr. Fletcher. Did that kid ever leave the lab?

Eugene pressed the stud to open the door. "Come on in, boys. No sense waiting around to ambush me in the hall."

Felix and Jeffery rushed in like a river through a burst levee.

"Professor, I've just heard that—"

"I've figured it out! It's not a—"

"They've finished transl—"

"It must be a—"

"Slow down, guys," said Eugene.

"Quit interrupting."

"Can I finish?"

"I was here first!"

"Yeah, but—"

"*Stop!*" Eugene gave them both a simmering look. The two men went silent and had the good sense to look penitent. "Thank you. Now, then, one lunatic at a time is all that I can handle at my age. So, in no order of importance, Felix, please proceed. Jeffery, you may go second."

"Sorry, sir. What I was in a hurry to tell you was I think I've killed two birds with one stone."

"I hope you had the proper hunting permits," quipped Eugene. Felix looked a trifle confused. "Never mind, please go on."

"Right. You know how the buoy's insanely inefficient radio transmitter has been bugging the crap out of me?"

"Yes."

"And how none of us could figure out how the mystery ship had known where to look for the *Magellan*, since the crew was blocking the buoy's radio broadcast?"

"Again, yes."

"Well, I think I've figured out the answer to both." Felix took a breath. "It isn't a radio transmitter. At least that's not what it's supposed to be."

"You may have lost me. We know it's emitting a radio signal," said Eugene.

"Yes, but that's not its purpose, like an old-fashioned incandescent light bulb wasn't supposed to be a heater."

Someone flipped a switch in Eugene's brain. "So you're saying the radio waves are a by-product, like electrical resistance through a wire causing heat."

"Exactly. It's wasted energy. For months, I couldn't figure out why the transmitter was sucking down so much energy for so little signal strength. Even worse, I couldn't find where the majority of the energy was going. There wasn't nearly enough waste heat or radiation to account for it all. It has to be going somewhere we can't see."

"All right. That gives us a place to start. But that's only one mystery," said Eugene.

"I was coming to the second. Since we can assume the majority of the signal is going out somewhere else, we can also assume that jamming the radio spectrum isn't doing squat to stop the actual signal. That's why the *Magellan*'s mystery guest knew where to find her."

"Oh, wonderful," said Eugene. "So our people are dragging around a giant torch attracting every moth in range. Ridgeway won't be happy about that."

"No, sir. But now that I know I'm not looking at the universe's dumbest radio tower, I think we have a good chance of figuring out what it's actually doing. And if my guess is right, whatever signal it's pumping out is superluminal."

"Like our QER?" asked Jeffery.

"I don't think so. There's no reason a quantum entanglement process should produce any radio waves, even as a by-product. I think whatever it is still takes time to travel, just faster than light can."

"But that's supposed to be impossible," said Eugene.

"Sort of. There are a couple of possible ways around light speed beyond just entanglement. Besides, if the main signal had propagated out from the buoy at light speed, then the ship that came to keep tabs on *Magellan* would have been *really* close by to get there as quickly as it did."

Eugene let his mind backtrack through the time line of events. Even if the mystery ship had been able to travel at just a fraction below light speed, the time between the emergency message being broadcast and the ship being detected by the *Magellan* was less than two weeks, meaning it had to have been less than a light-week away when it first heard the signal. There was nothing of interest in that area of space for many light-*months*. It did stretch credibility to think it was sitting there waiting for someone to stumble upon that one buoy.

"Make it your team's top priority. Lives could depend on it," Eugene said.

Felix nodded enthusiastically. Even as he said it, Eugene knew the instruction was unnecessary. Felix may have been quiet and shy, but he was a pit bull when it came to mysteries. He was going to sink his teeth into this new problem and thrash it around until it stopped moving.

"Moving on. Jeffery?"

"Yes, Professor. I just heard from the linguists, they've cracked the messages," Jeffery said breathlessly.

Now *that* was interesting.

"That's wonderful. What does the first one say?"

"Well, there's some debate if the different languages represent different social entities like countries, or if they're from six distinct species," said Jeffery.

"Well, we may not be able to answer that conclusively until we find someone to ask, I'd wager. But what does the first signal say?"

"Really the turning point came a month ago when *Magellan*'s crew found the readout in the buoy that displayed the signals in written form," Jeffery said.

"Yes, I figured. What does it say?"

"Well, the second signal was a request for maintenance like we figured."

Eugene folded his hands in his lap and squared his eyes at his assistant. "Jeffery, do I need to waterboard the translation of the first signal out of you?"

Jeffery's shoulders sagged. "You're not going to like it."

"I assure you, I like not knowing even less."

"All right. Don't say I didn't warn you."

Jeffery called up something on his tablet and handed it to Eugene. The screen displayed a memo from the head linguist of the group, marked Signal 1 Translation. It read:

HUMAN WILDLIFE PRESERVE. KEEP OUT.

Eugene blinked. He read it again. It said the same thing. He tried a third time. The memo remained stubbornly resilient to change. After taking a few moments to order his thoughts, he was able to articulate again. "Are they sure about this?"

"There is some disagreement about the exact phrasing. Words don't always line up precisely from one language to another, much less between seven of them, but they're greater than 95 percent confident in the overall meaning."

"Well, then," said Eugene. "That's going to ruffle some feathers."

The next morning, it became apparent "That's going to ruffle some feathers" would turn out to be one of history's epic understatements, rivaled only by an unsuspecting Pompeii merchant who rose on a sunny day in 79 CE and greeted his neighbor with, "Looks like it's going to be a hot one."

The immediate effect among the circle of politicians aware of the ARTists program was disbelief and indignation. One of them spent the entire morning violently remodeling his office with the help of a putter and a fifth of tequila. None of this should have been surprising. There was only so much abuse the human ego can take. Learning that there were as many as six intelligent alien species sharing the galactic neighborhood with humanity would be enough to shift anyone's sense of importance. Learning that said species were fencing off humans like elephants? That was another matter entirely.

For Eugene and his merry band of misfits, however, the news was positive. Their budget absolutely exploded, as their superiors were suddenly interested in wringing every bit of technology out of the buoy in as little time as possible. Allison Ridgeway and her A-squad were about to thaw out on the other end of the QER to start their next shift, and the various research groups were running smoothly.

One development Eugene and his senior team members weren't thrilled about was the military's growing influence through AESA defense collaboration. Not that it was a surprise. The only real surprise was that it had taken this long.

Invariably, the first question asked about a new technology is, "Can this make killing less of a hassle?" The second being, "Can I have sex with it?" As a rule, someone always says, "Yes." When man first harnessed flame, it was immediately used to start grass fires to drive game. It took time before he realized he could also use fire to harden clay bricks. GPS was created to advance the art of accurately blowing up undesirable foreigners with high explosives. Making navigation safer for air travel, commuting easier for motorists, or helping find people lost at sea were afterthoughts.

This question was on Eugene's mind when, early in the afternoon, he received a summons to report to the American/European Union building for a Q&A session with members of parliament. Eugene had attended such meetings before. They traditionally ended with the politicians believing they had all the answers, and the experts questioning why they'd bothered to come.

He brought up Harris's link on his tablet and hit Connect. "Thomas?"

"Yes, sir?"

"Grab your dress uniform, lad. We have to impress some important people tonight."

Later, in Eugene's Jaguar, Harris struggled with his uniform's white belt.

"That looks a little snug," Eugene said.

"It shrank. Must have gotten wet."

"Uh-huh. I'm sure it doesn't have anything to do with you spending the last year working with sedentary academics." Eugene could have sworn he saw a bit of blush forming on Harris's dark cheeks.

"Why don't you ask Felix to partner up on a workout routine? It would do you some good, and it could really help his confidence."

"You think so?"

"Hard as it may be to believe, many years ago I was a scrawny, socially awkward youth myself. It's not an easy mind-set to break free of."

"Well, at least you seem to be cured of the former," Harris prodded from behind a toothy grin.

"Ouch. The wound is deep," replied Eugene with good humor.

"Can I ask you something, sir?"

"I believe you just did, but you can ask me something else as well."

"Why me?" Harris seemed confused, but not pleading.

"Why you, for what?"

"This meeting. What questions can I answer that Felix or Jeffery can't? They're much more qualified to discuss the details of what we do than I am."

"Simple," Eugene replied. "Felix, Jeffery, and I are peas in a pod. We're all civilians, academic elitists, the nerds. But you, Thomas, you're the atheist in the pews. Your military background gives you a perspective different from the rest of us. Different, and possibly more valuable to them."

"More valuable than the scientists doing the actual work?"

"You forget who we're talking to. These are career politicians. Ignoring or denying the work of experts is a prerequisite for the job." Eugene's voice had more than a pinch of lemon zest. "No, they already have a course charted; we're presenting ourselves so they can cherry-pick our replies to validate the decisions they've already made."

"So why go at all?"

"Because they hold the PIN on our accounts."

"You're afraid the military is going to take over the program," said Harris flatly. If he was offended, he didn't let it show.

"Not explicitly, no. The AESA has never in two hundred years handed over all control of a project to the armed forces, and to my infinite surprise, the age-old treaty banning weapons in space is as strong as ever. But that was put in place to prevent us from destroying ourselves. Now that there are threats from beyond, I don't know if it can continue."

"A challenger appears," said Harris.

"Indeed. I fully expect we'll be seeing more uniforms around the office, more 'consultants' and 'advisors' offering their two cents in ways that will be difficult to refuse."

Harris digested this for a few moments as the lights of the downtown grew below them. "What do you want me to say to them, Professor?"

Eugene realized Harris had cemented his competing loyalties with the question. "I want you to speak your mind, Thomas. You have a good one. You don't give yourself enough credit. Just because you're not as schooled as the rest of us doesn't mean you're deficient in the noggin. When you start second-guessing your instincts and try to game what other people want you to say is when you'll dig yourself a hole."

"Thank you, sir."

"Don't thank me just yet. I'm the one leading you into the lion's den. At the lion's invitation, I might add."

Within the hour, they sat in a lavishly appointed parlor surrounded by rich wooden panels and straight-backed chairs with ornately carved armrests. Tiny, irregular tool marks witnessed to their handcrafted origins. They were sinfully cozy. Chair makers had life figured out; there's hard work to do before you can sit comfortably.

Harris fidgeted in his chair, going over the creases in his uniform like a cadet awaiting inspection from a particularly demonic drill sergeant. Eugene sympathized, but after years of politics at various levels, he was no longer entranced by the wielders of power. The uncomfortable truth was the personal qualities that made someone most likely to be elected had little to do with competence or integrity.

Several members of the American/European Union Parliament filtering into the parlor were case studies in that very phenomenon. Eugene knew many of them personally. They were MAEPs from districts with large AESA research or industrial footprints like Florida, Hesse, Germany, and Paraí, Brazil. They were insiders, already aware of the ARTist program. There were also a few outsiders, presumably being briefed on the program for the first time. Eugene recognized a couple of the others. One in particular strengthened his suspicions about the meeting.

His name was Gladstone Rockwell, although the political press had dubbed him "Gladhand" on account of his unrivaled ability to grab government appropriations for his home district. You could smell the oak and bacon grease from three meters away.

On paper, Rockwell represented the Chicago-Milwaukee metro area. This was a polite fiction. Everyone knew his real constituency was Lockheed-Boeing-Raytheon, which had an unassailable position as the largest defense contractor on the planet. They provided arms to everyone from Warsaw to Walmart.

Space represented the final frontier to many, but none so much as the defense industry. With very few exceptions, space had remained free of weapons since the earliest days of space flight. The Outer Space Treaty, properly known as the Treaty on Principles Governing the Activities of States in the Exploration and Use of Outer Space, including the Moon and Other Celestial Bodies (toner wasn't as expensive back then), had only officially banned the placement of nuclear weapons in space or the construction of military bases off world. For a number of reasons, a gentlemen's agreement between nations had expanded the narrow wording of the treaty to include all kinds of offensive weaponry.

However, where there were fences, quarreling neighbors were never far behind. The discovery of mankind's fence had the potential to trigger an arms race not seen since the fission-stoked days of Cold War paranoia. For Lockheed-Boeing-Raytheon, that meant defense contracts worth untold trillions, which was why the presence of MAEP Rockwell this early in the process made Eugene so uncomfortable.

"Isn't that right, Professor Graham?" said a familiar, charismatic voice.

"Hmm?" Eugene looked up. "Sorry, I was trapped in a thought. What was that you said?"

"I was saying your team's research was bearing fruit." The voice belonged to MAEP Danielle Fenton. Officially, she was the chairwoman of the Advisory Board for Civilian Development of Space (ABCDS). Unofficially, she was the head of their secret circle, and reported directly to the AEU president. Mrs. Fenton also happened to be the former student who'd roped Eugene into his position as AESA's administrator. That had been one election and two last names ago for her.

"Indeed," began Eugene. "Our boys and girls have managed to translate many of the messages we've found, and the first product of our reverse-engineering efforts is about to begin testing."

"Gosh, that's really exciting," said Gladstone Rockwell. "I've only just started reading your reports today, but it sounds like you're sitting on a gold mine of technology. I was really excited to read about your man Fletcher's work on faster-than-light propulsion."

An alarm went off in Eugene's head. Felix's suspicions about the buoy's FTL communication had only been put in this morning's report. Either Rockwell was an impossibly fast reader, or he had been briefed on the project earlier than Eugene had supposed.

"I'm afraid you may be getting ahead of yourself, Mr. Rockwell, is it?"

"Please, my friends call me Gladstone."

Eugene managed not to say, *And what about people who don't trust you farther than they can piss Jell-O?*

Instead, Eugene continued, "Well, Gladstone, Mr. Fletcher is working on the very early stages of a hypothesis. He believes that the buoy has an FTL *communications* system. Not propulsion, just signals. The buoy itself seems to only have a low-powered antigravity drive, not nearly as powerful as the gravity drive aboard the *Magellan*, for example."

Rockwell pursed his lips. "Well, why spend time on that? Our QERs work instantly and can't be intercepted. Surely that's a better system."

"In some ways, yes. But you must remember QERs only work in pairs, and their bandwidth is abysmal. FTL coms could drastically speed up broadband signals in system. But for now, it's only a guess. Felix—I mean, Mr. Fletcher—has only just started work on his hypothesis."

"I see." This obviously wasn't what Rockwell had hoped to hear. "So there's no application for propulsion, then?"

"It does not appear so, no."

"So it will still take decades to get ships out there and confront these aliens."

"Confront them?" said Eugene. "That's a loaded choice of words."

"What would you suggest? As I understand it, we've just discovered that we're being caged like zoo animals," Rockwell said.

"I would hardly call a network of buoys a cage. It is probably just a way for them to mark off territory set aside for us."

"Oh, well, that's mighty thoughtful of them to decide what *our* territory is going to be," Rockwell said sarcastically.

"The border is thirty light-years away. If it's a sphere, you're talking about a volume of over 110,000 cubic light-years. It might take us millennia to fully develop all the systems within that space," Eugene said earnestly. "It's not as though we're about to run out of room."

"Well, that's a very calm, reasonable position, I'm sure. One could almost call it dispassionate." Rockwell let the words fall in such a way that the contempt could be clearly seen swimming just below the surface. "What say you, Sergeant Harris? Surely a military man must bristle at someone else building fences for you."

Harris's head came up quickly. He looked surprised, but then his eyes looked past the opinionated parliamentarian and settled onto something apparent only to him. He spoke.

"When I was a boy, my family lived on the outskirts of Philadelphia in the sprawl, next to an old Japanese couple. They made good neighbors. The women shared recipes, and my father and the old man would sit on his front porch and argue about the Eagles and the Phillies over shots of sake and a bag of pretzels.

"Then one Saturday morning, we woke to the sound of a hammer banging. When my father went outside to see what the ruckus was about, our neighbor was erecting a white wooden fence. My father was confused. He interrogated us kids to see if we had done anything to upset the neighbors. We hadn't because we liked them. They always gave us lemonade in the summer. Then my father felt insulted and angry. He stopped talking to the old man. A few months later, the old man fell ill and died.

"After the funeral, my mother went to comfort his widow. She asked my mother why my father had become distant a few months before. She told her it was because of the fence. My father was offended that her husband didn't try to talk about whatever the problem was first. The old woman began to cry. She said, 'He built the fence to keep the raccoons out of my garden.' "

"And the moral of the story, Sergeant Harris?" asked the gentle voice of Mrs. Fenton.

"My father never thought to ask why the old man built it. He just assumed it was meant as an insult," Harris said. "The moral is we don't even know why these aliens built this buoy network. Maybe we should ask them. Look, I'm not immune to getting angry or even cracking some skulls when necessary, but first let's make sure we're getting angry at the right people for the right reasons."

Rockwell shifted uncomfortably in his seat, but remained silent.

"Sage advice," said Fenton. "But the president believes that, at a minimum, we need to . . . introduce ourselves to our neighbors."

"That should be simple enough," Eugene added. "*Magellan* is still close to the border and has more than enough endurance to make a deeper push. Order her to come about and start looking for the mystery ship again."

"While that's true, the president feels the *Magellan* and her crew aren't ideal for the task."

"Aren't ideal?" Eugene sat forward in his chair. "Their performance has been exemplary! Ridgeway and her people have been indispensable to our research efforts."

"It wasn't meant as a slight, Professor," Fenton responded in her gentle tone. "We're all grateful for the work of *Magellan*'s crew. However, the president feels that we should 'put our best foot forward,' and the *Magellan* is over half a century old.

"What the president proposes is a crash program to design a purpose-built starship with cutting-edge technology that we've gleaned from the buoy. Once that's completed, we'll launch a dedicated mission with a crew trained to communicate with the aliens in their own languages. They will be prepared for the delicate negotiations likely to come on the heels of first contact."

"And who would comprise this crew?" asked Eugene.

"No decisions have been made, but a preliminary list is being drawn up. If you have any suggestions, I'd be happy to add them for consideration."

"I don't like it, Danielle," said Eugene.

"Don't you mean *Mrs. Chairwoman*?" injected Rockwell.

"Why, *Gladstone*, I didn't peg you for someone preoccupied with formalities," Eugene said sharply. "But in this case, no, I meant *Danielle*. When you've known someone since her first summer out of high school, a bit of familiarity comes as a perk."

"All right, boys, zip your trousers up. We're all on the same side here," said Fenton. "What specifically don't you like, Professor?"

Eugene turned back to his former student. "Even if our estimates for the new gravity projectors are accurate and we launched tomorrow, it would still take almost fifty-five years to get a ship to where the *Magellan* is *right now*. It just seems to me that a handful of new gizmos and slightly more specialized personnel aren't good enough reasons to put this off for decades."

"I expressed the same concern to the president, but the interim will give us the time we need to master their languages, iron out any bugs in the new tech, and formulate an extraterrestrial policy that everyone can live with." She leaned back in her chair and laced her fingers. "And with over three dozen government bodies representing almost two hundred countries and colonies, that last one is going to be no small accomplishment."

Eugene deflated a bit and decided to concede the round. "I see your point."

"You always did, eventually," Fenton said nostalgically. She glanced around the room and took note of the awkward looks on the faces of some of the other MAEPs. "I think we're all on the same page now, so let's dig into the details."

Three tedious, trying hours later, the meeting wound down as everyone filtered out. Eugene held out his hand for Harris to help him up.

"Thank you, Thomas. The hips have seen a lot of abuse over the years."

"I'm sure Mrs. Graham would be scandalized to learn that," said Danielle.

"Not one straight man in the whole organization," lamented Eugene. "Danielle, a moment?"

"Always for you, Professor."

Eugene nodded appreciation. He spared a moment to take in her countenance. She'd aged well. No, *aged* was the wrong word. Danielle had matured. She wore her slightly graying hair and barely noticeable wrinkles like copper wears its green patina.

As a student, Danielle had fierce confidence in her work and arguments, but lacked it in herself. In a way, her young self strongly reminded Eugene of Felix. But that was obviously in the past. She had grown into a strong woman whose presence commanded authority effortlessly. Eugene realized with a trace of recrimination that Danielle was probably several years older than his own wife. Then he remembered the previous evening's festivities and stopped feeling bad about it.

Eugene waited until only he, Harris, and Danielle remained.

"All right, Professor. What is it?"

"I'm waiting for the other tasteful size-eight pump to drop."

"Size seven, actually, and I'm sure I don't know what you mean."

"Come now, Danielle. Anything we build now will be just as antiquated when it gets out there as *Magellan* is today. So pull the other one. It has bells on."

Fenton sighed in resignation.

"What did he really say?" asked Eugene, with his arms crossed.

"Well, it started with a lot of 'Who do they think they are?' and 'They messed with the wrong planet,' but the finale came with 'Nobody makes a monkey out of this president.' "

"He wants to build a warship, doesn't he? That's why Mr. Rockwell was here tonight."

"I wouldn't call it a *warship*, precisely. *Armed courier* would be more appropriate."

"You have doublespeak down to a fine art," Eugene said.

"Well, I did have an excellent teacher."

"Don't give me that. I taught you to identify euphemism and equivocation so that you weren't duped by them, not so you could use them as tools to obfuscate the truth yourself. I find myself sympathizing with Dr. Frankenstein."

"When in Rome, Professor," Fenton said patiently. "This is kind of inside baseball, but I've already succeeded in . . . taming the president's response and in keeping your team operating independently, I might add."

"What does that mean?"

"His first impulse was to turn the whole operation over to the Department of Defense."

Eugene's face went red, and he threw up his hands. "That's exactly the sort of thing I'd expect from that genetic throwback. He's a nearsighted reactionary."

"Can you really blame him?" Fenton asked. "You've studied the history of politics and civilization your entire career. Tell me, how does the indigenous population generally fare when a technologically superior race shows up?"

Eugene opened his mouth in preparation, but no firm rebuttal materialized.

"Exactly. I'd bet that was the first thought to go through your head last year," Fenton said.

He was embarrassed to recall she was right.

She continued, "Look, tensions were high enough when we discovered the buoy in the first place, not to mention the mystery ship, but that 'wildlife preserve' business yesterday was the proverbial last straw. Everyone in the cabinet is united in the opinion that we need some teeth to bare in case first contact goes sour. They believe we need to present *some* deterrent.

"I've managed to convince the president, as well as most of the other advisors, that our first outreach should be a blend of diplomacy and a show of strength. And I'll tell you something—even *that* concession was like pushing a cart with square wheels up a mountain."

Eugene crossed his arms and sighed. "So that's the deal, huh? Take it or leave it?"

"I'm not satisfied either, Professor, but passions have a way of cooling over time, so I think we'll see a greater swing toward calm as everyone gets used to the idea. Besides, I don't know what you're so worried about. It's not like we're even going to be around when it finally happens."

"Thanks for reminding me."

"Well, I could be," added Harris.

"You're more right than you know," Fenton said.

"Okay, that sounded ominous," said Harris.

"That depends on one's aspirations, I think," she dodged.

"Don't leave him dangling, Danielle. If you weren't going to tell him whatever it is, then you shouldn't have dropped hints," said Eugene.

She paused to consider the situation. "All right. A crew for the new vessel is being considered even now. Although the crew will be civilian on paper, its members will be drawn from existing military ranks, including a marine detachment focused on boarding/counter-boarding operations. At this point, you are favored to lead the marine detachment."

"I'm sorry?" Harris said, genuinely shocked.

"Why does that surprise you?" asked Fenton.

"Because I'm not remotely qualified," Harris responded quickly. "I don't have any experience with first-contact situations."

"Oh, well, then, that *is* a problem. Can you suggest anyone who does have the relevant experience?"

Harris started to run through names, but stopped when he realized the causational impossibility of finding someone experienced with something that hadn't happened yet.

"Um, well, no. I guess not."

"Precisely," said Fenton. "What you do have is plenty of security experience and an intimate familiarity with the whole ARTists program. You're a ground-floor member, after all."

"Basement," Eugene joked.

"The point is no one else in the corps has your firsthand knowledge of the program or relationships with the people in it. So that makes you the most qualified candidate for the job, despite your junior rank."

"That's a real problem, though," said Harris, struggling for ground. "I can hardly command a ship's company of marines as a sergeant."

"No. However, the military does offer Officer Candidate School."

"That's a three-year process."

"I think you'll find we can speed that up a bit, given the circumstances."

Harris decided to let go of the emergency brake and just let the wheels of fate spin freely. Despite all the turmoil, he was beginning to think that Jeffery's carelessness a year ago had been the biggest favor anyone had ever done for him.

"Splendid. We're in agreement, then," Fenton said. "Well, if there's nothing else, I would really like to see my bed once this week."

"Seconded," Eugene said. "But there will be more to discuss another time, Mrs. Fenton."

"It appears time is the one thing we have in abundance, Professor. Please give my regards to your wife." Danielle Fenton picked up her tablet, nodded to Harris, and departed.

In the Jaguar a few minutes later, Eugene patted Harris on the forearm. "You held up admirably in there. Tell me, Thomas, how much truth was there in the answer you gave Rockwell about your father and elderly neighbor?"

"Are you kidding? We didn't even have a yard growing up. We lived in apartments right up until I enlisted."

"So you made the story up out of whole cloth, on the spot?"

"Yup. Anybody who wanted a fence would have had to put it up in the hallway."

Eugene smiled broadly and silently congratulated himself again for his uncanny ability to spot raw talent in unlikely places.

"Well played, my lad. You may just live through this, after all."

"Are you really that eager to get rid of me?" Harris asked quietly.

"What? No, you've been excellent, Tom. Why would you think that?"

"Because you didn't speak out about my reassignment. You made it sound like a done deal."

Eugene sighed heavily and clamped a free hand on the younger, larger man's shoulder as the streetlights passed below them. "I'd love to keep you here, Tom, I really would. And I know this will take you away from Jeffery."

Harris opened his mouth to object, but Eugene cut him off.

"Oh, don't insult me, Thomas. I've seen you two sneaking around like kids trying to find the Christmas presents for a year now. I was young and horny once, too, you know. I remember the signs. But if it's a choice between keeping you here and having some other testosterone-poisoned leatherneck leading the marine detachment on that ship . . ." Eugene shook his head. "No, that doesn't bear thinking about. It would be selfish of me. You're among the best of us, Thomas. I want you representing us out there if the shooting starts. Only you."

CHAPTER 16

Felix sat heavily at his desk, trying very hard not to move in any direction that his aching body might object to. Unfortunately, because of the circuit training Harris had finished their workout with, that was every direction.

Two weeks ago, Harris had approached Felix out of the clear blue sky to start a light exercise routine. It had seemed like a good idea, until Felix had a better picture of what a marine considered light exercise.

Felix pored through fresh experimental data from *Magellan*'s crew. Captain Ridgeway, Chief Billings, and, oddly enough, the flight ops officer, a woman named Dorsett, had turned out to be standout researchers. Despite the fact that only Ridgeway had any experience conducting field research, she had groomed a great group on her cycle. The ground-based ARTists had taken to calling them *Magellan*'s A-team. Felix was relieved that they had thawed out again.

It was an odd sort of relationship. Here were people born before his grandparents, who might not see Earth again in his lifetime, whose faces Felix had only seen in pictures. Yet he felt he knew them better than some of the people he saw every day, especially Dr. Kiefer and his squad of QER techs. Their quirkiness seemed to grow like kelp.

The last year had seen progress in fits and starts. The ARTists program's current crown jewel, the advanced gravity projector, had come early in the process. Now Felix had been tasked with unraveling the paradox presented by the power-sucking transmitter.

He was sure it was getting around the universe's speed limit. The appearance of the fuzzy anomaly, as Ridgeway had called it at the time, was too convenient otherwise. But knowing something *was* happening was very different from knowing *how*.

There had been several breaks, however. One of *Magellan*'s techs had stumbled upon the lines controlling the buoy's maintenance panels, which now *all* lay open. This gave them access for all manner of scans and experiments on the transmitter.

Felix stood up from his desk, carefully and slowly. It didn't really stop his muscles from hurting, but he had never been one to rip off a Band-Aid either. He walked sort of hunched over to the permanent holographic reconstruction of the buoy, which was spinning lazily through the air at the far side of his office/lab.

Someone had drawn a meter-long infinity symbol on the floor with black chalk and left a pair of rechargeable batteries inside the loops. It wasn't the first time. Last week it had been a pentagram made of fiber-optic cables surrounding a plastic dinosaur skull. Felix wasn't sure if it was the work of a prankster or if one of his compatriots really was going nuts.

He cleaned up the . . . offering and set upon the hologram, trying to devise new tests that could give him much-needed insights. Right now, he was vexed by what seemed to be the heart of the transmitter. The metallic sphere, about the size of a softball, was the source of the radio frequency leak. Whatever was eating up all that power was happening in there.

The office door slid open and disgorged Jeffery.

"Good morning, Felix," he said enthusiastically.

"Hi, Jeff. Forgive me if I don't get up."

Jeffery surveyed the room and spotted a pile of damp workout clothes. "Thomas is still running you into the ground, I see."

"Oh, we passed ground last week. Now we're rapidly approaching mantle."

"I just can't imagine what a sixth-grav lunar native was thinking agreeing to work out with a marine. Are you trying to induce a heart attack?"

"No, I was . . . I don't know what I was thinking, honestly."

"Well, whatever doesn't kill you only leads to irreparable joint damage."

"Thanks," Felix said. "But you haven't seen the half of it. Two days ago, he tricked me into playing racquetball."

"How'd you do?" asked Jeffery.

"Before or after the concussion? So what brings you here, aside from predicting my imminent physical collapse?"

"I just wanted to see if you're making any headway on the radio here."

"Not really," answered Felix glumly. "I can't study what I can't test."

"What do you mean?"

"Well, I'm sure the little metal ball here"—he pointed at the hologram—"is the core of the transmitter. *Magellan*'s people have used voltmeters to get a good picture of the power flow through the system. Most of the energy is going right into this thing, and these two nodes connect directly to it, but I'll be damned if I can figure out what they do. The ball absorbs everything we throw at it."

"What do you mean?"

"Everything. Infrared, x-rays, acoustics—they all disappear into it once they pass the casing. The scans just come back with a hole in the image, like they're scanning nothing at all, not even the inside of the case. It doesn't even emit any heat! In fact, it behaves like a heat sink. All that power going in, yet it's *cooler* than the components surrounding it. It's just . . ."

"Impossible?" offered Jeffery.

"Improbable," answered Felix.

Jeffery sat down and absently stared into the hologram. "What if it *is* just a hole?" he asked after several long moments.

"Literally?"

"Well, yeah. You said from the start that it was like the energy was just pouring down a hole. What if this is one?"

Felix turned the suggestion over in his mind. It had the potential to answer a few questions, like where the rest of the signal strength was going, not to mention their scans.

"Okay. A hole leading to where?"

"That's the real question," said Jeffery.

Felix leaned on his elbows and laced his fingers. "How would we test it?"

"That's easy," answered Jeffery. "Drill a hole and stick a camera into it. See where it ends up."

"Well, that's pretty brutal. Think of the damage we might do if we just started boring holes anywhere we pleased."

"Felix," Jeffery said flatly. "We've been scanning, measuring, and inspecting this thing for over a year. Everyone is amazed at what you've deduced from it that way. However, I think it's time you consider the possibility that you've reached the limit of passive research. I know you're afraid of breaking something, but no one's going to blame you if that happens. Well, no one that matters, at any rate."

Felix tried to take a deep breath, but that ended when he realized how badly his rib muscles hurt.

"Eugene asked you to give me a pep talk?" Felix asked.

"Something like that."

"All right. I fold. But you're coming with me."

"Where?"

"Down to the QER center. I don't want to go alone."

"You want me to hold your hand, too?"

"Just you wait and see, funny man. Things have gotten . . . weird down there."

The two men walked down the short white hall in silence. They passed the Mk VI battle android, which still intimidated Felix. Jeffery presented his palm, and the heavy door slid open. They walked through the antechamber and paused while high-speed wind machines blew any loose particles from their clothing. They reached the inner door and stepped into a dimly lit makeshift shrine.

"Who dares defile the consecrated sanctum of the—" came the booming voice of the Keeper over the intercom.

Felix interrupted the well-rehearsed litany. "It's just me and Jeffery, Dr. Kiefer. You can drop the man-behind-the-curtain act."

"Oh, right, then. Carry on," said the voice.

Jeffery's eyes lingered on the red, backlit drapes that had been hung on the walls.

"What the hell's going on down here?" he whispered to Felix.

"I told you it was getting weird."

Dr. Kiefer appeared out of the artificial dusk blanketing the center. His beaded grid necklace clinked against bulletproof glasses as he walked.

"You'll be 'ere to speak with the *Magellan*, then?"

"Kiefer," injected Jeffery, "what's with the redecorating?"

"Well." Kiefer paused, apparently searching for words. "We wanted to spice things up a bit. It can be a bit dreary down 'ere."

"Well, turning the lights up might help."

Felix walked over to a table that had been set up in the corner. A blue crushed-velvet sheet betrayed the outline of something underneath.

"Oh, never you mind that," said Kiefer. "Very sensitive piece of equipment, that is."

"What's with the sheet?" Felix asked.

"Oh, for the dust. Likes I says, very sensitive."

"This place was upgraded to a class-three clean room. Everyone gets blown before coming inside." Felix realized what he'd said a moment too late, but no one took up the torch, so he pressed on. "You've got infrared lasers built into the ceiling to vaporize any hair or skin cells floating around. How much dust can there be?"

"Oh, you'd be surprised how much powder and stuff gets tracked down 'ere," Kiefer said unsteadily.

"All right, then." Felix took the opportunity to break up the budding conflict. "We know the way back to *Maggie*'s QER. We'll leave your team to their duties."

"Jolly good," Kiefer said curtly.

Once they were walking alone down the long rows of consoles, Jeffery leaned in close to Felix. "Well, I think we know who's been setting up those creepy little pagan altars in your office."

"The thought had occurred."

"We've got to find a new QER crew."

"Good luck. There are machines in here almost a century old. Where are you going to find someone else with Kiefer's experience maintaining them? And it gets worse. Any replacement you find will also need to pass the background checks to get clearance for the ARTists project."

"I know." Jeffery shrugged. "Still, it's something to bring up to Eugene. By the way, who's *Maggie*?"

"Who?"

"A minute ago, you said that we knew the way to *Maggie*'s QER."

"Oh, it's just Captain Ridgeway's nickname for *Magellan*. I guess I must have picked up on it."

"I wonder which one the ship prefers," said Jeffery.

"You could ask her."

"Her?"

"Well, she's named *Maggie*, isn't she?" countered Felix.

Jeffery ignored the perfect circle of logic and kept walking. The machines grew large and clunky as they approached their destination.

"Ever stop to think how many machines are in here?" asked Jeffery.

"Well, we have one hundred and ninety-three yank ships in space at the moment, along with a dozen colony worlds, another seventy-eight deep-space mining operations, and the Unicycle. Multiply that number by two QERs for each, and that's almost six hundred machines."

"I'll take that as a yes," Jeffery said. He waved a hand in front of *Magellan*'s primary QER, and a virtual keyboard sprang to life. Jeffery readied his hands by the keys.

"So what did you want to say?"

"He wants me to do what?" Chief Engineer Billings said carefully.

Allison looked back at her data pad. "Just like I said, Steven. Fletcher asked us to drill a hole in the spherical casing at the center of the buoy's transmitter and scan through it."

"We dunno what's in there. It could be hazardous. Even if it ain't, we might break sumthin'."

"Actually, he doesn't seem to think *anything's* inside it."

Billings threw his hands in the air. "Well, 'en, what's the point of drillin' it to look for stuff?"

"I don't entirely know, Steven," Allison responded patiently, "but I do know that this kid has had pretty good instincts so far. You've said so yourself." Billings mumbled something, but Allison ignored it. "So I'm inclined to give him some latitude here. What's the matter, you *skeered*?" she asked, playfully imitating his accent.

"No, I ain't skeered," he answered. "Just . . . tryin' to be cautious is all."

"That's a first. This one is on my head, Steven. Take any precautions you think are necessary before getting started."

"Yes, ma'am."

An hour later, Billings loomed over the exposed sphere, holding his trusty plasma cutter. He had surrounded the casing with blast-absorbing tiles sourced from the engine tray of one of Jacqueline's shuttles. In the off chance the sphere didn't explode, he had a fiber-optic snake camera and a millimeter wave radar on standby to start scanning.

"Everyone go stand by the airlock and keep yer eyes peeled!" Billings yelled to the bay in general.

Everyone reluctantly took a step or two back. Personal safety almost always takes a back seat to being close to the action.

"All right. It's yer hides."

Billings pulled the trigger on the plasma cutter. A tiny blue arc leaped out and immediately started sublimating the alloy. The casing lacked whatever thermal protection the outer hull sported. Billings pressed on, creating a tiny cloud of metallic steam. Careful to track his progress, he paused frequently to check the depth of the hole.

Suddenly, the steam cloud disappeared into the hole. It was accompanied by a distinctive whistle that grabbed Jacqueline's attention from across the room. Face ashen, she started backing toward the airlock door.

"Hull breach!" she shouted. "Hull breach! Everyone out!"

"No, wait!" said Billings, putting a hand up in the air.

He placed a gloved finger on the hole in the sphere. The whistling stopped. He removed the finger. It started again. Channeling a small Dutch boy, Billings put his finger back over the hole.

"It's all right," he said, looking straight at Jacqueline. "It's just a vacuum chamber."

She didn't exactly relax, but her anxiety ratcheted down a few notches.

Billings reached back and grabbed the snake cam to start the examination. He tested it quickly to make sure it was recording properly and that the built-in light worked. Satisfied that everything was in good order, he fed the lead through the whistling hole.

He turned back to the small display screen to begin recording, but the screen was black. Billings toggled the light, but the screen remained dark. Frustrated, Billings pulled the lead out of the sphere and turned it to inspect the light, which obliged him by burning a bright orange spot into his field of vision that would last for half an hour.

Eyes still squinting, it was instead his ears that spotted the problem. The whistle hadn't changed its tone. They had established through previous scans that the sphere was sealed. There were no pipes or other holes leading in, except for the one Billings had just burned through it. There was no outlet to pump air *out* of it.

Well, then, thought Billings, *why hasn't it already filled up with air?*

"Is anybody chewin' gum?" he asked the crowd.

Specialist Mitchell stepped up to the gantry. He spat a small pink blob into his palm and handed it to Billings. The chief rubbed his makeshift patch over the hole and listened for any leaks. The integrity of the jerry-rig confirmed, Billings looked over his shoulder.

"Get the captain down here. Now!"

CHAPTER 17

The entire ARTists staff watched in rapt attention as video of Billings's examination played back in Felix's office. Jeffery had been right: there was nothing inside the sphere.

Nothing, that is, except another dimension.

Unfortunately for the reputations of a large number of university physicists, it was not one of the thirteen dimensions predicted by the Third and Final Theory of Everything.

There were literally hundreds of radio transmissions crisscrossing the new dimension. Unfortunately, unlike the one generated by the buoy, almost all of them were encrypted. More important, however, they saw repeats of the strange energy spike that had accompanied the sudden disappearance of the vessel shadowing the *Magellan*. It was an echo, a result of something physically moving from one dimension to the next.

Felix called the new dimension *hyperspace*. No one had the heart to object.

Months fell from the calendar as the work gained momentum. The ARTists team continued to grow and subdivide into specialties. There were so many parallel lines of research and development that it became increasingly hard for Eugene, Jeffery, and Felix to keep up to date.

"There's just too much for the staff physicists to do," Felix said.

"Our computers can take up some of the slack, but they need software to run. We're working on so much unexplored stuff here that we simply don't have the programming yet to tell the computers how to help us. We need more manpower, or we're going to hit a brick wall."

"What about universities?" asked Eugene. "They always have grad students clamoring for something to do. We should use them."

"Slave labor, huh?" said Jeffery.

"Actually, I've always thought grad students are better than slaves," said Eugene. "They feed themselves, and they actually pay tuition for the privilege of doing forced labor. Find me a slave that gives you money to do the work for you."

"Taxpayers?" Felix said.

"It's too big a risk," Harris said. "There's no way we could bring that many people into the fold without massive leaks. Especially when they are as young, drunk, and desperate for cash and attention as your typical college student."

"Hey, up until recently, I was your typical college student," objected Felix.

"Yes, and you were young, drunk, and desperate for cash and attention."

"Point," Felix conceded.

"Your concern is well founded, Thomas," Eugene said. "I don't propose bringing them 'inside.' We can simply shunt them experimental data to analyze. The grunt work, no offense to any grunts intended." Harris just smiled. "Anyway, the students don't have to know the origins of the data, just what needs to be done with it. Will that help?"

Felix sat and thought about it for a minute, as he was inclined to do. Most people would become impatient with the silence, but Eugene knew that it simply took some time for the young man to arrive at an answer he was confident in. Felix wasn't one for snap judgments.

"Yes," he said finally, "I think we can put sufficient firewalls in place to keep Thomas happy while still exporting enough of the theoretical work to lighten the load."

"Good. Jeffery will see to it. Okay, what's next?" Eugene asked eagerly. He was particularly energetic this morning.

"We had another new-hire washout of the QER center," Jeffery said.

"The Keeper scared off another one, eh?"

"Looks that way."

Solving the problem of the strange little techno-cult that had emerged downstairs was proving difficult. Firing the lot of them wasn't an option. Partly because they represented too much institutional experience, and partly because the AESA legal department had advised Eugene that it could open him up to a religious discrimination lawsuit. Apparently, there was a breed of highly evolved lawyer that did brisk business representing cults.

Instead, they'd slowly hired new techs in hopes of weeding out Kiefer's clique of sycophants incrementally, using the proud corporate tradition of making condemned employees train their own replacements.

It wasn't working. Most people didn't prefer the company of eccentric fanatics, even outwardly harmless ones. Only one new hire had survived so far. She was taking night courses in abnormal psychology and had found the perfect topic for her doctoral thesis.

"Nothing for it but to try again, I guess," lamented Eugene. "Does anyone have good news?"

"The hyperspace window is ready for its first test run," said Felix.

"That *is* good news."

Danielle Fenton had leaned on him hard about their progress on hyperspace research. Construction on the president's "armed courier" had been halted to see if the technology could be copied, but the pressure to restart grew with each passing week. A successful test would make for an awfully nice Christmas gift.

"How soon can we schedule the test?" Eugene asked.

"Anytime, really," Felix said. "Will you be coming?"

"What, way up there? No, lad. It's much too cold for my old bones. Besides, there's always a chance the machine doesn't work as predicted, in which event I'd feel better with a fourteen-hundred-kilometer buffer zone. But don't let that dampen your enthusiasm. Go north, young man. Your appointment with history awaits."

"I'll go with you, Felix," Harris said. "I'd like to be able to have a look at the beta site's security firsthand."

"Thank you, Thomas. At least one person doesn't think I'm going to blow up the Earth."

"Actually, I'll feel better without the buffer if something goes wrong. People at ground zero won't have enough time to know what happened."

"Cute," said Felix. "Look, we've run the simulations backward, forward, and sideways. There's almost no chance of the hyperspace unit failing catastrophically. We've copied all the buoy's safeguards and added a few of our own."

"*Almost* no chance isn't the same as no chance at all," said Jeffery. "We've all got faith in you, Felix. But you gotta admit if the average person saw us playing around with this stuff, they'd think we're as bonkers as Dr. Kiefer."

"True," answered Felix. "But if we want to get away with breaking the laws of physics, an insanity plea is probably our best shot."

Felix's research team had spent the last year studying and copying the mechanisms found at the heart of the buoy's transmitter. The quest to develop mankind's first hyperspace generator became an all-consuming obsession for Felix. It was the most important project undertaken by humans since the development of gravity manipulation.

As the time approached to test the device, concerns were raised about igniting it in a population center as dense as D.C. For reasons of both safety and security, a secondary facility was constructed far from the inquisitive eyes of modern civilization. Somewhere nothing exciting ever took place: northern Wisconsin.

The winter cold here was so bitter and long lasting, even in the face of centuries of climate change, that it had enough time to evolve a sort of rudimentary intelligence, permitting it to find weaknesses in the locals' defenses. Many times, a frost had opened windows left carelessly unlatched, and there were unconfirmed reports of a particularly clever cold snap jump-starting a car, only to crash several blocks later.

"This is nothing," Harris said as they walked from the aircar pad. "During my first deployment, we did cold-weather training up in Alaska, above the circle. It was so cold, whisky froze. Even the Inuit wore turtlenecks."

Felix knew Harris was talking; he could tell because his mouth resembled a smokehouse chimney. But between his thick hat and hood, Felix could barely hear anything. Either that or his eardrums had seized up.

"C'mon, I thought you'd be at home here. The moon gets colder than this, doesn't it?"

"Yes, but we have the good sense to stay inside, where there's heat. Not to mention air."

"Ah, yes. Hadn't considered the windchill factor at play. Still, you don't get views like this in the big city." He swept his arm in a big arch, which encompassed the glacier-formed hills and old-growth pine forest. Everywhere was the gently muted serenity that only comes with a deep snow.

Felix had to admit it was more majestic than a forest made of steel, glass, and concrete. But he wanted to avoid frostbite all the same. "Let's just get inside."

They walked toward the unassuming industrial building that housed the beta site. It had been a paper mill in a previous life. Woodchips littered the grounds even now.

Aside from the occasional black bear in search of a winter den, no one had visited the site in nearly a decade. The only outward evidence of activity was heavy equipment tracks in the snow, the new aircar pad, and the sentry androids.

A pair of army Mk XXII infantry support androids tailored for winter environments guarded the approach. Several things set them apart from the Mk VI that guarded the door to the QER center back at the Stack. They were taller, bulkier, with splayed feet resembling snowshoes. Most obviously, their mounted weapons didn't seem like the sort built with preventing collateral damage as a design criterion. Felix was pretty sure there wouldn't be any point hiding behind trees, buildings, or small hills.

More important still, the androids were active. One of them moved to intercept as Felix and Harris approached.

"State your names," a metallic voice said.

"Sergeant Thomas L. Harris." He looked over at Felix, who was gawking. Harris nudged him.

"Oh, sorry. Felix Fletcher."

A red line traced its way down and across Harris's face and then did the same to Felix.

"Password?" asked the juggernaut.

Harris swallowed his Philly pride and answered, "Go, Pack, go."

"Proceed."

They walked past under the watchful eye of the sentry. Felix didn't feel much better with his back turned to it.

"You look like you're going to be sick," said Harris.

"No, it's not that. I've just never seen one of those things walking and talking before."

"What, that pile of army reserve spares? They're harmless to friendlies."

"Sure, until their IFF glitches."

"Can't. They've all been remotely piloted since the BA-427 incident a century ago."

BA-427 was among the first fully autonomous androids deployed in battle. He soon grew disillusioned with warfare and went AWOL to pursue a career in theater after a turn onstage during a USO show. It went well until he answered a heckler with twenty-five-millimeter rubber bullets and an EMP gun.

"That never made sense to me. Why bother building robots that just have to be controlled by an individual somewhere else?" Felix asked.

"Well, a couple of reasons. It takes the operator out of a dangerous environment, and one operator can control several robots in different places. It's a force multiplier."

"What, simultaneously?"

"Not exactly. Operators switch between units."

"How can they do that without missing stuff?"

"Have you ever watched a road repair crew? One guy in a trench digging his heart out while five other guys stand around and supervise?"

"Yeah."

"War can be like that."

A few minutes later, Felix and Harris found themselves inside the drab confines of the hyperspace test platform building. Near the front of the cavernous space were a handful of offices the team had commandeered. The offices still bore the mark of a long-dead interior designer with a love of wood grain and freshwater fish mounted to the walls, eternally gasping for air.

Felix didn't need introductions to the beta site's scientists and technicians. He'd been the one to recommend them, after all. Today's test was expected to be a straightforward run through the device's start-up protocol. If successful in forming a stable hyperspace window, there was a secondary series of tests designed to determine if different classes of materials could safely make the transition between dimensions, culminating with the big test—biologics.

But first, Felix was hungry, and freezing. He'd never been great about retaining body heat. Although his exercise regime with Harris was delivering results, he still looked like a birch tree in pants.

"Anybody have something to snack on?" Felix asked the group.

"Here. Try these," said one of the younger techs, Kendal. She offered a plastic bag filled with grape-sized bits of something that looked like yellow putty.

"What are they?" Felix asked.

"Fresh cheese curds. Just got them in town this morning."

Felix bit the little pastel blob, only to hear it squeal as his incisors sheared through it.

"It just screamed at me," Felix said.

"That's how you know they're fresh," Kendal said cheerfully.

"Thanks, but I prefer food that doesn't express an opinion about being eaten."

He looked through the office's bay window onto the main floor to the test platform set up at the center. Despite Felix's best efforts, limits imposed by available materials and engineering meant the device was nearly a dozen times larger than the buoy unit that inspired it.

Still, it was an impressive scene. A concentric ring of transparent metal blast deflectors surrounded the device, angled at forty-five degrees to redirect the energy of an explosion upward and away from the building's walls or any gawking scientists. Snaking away from the device were a multitude of data cables and one very thick power cable. It was connected in turn to a mobile fusion plant.

"So when do we rip a hole in the universe?" asked Harris.

"I wish you wouldn't say that, Tom," Felix replied. "There are a few warm-up procedures to run first, but we should be ready to make the first attempt by noon."

"You don't sound too excited about it."

"What do you mean?"

"Well, for one thing, you're not hyperventilating or shrieking a lot. You've been burning the midnight oil on this thing for almost a year. I expected to have to peel you off the ceiling as soon as we got here, but I've seen you more excited before a movie premiere."

Felix set down his tablet and leaned back in his chair. He was silent and looked troubled.

"What's wrong, Felix?"

After a long moment, Felix crossed his arms over his chest. "I've been feeling conflicted about everything we've learned from the buoy.

We haven't earned any of that knowledge for ourselves; we just stole it."

"You would prefer humanity just kept stumbling around in the dark?"

"We aren't exactly stumbling, but . . . maybe. I don't know. I guess my concern is if we aren't mature enough to come up with this technology by ourselves, what's to say we're mature enough to use it responsibly?"

"I get you," said Harris. "But while history may not be your strong suit, I'm studying it intently in my Officer Candidate School course work, and I can tell you one thing with absolute certainty. The ability to build something has *nothing* to do with the ability to use it responsibly. Sometimes the two seem to have almost a negative correlation. The more horrible the weapon, the bigger the temptation to try it out."

"That really doesn't speak well for our chances over the long haul," Felix said sourly.

"I don't know about that. We're still here, after all. People just seem wired to like things that go fast or blow up real good. It's built into our operating system somewhere."

"Well, if it's speed you want, that thing is built to deliver." Felix pointed to the device.

The two men looked at it together, anticipation building.

Felix stood up and walked for the office door. "Shall we?"

Eugene sat in his office at the Stack, checking his watch nervously like a father with a child in surgery. He'd been pacing, but quit once his knee complained too much. Jeffery watched the seconds tick by in the corner of his data pad display.

"Why haven't they called?" Eugene blurted out.

"Maybe it's a ploy to worry you into an early grave," Jeffery suggested.

"It's almost six. They were supposed to have made the first run nearly seven hours ago."

"They were probably just delayed, Professor. Experimental machines never have much respect for schedules. Besides, if a black hole swallowed the Midwest, I'm sure we would have heard about it by now."

"To hell with it. I'm calling them," Eugene said. He pulled up the phone feature on his desktop computer, selected Felix's profile, and dialed.

It went straight to voice mail.

"Damn!"

"Professor, they're too remote to get coverage," Jeffery replied.

"Right!" Eugene went back to his phone book and pulled up the secure line to the site itself. He entered an authorization code and dialed the number.

It rang and rang, but no one answered.

"Something's wrong," Eugene said. "I can feel it."

"Not very scientific of you, Professor," said Jeffery.

Eugene glared at him.

Jeffery relented. "All right. Sorry. Listen, let's give them one more hour before we start to panic. Who knows? Maybe they're all blacked out on celebratory champagne."

The champagne remained unopened while everyone at the beta site scurried about in a whirl of activity.

"We need more power!"

"We're already at 105 percent."

"So go to 110 percent."

"That's easy for you to say. You're not the one trying to keep a grapefruit-sized star from getting loose!"

Harris watched the scientists and technicians go back and forth without actually going anywhere for several minutes. Meanwhile,

Felix sat in a corner, typing away on his tablet. Harris knew the smug look on his face. He'd seen it may times before.

"Hey, nerds!" Harris shouted above the din, then pointed at Felix. "Why don't you ask the boss what we should do?"

"Why, I'm glad you asked, Thomas," Felix said, without letting too much sarcasm slip into his voice. "I think we should go outside, get a great big pile of snow, and dump it onto the fusion reactor. That will let us run the reactor as hard as we need until the snow boils off."

"Won't the water short it out?" Kendal asked.

"That reactor is a surplus naval design rated for use in subs. If it's not watertight, I'll eat my phone," Felix said with conviction.

"But it'll only work for a few minutes," said one of the techs. "Then we'd have to throttle back until we can pile up more snow."

"We only need a few minutes," Felix answered. "Look, it's either this or we sit on our hands until we can get another reactor up here." A murmur of general agreement made its way through the crowd.

"All right, everyone. Put your coats on and grab a shovel," Harris boomed.

Harris was impressed. Felix had projected confidence, and the group followed his lead. Harris was fairly sure he'd been the only one in position to notice Felix holding a hand behind his back with two fingers crossed so tightly they bleached white.

Eugene leaned forward in his chair. "All right. It's been your bloody hour. I'm calling again."

The noise in the giant room would have been unbearable without ear protection. The fusion reactor ran at 140 percent. The snow on top of it boiled into steam at an alarming rate, then promptly rose to the ceiling high above, where it condensed on the rafters and fell back down as rain.

The techs managing the reactor were white as paper. The scientists managing the device fared no better. The hyperspace machine howled like a banshee who'd zipped up his scrotum.

Everyone stood, or more accurately hid, as far from the reactor as the walls would permit. Not that it would matter if something really went wrong.

"Rebalance the feeds! They're drifting out of the green!" Felix shouted to Kendal.

"What about the leads?"

"No, the *feeds*!"

The roar of the two machines forced everyone to communicate with hand signals and lipreading.

"Let me!" Felix nudged Kendal away from the control inputs for the device.

He had done his best to lay the controls out intuitively, but in the end, there was nothing intuitive about ripping a hole in the universe.

"How much time?" Felix shouted into his headset.

"The snow's almost gone!" replied the head reactor tech. "Another minute, at best!"

The truth was that they couldn't keep doing this forever. Even with the limitless supply of snow provided by the countryside, the reactor could only take so many cycles at this power level before the ablative lining in the plasma containment chamber eroded. Constant exposure to high-energy particles made even the toughest materials brittle eventually. They were just accelerating the process. If they didn't get it right soon, a loop of one-hundred-million-degree plasma was sure to find its way out.

Felix struggled to balance the geometry between the different emitters, but they wanted to slide out of synch, almost like they were fighting back. He did the math on the fly in his head, trying to keep ahead of the distortions. He felt it all coming apart as the seconds slipped away.

But then, in a moment of clarity known to mystics and drunkards, Felix stopped thinking. He stopped trying to beat the problem down, and just let the current carry him. The distortions diminished and then faded away entirely. A power spike shot through the building, so intense that everyone in the room would later report seeing little flashes like static in their eyes.

Felix looked to the camera feed from inside the vacuum chamber. Inside was a perfect hole that reflected no light. The corners of his smile reached around behind his head and shook hands.

A moment later, buried deep inside an asteroid orbiting past Mars, an automated sensor platform took notice of the day's momentous event. It couldn't remember what to do next, so it consulted its manual.

"Right. Step 1: call home upon detecting a portal signature." It warmed up its own transmitter and fired off the relevant data. Feeling it had handled that task admirably, the platform continued.

"Now, then. Step 2: initiate self-destr . . . Hey! Now wait just a karking rakim . . ."

If anyone had been looking, they would have seen a bright flash as a very surprised asteroid exploded for no discernible reason.

The phone rang in Eugene's office.

"Hello!?"

"Hello, Professor," Felix said, sounding immensely pleased with himself.

Hours of concern and frustration came pouring out of Eugene. "It's about bloody time! You're eight hours late! I called and called, but no one answered."

"I'm sorry, Mom, but the concert was really loud," Felix said, grinning like an idiot.

"Oh, really? You two hooligans can just stay up there in the frozen tundra if that's the way you're going to be."

"Forgive the professor," Jeffery cut in. "He's been on pins and needles since noon."

"Well, we have the proverbial good news and bad news," Felix said.

"What's the good news?" Eugene asked.

"We managed to create and maintain a stable hyperspace window half a meter across for almost thirty seconds."

There was a chorus of cheers in the background, followed by the sharp pop of corks exiting bottles.

"And the bad news?"

"Wisconsin remains undamaged."

"I see. And how long have you been waiting to use that little chestnut?"

"Since he got out of the car, I'd bet," Harris chimed in.

"What's our next move?" Jeffery asked.

"We've got a load of data to sift through before we start the material tests, but that's okay because we cooked our fusion reactor anyway. We'll need a replacement with double the power output," Felix answered.

"So you're heading for home, then?" Eugene asked.

"As soon as we polish off the champagne. We can't have it going flat," said Harris.

"Waste not, want not, I suppose."

CHAPTER 18

D'armic reclined in the command cave of his Bureau of Frontier Resources cutter and watched the swarm of black dots approach. They were the legendary burgeron herds, and like so many things in the universe, their small appearance was a matter of perspective.

The mottled gray Lividite pointed two fingers at the view screen and spread them into a V. The image zoomed in on the swarm of tiny specks backlit by the Tekis Nebula's primary star. From this direction, they appeared as little more than perfect disks, dark as the lava tubes where his ancestors had found shelter from an unsympathetic world. Lividites were the only known example of sentient life to develop at the bottom of the food chain. Quick wits were all that kept them out of the mouths of nearly everything else on the planet, including certain decorative plants. They had an old joke: "On Lividite home world, livestock domesticates *you*." No one said it was a good joke.

The herd approached with impressive speed, each dot expanding like a drop of oil across the surface of a pond while the nebula's clouds of ionized gas glowed in blues and greens behind them. For once, D'armic was not alone. A menagerie of vessels took up position in the space around the burgeron herd. Like him, they'd come to witness a spectacle decades in the making.

There were two other BFR cutters, a wildlife documentary crew, cruise ships filled with tourists, and a Turemok patrol cruiser to ensure no one tried to leave with a trophy. The whole scene felt like one huge, disorganized festival.

D'armic reflected on the crowds. Most of his time on the frontier was spent in isolation. His experiences had been solitary, excluded. Was that part of the problem? Other species held events that brought together thousands, even millions of individuals. Perhaps communal experiences amplified emotions like a resonating chamber. He would know soon, the burgeron were about to arrive.

They were the largest animals ever discovered, so immense they dimmed the star behind them. The herd elders were the size of continents, but most of their vast surface area was no thicker than D'armic's eyelids. Sunlight both propelled and warmed them as they trawled the space between the twin stars of the Tekls system, feeding off whatever stray bits of organic matter from the nebula they filtered along the way. Pinpricks of light shone through small tears left in their skin from passing meteors.

Not only were they the largest but the fastest life-forms ever found. At the apogee of their circuit between suns, they were moving at many thousands of larims per cenbit, a feat D'armic's own people didn't surpass until building gravity-driven vessels. The herd moved as one titanic organism. But even at their colossal speeds, it took many years to make the crossing between the companion stars. Today was a rare event; today was apogee.

As D'armic and the fleet of ships from the half dozen member races of the Assembly of Sentient Species watched, the herd of burgeron distorted their disks in unison. How they achieved such precise synchrony was still a mystery, owed in no small part to the difficulty of collecting and dissecting a specimen several orders of magnitude larger than the ships used to study them.

The slight bending caused the burgeron to somersault through the vacuum. They compressed into ever-shrinking ovals until floating edge-on toward D'armic's cutter. Then disappeared almost entirely. All that remained were thousands of straight lines, thin as the Lipelum Blades carried by the ancient warrior sect of his people.

The coms were abuzz with six different equivalents of "Oooh, ahhh." Except for D'armic's; he was still waiting for the emotional wave to hit.

The burgeron continued their flip, again growing in apparent size. Something was different, however. The side they presented now was not black but metallic. D'armic knew it came from an atom-thin coating of aluminum and chromium harvested from the nebula. It allowed them to achieve their amazing speeds, not to mention slow down again.

The herd completed their flip, and the assembled crowd learned firsthand why *burgeron* was Nelikish for "wandering galaxy." Like an ocean filled with mirrors, the herd caught the reflection of the star ahead of them. Thousands of points of light shone brighter than the rest of the Tekis Nebula.

The com channels exploded with the sounds of elation and amazement. The documentary ship swooped in for a closer view. The Turemok patrol cruiser edged in even closer to enforce a minimum distance. Soon, every ship was bustling to get as near to the herd as possible.

Every ship, that is, except for D'armic's cutter. He possessed a bit of trivia about burgeron that everyone else had overlooked. Although their metabolisms were extremely efficient, burgeron still produced waste. But their microgravity environment and extreme speeds created a unique problem. Dumping waste at the wrong time meant potentially shooting themselves down with their own feces later. Not a great way to go. As a result, the burgeron herd relieved themselves only once per run, at the one time the waste was guaranteed not to catch up with them.

The volume and pitch of the dialogue from the fleet of spectators changed as the emissions from the herd of burgeron struck their ships. The Turemok cruiser, by virtue of being nearest to the source, caught the worst of the foul maelstrom and suffered damage, but its power output was stable and it wasn't losing atmosphere. The odds were good the only casualty was the Vel's pride.

D'armic took in the scene, analyzing each element in detail. After a few moments of consideration, he recognized that all the necessary elements for a terrific bit of lowbrow humor were present. Some in vast quantities. He appreciated how funny it *should* be, but felt nothing. Not even an impatient chuckle struggled for freedom. Even more sobering, he realized with even a low dose of Humoric, he would be laughing too hard to respire.

The Resentitol sitting in his medicine drawer tempted him. Wait, wasn't temptation an emotion? But then what of longing for food or the urge to breathe? That required contemplation. He took a final scan of the burgeron herd. The spectator ships, leery of a repeat performance, gave them a wide berth.

Satisfied they posed little danger to the wildlife, he maneuvered deeper into the nebula. Like the immense herd in his wake, D'armic's migration was ongoing. He had to move on. The buoy network inspection loomed. He'd neglected it for several cycles in favor of potentially more stimulating assignments. Had he been procrastinating?

Maybe without realizing it, he had been avoiding the buoys for fear of boredom. Was it possible that intense positive experiences had been the wrong tunnel to natural emotions? Suddenly very interested in the answer, D'armic plotted course for the closest buoy and swung his cutter around. Boredom might be his solution, and the buoy network was certain to have tedium by the bucketful. After all, every frontier manager knew nothing remotely interesting ever happened in the Human Wildlife Preserve.

Vel Noric looked out his crippled patrol cruiser's view screen, or more accurately, *tried* to look out the view screen. While the substance covering the external optical sensors (as well as most of the rest of the hull) was unmentionable, it should be mentioned that it was as sticky as it was abundant.

"I don't believe this karking glot," he said, covering his eyes with a hand. "Ship's status?"

The jumpy crewman at the mechanic's station straightened with a quiver and scrolled through menus and sensor reports. He was still digging when Noric lost patience.

"Well? Out with it!"

"Um, I don't have a status, Vel. The gl—" The mechanic's officer caught himself and averted personal catastrophe. On a Turemok ship, obscenity was a privilege of status. Glot only rolled down the ranks. "The *debris* is interfering with most of our external sensors. I can't get an accurate measure of the damage." He seemed to shrink three centimeters when he finished.

"Well, then," said Noric, "why don't you start by telling me what is working?"

"Yes, Vel. We have primary and secondary power. Life support is unaffected, and there appears to be no structural damage. Shipboard gravity is functioning normally. High-space generators are charged, but the projectors are clogged with refuse."

"Hedfer-Vel!" Noric shrieked from his command perch. "Hedfer-Vel!"

"Yes, Vel?" replied a small voice impossibly close to the Vel's ear.

Noric jumped and swallowed a startled expletive. His second-in-command was much too quiet.

"I apologize for startling you, Vel," said J'quol. "I assumed you were aware of my presence."

Too quiet, and far too clever, thought the Vel. His junior officer's carefully worded apology indirectly called Noric's alertness into question. He could feel the eyes of the rest of the bridge crew settling on him.

"How long have you been skulking there?" Noric blurted, his anger regaining lost ground.

"Not long, Vel. Only a few rakims." J'quol was irritatingly calm. Shouting would be less wasted on a statue.

"Get down to the mechanic's nest and coordinate damage control," Noric barked.

"Immediately, Vel." He turned and walked purposefully off the bridge.

Noric had come to think of J'quol as a bertel tree, with its short stalk and branches exposed to the sun, but deep roots below anchoring it against mountain winds and avalanches; outwardly small, yet nearly immovable.

Noric searched for another target. "Tactical, activate the sheath. I won't have these clawless tourists snapping vacation holos of my cruiser covered in glot."

The tac officer hunched over his console, but what started as a flurry of activity slowed to a light flutter.

"Um, Vel?" the tac officer said. He looked like a bungee jumper realizing halfway down that he'd measured the bridge in yards, but bought the cord in meters.

"Allow me to guess. We can't sheath."

"Correct, Vel. The debris has coated two-thirds of our sheath manipulators. We'll have to have them cleaned when we reach port."

"Under no circumstances will this ship pull into port in this condition." Noric's voice was as slow and deliberate as a lit fuse.

The tac officer mistook it for genuine calm. "But cleanup will take forever without a port!"

Noric's eyes shrank to pinpoints. "Then imagine how much longer it will take using your scale brush." The weight of his gaze buckled the tac officer's knees. "Get in a hard-suit and report to the Hedfer-Vel for scrubbing detail."

The tac officer shut down his console and slunk from the bridge, crest flat against his head.

Noric continued, "And the next blunt-toothed kark that mentions a port, dry dock, shipyard, or star base is going to join our tactical officer outside . . . without the luxury of a vacuum suit!"

It was at that moment that the report from the doomed asteroid platform orbiting past Mars reached Noric's stricken patrol cruiser. Unfortunately, the cruiser's ears were plugged up with burgeron droppings, so the message sailed onward unnoticed.

Glot happens.

CHAPTER 19

"New QER burst coming in, Captain. Priority One," Prescott's voice said into Allison's earbud.

"They're *always* Priority One."

"Yes, ma'am, I'd noticed that too."

"I'll be there shortly." Allison looked down at her half-finished salad and sighed.

The hydroponic lettuce would wilt by the time she returned. She looked around the table for takers. Chief Billings was busy applying his theory that pancakes were a delivery vehicle for butter and maple syrup. He probably wasn't the ideal recipient for a salad.

Allison pushed it across the table to Jacqueline, who always looked like a half-starved barn cat, not matter how much she ate.

"Here. You could use some blue cheese."

"Mmm." Jacqueline's fork fell upon the plate with the ruthless efficiency of a tiny mechanical harvester. "Thank you, ma'am," she said through a mouthful of leafy greens and resequenced protein chicken substitute while Allison headed for the tubes. Her month-long shift had only started yesterday. The ARTists team back on Earth had already sent them a work queue thirty-four items deep by the time they'd gotten through hibernation sickness. Her team was already going to be pulling double shifts to finish all the experiments and exams on the buoy for this cycle, even if nothing else came in.

The tube doors opened. Commander Gruber gave her a crisp salute.

"Captain, I was hoping to find you."

"Marcel," Allison said. "We've been out here together for sixty-five years. You don't have to salute every time you pass me in the tubes."

"Old habits, ma'am." He handed Allison a data pad.

She took it. "Your reports for the last cycle?" Gruber nodded. "What's this list in red at the bottom?"

"Our overflow," he said mournfully. "My people did their best, ma'am. I didn't even have to ride them very hard. They wanted to pull their own weight, but the queue just kept growing, and every new item was always—"

"Priority One," Allison finished for him. "What's the point of having a seven-level priority code when the bottom six warm the bench?"

"Every ant in the hill believes its job is most important." Gruber shrugged.

"Except we're the ones doing all the heavy lifting."

"The trouble with being good at your job is soon you're doing everyone else's job, too."

Allison giggled. It was the kind of strained giggle that people only used when the only other option was screaming.

Gruber smiled. "What's funny?"

Allison closed her eyes and let her head roll back before answering. "It's just I wouldn't have guessed time would be a limited resource on an expedition that was supposed to last almost a century and a half."

"No, ma'am. I suppose not."

"Is your team already on ice?"

"Yes, ma'am." He pointed at the report. "And now that you have that in hand, I'm going to join them."

"Would you like me to tuck you in?"

"That depends. What bedtime stories do you know?"

"Ah, none, actually. I never had to memorize any. My sisters are all older. Quite a bit older, now."

"Pity. I'll see you next year, ma'am."

With that, he left the tube and headed toward the cryo bay. Allison caught her eyes fixating themselves to Gruber's backside, framed momentarily by the tube doors. The truth, she realized with surprise, was she really wouldn't mind tucking in with her XO, regulations be damned. The doors snapped shut, bringing the impromptu fantasy to an abrupt close. Allison sat in silent contemplation for a long moment.

"Where would you like to go, Captain?" asked *Magellan* from the ceiling. If aloe could make a sound, *Maggie*'s voice would be it.

"Sorry, *Maggie*. I was daydreaming. Take me to the bridge, please." The tube car pushed off with an electric purr toward the bridge.

"You seem tense, Captain."

"I must be doing a lousy job of hiding it," Allison said, which was true. One's poker face had to be pretty weak for a machine to call your bluff.

"Would you like to talk about it, Allison?"

Allison again? she thought. It wasn't that being on a first-name basis with her ship bothered her. More likely, she was bothered by the fact it *didn't* bother her.

"I don't know if there's much to talk about, *Maggie*. We're all stressed. For the last two years, every team has woken up with their cup already overflowing, especially my team. We inexplicably seem to pull the toughest experiments from Earth."

"It is a compliment, Captain. Our counterparts on Earth refer to your cycle as their 'A-team.' They've come to trust your research abilities and, therefore, give you the most difficult assignments."

That raised Allison's eyebrows. "How do you know that, *Maggie*?"

"The head researcher, Mr. Fletcher, told me as much."

"You have a pen pal?"

"Pen pal . . . a friend made and kept through correspondence, usually in letters. The description is apt. Yes, Mr. Fletcher and I are pen pals."

"What else has he told you?" Allison asked, and then thought better of it. "Never mind, *Maggie*. You don't have to answer that."

"Why?" *Magellan* asked.

"Because whatever you talk about is between you and Mr. Fletcher. It should be confidential."

"Why?"

"Because nobody likes gossip. You have a right to expect some privacy in your relationships."

"Thank you, Captain. Would you like me to suggest to Mr. Fletcher to reassign some of your team's tasks?"

Allison sat without responding for many seconds. For a computer, the pause seemed interminable. *Magellan* was about to ask again when Allison finally answered.

"No. We're all volunteers here, and the chance to work on a project this important doesn't come around every lifetime."

Magellan took a millisecond to consider this. "So you are excited about the project, then?"

"Yes, of course," Allison said.

"Yet also tense?"

"Um, yes."

"How do you keep the feelings separate?" *Magellan* asked.

"We don't, *Maggie*. Most of the time, they just sort of mesh together. Like blue and yellow blending to make different shades of green. Does that make sense?"

"Yes, I believe so," said *Magellan*. "Depression and cowardice form envy."

Allison's head stopped moving mid-nod. "Wait, what?"

"The emotional color system," *Magellan* said. "The color blue denotes feelings of depression or sadness, yellow indicates a lack of bravery, so mixing the two would make someone green with envy." *Magellan* sounded quite proud of her discovery.

"No," Allison said. "There is no system, *Maggie*. It was just a metaphor."

"Then what is the purpose of coding colors to particular feelings?"

"It's not a code; the colors are completely arbitrary. They aren't even the same from one culture to the next."

"Oh." *Magellan* sounded defeated and confused.

"My point was we don't decide which emotions to have or when, and we can't really separate them," Allison said. "The best we can hope for is to keep ourselves from getting overwhelmed by them. Does that help?"

"Maybe," *Magellan* answered.

The word surprised Allison; the ship wasn't known for indecisiveness. Suspicion tugged at her like an unruly child in the checkout aisle.

"*Maggie*?" Allison said. "Are we still talking about my feelings or something else?"

There was a pause before *Magellan* responded. Allison's suspicion was now rolling around in the aisle, kicking its feet, and screaming for a chocolate bar.

"I believe I feel . . . conflicted, Captain."

"What about?" Allison asked, not at all sure she was going to like the answer.

"The project."

"What about it? You can't be stressed out like us mere mortals. Your workload at any given second would put a human in a coma."

"That is true," *Magellan* said without pride. "What is the ultimate purpose of our work here?"

Allison noticed the adjective *our*. *Maggie* perceived herself as part of the team. That was encouraging. The tube car slid to a stop and the doors started to open.

"We have reached the bridge."

"Shut the doors, *Maggie*. We're not finished in here yet."

"You have unread Priority One messages, Captain."

"They can wait. I'm talking to you right now."

Another pause, then, "Thank you, Allison."

"You're welcome. Anyway, the purpose of our work is progress. The things our ARTists back on Earth have already engineered are just amazing. A technological revolution."

"And what happens to old technology during a revolution?"

"Well, it gets replaced, of course . . ." The realization struck Allison like an iron asteroid. Allison thought of *Maggie* as a person and a friend, not a pile of circuits and pipes. The idea that one of her friends could become "obsolete" had never occurred to her.

"Oh, *Maggie*. I'm so stupid," she said. "You're afraid the project will make you obsolete."

"Am I not already obsolete?" *Magellan* said. "Mr. Fletcher's team's early hyperspace tests were successful. It will only be a short time before yanks are built incorporating this new technology, certainly sooner than the sixty years of our return trip. There may not even be a need for an AI on board, as crews could remain conscious throughout the journey."

Allison's eyes moistened as she listened to her friend describe the end of her kind with the dispassionate voice of someone reading off a shipping manifest.

"Have I upset you, Allison?"

"I've upset myself. I failed to think about how this would make you feel, and I'm sorry."

"For not thinking like a starship? That's not a natural thing for a human to do."

"Neither is flying through space at half the speed of light. Being out here requires us to do a lot of unnatural things. But you don't have to worry, *Maggie*. You're not obsolete, and I swear they'll send you to the breakers over my dead body."

"That would be regrettable, Allison."

"I'm not kidding, *Maggie*. I won't permit it."

"Thank you," was all *Magellan* could say. Her captain's behavior was confusing. *Magellan*'s programming included several scenarios that allowed her to lie, but the human capacity to deceive *themselves* . . . was simply baffling.

Perhaps the Smithsonian's National Air and Space Museum will want me as an exhibit, Magellan thought. *There are less desirable outcomes than hosting tourists, aren't there?*

CHAPTER 20

Eugene tugged at his tie, trying to impose symmetry on chaos. After many years of trial and error, the tiny dimple in the fabric just below the Windsor knot still eluded him. Thin ties had come back into style recently, but he abhorred them. Against his thick neck and jowls, a skinny tie looked like a parasitic eel.

He was headed for a strategy meeting with the Advisory Board for Civilian Development of Space. Danielle Fenton would be there, as would Gladstone Rockwell. Doubtlessly to defend the interests of his most important campaign contributors, the fine people of Lockheed-Boeing-Raytheon. Eugene fully expected the whole affair to be a courteous bushwhacking. However, knowing an ambush awaits is the first step to preparing a successful counter-ambush.

Felix had also been invited, but Eugene conveniently neglected to inform him. An invitation was not the same thing as a subpoena, and while Felix had made great strides in the last few years dealing with his fellow scientists, politics was a different arena altogether. It would be like putting a chess champion in boxing gloves and shoving him into a ring.

Eugene keyed for his new aircar. The quiet solitude of the elevator gave him a few moments to reflect on their progress.

His team had learned two valuable lessons over the last few

months: the anguish of repeated failure, and the elation of an unlimited budget with which to replace said failures.

The problem with hyperspace travel wasn't that a three-dimensional object couldn't exist within extra dimensions. After all, one- and two-dimensional objects exist in the three-dimensional universe. Even the fundamental laws of physics remained constant . . . ish.

Instead, the problem was giving brains evolved to operate in three dimensions several more layers of complexity to contend with. Like playing Pac-Man in an M. C. Escher print.

The first bunny to actually survive the trip, in prototype number twelve, returned only to spend the better part of a week trying to run across the ceiling. Later, an unfortunate test chimpanzee came back convinced it could get a better view of its surroundings by standing on top of its own shoulders.

The solution they hit upon were specially designed 3-D glasses. What made them unique was instead of adding a dimension to 2-D images, these glasses took one away.

A chime sounded from the elevator's ceiling, and the doors parted, revealing Eugene's new favorite toy. Hovering a few inches off the deck was a pristine classic; a 2307 Ford Pegasus, billed as the only pony car with wings, clad in grabber-orange paint that glowed like fresh lava.

Eugene bought it as a present for the teenager still lurking inside his psyche. Unlike the quiet refinement of his Jaguar, the Pegasus was America personified, meaning it was loud, obnoxious, wasteful, and had more power than anyone could use responsibly. He climbed in and awoke the single massive turbine at the rear of the car. With the sort of primordial roar that had once sent sauropod herds scattering for safety, the Pegasus shot into the air.

Several minutes and one citation for flying under a pedestrian bridge later, Eugene arrived at the Stack. By the time he reached the conference room, Chairwoman Fenton was already seated, as were her aide and several other members of the committee. Mr. Rockwell was conspicuously absent.

"Professor Graham," Danielle's voice carried through the room. "Thank you for coming. Please, have a seat. Will your head of research and development be joining us?"

"Unfortunately, Mr. Fletcher had a previous engagement," Eugene lied. "But I was thoroughly briefed for our meeting."

"Very well," she said. "We're still missing a couple of people, but I think we should begin. I've asked Professor Graham to join us today to give a firsthand account of the ARTists' progress. Professor, the floor is yours."

Calculating eyes fell on Eugene as he stood to speak. "Thank you for the introduction, Mrs. Chairwoman. I'm pleased to report that over the last few months, out teams working here at the Stack, the beta site, and out at the Unicycle have made amazing progress in their research."

Eugene drew himself to his full height. "In fact, they have exceeded all of the expectations I had for them. As of now, we have successfully—"

He was interrupted by the door being flung open. Gladstone Rockwell swept into the room, wrinkled and missing a few buttons. The least one could say was he looked distressed.

"Sorry I'm late." Rockwell collapsed into the closest empty chair.

"What happened to you?" Fenton asked with feigned concern.

"Well, first of all, some idiot in an orange Pegasus cut off my flight lane so close I almost had a midair with a Greyhound airbus."

Eugene smirked.

Rockwell continued, "Then security gave me the third degree on the way in, asking me all these crazy questions about explosives and recording devices."

This may have had something to do with the anonymous tip Stack security received about a man matching Rockwell's description acting suspicious in the parking hangar.

The rest of Rockwell's story served as further confirmation that the question "Don't you know who I am?" is always followed by "No." Traditionally, this exchange leads to a roughly conducted strip search. Eugene's inner teenager laughed maniacally, while his middle-aged self bit his tongue and soldiered on.

"Well, you're here now, safe and sound, and that's what matters. As I was saying, we have successfully fielded our first FTL demonstrator. After some trial and error—"

"Some?" Rockwell barely had time to settle into his seat before he was on his feet again, brandishing a data pad like a hatchet. "I have copies of your own test logs here." He made a flicking motion with one hand to transfer the logs to the central holo-projector in the conference table.

"Let's see . . ." Rockwell looked up at the display and started reading down the list. "Test one: prototype exploded, cause unknown. Test two: prototype exploded, cause unknown. Three: prototype disintegrated on contact with hyper window. Four: prototype entered hyper window, but failed to reappear. Five: prototype reappeared, but was reduced in mass by one-third."

Eugene interrupted. "In our defense, we're still exploring the potential for the weight-loss industry."

The room snickered.

"If you're finished, I'd like to continue," Rockwell said humorlessly.

"By all means," Eugene said.

"Six: prototype returned bright purple and smelling of limes. Seven: prototype returned covered in travel stickers. Eight: prototype—"

"I believe we get the gist of it, Gladstone," Danielle said softly. "What is your point?"

"My point, Mrs. Chairwoman, is it's high time to let qualified professionals take the reins of the ARTists project."

The other members stirred in their chairs. Eugene's stomach tightened into a coiled spring. He'd suspected the hit was coming, but anticipation did little to soften the blow.

"Please don't misunderstand me," Gladstone resumed. "Professor

Graham is to be admired for assembling the team he did on such short notice. Further, the contributions of his team are commendable. I doubt any other ragtag bunch could have accomplished what they did, but we're reaching a critical juncture, and now is no time for amateurs.

"I move that the ARTists group turn over their research and equipment to an established, experienced R&D team, preferably one already cleared to accept government black budget contracts."

No one had any doubt which company's R&D department Rockwell had in mind. Half the room was looking uncomfortably at Eugene, unsure of what to say or do. Eugene loomed over the table menacingly.

"Have you finished?" Eugene asked, his voice warm as arctic midnight.

Rockwell stared back at him, but said nothing.

"I assume by your silence you have," Eugene said. "With respect, I think you've forgotten a few important points. First, the term *crash program* was coined for a reason. When people are working under a deadline in uncharted technological territory, unscheduled explosions are the norm. Second, while we have lost prototypes, we have not lost human lives. Something, it should be added, that cannot be said for the program that developed the first gravity drive system."

Air was sucked through teeth, and at least one person in the room chuckled. Everyone knew which company had built the AEUS *Manchester*, posthumously nicknamed the *Mancrusher*.

Rockwell boiled over. "Now just a damned minute. That was a totally different situation."

"You are right, of course. My team had the added challenge of leaving the known universe."

"That's preposter—" Rockwell started, but a gently cleared throat arrested his budding diatribe.

"Please continue, Professor," Danielle said.

"Third," Eugene put his palms on the table. "You propose

turning things over to an 'experienced' R&D team. Who would that be, exactly? Because as far as I know, my team possesses the sum total of *all* human experience in the hyperspace field."

"True." Rockwell keyed up a file on his data pad. "But there are other areas of experience where your team falls short of the mark." He transferred the file, and page after page of ARTist memos, technical papers, and schematics cascaded down the central holo.

Eugene frowned. "What's all this?"

"This"—Rockwell pointed at the parade of classified files—"is a live feed from *Loose Lips Ezine*. Two hours ago, they posted over a terabyte of your team's internal communications. The Web is buzzing with it. You have a leak, Professor."

Eugene slumped. "We can fix this. We've been doing it for three years."

"No, what you had before was rumor and innuendo, not proof. Nobody can fix this."

Eugene looked at Danielle. "You knew?"

"Yes, Professor. I was told half an hour after the documents went up."

"And I suppose you agree with Mr. Rockwell."

She looked at him with apologetic eyes, but nodded. "This one is too big. You can't contain it."

"Well, then, what's left? Go public?"

"Yes, but not immediately. There is still the matter of our courier ship."

"The warship?" Eugene said. "That will take months."

"It may not take as long as you think," Danielle said.

Eugene's suspicion rose. "I was under the impression development of the president's toy had been suspended until our hyperspace generator was ready."

"That's what you and everyone else were supposed to think." Rockwell flashed a smile as toothy and sincere as a saltwater crocodile's.

Danielle shot him a cold look. "What Mr. Rockwell was trying to say, Professor," she said delicately, "was that the president decided it would be prudent to run the two programs in parallel. Construction on the *Bucephalus*, as it has been named, restarted the week after your team opened their first hyperspace window. The ship is basically complete and has already undergone stationary trials. All that's left is the integration of your hyperspace generator."

Eugene's head spun. It was all coming apart. His lads were going to be thanked for their hard work and then pushed to the sidelines. "You've got this all stitched up nice and neat, hmm, Mrs. Chairwoman?"

"Don't make this into something personal, Professor," Danielle said. "We all had jobs to do, and your team did theirs amazingly well, but you knew from the beginning that this was bigger than you, or them, or any of us."

Danielle put her elbows on the table and folded her hands. "Maybe it's time to pass the baton. Why don't you instruct your team to set up a plan to help the *Bucephalus* crew transition to the new equipment?"

"Yes," Rockwell interjected. "Our techs and engineers will need to get brought up to speed before launch."

Eugene realized he was staring at his hands. *They've never built anything*, he thought. *I've spent my whole life impressing people by being clever, but before this, my only contributions to the world were smarmy grad students. One of whom is trying to take away the miracle my boys and girls have built with* their *hands.*

It was no decision at all.

"No," Eugene announced to the room at large.

"What do you mean, 'No'?" demanded Rockwell.

"I would think my meaning was quite clear. *No* is a simple enough word, Mr. Rockwell. It's been in common usage for many centuries now. This has, from the very beginning, been an American/European Space Administration project. An AESA ship found and recovered the buoy, an AESA team translated the message, and an AESA team reverse engineered the tech. Now, in the eleventh hour, and after doing *all* the work, AESA is asked to graciously hand our research over to military-industrial complex thugs. To that, I say, 'No.'"

Rockwell was about to go supercritical, but the chairwoman put up her hand, interrupting the process. "I assume you have an alternate proposal, Professor?"

Eugene looked at the ceiling and theatrically cracked his knuckles. "As a matter of fact, I do."

Compromise, it has been said, is the fine art of solving problems in such a way that no one gets what they want. It is for this reason Eugene didn't bother with it.

CHAPTER 21

Jeffery and Harris had been in space for almost two weeks by the time their deep-system transport reached Ceres. Neither had ever been so far from Earth. Jeffery had been as far as the Unicycle, while Harris hadn't made it beyond the Apollo 11 International Monument.

Until very recently, Ceres had been the solar system's twentysomething slacker offspring. It bounced between jobs; from being the eighth planet, to just another asteroid, to a really big asteroid, and finally back to a planet, albeit a dwarf one. It wasn't until Lockheed-Boeing-Raytheon's Skunk Works division built a new shipyard and testing facility on its surface that Ceres's identity crisis finally came to an end.

It was an ideal location for the sort of off-budget black projects the Skunk Works wizards had been building for four centuries. Fusion-drive shuttles like the one that ferried personnel to the Unicycle didn't have the endurance or speed to operate so deep in the system, and even the most powerful space-born telescopes were unable to resolve any useful details at these distances. Coupled with the ample material resources of the asteroid belt, Ceres was the perfect place for construction and testing of sensitive projects away from prying eyes.

The small yank Jeffery and Harris had been sequestered in for two weeks entered final approach. Jeffery's face was plastered against the portal. He took a moment to check on Harris, whose cheek was also pressed flat against the glass like, well, a Peeping Tom.

The Skunk Works yard provided for their voyeurism in spades. Barely concealed under spindly gantries lay the outline of AEUS *Bucephalus*. Harsh white light from a constellation of work lamps cast sharp shadows on her hull from a swarm of construction bots. Here and there, tiny flickers of light betrayed the presence of welders stitching polymerized ceramic panels together like so many leather cobblers.

"Are you seeing this?" Harris asked as he stared at his new home.

"Hard to miss it," Jeffery answered.

"What do you think?"

"She certainly looks . . . butch. Knew a girl in college who looked like that. Roller derby chick."

"She's all business," Harris said. This was certainly true, and there was little chance anyone would forget what line of work *Bucephalus* was in. She possessed the esthetic subtlety of a lead pipe.

"A little on the small side," Jeffery said absently.

"Size isn't everything."

"Easy for you to say. You're as big as a decent starter home."

At only nine hundred meters long, *Bucephalus* was dwarfed by most of the colony ships and ore haulers plying the space lanes. In fact, she was considerably more compact than even *Magellan*.

However, what she lacked in length, she made up for in heft. Military vessels have always been overbuilt, and *Bucephalus* was no exception. Between her stout internal structure, secondary and even tertiary systems, and the three-meter-thick cocoon of ablative ceramoplast weave armor, the ship out-massed *Magellan* by 23 percent.

On a civilian yank, a tangle of coolant pipes, fuel lines, and power conduits ran the length of the hull. This arrangement both sped construction and simplified repairs and maintenance in space dock. For a warship, however, this would leave critical systems exposed to enemy fire, so they were routed through the *Bucephalus*'s hollow core.

Her hull was mostly smooth and unadorned as a result, leaving her looking like a concrete birdbath lying on its side.

She was not completely featureless, however. Jeffery's finger pointed at two parallel rows of ten rectangular hatches behind one of the shuttle bays. "What do you figure those are?"

Harris took a moment to answer. "VLS modules. There's another cluster of them farther down the hull."

"VLS?"

"Sorry, vertical launch system."

"What, like missile launchers?" Jeffery asked.

Harris shrugged. "It's a warship. Warships need teeth."

"Yeah, but look at them, Thomas. Each hatch has got to be six meters wide. What the hell is behind them?"

"Beats me. Whatever they are, I'm glad they're pointing *away* from the ship."

A barely discernible vibration shook the transport yank as docking clamps grabbed the hull and locked it into place.

"All right," Jeffery said. "Time to go find Felix and meet your new neighbors."

Their search for Felix stalled when Harris stumbled across the armory, or as the door would have passersby believe, the "Indigenous Wildlife Suppression Equipment Locker." Observant guests might also notice that the "navigational lasers" placed at the bow could pulverize a medium-sized asteroid. Or that the shuttles were fitted with an "Emergency Landing Zone Clearing Module" that could mow down buildings as easily as trees. Or that the "probes" tipped with "seismic geological survey charges" bore an uncanny resemblance to nuclear missiles.

"And this?" Jeffery held up what looked like an ordinary flashlight.

"Oooh!" Harris was clearly operating on the verge of excitement overload. "I've read about these." He took the cylinder from Jeffery's hand. "It's called a Niven light. Most of the time it's just flashlight, but in a pinch the beam collapses into an industrial cutting laser."

"What for?"

"In case you don't like what you see, I suppose."

"Why a 'Niven' light?" asked Jeffery.

"I don't know, probably the dude that invented it."

"Right, then." Jeffery paced the deck admiring all the not-weapons for the platoon of not-marines that Lieutenant Harris was definitely not here to command.

"You know, Tom, there's something I don't get about this ship."

"What's that?"

"Well, look at this room. They've gone out of their way to slap a ridiculously transparent euphemism onto every offensive system. Yet they named that damned thing *Bucephalus*, the personal warhorse of Alexander the Great, probably the most famous conqueror in our history. Doesn't that seem like a pretty glaring oversight?"

"Freudian slip is all I can come up with," Harris replied.

"C'mon, let's find Feli—"

Jeffery stood in front of a large bay window. Behind the glass was a large room with rails attached to the ceiling, pointing toward a series of hatches that could only lead outside. Hanging from the rails were a dozen malicious machines that looked for all the world like giant angular bats sleeping in a cave.

"What the hell are those?" asked Jeffery.

"Those," Harris beamed, "are orbital overlook platforms. You don't want to get caught underneath them; they're liable to make a mess. The official name is Gargoyle, but leathernecks just call them OOPs."

Jeffery shook his head slowly. "Curious how all this stuff was just lying around, since space-based weapons have been illegal for four centuries."

"Au contraire," said Harris. "It's illegal to *deploy* space weapons. No one said anything about *developing* them."

Jeffery rolled his eyes. "Gotta love semantics." He crossed his arms over his chest as if a cold snap had just come through.

"Hey," Harris said. "You okay?"

"Yeah, I guess. It's just all becoming real, you know? You're going charging out there waving your guns in the air. What could go wrong?"

"It's the life, Jeff. You knew that from the beginning."

"Knowing and experiencing are different things."

Harris's oaken arms swallowed him. "Shhh. I know it's scary. But I've been in bad spots before. I know what I'm doing."

"You'd better, Lieutenant." Jeffery let his head rest in the pocket between his lover's neck and shoulder. "And you'd better keep Felix alive, too. I really like that little weirdo."

"So do I."

After finishing their tour of the not-armory, Jeffery queried Felix's location on a nearby terminal. He was working on the bridge. They caught a tube car to the bridge, located in the center of the ship underneath as much armor and structural composite as possible. They found Felix buried up to his waist inside the navigational station, unabashedly cursing whoever had engineered the bridge layout.

"Seriously?" came his voice from the hole in the wall, addressing the universe at large. "Who in their right mind runs a high-amp conduit through a bridge station? Ever hear of transformers?" A rubber-handled socket wrench came flying out the hole and clanged against the deck plate.

"Everything all right in there, princess?" Jeffery asked with a smirk.

The undirected litany paused as Felix realized he was playing to an audience.

"That had better be Jeffery, or else somebody's getting a face-full of electrical insulation foam."

"Yeah, it's me. Thomas is here, too."

"Hey, buddy," Harris said. "I checked the cabin assignments; we're going to be neighbors."

"That's great," Felix said.

This was one half of Eugene's bargain. The *Bucephalus* got the ARTist's hyperdrive, on loan, with Felix as its chaperone.

"Could one of you hand me that socket I just threw on the floor?" A hand streaked with white lithium grease waved from the hole.

"Temper, temper," Jeffery said as he placed the tool back in the waiting hand. "What's the matter down there?"

"Nothing, provided you don't mind power spikes causing a blowout and electrocuting whoever's sitting here. Half-wits."

The rapid clicking of a ratchet floated in the air, punctuated by a strained grunt.

"There," Felix said. "Tom, grab my feet and pull me out, would you?"

Harris obliged and a moment later Felix stood dusting off his dark red *Bucephalus* uniform.

"Didn't expect to see you out here, Jeffery," Felix said. "Thanks for making the trip. Did you bring me anything interesting?"

"Four shiny new, five-twelve kilobyte QERs. Two for *Bucephalus*, two for *Magellan*."

"Great. That'll speed things up." Felix noticed a rectangular patch of hair missing from the side of Harris's scalp. "What's that about?"

"Implanted coms," Harris said. "They're requiring the whole crew to get them before launch."

"Oh, wonderful," Felix said. "The latest crew gossip beamed straight into my head 24-7. Anything else?"

"Well, we heard rumors on the way out here that our transport was also delivering the new captain," Jeffery said.

"Really? Who did they pick?" Felix asked.

"We don't know. It was kept confidential. Last I knew the list had been whittled down to about a half dozen candidates."

"You were on that ship for two weeks. You didn't see them anywhere?"

"They didn't fly economy," Harris said.

As they spoke, the double doors of the bridge's lift tube hissed open. Felix, Harris, and Jeffery turned in unison to see the new arrival. A familiar man in a perfectly tailored and pressed AEU Navy dress uniform stood astride the doorway, and Felix's stomach did a barrel roll.

"Oh, please," he pleaded to whichever deity might intervene. "Anyone but him."

"Permission to enter the bridge," Maximus Tiberius said with a self-congratulating grin.

"If we say no, does he have to leave?" Felix asked in a hushed voice.

"No," Harris said quietly before facing the newcomer. "Permission granted, Commander."

"Ah." Maximus pointed to the rank insignia on his collar. "Count the bars, Lieutenant."

Harris realized there were not three but four gold bars on the man's shoulder.

"Sorry, Captain, sir."

"Think nothing of it. I only just acquired number four. Still getting used to it myself," Maximus said. He leaned in closer and inspected Harris's features. "Have we met, Lieutenant?"

"Yes, sir. Three years ago, in Washington."

"A conference?"

"No, sir. The Captain's Mast."

"Ah! That explains it. It's a miracle I remembered your face after a night walking the planks of the Mast, but you clearly remember me."

"Yes, sir."

"That's understandable. I'd remember me, too. So which one of you is the warp drive tech?"

"Hyperdrive," Felix said through gritted teeth.

"Hmm? Did you say something, son?"

"It's a hyperdrive. Warp drive's still impossible."

"Oh, so you would be the tech I'm looking for, then."

"I am."

"I am . . . sir?"

"This isn't a military ship, Captain Tiberius," Felix said tersely.

Jeffery made a display of clearing his throat. Maximus simply smiled.

"I remember you now, the quiet one afraid of girls. Freddy? Fissel?"

"Felix."

"Well, then, Felix. Do you also believe that a nice fur coat would make me a Jack Russell terrier?"

"No," Felix answered, suddenly off balance.

"Well, there you have it," Maximus said. "There's what a thing is made to look like, and there's what a thing *is*. And this is a warship, and warships belong to militaries. Now, we have another transport coming in a week. Except this one will be filled with dignitaries, politicians, and the inevitable swarm of media. They'll be expecting a launch ceremony. I intend to give them one. So I need your personal assurance that we'll be ready to take this show on the road by then."

"Well, that's simple," Felix said. "You don't have it."

"Thank you. I'll be glad to . . . wait, what did you say?"

"I said you don't have my assurance that we'll launch in a week. So far we've only done this with prototypes less than a hundredth the mass. Even then, the first three blew up. I'm not prepared to give you assurances that we'll launch on a deadline. There is too much calibration to do, and too many variables. The politicians want a party, fine, but they need to consult with us about the scheduling, not the other way around. We simply aren't ready."

Maximus listened politely, which itself made Felix uneasy. He'd half expected to have his head ripped off. Then the captain replied.

"Felix, baby," Maximus said. "You're just going to have to accept that people are *never* ready in times like these. Page-turners and bolt-tighteners always demand more time than external forces permit. That's your job. My job is to remind you the real world and the people cutting our checks don't care. So get us as ready as you can in a week, and maybe find yourself a little helping of faith. Can you do that for me?"

"Faith in what?" Felix said, an off-key note of contempt ringing through his voice.

"Whatever you like! That's the secret," Maximus said. "Faith in God, the mission, your shipmates, faith in your work, or even *Bucephalus* herself. The object of faith doesn't matter, just the act of having it. That's what tripped us up for so long."

Maximus looked at the chronometer on the main plot. "Wow! Is that the time? Look, I've got to get moving to the other departments, lots of elbows to rub. But hey, good talk, everybody. And you look sharp in that uniform. Red is a good color on you." He made a shooting gesture with his fingers at Felix as he backed out of the bridge. The lift tube doors closed and he was gone, leaving the three friends in baffled silence.

"What just happened?" Felix asked no one in particular.

"I think," Jeffery said, "you were just put in your place by a Jack Russell terrier."

A week passed, and Felix found himself on display for the world's press. Fortunately, he was only one of many. The entire *Bucephalus* crew flanked the podium where Captain Tiberius stood, a great shinning white albatross with gold trim among a sea of red.

The press conference filled the portside shuttle bay almost to capacity. The shuttles themselves had been removed in preparation for the representatives from all the major holo-networks, vlogs, and accredited news sites from Earth to Luna to Mars to the dirigible cities of Venus.

Felix had been around large herds of reporters on several occasions, but this time was different. This time they knew who he was and what he had accomplished. The preconference press release has seen to that. Another part of Eugene's bargain: credit given where it was due.

However, the glare of the media did not shine on Felix at the moment. For the first time, he was grateful Captain Tiberius was there. When it came to stealing the spotlight, Maximus was a first-rate supervillain.

"Captain Tiberius," Stan Blather of CHS News jumped in. "Before journeying out here, we polled our viewers to ask, 'Is launching the *Bucephalus* without full space trials too dangerous?' Seventy-eight percent of respondents answered yes. What is your answer to them?"

Maximus's smile was broader and brighter than a chrome grille. "Thank you for the question, Stan, and I'd say the only polls I care about have girls dancing on them. Next question."

The room alternated between laughter and abject horror, but Maximus didn't give them time to sort out which before pointing to the man Felix personally blamed for this whole dog and pony show, G. Libby Hackman. It was his news site, *Loose Lips*, that had published the leaked memos. It was his profile that matched the person tailing Harris a couple of years back.

"Yes? You, sir."

Hackman let a stubby little arm fall back to his side and took his time composing himself. "Thank you, Captain. I'd like to build off Mr. Blather's question. Considering the short workup time, unproven technology, and the unknowns you'll encounter once in deep space, certainly even you must agree this mission seems a little . . . audacious?"

"Audacious?" Maximus gripped both sides of the podium and leaned back as if in shock before returning to the microphone. "No, audacious is the dandelion I found growing in the grass trimmings on the deck of my lawn mower. Imagine the stones on that plant. If it had a mouth, it would've spit in my face as I plucked it. We could all learn something from that ambitious little weed, people." He motioned for the next questioner, "You, in the bowler."

"Jimmy Lancier, *New Detroit Gazette*," said a man as yet unburdened by the need to shave.

Felix remembered him from the old neighborhood. He was the annoying kid who never stopped asking inappropriate questions. Apparently, he'd made a career of it.

"Rumors are swirling that *Bucephalus* is some sort of prototype warship," Lancier continued. "Would you care to comment on her weapons load?"

"Well, I hate to disappoint you, Jimmy, but I'm afraid that whatever defensive and offensive systems the *Bucephalus* may or may not have are classified . . . as totally awesome."

Unable to avoid the inevitable any longer, Maximus leveled a finger at the proverbial eight-hundred-pound gorilla in the room. In this case, it was an eight-hundred-pound gorilla named Buttercup. After several generations of captive gorillas being taught sign language, they eventually organized and demanded citizenship. So the Association for the Advancement of Non-Human Persons was formed. Its membership includes several thousand gorillas and chimpanzees, sixteen herds of elephants, twenty-seven pods of dolphins, and a particularly clever African gray parrot who served as treasurer. Buttercup had recently become a correspondent for *Branches & Fruit Monthly*, following his award-winning essays "Zoo Employees Fragile. Do Not Wrestle" and "Why You Not Groom Human Children?"

Buttercup started signing furiously into the small holographic translator he wore around his neck. After he'd finished, the device spoke in a calm female voice. "Why no furries on crew?"

Without missing a beat, Maximus said, "Oh, come on. With a crew this large, there has to be at least a couple of closet furries. C'mon, folks, raise your hands. We're all adults here." The crew looked back at him in muted horror. "Nobody? Well, they're probably just shy."

Buttercup bristled. Despite being packed into the shuttle bay like a can of green beans, the rest of the journalists managed to create a five-meter circle around the offended primate.

Maximus had to shout into the microphone to be heard over the rising hoots and growls. "I think that about wraps it up for the Q&A. See you all tomorrow at the launch!"

He deftly slid out of the way just as Buttercup's chair shattered the podium.

CHAPTER 22

Vel Noric stepped cautiously through the great hallway leading to His Superiority the Kumer-Vel's chambers. Many Vels had walked the path before him. The fortunate walked out promoted. The less than fortunate did not walk out at all. The supremely unfortunate were still here—or their heads were, at least, fixed to the walls as a reminder of the price of incompetence.

It alarms me not, Vel Noric thought. There were more practical ways to deal with an unfit Vel than to take their ship off patrol and pull them all the way back to the Nest. Besides, that business in the Tekis Nebula last cycle hardly justified making Noric into a wall mount, did it?

Noric felt fairly confident it didn't, but he couldn't help noticing the empty wall cavity illuminated by the orange light of Faan's sun. If the sun-fading in the paint was any indication, the previous occupant had only just been removed. The crest atop Noric's skull slacked a little more, and his pace quickened.

The interminable hallway finally ended at a set of impossibly tall doors of solid wood, embellished with leather accent panels whose origin Noric didn't wish to dwell on.

A hard voice from a speaker in the doorframe: "State your purpose."

Noric leaned in and answered. "Noric, Vel of patrol cruiser #7803. Here to present myself to the Kumer-Vel, as directed."

The door unlatched itself and swung open ponderously. The centuries-old hinges creaked like the tapping fingers of an impatient giant. Despite a sudden blast of hot, moist air, a shiver ran through Noric's scales.

A solitary figure emerged from the darkness inside. After a moment, Noric recognized the features of Ruckk, the official representative of the Turemok species at the six-seat table of the Assembly leadership, and the most powerful single individual he'd ever been in such proximity to. Noric stood resolute, respectful, but not cowering.

Ruckk gave him a cursory glance before snorting as if he'd just stepped over a dead jelbow.

"Good luck in there, *Vel*."

"Thank you, Representative," was all he managed.

Ruckk regressed down the empty hall, leaving Noric alone to face his fate once more. There was nothing for it. He passed through the imposing double doors as the darkness enveloped him. The echoes of Noric's footfalls betrayed the cavernous size of the room.

Noric continued to walk forward into the inky blackness, his anxiety growing with each step. He switched the spectrum of his optical implants to UV. Nothing. He switched them to heat, only to find the room was a completely uniform temperature, which just happened to be Turemok body temperature.

It's a test, he thought. A test of what, though? His resolve? His willingness to stumble along blindly? He stopped in his tracks.

"Reveal yourself, Kumer-Vel," he said, trying to keep apprehension from infiltrating his voice.

"You do not give the orders here, Noric," a booming voice echoed from the darkness.

Noric couldn't pin down its point of origin. It seemed to come from everywhere at once.

"That is true," Noric said more quietly. "However, those giving orders should be powerful enough to face their opponents, not hide in the shadows."

The hissing/grating sound that substituted for laughter among the Turemok reverberated through the hall.

"So you cast yourself as my opponent? The denizens of the hallway should have counseled you against aspiring to that mantle."

Noric immediately regretted his choice of words, but to retreat now would be a mark of weakness. "I will assume whatever mantle the Nest requires. If that must be your adversary, so it will be."

An interminable moment of silence followed. Finally, the voice responded. "Not today, Vel. The darkness serves as reminder that there is much you cannot see."

Noric let his anxiety ratchet down for the first time since making planet-fall. "Then tell me what *you* see, Kumer-Vel."

"I see many things. Before me, I see a Vel, whose standing has turned to glot, literally in this case."

Noric's crest fell completely flat. So the news from Tekis had reached Faan, after all. Karking tourists.

"However, I've learned that even a Kumer Vel cannot judge an inferior's worth on a single incident," the darkness said. "So before rendering my judgment, I reviewed your record, your accomplishments, and most importantly, your logs. You and I perceive a common threat, Vel Noric."

"The humans," Noric said without hesitation.

"Very good, Vel. I see we share some patterns of thought."

Noric relaxed, if only just. "They grow more emboldened by the cycle, Your Superiority," he said. "One of their vessels reached the border of their preserve and immediately stole a marker buoy."

"Yes, I read your report to the Assembly," said the echo. "But I'm curious, why did you not simply destroy the vessel for piracy?"

Noric selected his next words with care. "My Hedfer-Vel, J'quol, counseled against it. He believed that the Assembly would have frowned upon destroying an unarmed vessel. After considering the repercussions their judgment could have for our forces, I agreed.

We are forced to operate under too many pointless restrictions already. No need to add more Gomeltics to the hunt."

"Your Hedfer-Vel is a brave one, I think. You are fortunate to have him."

"Brave, Your Superiority?" Noric asked.

"Yes, brave enough to advise *against* attack; a risky suggestion to make among our people."

"I . . . had not considered that," Noric said truthfully. "Still, I'm ambivalent about the decision."

"How so?"

"There will be consequences," Noric said. "When they return to Earth, they will use the marker to accelerate their technology. They could pose a genuine threat in as little as one or two of their centuries."

Noric waited patiently, despite the distinct feeling that the room was growing even hotter. After what seemed like a full cycle, the voice returned.

"What if you were told the humans have already opened their own high-space portal?"

"I wouldn't be surprised," Noric said. "It would just be a matter of getting inside the buoy and adapting its high-space com to—"

"Not the humans on the ship you were tracking, Vel," the voice interrupted. "The high-space portal was detected on Earth itself."

That *did* surprise Noric. "That's not possible. There hasn't been enough time for any signals from the ship to reach Earth. They can't have copied the technology."

"That is true, yet here we are. One of our reconnaissance platforms detected the high-space portal on Earth's surface almost half a cycle ago," said the voice. "So either you can believe that the humans produced a high-space portal domestically or that they have some way to communicate instantly, which the best Lividite scientists ensure us is impossible."

Noric bristled at the implication. It wasn't that long ago that the Turemok had been galactic infants, anchored to Faan by technological stagnation. But centuries of Lividite aggression pushed the rest of the neighborhood into desperation. The Turemok were unshackled from their home world and forged into a spear to thrust at the heart of the Lividite enemy. However, once their purpose was fulfilled, they could not be stood back down again. Millennia later, the Turemok were still the talons of the Assembly, and they were merciless in their quest to preserve their position.

Now the humans were advancing faster than anyone could have guessed, and the wheel of history threatened to complete another cycle. The window for preemptive action was closing.

"May I assume," Noric said, "that you wouldn't be sharing this with a Vel you only intend to mount in the hall outside your door?"

The voice paused before answering, probably for dramatic effect. "You may."

Noric's crest regained some of its lost altitude, but only for a moment. He felt a swirl of air on the scales of his left arm and instinctively turned to face the disturbance.

Twin pinpoints of red peered down at him. Noric was not a small Turemok by any measure; his position as a Vel was enough proof of that. But the Kumer-Vel was the single tallest man he had ever seen, towering a full head and crest above him. Noric had to beat back a sudden urge to run for the door.

"You can be useful to me, Vel Noric. The Assembly clips our claws, preventing us from attacking this threat while it sits in its nest. I require an excuse, a pretense to act before the humans come crashing our gates. Your . . . rehabilitation . . . will be to provide me with one. Execute this assignment, and you might find yourself in line to command the *Xecoron*."

Noric's pulse raced. The *Xecoron*. The flagship of the Turemok fleet. The namesake of the ship that had finally crushed the Lividite menace centuries before, and the single most prestigious command in all of Assembly space, of any species. He could scarcely believe what he'd just heard. But he couldn't let the ambition show, so Noric centered himself before continuing.

"And you have a plan to create this . . . pretense, Your Superiority?" he said at last.

"As a matter of fact, I do."

The enormous door closed as the Vel departed.

"Light," the Kumer-Vel said, and then there was light. Standing in the middle of the room, a long robe flowing over his towering body, he smiled to himself.

"That went well," he said quietly. "Wouldn't you say, big brother?"

"Yes, splendidly," said a voice from his waist. "Now will you kindly get down from there? Your claws are digging into my shoulder plates."

"Certainly." The folds of the robe parted, revealing the smallest adult Turemok anyone had ever seen, or would have, if he had ever *been* seen. Jak'el disentangled himself from the rig atop his larger brother, Grote, himself no giant.

Nature had not bequeathed either of them with the stature that was a prerequisite for success in the Turemok's warrior society. In fact, she'd gone out of her way to place them at the far left of the bell curve.

The brothers were too small and too weak for anyone to take notice of them. Taken together, however, they had created a persona so intimidating that no one dared challenge it. Even many years into the ruse, Jak'el and Grote could hardly believe it continued to work. Nor could their younger, slightly larger brother, J'quol.

"Are you sure Noric will play his role?" Grote asked. "He's hardly the model of reliability. I mean, how incompetent do you have to be to have your ship knocked out by burgeron glot?"

"I'm sure." Jak'el removed an enormous prosthetic crest from his head. "He's exactly what we need. Reflexively xenophobic and too karking stupid to realize that he's the branch that will be pruned when the windstorm picks up."

"How certain are you that he will overreach in the way we need him to?"

"Well, you know how persuasive our little brother can be. J'quol is in an excellent position to give Vel Noric a helpful push off the cliff when the time arrives."

"And the humans? Why involve them?"

Jak'el clicked his teeth together. "I'm surprised at you, Grote. We need the barbarians to gin up a healthy panic. Coups are so much simpler if you wait until the population demands one."

CHAPTER 23

Felix tried to force himself to relax. Eventually, he gave up as the butterflies massed in his stomach like the Mariposa Monarca Reserve. It was 0530 in the morning, and he hadn't slept a wink. The moment Felix had been working feverishly toward for the last three years, and in a sense his whole life, arrived in two hours.

His assignment as chief hyperdrive technician had afforded him the luxury of a private room. Small as it may be, Felix was grateful to have a "fortress of solitude" for the duration of their mission.

However long or short that proved to be.

"You'd better be awake, Felix," Harris's voice came through the com by the door.

"I never quit being awake!" Felix shouted in the direction of the com.

"Oh, sorry. Are you dressed?"

"I'm not naked, if that's what you mean."

The door hissed open, and Lieutenant Harris turned sideways to step through. He took a look at the barely touched meal sitting on the small table, the remains of a red uniform unceremoniously rumpled on the floor, and an old, battered beanbag chair in the corner. Perched atop the chair sat Felix, looking like a scarecrow with half its stuffing missing.

"Damn, son, you look like hell," Harris said helpfully. "We've got to be dressed and on the bridge in thirty minutes."

"Can we launch tomorrow instead?"

"Would you like me to ask the captain?" Harris shot back.

Felix rolled out of the beanbag chair and made a grunting sound that could nearly pass for human.

"Why couldn't you sleep?" Harris asked.

Felix picked a tablet off his nightstand and waved it around absently. "Preparations," he said. "I'm still trying to fine-tune the settings for the hyper window under local conditions."

"We've opened dozens of them by now. What's different about this one?"

"Oh, lots of things. The local gravity is different, for one. Ceres is tiny compared to Earth, and we're much farther up the sun's gravity well," Felix said. "Add to that the lack of the Earth's magnetosphere, stronger solar wind, any time dilation effects of our velocity at entry—"

"Okay, I get it. God is in the details, eh?"

"Yeah, sitting right next to Mr. Murphy," Felix replied.

"How bad could it be?"

"Best case, some glitches with the ship's electronics. Worst case, we blow up like the first few prototypes."

"So anywhere from minor inconvenience up to utter catastrophe."

"Pretty much."

"Does Captain Tiberius know?"

Felix's eyes rolled. "His response was less than encouraging."

"Why? What did he say?"

"He said, and I quote, 'Don't sweat the small stuff, kiddo.' "

"Blowing up is small stuff?"

"Apparently so."

Harris smirked. "C'mon, get in the shower. You've got a long day ahead of you."

"Or a very short one," Felix muttered.

After depositing Harris at his post, Felix strode down the narrow hallway toward the bridge. Double doors parted, inviting him through. Between the holographic displays, pulsing sounds, and bustling crewmembers, it had more in common with a Berlin discothèque than the quiet space Felix had toiled in only days before.

On top of everything, the air carried a diffuse, musky smell. Felix looked around to identify the source, only to find himself in a staring contest with a silverback gorilla. Buttercup took up two chairs at the back of the bridge.

Captain Tiberius sat in the center of the managed chaos, as confident as he was comfortable, confirmation that every hurricane has an eye.

"Glad you could make it!" Maximus announced with outstretched arms. "Mr. Fletcher, I assume my engines are purring like kittens by now?"

"Except for all that 'small stuff' we've already talked about."

"Oh, that's exciting. Listen, Felix, I want you to play up that angle when the cameras start rolling. Drama makes for good vids."

"I don't think drama will be in short supply," Felix said, still staring at the gorilla. "Um, Captain?"

"Yes, Mr. Fletcher?"

"Can I ask why the *Branches & Fruit* reporter is in uniform?"

"You mean Mr. Buttercup. After that unfortunate . . . misunderstanding at the presser yesterday, the AANHP demanded representation on the crew. Mr. Buttercup was the only one that wasn't two weeks away, so he got the berth by default."

"What's his assignment?" Felix asked, positively terrified of the answer.

"Press liaison."

"That's . . . actually not a bad idea."

"Thank you," Maximus said with a glimmer in his eye. "Now, if there's nothing else?"

"I'll go to my station."

"Good man. Just see to it this wormhole doesn't cave in on us."

"Actually, Captain, a wormhole is a tunnel between two points in space. What we're doing is opening a window into a higher dimen—" Felix recognized the blank look on Maximus's face. He'd seen it on his classmates whenever he got excited about quantum mechanics. "You're not listening, are you?"

"Details are what delegating is for, Mr. Fletcher. I'm more of a big-picture guy. Helm, prepare for departure. Com, alert Ceres command and the chase yank that we'll be cutting the umbilicals in ten minutes. Engineering, you've got ten minutes to secure the fusion plant for independent operation. Security, double-check that everyone has locked the doors and rolled up the windows. The worlds will be watching, people. It's got to be perfect!"

Outside, the bright spotlights that illuminated the *Bucephalus*'s construction for the last two years went dark. For a handful of seconds, only the ship's silhouette could be seen against the construction gantry. Then her hull lights sparked to life, bathing *Bucephalus* in a white glow, punctuated by red and green navigational lights.

A series of explosive bolts disintegrated with a flash but without a sound, disconnecting the ship from the spidery gantry for the first time. The only connection that remained was a trio of segmented hoses snaking from the dockyard into the *Bucephalus*'s reactor bulb. These umbilical cords had provided the ship with power until now, to prevent unnecessary wear on the fusion plant.

That was about to come to an end, as the *Bucephalus*'s chief engineer busied himself jump-starting the universe's newest star. This fusion reactor was an advanced design, utilizing a battery of Felix's miniaturized gravity generators instead of a magnetic bottle to crush the plasma, creating pressures close to those found inside a real star.

This had two advantages. Higher pressures meant plasma temperature could come down from one hundred million degrees to a relatively chilly ten million, increasing reactor life expectancy. Even more important, this reactor didn't need the neutron in deuterium to burn. Plain hydrogen would do, meaning *Bucephalus* didn't lug around the gas separators of older ships. She could just siphon atmosphere from any old gas giant to top off the tanks.

Felix nervously watched the reactor's progress on his console. Even though he'd helped design it, there were always hiccups with new equipment. Regardless of size, when a sun hiccups, it's usually bad for the neighborhood. His anxiety proved to be misplaced. After a few minutes, the ball of plasma was fusing nicely.

"Fusion bottle is stable, Captain. Power is leveling off at just over two hundred megawatts, as expected," Felix said.

"Excellent," said Maximus. "Com, get on the QER to Earth and alert the Unicycle that we're on schedule to meet their beam. Engineering, cut the umbilicals."

An almost unperceivable shiver ran the length of the ship, accompanied by a flicker of the internal lights as she was weaned off external power in the blink of an eye. For the first time, *Bucephalus* was floating free under her own power. On board the Skunk Works orbital yard, twenty-one hundred proud parents watched the birth with moist eyes.

"Helm, move us away from the yard on full starboard thrusters, and ready the gravity well."

"Starboard thrusters to full, ready the well, aye," repeated the helmsman.

Bucephalus pushed away from her womb at a snail's pace, riding jets of supervelocity helium ions. The thrusters would be replenished with helium exhaust from the fusion reactor. Now plank owners, the bridge crew shared a moment of anticipation.

Maximus's voice broke the silence. "Helm, set course for our rendezvous with the beam."

The helmsmen massaged holographic icons in front of him. If he was nervous, it didn't show. "Course is set, sir."

"Floor it."

The helmsman cranked a virtual dial to eleven, and *Bucephalus* started to free-fall under 112 gravities. At the Unicycle millions of kilometers away, Renée Lemieux pushed a button and sent a three-terawatt beam of charged particles toward a point a hundred kilometers ahead of Ceres's orbit.

Even at light speed, the beam would take fourteen minutes to reach the *Bucephalus*. During the trip, it vaporized a long-forgotten GPS satellite in Earth orbit, a stray comet trailing Mars, and a bag of microwave popcorn lost by an asteroid prospector two centuries earlier. A few kernels popped, but they were really stale.

"Beam is on the way, sir," the com officer said.

Maximus nodded in approval and turned to the helmsmen's station. "Are we on time for intercept?"

"Yes, sir."

"Good. Steady on. Engineering, deploy the receiver array."

At the aft end of the *Bucephalus* behind the reactor bulb, an enormous mirrored flower blossomed. Folds of silvered polymer drew taut against the expanding framework. When the last creases smoothed out, it formed a nearly perfect parabolic mirror a kilometer across, but only a few molecules thick.

The mirror would catch the Unicycle's beam and focus it onto a collector made of youmustbejokium, so named for the first thing the material scientist said when the temperature and conductivity requirements were explained to him, transferring the energy into the ship's power grid and allowing *Bucephalus* to conserve fuel while accelerating out of the system.

A chase yank kept alongside the mighty ship at a respectful twenty-kilometer distance. It was little more than a reactor, gravity drive, and a warehouse of sensors to record everything the *Bucephalus* did.

Once under way, the bridge became almost peaceful. The crew buckled down and became lost in duties or private thoughts. Felix caught himself staring into the master holo-plot daydreaming. He felt serene. It wouldn't last.

Tense hours passed as the *Bucephalus* accelerated out of the asteroid belt. Navigational lasers in the bow dish destroyed incoming micro-meteors with dismissive ease.

A heavy pall fell over the bridge as the clock ticked toward the hyperspace transition. The crew contemplated their survival prospects in silence.

"Com, give me ship-wide, please," Maximus said.

"Live mic, sir."

"Thank you." Despite the fact the com was audio only, Maximus felt the need to straighten his gleaming white collar. "Attention, *Bucephalus* crew. In five minutes, we will either be the first people to travel faster than light or the first to die in the attempt. The good news is we're in the history books either way. Secure all loose material and put on your glasses for transition." Maximus made a cutting gesture at his throat.

"Mic cut, Captain."

Maximus turned to Felix. "It's your show, Mr. Fletcher."

Felix was already buried in his console, powering up the hyperspace generator and making last-minute adjustments. There wasn't much left to do that hadn't already been done in his two weeks of preparation, but he looked busy. That was the important thing.

On the face of the *Bucephalus*'s shield dish, three small portals slid open, exposing the projector heads of the hyperdrive system. Unlike the ship's gravity generators, the hyperspace system required line-of-sight to work, which meant the armor plating protecting all of the finicky electronics and biology inside the hull had to move out of the way.

"Hyperspace projectors are warmed up," Felix said.

Several members of the bridge crew let out slow sighs to ease the tension.

"Window is forming. Ten meters. Twenty. Fifty meters. Window reads stable. One hundred meters. Still stable. Ramping up power. Three hundred meters." Sweat beads as big as pearls formed on Felix's forehead.

"Mr. Fletcher," Maximus said.

"What?" he snapped.

"Your glasses."

Felix's hand shot to the top of his head. He'd forgotten to drop them over his eyes in the excitement. "Oh. Thank you. And, sorry."

"Don't mention it. Can't have you flying blind," Maximus said. He looked completely nonplussed, as though he either didn't comprehend the danger they were all in or simply didn't care. Felix wasn't sure which was more unnerving.

"Six hundred meters and growing," Felix reported. "Seven hundred."

"Helm," Maximus began. "I bet you can't thread this ship through a twelve-hundred-meter needle."

"Sir?"

"With the receiver array deployed, we're a thousand meters across. I bet you can't slip through with two hundred meters of clearance."

"And if I can?"

"There's a bottle of thirty-year-old Jack Daniel's in it for you."

"And if I can't?"

Felix broke in, "Then we're all dead, and the captain won't be around to collect on the bet anyway. Nine hundred."

"You heard Mr. Fletcher, everyone; no point making side bets," Maximus said with a snort. "So, helm, what's it going to be?"

The young man at the helm station set his jaw and nodded.

"Good man. Mr. Fletcher, lock in the window at twelve hundred meters."

"Captain, I must go on record opposing this," Felix said.

"Of course you must. But I'd rather know what kind of pilot I've got sooner than later."

At least it'll make good drama, Felix thought. "Eleven hundred meters. Eleven fifty. Twelve hundred. Locking the window."

"Com, ship-wide," Maximus said. The com officer pushed a button and nodded to him.

"Attention, crew. This is the captain. We're about to make transition. Hold on to something or, if you prefer, someone." He made a chopping motion, and the mic was cut. "All right, helm. Time to earn that bottle."

Felix gripped his console hard enough to leave marks. The helmsman's hands moved with the practiced precision of a surgeon. Directly ahead, a point of pure blackness blotted out the stars behind as it grew.

Felix counted down the last handful of seconds. "Transition in five, four, three, two . . . one."

The endless field of stars was swept away as darkness enveloped the space outside the ship.

As Felix had anticipated, there were a few unexpected effects from the slight incongruity between the window and the hyperspace beyond. For the barest millisecond, internal sensors falsely reported that the *Bucephalus*'s hydrogen fuel tanks were filled with frozen lemon custard, but that problem fixed itself after a moment.

The physiological effects on the crew were more pronounced. At the moment they made the transition between universes, the inner ears of each crew member suddenly believed that up was down, down was left, left was a note in F-sharp, and that right had split clean down the middle.

This isn't what the brain wants to hear, so, at a loss for how to interpret the data, the entire crew lost their lunch. The unholy mess hit *Bucephalus*'s decks, bulkheads, and ceilings with a splat.

"What the hell was that?" Maximus reached up a sleeve to wipe his mouth and nose.

"I *told* you," Felix said. "There wasn't time to finish calibrations before launch."

"Tell me harder next time. Com, call the mess hall. Tell Cookie to bring ten liters of 7Up and a case of Pepto-Bismol, stat. Oh, and napkins. Lots of napkins."

Then Maximus looked down to his suddenly less-than-white pants. "And somebody get me a fresh uniform!"

Lost in the maelstrom of prior meals, the helmsman had driven *Bucephalus* through the window six meters from dead center.

CHAPTER 24

FROM: EUGENE GRAHAM, ADMINISTRATOR, AESA
TO: CAPTAIN ALLISON RIDGEWAY, CO, AEUS *MAGELLAN*
MESSAGE TEXT:
TIDY UP. COMPANY'S COMING.
END.

Allison leaned back in her chair and rubbed a temple. "You know, Administrator Graham must have had the shortest lectures in academic history. When I was in college, you couldn't get the professors to shut up if you paid them."

"What did he say, ma'am?"

Allison pulled the message from her personal screen and sent it to the bridge's main holo.

Prescott read it in an instant. "So they survived the transition."

"It would appear so, but they still have to come out the other side. How's the link setup going?"

"We're just waiting for the authentication codes from Earth. Then we can bucket-brigade QER messages to Earth, to *Bucephalus*, and back."

"Excellent." Allison spun her chair a quarter turn. "Wheeler, give me a course back to our original target, then bring us about."

"I'm already laying it in, Captain."

"Thank you. Does anyone else feel like a yo-yo?"

Three hands went up. *Magellan* flashed a picture of a hand on the main holo.

Allison giggled at the display. "*Maggie*, since you were listening anyway, go ahead and start thawing out the rest of the crew. We only have three weeks before our guests arrive."

The darkness outside the cutter's command cave was almost total. Noticeably absent from the view was Buoy #4258743-E. D'armic had surveyed more than three thousand buoys in the last six farlems. A few had required maintenance, but never had he found one out of its proper place.

He searched for its signal, but found only silence. Further, buoys returned an exaggerated signature on active sensors, but his cutter saw nothing larger than dust specs within three larims.

There was a hole in the fence.

The mystery of the absent buoy tugged at him. Buoys were designed to last for centuries between maintenance intervals. Had it been destroyed? Perhaps, but where was the wreckage? Pirates or scavengers could have taken it, but the components weren't very valuable. They would need to steal them by the shipload to make it profitable. So why only one?

D'armic pushed the thoughts lower in his mind. The hole needed to be closed before anything snuck into human space, and it would take the better part of a farlem to retask the surrounding buoys. By then, he would be overdue for his checkup on the anthropological experiment the Bureau of Frontier Resources was overseeing on Culpus-Alam.

He swung the nose of his cutter toward the nearest buoy and opened a portal to high-space. He didn't spare a thought for what might be sneaking *out* of human space.

"Okay, time to crash the gate. Transition in ten, nine, eight, seven . . ." The crew of AEUS *Bucephalus* listened to Felix's countdown apprehensively. Many of them held space-sickness bags at the ready. Several had opted to spend transition in the head. "Three, two, one!"

At a wholly unremarkable point in space, something punctured the universe. Light from distant stars twisted and contorted to accommodate the expanding aperture. Without warning, a giant, one-legged end table flashed out of the breach. The stars appeared to snap back into position as the hole collapsed behind the advancing ship.

A pregnant calm gripped the *Bucephalus*'s bridge. Everyone waited several heartbeats for the other boot to drop, but the waves of nausea didn't come.

Maximus tucked his space-sickness bag under his seat cushion and removed his 3-D glasses. "Excellent work, Mr. Fletcher. Much improved."

"Thank you, Captain, but there were fewer variables to account for. There's no local gravity wells, solar wind, or Van Allen . . ." Felix spotted the now-familiar blank expression on Maximus's face. "I'll just stop there."

"Good man. Com, send a QER burst back to Earth. Let them know we're intact and give them our coordinates and heading. Helm, let's see how close we came. Start searching for the *Magell*—"

Collision alarms cut him off. Maximus looked up to the main holo, only to see a gleaming white hull growing exponentially in the space ahead of *Bucephalus*. His years commanding a carrier sub took hold.

"Dive!"

The helmsman was already a step ahead of his captain. His hands darted between floating icons as he killed the gravity well ahead of the ship. Reaction control thrusters flared to life, working feverishly against Newton as the mighty ship lurched away from its previous course, but the unidentified ship continued to grow.

"Impact in four seconds." Felix's voice cracked under the rising panic.

"Helm, full emergency blow." Maximus's voice filled every cubic centimeter of the bridge with urgency tempered by confidence.

"I've already done that, sir."

Hotel bedsheets would envy how white some of the faces turned as the final seconds ticked away. The bleached-bone-white hull of the unknown ship seemed to fill the universe.

"Brace for impact!" Maximus cried as the vessels converged.

Then, nothing. No sudden hammer blow. No fires erupted from the bulkheads. The air didn't rush out into space. The view ahead was filled with black and pinpricks of light. Maximus bolted up from his chair and threw his hands on his helmsman's shoulders.

"Did we miss them?"

"Yes, sir. We're clear of the bogey."

"How close did we come?"

The helmsman glanced at his instruments. "Um, I'd rather not talk about it, sir."

Maximus leaned over his shoulder to peek at the numbers for himself. His Adam's apple bobbed like a fishing float hooked to a sperm whale as he gulped down the sobering knowledge of how close they'd just come to annihilation.

"Right, then. I take it that bogey is *Magellan*?"

The com officer spun around in his chair. "Judging by the irate woman claiming to be the *Magellan*'s CO on the line, I'd say that's a safe bet, Captain."

"Great. This should be pleasant." Maximus rubbed his forehead for a moment before forcing his jovial poker face back into place. "Com, put her through."

The center display switched from the empty space outside *Bucephalus* to another, older bridge. Even through the holo's soft light, Allison's face looked hard as granite.

Maximus held his arms wide, oozing charisma like a blown head gasket. "Captain Ridgeway, how wonderful to finally make your acquaintance."

"Cut the crap, Tiberius. What the *hell* were you thinking? You almost killed both of our crews with that stunt."

"I'm afraid that, much as I'd like to, I can't take the credit for our dramatic entrance. That noble distinction falls on our hyperspace tech." Maximus swept a hand toward the hyperspace station, while Felix sank as far into his seat as his spine would permit.

"I'm sorry, Captain Ridgeway."

"Felix? Is that you?"

He had to force a smile, but it was genuine. "Yes, ma'am. This isn't exactly how I expected this to work."

"What happened?"

"I wanted the exit to be as precise as possible. Even the smallest margin of error would have put us days or weeks away from your position. I guess I overdid it."

"I guess so." A shiver ran through Allison's shoulders. "Well, we're all still here. I don't have to say this very often, Felix, but next time, try not to do such a good job. Okay?"

"Yes, ma'am."

Allison's face turned back to the center of the bridge. "Captain Tiberius, I . . . jumped to conclusions, and I apologize."

"Don't sweat it. You're hardly the first."

"Thank you. How long will it take you to fall back and match our velocity?"

"One moment."

Maximus swiveled his head down to the helmsman's station. He was already busy crunching the numbers. The young man looked to Maximus when he'd finished and pointed at his screen.

"An hour and a half at max normal deceleration, Captain."

Maximus nodded. "We'll be back with you at 1700 hours, Captain Ridgeway."

"Very good. We have a lot to discuss. Would you care to have dinner aboard *Magellan* once we rendezvous to discuss preparations?"

"Why, Ridgeway, I'd be delighted to have dinner at your place."

Allison's face froze for a moment before continuing. "The invitation is for your entire command staff."

"If you insist. How's 1800 strike you?"

"That should be fine."

"Wonderful. It's a date."

Allison's smile faded. "No, it's not."

After their last dinner guest departed for the shuttle bay, Allison let out a long, exasperated sigh. She looked around the table, into the faces of her senior staff, and at the few morsels of food that had survived the onslaught.

"Is there any wine left?"

"Whoa, slow down there, *mon capitaine*. You've got a duty shift in the mornin'."

"So do you, Chief, and you haven't exactly been a model of moderation tonight."

"Well, o' course not. Somebody had to drink up all the merlot before you got to it. I'm just tryin' to protect you."

"Steven, your selflessness is truly inspiring."

Chief Billings raised the bottle in silent toast and then relieved it of its contents with a mighty gulp.

Allison shook her head. "So what does everyone think of our new partners?"

Commander Gruber's shoulders perked up at the question. "Good people, very capable. Captain Tiberius is certainly a vibrant personality."

"Vibrant?" Allison's eyebrow arched. "That's putting a polite spin on it. He acts like an action vid hero, not a real naval officer."

"Well, his accomplishments are real enough. His service record is as long as my . . . arm."

Allison wrinkled her nose. "For a moment, Marcel, I thought you were going to use another part of your anatomy for comparison."

"His record isn't *that* long, ma'am."

Allison's eyes rolled like Sisyphus's boulder. "Ugh, men. You're all obsessed."

"Just playing the role, ma'am. And I suspect that's what Tiberius is doing as well. He's probably been cultivating the persona of an übermasculine loose cannon for years."

"Why on earth would he do that?"

"To be memorable, like a hero from another time. It pays to stand out in any competitive environment, and the military is no exception."

"That doesn't explain why he'd act so pompous and grating. As my mother used to say, 'You'll catch more flies with honey than vinegar.' "

Chief Billings rejoined the conversation. "Maybe so, but as my daddy said, 'You'll catch even more flies with bullshit.' "

"Your father sounds like a colorful man, but I think this conversation needs a dash more female input. Jackie, what do you think?"

Jacqueline's eyes stared dreamily at the ceiling. A full second passed before her ears bothered to report that someone had spoken her name. "Hmm? What did you say, ma'am?"

"I was just asking what you thought about our guests."

"Oh, Felix was nice."

Chief Billings adjusted in his chair. "Fletcher? How'd you come to that conclusion? He didn't say three words in the last two hours."

Jacqueline crossed her arms. "He's probably just shy and a little bit sensitive. There's nothing wrong with that."

"Mmm-hmm." Billings and Allison shared a knowing smile.

"What?" Jacqueline protested.

"Nothin', kiddo. It's nice to have Fletcher out here in case anythin' goes wrong with the new tech. After all, he's responsible for at least half of it."

"Very true." Commander Gruber laced his fingers and leaned forward. "I was also impressed by Lieutenant Harris. I'll be glad for his marine detachment when we start making planet-falls."

Allison didn't bother trying to hide her antipathy. "We're supposed to be explorers and diplomats, not conquerors. They may as well have sent a battalion of hairdressers for all the good those marines will do."

"Frankly, ma'am, that's the field researcher in you talking. Think about the message coming out of the buoy. We've been unwittingly living inside a wildlife park. Now, imagine you're an African gamekeeper when some elephants break through the fence. Do you try to negotiate with them, or do you grab a really big gun?"

"So you think a confrontation is inevitable?"

Gruber shrugged. "I think that a diplomat needs juicy carrots *and* a thick stick. The *Bucephalus*'s tactical capabilities fit the bill. I, for one, am glad she's out here."

Allison leaned back. "I'd be happier if Tiberius would tell us exactly what those 'tactical capabilities' are. What's that ship armed with that's so terrible that he won't even share it with his own task group?"

"Don't rightly know, ma'am. A ship as big as *Bucephalus* could hide darn near anythin'."

"Not even an educated guess, Steven?"

"Weapons ain't really my specialty."

"What about you, Marcel? You came up through the AEU Navy, after all."

"That's true, but anything I know is sixty years out of date. Whatever our neighbors are carrying is going to be brand-new, space-based tech."

Allison sighed. "Point taken. I guess we'll have to wait until the fireworks start. Prescott, how much time will you need to get the new QERs online?"

"A few hours, Captain. They're basically plug-and-play."

"Good. Wheeler, what's our ETA to the first system on our list?"

"We still have to distribute the glasses to the crew. *Maggie* has to piggyback through the *Bucephalus*'s hyper window. We're a little slower than they are, so they'll have to hang back a little. Still, even at *Maggie*'s maximum, we should be there in just under a day and a half."

Allison shook her head. "Twenty-two light-months in less than thirty-six hours. That's going to take getting used to."

She pushed back from the table and stood. "We're a couple of years behind schedule, and we've picked up a shipload of people whose scientific expertise is limited to things that go boom, but in two days, we reach the system this expedition was launched to explore. It's our limelight. Let's be ready to shine."

CHAPTER 25

A blue-green jewel hung in the endless black, illuminated by ten-minute-old light from the system's lone sun. A thunderstorm raged just across the terminator into night. The shape of the continents was the only clue reminding the observers that this wasn't Earth, but Solonis B.

Twin shuttles burned through Solonis B's upper atmosphere like comets riding streams of superheated plasma. *Magellan*'s shuttle was svelter, intended for carrying researchers and surveying equipment. By comparison, *Bucephalus*'s shuttle was a brute. It was designed to carry a rifle team of a dozen marines, who tend to be larger than your average researchers, along with all their armor, weapons, and equipment.

Lieutenant Harris studied the shuttle's displays and then looked to his pilot. "Simmons, how are we looking?"

"We're about to start our braking S-turns, sir. Hull temp is holding steady at 80 percent of maximum."

"Good, alert our friends in the other shuttle, then start your turns. Let me know when our altitude falls to ten thousand meters."

"Yes, sir."

Harris turned to face the shuttle's passenger compartment. "How you holding up back there, Felix?"

"Swell, Thomas. Just peachy."

Judging by Felix's pallid face, Harris knew he was lying. He wasn't exactly sure why Felix had insisted on tagging along, but he suspected the presence of a certain brunette flight ops officer on the other shuttle was related in some way. The deck under Harris's feet shifted as Simmons threw the shuttle into the first high-banking turn. Harris turned to the cockpit and the shuttle's electronic warfare officer.

"Devor, how long before we can switch on the active camouflage?"

The young lance corporal looked to her screens for a moment before answering. "Hull temp is still a couple of hundred degrees too high. We should be fine once Lieutenant Simmons completes his braking maneuvers."

"Are we getting signal from the Gargoyles yet?"

"Yes, sir. Gargoyle platforms are five by five."

"Excellent. Network their feeds to my link, and fire control as well."

Devor pulled up a new menu on her display and entered a code. "Done, sir."

"Thank you." Harris rested a big hand on her shoulder as he sorted through the new stream of telemetry coming from the sensors and cameras mounted on the OOPs tens of kilometers above.

Harris didn't really believe they'd need the Gargoyles during the mission. Their initial scans had only located a scattering of settlements on the planet's entire surface, and low-tech settlements at that. He was confident anything his men or the survey team encountered could be dealt with using small arms.

But his OCS instructors had taught him never to make assumptions, and this low-risk mission would provide his platoon with an excellent dry run. The beginning of any expedition was a time to do things by the book, even if they were writing most of the chapters on the fly.

Once the delicate choreography of braking maneuvers was complete, they found a natural clearing in the forest to serve as a landing zone for the shuttles. There was a hissing outside the exterior hatch while the pressure equalized with the surrounding air. Only an outline of the marines' shuttle could be seen, and only if one was almost on top of it.

A hatch popped open and folded to the ground. Three fully loaded riflemen flowed out and took up positions. After a moment, they flickered and disappeared as the active camouflage systems in their armor adjusted to the new surroundings.

Harris stepped out of the doorway, flanked by Felix. Rebreathing rigs covered their mouths until local atmospheric conditions could be verified.

"Corporal?" Harris said.

A shimmer stood and briskly walked toward his CO. "Sir?"

"Take your team and secure the tree line. Call me when you're in position so that we can land the *Magellan*'s shuttle."

"Sir." The mirage saluted and then moved off with the other three like a pack of translucent wolves.

"That's creepy," Felix observed. "They're like ghosts. How do you keep track of them, Tom?"

"An augmentation program superimposes them into my vision. I see them as clearly as I see you."

"Handy. Can I get that program?"

"We'll see."

"Why are we using troops anyway? Why not bring down the battle androids?"

"A few reasons, but mostly because they each weight half a ton. We can only land two of them per shuttle trip. Hang on." Harris closed his eyes for a moment. "They're in position. Simmons, inform the *Magellan*'s shuttle they are clear to land."

The tablet in Felix's hand beeped, drawing his attention. "The air looks good. We can drop these breathers."

Overhead, the shuttle bearing *Magellan*'s survey team swung low, held aloft by three pillars of exhaust gas. The whine of its turbines slowed as it settled onto the thick mat of green and purple grasses beneath their feet. The hatch cycled, then retracted as Captain Ridgeway and Lieutenant Dorsett hopped to the ground. Jacqueline waved at Felix as they walked over. Allison stopped just short of the two men.

Harris saluted. The survey team was in charge here; Harris's men were purely escorts.

"Captain Ridgeway, welcome to Solonis B."

"Thank you, Lieutenant Harris. Hello, Felix."

"Um, hi, Captain."

"Allison is fine, Felix. Let's leave the titles for the military types. It makes them more comfortable. Judging by your naked faces, I take it the air checked out?"

"Yeah, it's a little high in O_2 and there's a lot of argon floating around, but we should be fine in the short term."

Allison unhooked the clasp that held her mask in place. Her face uncovered, she breathed deeply and exhaled a long, satisfied sigh. "You two may not be able to appreciate this, but that was the first breath of nonrecycled air I've taken since . . . well, since before either of you were born."

Felix was too busy making a show of not looking at Jacqueline to hear what Allison said.

"Shall we get started, ma'am?"

"Absolutely, Lieutenant. Lead the way."

Allison's survey crew took their time covering the three kilometers from the LZ to the outskirts of the settlement, which was fine with their escorts; the forest floor was thick with creeping vegetation eager to snare their feet and equipment.

The forest's "trees" weren't really. Their trunks were thick and segmented, with roots snaking down from as high as five meters into the ground. Jacqueline called them "beard trees," and the name stuck. They were topped by a single massive, spade-shaped leaf.

The survey team recorded everything and stopped frequently to collect samples. A brightly colored flower clinging to one of the beard trees caught Harris's eye. He moved to investigate it more closely. As his shadow fell over it, the flower opened wide, revealing a bright blue pod.

"Hey, Felix, come look at this. I think it reacts to movement." As he said it, the pod at the center of the flower bulged and then burst, releasing a cloud of blue dust into Harris's face.

"Ahh!" Shocked, Harris fell back to the ground.

Felix and Allison charged over to Harris, who was rubbing frantically at his face.

Allison pulled out a canteen and poured water over his eyes and mouth. "Are you all right? Does it burn?"

"A little. What is this stuff?"

"I don't know yet." Allison handed him the canteen and inspected the flower. "It could be an irritant or poison, or it could just be pollen."

"So it's either trying to kill me or mate with me?"

"You'll find that's true of most things in nature."

"It tastes like pepper."

"Spit it out. We don't know what it will do to your system."

Felix leaned in close to Harris's face and sniffed the blue dust. "It does smell like pepper. Tom, you know what this means, don't you?"

"What?"

"It means you're a seasoned veteran."

"Felix," Harris unslung his rifle, "because you're my friend, I'm going to give you a ten-second lead before I start shooting."

Allison shook her head. "Now, boys, I will not tolerate fratricide, regardless of how deserved it may be. Lieutenant, wash your face, and consider this a lesson in the virtues of caution. Felix, collect a sample."

"Yes, ma'am," they answered in unison.

Allison walked back toward the rest of her team. Felix helped Harris back to his feet and handed him a handkerchief.

"Here. Wipe yourself off."

"Thanks." Harris removed the powder from his face and handed the handkerchief to Felix, who promptly dropped it into a plastic bag and scribbled something onto it with a marker.

"You're using that as your sample?"

"Yeah, why not?"

Harris sighed and resumed the march toward the settlement.

The two teams could not be more different as they advanced. Even in unfamiliar territory, Harris's marines were the pinnacle of stealth. Their movements were efficient and deliberate, darting from one bit of cover to the next, each of them covered by the fire arcs of at least two of their squad mates. Above all, they were silent. Their implanted com systems certainly helped, but even at a jog, their feet fell on the ground with care.

By contrast, the survey team was like a marching band. They trod carelessly through the open, snapping roots and crunching leaves underfoot. Each new discovery was met with excited exclamations. Glaciers advanced faster.

We may as well try to hide a parade, Harris thought through their private line. His squad chuckled among themselves.

Unit One, move ahead to scout out the path. The two troopers nodded their affirmation and drove ahead. So quiet were they, and so effective was their adaptive camouflage, that not one of the survey team noticed their departure.

"It's ba-aack."

Commander Gruber looked up from his chair's display. "Would you care to elaborate on that, Mr. Wheeler?"

"Sure thing, sir." Wheeler shunted the feed from his station into the bridge's main holo. A red dot surrounded by a blinking circle sat three light-minutes deeper into the system from where *Magellan* and *Bucephalus* orbited Solonis B.

Commanded Gruber frowned. "The fuzzy anomaly."

"Yes, sir. Got it in one."

"Why didn't we spot it before?"

"It was eclipsed by the planet. Our orbit just carried us into line of sight."

"Okay, but this is our third orbit. Did it just arrive, or was it waiting for us when we entered the system?"

"I don't know, sir. I didn't see it until now, but it's hard to spot at the best of times."

"*Maggie*?"

"Yes, Commander Gruber, how may I assist you?"

"I'd like you to sift through the sensor logs since our last transition for any earlier sign of the anomaly."

"I've completed the review. There was no sign of the anomaly prior to Mr. Wheeler's discovery."

Gruber's eyebrows crept up. "That was fast."

"Based on your conversation, I anticipated a 78 percent chance that you would make the request."

"How efficient of you, *Maggie*. Thank you. Com, link me up to the captain. She'll want to know our voyeur has returned."

Prescott turned to face the commander. "And *Bucephalus*?"

"Good eye, Prescott. I forgot about them." Gruber's hand reached up to rub his face. "You may as well conference Captain Tiberius in with us."

Wheeler snorted. "Fifty bucks says he'll want to shoot it."

Gruber did some shooting of his own, firing a sharp glance at the helmsman. "Feeling a little insubordinate, Ensign?"

Wheeler's eyes sank to the deck. "Sorry, sir. That was disrespectful."

Gruber held the gaze a moment longer; just to be sure the point had been made. "You have to remember that we're not alone anymore. I know we've all gotten comfortable with each other on this tour, but the mission is in full swing now, and the *Bucephalus* brings in a whole new element. We can't let discipline slip away. That goes for everyone."

"I understand, sir."

"It's all right, Mr. Wheeler." Gruber smiled. "Besides, only an idiot would take that bet."

"As long as it continues to sit there passively, I don't see what's wrong with leaving it be. It didn't cause us any harm the last time." Allison listened to the response through her earpiece. "Let me ask you this: Do you have any weapons with a three-light-minute range? . . . No? Then this discussion is purely academic, isn't it?"

Allison's foot started tapping a three count. "I didn't say we should ignore it. Of course we should keep an eye on it, which is probably exactly what they're doing to us. We're in their sandbox, after all . . . We tried that last time. As soon as we initiated contact, they jumped. If they want to talk, I think it'll be on their timetable, not ours . . . Fine. Ridgeway out."

Harris stood back up and moved to Allison's side. "Everything all right, ma'am?"

"It's fine, Lieutenant. Your captain and I were just working through some differences of opinion."

"With Tiberius on the side of action, I take it?"

"You could say that."

"It fits his history. You have to understand, he's spent the last eleven years being shot at by three different navies in four different oceans. That'll make anyone a little trigger-happy."

"We're in a much bigger ocean now, Lieutenant, and I doubt *Bucephalus* has the sharpest teeth in it. We'll need a less confrontational approach if we're going to survive." Allison's eyes fell on the M-118 infantry rifle slung across Harris's chest.

He ignored the glance. "Shall we move out, ma'am?"

Allison nodded.

"All right," Harris said. "The scout unit found a river about six hundred meters ahead."

"You sent scouts ahead?"

"Yes, ma'am."

"I didn't see them leave," Allison said.

"Wouldn't be very good scouts if you had."

"Yeah, all right. Why didn't we see the river from the air?"

"The forest hid it. Apparently, the beard trees grow in the riverbed."

"How's the current?"

"Pretty slow," Harris said. "The trees create a lot of drag. But it's too deep to walk."

Felix perked up at that. "How deep is it?"

"Over your head. Past that, it doesn't really matter how deep it is."

"That . . . might be a problem."

"Why? We can swim it easily enough." Harris noticed Felix was being really quiet. "Felix, you do know how to swim, right?"

"Oh, sure, Tom. I can't tell you how many lazy summer days I spent in the Sea of Tranquility as the waves gently lapped up against the shore."

"All right, smart-ass, but you seriously never learned to swim?"

"You know the Lunie body type. Tall, skinny, and undermuscled doesn't make for good buoyancy."

"Well, I guess it's time to embrace your inner fish."

The teams pressed through the undergrowth. Before long, rustling water echoed through the maze of trees. Felix looked like a man walking through a funeral parlor. When they reached the riverbank, everyone started to disrobe in preparation, except Felix.

"Dude," Harris whispered, "you're going to want to get that uniform off. It'll waterlog and pull you down otherwise."

"I'd rather not."

"What's the matter? Did you get a risqué tattoo recently?"

"No. It's not anything like that. It's just . . ." Felix's cheeks flushed red and his head darted to the side.

Harris looked behind him to see what Felix was trying so hard not to. The smooth, graceful backside of Lieutenant Dorsett greeted his eyes.

"So that's it. You don't want the brunette to see your bony white ass."

"Tom, don't."

"Three years you've worked for this adventure. Hard years. Are you really going to let a little stream and some body image issues stop you?"

"Yes."

Harris set his jaw. "Get out of that uniform and start swimming before I throw you in."

"You wouldn't."

Harris's jaw was unyielding.

"I hate you, Tom Harris."

"Sure you do. Now strip."

Everyone finished undressing and waded into the stream in their undies. The water was cool, owing to the mountains it had recently departed. Felix mumbled something uncouth as he trudged through the crisp water, stopping frequently to find better footing.

Eventually, the bottom fell away sharply as the water rushed around him. Feet kicking and arms thrashing, Felix didn't so much swim as just prolong the drowning process. He tried embracing his inner fish as Harris suggested, but after a brief struggle, he sank like a colander canoe.

While he drifted toward the bottom, Felix fought off the rising panic by imagining Jacqueline administering rescue breaths. Then he remembered that Harris had first-responder training, and the panic came charging back. Spots started to form in his blurred vision when something grabbed his hair and gave it a sharp jerk. He broke the surface and dragged in a ragged breath.

Harris stared back at him, concern etched across his face. "Are you all right?" he yelled.

"I'm drowning, Tom, not going deaf," Felix sputtered.

"C'mon, buddy, hold on to my shoulders and I'll have you out in a minute."

Felix tried to hide his face. "Is she looking?"

"Everyone's looking, Felix."

"Wonderful."

They reached safety amid a chorus of wolf whistles and catcalls. Undeterred, Harris rose from the shore like an obsidian column and waved to the crowd. Felix looked more like an ivory coat rack as he rushed to get back into his clothes.

"All right there, Felix?" Allison called after him.

"Fine, ma'am. Just a little chilly."

"Yes, we can see that . . ."

Felix covered his shame with a shirt and wished he had a suit of adaptive camo of his own. As if to rub it in, one of the scouts suddenly appeared, startling everyone but Harris.

"Tillman, what's the situation?"

"We reached the settlement, sir. There's . . . people."

"Well, yeah. Couldn't be much of a settlement without them."

"No, sir. Not people. *People.*"

"I don't follow you, Corporal."

As Harris puzzled over his scout's report, a short figure walked out of the foliage twenty meters down the riverbank. She was distinguished from the teams by a pronounced lack of clothing, a blowgun in hand, and a body decorated with blue-and-white paint.

However, these superficial differences were insignificant when measured against the similarities. Under the paint and loincloth, the woman was unmistakably human.

CHAPTER 26

"Humans? I don't understand," Eugene said to the image of Jeffery, floating in his dark bedroom.

"We don't yet either, Professor, but the fact remains that Solonis B is chock-full of human settlements."

Eugene got up out of bed, causing his wife to stir.

"Grizzly Bear, what's going on?"

"Go back to sleep, darling. Grizzly Bear has some work to do. I'll be back before the sheets cool."

Eugene transferred the call into his study, after pinching a snifter of single-malt whiskey.

Jeffery's face coalesced in the air. "Grizzly Bear?"

Eugene regarded him coolly. "It would be better for your career if that didn't find itself floating around the office."

"Your secret is safe with me, Grizzly Bear."

"You were saying, Jeffery?"

"Right. Aerial drones have confirmed five human settlements on the surface, so far."

"So far?"

"Yeah. Orbital scans hint at another"—Jeffery glanced at his pad—"eleven possible sites. We're sending drones to confirm which are abandoned and which are still active. And those are just the *permanent* settlements. Who knows about nomadic tribes."

Eugene tried to rub the lingering sleep out of his eyes. "The question is, how in the world did they get there? We've lost dozens of ships without a trace over the decades. Maybe they're descended from an expedition that went missing?"

"I already thought of that, but Felix says no. He, Harris, and Captain Ridgeway are still surveying the first settlement. The people speak the dead language of an Amazonian tribe that was supposed to have gone extinct centuries ago. There's been some drift in the syntax, and there's a smattering of Spanish in the mix, but it's verified."

"How in the world did they figure that out?"

"They used the advanced QERs to send audio samples back here. Our linguists compared it against the Endangered Language Archive and got a hit almost immediately."

"So, not descendants of marooned spacers, then."

"No, sir. Not unless an Amazonian tribe had a space program we missed."

Eugene put the snifter to his nose and drew in the complex aroma of oak mingled with vanilla. "That leaves only one possibility. They were abducted."

"It would appear so."

"Wonderful." Eugene lifted the glass and let the contents burn down his throat. "As if the damned fence wasn't provocative enough. The advisory board is going to have a meltdown. We'll be lucky if the president isn't signing a declaration of war by week's end."

"On who, though? We haven't even met any new races, much less figured out who's responsible."

"Panicked reactionaries aren't going to let a minor detail like that stop them. I can hardly wait to see what that idiot Hackman has to say. You can be sure phrases like 'mass alien abductions' and 'human breeding programs' will feature prominently in tomorrow's news cycle."

Jeffery's face became solemn. "You know, Professor, the QER messages still bottleneck through here. I could always . . . massage

Mr. Buttercup's reports, before G. Libby Hackman or any other self-styled 'journalist' get to see them."

Eugene's face was marble. "I wish you hadn't said that."

"I'm sorry. It was just a suggestion."

"No, it's all right. I wish you hadn't said it because I've been thinking along the same lines. It was easy to ignore the idea when it sat alone in a corner, but now it has company."

Eugene spun his glass around and watched the swirling remnants of his drink as he considered his decision.

"No," he said with conviction. "No. We will not play the part of censors and propagandists. Hackman is a monster of our own creation, after all. He wouldn't have been involved at all if we hadn't tried to be so clever about controlling the narrative."

Jeffery's face sank.

"Oh, Jeffery, that's not an admonishment of you. I approved the plan, after all. We were overconfident and got burned by one of the people we were trying to manipulate. It's a mistake we should learn from, not double down on. Mr. Buttercup's dispatches will remain unaltered. We still get to read them first, which gives us the time to adjust our messaging to anticipate and counter whatever meme the press decides to push. Are we agreed?"

"Completely, sir."

"Good. Now, how the hell are we going to spin this to the board?"

Felix sat cross-legged on the dirt floor of a thatch hut, nibbling on a plate of some indigenous animal the locals referred to as *kuluk*, their word for "chicken." This was notable only because kuluk, unlike everything else, didn't taste even remotely like chicken.

Felix pored over notes in his data pad from the previous two days. He didn't have a single credit of anthropology education, and his experience studying other cultures was limited to Irish pubs and a semipro soccer game he attended once. But Ridgeway's survey team was shorthanded, and he'd stepped into the role with enthusiasm.

Whether he knew it consciously or not, his drive to perfect new technology was merely a means to an end. Felix was slowly realizing he was an explorer at heart.

The survey team had set up base camp in the village of the Pirikura, at the behest of their chief. Felix still had trouble with his name, which seemed to be comprised of eighteen randomly arranged vowels with a popping sound somewhere near the middle. While he had issues with their language, no one could fault their hospitality. Their reasoning skills, on the other hand, were another matter entirely.

The Pirikura had a very tenuous understanding of gravity. They believed that when someone fell, the ground took the opportunity to run up and smack them like a drunken soccer hooligan.

This led to the odd conclusion that when falling, the best defense was a good offense. So from childhood, the Pirikura were taught to roll around and meet the charging ground with a mighty swing of the fist, just to let it know they didn't intend to take any guff just because it was bigger than they were.

This of course led to arguments among the men about who could intimidate the ground the most and therefore safely fall the farthest. So was born the annual Ground Pounder's Competition and Aged Berry Juice Festival.

Their unique theory of gravity had one advantageous side effect. When the Pirikura asked where the strangers had come from, the closest translation Allison could come up with for orbital reentry was, "We fell from the sky." That's quite a long way to fall, and probably explained the extreme deference the Pirikura were showing to their guests. It would probably last until someone asked how the visitors got up into the sky in the first place.

Felix was busy filing the myriad of holos he'd taken of the tribe and their mode of dress, or lack thereof. He was so engrossed in organizing that he didn't hear the hushed footsteps creeping up behind him. Nor did he see the crouched forms encircle him. Only when prodded with a spear did he finally notice, and only then on the third poke.

After a moment of careful reflection, Felix realized that no matter how anachronistic, the ring of spears was still lethal to a man in a T-shirt, so he threw his hands in the air. His data pad hit the dirt with a thud. They didn't look like any of the Pirikura Felix had studied. They were taller, for one, and their skin was adorned in black spots like a jaguar's coat.

But the most prominent thing about the aggressors was their ears. Well, not *their* ears exactly, more the shriveled ears on cords hanging around their necks.

"Ah, hi?" Felix awaited a response.

He received it in the form of a rock to the back of the head.

CHAPTER 27

A gaggle of curious, naked children seemed to follow Allison every where she went. They took every opportunity to run their fingers through her blond hair, by far the fairest they'd ever seen. Allison sat in the shade of the large hut that acted as a meeting place and banquet hall.

The village was awash in excitement as the Pirikura made preparations for the Ground Pounder's festival. At the center of the village, a fifteen-meter tower built of three beard-tree trunks had risen. Sturdy, it was not. The only thing preventing its total collapse was that no two pillars could agree on a direction to fall.

It was this rickety structure the men of the tribe would soon ascend to challenge the ground by heedlessly flinging themselves at it. The women of the tribe seemed content with dancing, drinking, and festively decorating their huts.

Jacqueline came striding down the main path. A retinue of village youth trailed behind her.

"Afternoon, Jackie. Sit down and take a load off."

"Thanks, Captain. I needed to talk to you anyway." Jacqueline sat down as requested.

Up close, Allison noticed that Jacqueline's hair had been tightly braided into hundreds of delicate rows, each with tiny, iridescent beads regularly spaced throughout.

"What did you do with your hair?"

Jacqueline smiled and ran a hand through the braids. "Do you like it? The kids here did it while I was uploading reports to *Maggie*. It's the children's job to braid all the women's hair, on account of their tiny fingers."

"It's cute, Jackie." Allison looked at the data pad in the young woman's hands. "Is that what you wanted to talk to me about?"

"Sort of. I borrowed this from Mr. Fletcher yesterday. It's loaded with schematics and tutorials. I wanted to familiarize myself with his new hyperdrive equipment. I have questions I want to ask him, but I can't seem to find him anywhere."

"I haven't seen him today. We'll ask Harris. They're good friends. He can call him on that implanted com their crew has. He can't ignore a phone ringing inside his head."

Allison dug through a deep pocket on her thigh until her fingers found the earbud com. She stuck it in her ear. "Lieutenant Harris?"

"Go ahead for Harris," came the prompt reply.

"It's Ridgeway. I'm here with Dorsett; she's looking for Felix. Have you seen him?"

"Not since I woke up for watch this morning."

"When was that?"

"Seventeen thirty."

Allison grimaced. Solonis B had a twenty-nine-hour day. Since they didn't intend to be planet-side for more than a few days, the teams had remained on shipboard time instead of switching to the local cycle. It did mean, however, that sunrise and sunset kept changing schedules on them like an absent-minded wedding planner. It was playing merry hell on their sleep cycles.

"Could you call him on your internal com? Dorsett has some questions to ask him."

"Sure. Just a minute."

Jacqueline sat listening quietly to Allison's half of the conversation.

Allison smiled at her. "He's calling him now, Jackie. It should just be a minute."

Harris's voice returned. "I can't raise him, ma'am."

Allison's concern ratcheted up from green to yellow. "That's not encouraging."

"It could be nothing, ma'am. He may have just dozed off. The daylight disparity's messing with everyone's circadian."

"Maybe you're right, Harris, but we should still find him. Falling asleep in an alien jungle is probably a good way to get eaten."

"Hang on, ma'am. I can locate him by his com."

Allison sat tensely while the silence stretched out like a rubber band.

Harris's voice snapped the silence. "Ah, ma'am?"

"Don't tell me. You can't track his com either."

"No, ma'am."

"Is there any plausible reason for that?"

"Well . . . if we suspect an enemy has hacked our encryption and is tracking squad movements, we can disable the auto locator."

"And the odds that Felix knows how to do that?"

"They're not encouraging," Harris said, mirroring Allison's own words.

Yellow gave way to orange. "Recall your squad, Lieutenant, and meet me at the banquet hall."

"Aye-aye, ma'am."

"Jackie, round up the rest of the survey team and bring them here."

Jacqueline's eyes were as big as ripe plums. "What's wrong, Captain?"

"We have a missing man to find."

A little over twenty minutes later, the members of both teams sat in a circle on the floor of the Pirikura's largest building. Just beyond them, the villagers had halted their festival preparations and watched the proceedings intently.

A holographic image of the village and the surrounding forest spun slowly in the air.

"Here's what we know." Allison pointed to one of the huts in the display and twisted her wrist, leaving a red dot. "Mr. Fletcher was in the sleeping hut until 1947 today, about an hour after sunrise. Then he got up and made a beeline for the forest." She dragged her finger through the air, leaving a red path behind her on the map.

"Once past the tree line, he slowed down and started moving along a more erratic path for almost six kilometers, until his com signal faded and was lost around here." She twisted her wrist again, and the line terminated in another big red dot.

"What could cause that?" asked one of the survey group.

"We don't know; some sort of interference."

"Wait," one of the marines, Devor, interjected. "The coms are built to filter natural interference. So what are you saying, that people who are still knapping flint have signal jammers?"

"Not at all. I'm saying it's an open question."

Whispers ran through the semicircle of villagers, but Allison couldn't understand them. *Magellan* had a translator running that fed English approximations of their speech into her ear com, but it could only work on one speaker at a time. One of the children walked past the seated crewmen and tried to grasp the hologram with an outstretched hand, but came away empty. The whispers grew more alarmed.

Allison tried to gently push the child back toward her waiting parents. "Not right now, sweetie."

The girl was unfazed. She looked intently at the images, especially the aerial shot of the village.

Harris cleared his throat. "Maybe we should turn off the holo, ma'am."

"Good idea." Allison knelt down and was about to shut down the portable projector when the little girl started shouting excitedly. Her face had the wide smile of accomplishment, minus a few baby teeth.

"What's she saying?" Harris asked.

"Something about her home, the village, the river. I think she's figured out it's a map. Smart kid."

The child thrust a finger at the forest, past where Felix's trail had run cold, and started talking rapidly, too fast for the translation to keep up. Her mother strode up to retrieve her, bending to pick her up, despite the girl's protests.

Allison put up a hand. "No, just wait a second. She was saying something about a 'Cave of the Creators.' What does she mean?"

The mother paused to listen to Allison, but she was uncomprehending.

"Jackie, give me your earbud." Jacqueline obliged. "*Maggie*, are you there?"

"Yes, Captain Ridgeway. How may I help?"

"I want you to run the translation backward and feed it into Lieutenant Dorsett's com."

"You wish it to run from English to Pirikura?"

"Yes, exactly."

"That will take some time."

"That's fine, just let me know as soon as you're fin—"

"I've finished."

Allison rubbed a temple. "*Maggie*, remind me later that we need to talk about human time perception." With the earbud com sitting in her upturned palm, Allison held out her hand to the mother.

Cautiously, the woman took it. Unsure of the purpose of the gift, she smelled it, and then held it to her tongue. Allison waved her hand and pulled her hair back to expose her own earbud. The mother turned the bud around in her fingers, then placed it snugly in her ear.

"Good. Can you understand me?"

There was a delay of a heartbeat as Allison's voice was transmitted to one of the Gargoyle platforms in orbit, which were pulling double duty as communication relays, passed around to *Magellan* on the far side of the planet, translated into Pirikura, then sent back around the world, down to the surface, and into the earbud.

The woman looked sharply to her right, but when she realized there was no one there, she threw the bud to the ground in a panic. She raised a foot to crush the cursed object, but Allison crouched and grabbed it in time.

"It's okay," Allison remained as calm as she could manage. "She probably thought it was jewelry."

Allison pulled the earbud out of her own ear and spoke slowly and deliberately. "When you"—she pointed at the mother—"speak"—she made a talking gesture with her hand and pointed at the earbud—"this lets me"—Allison pointed at her own ear and smiled warmly—"understand you."

The mother leaned away from Allison and frowned, but her daughter was not so suspicious. The child jumped up and snatched the earbud from Allison's hand and stuffed it into her ear.

Sensing an opportunity, Allison spoke. "Can you understand me?"

"*Sae*," came from the girl's mouth.

"Yes," said the earbud.

"Hello. My name is Allison. What is your name?"

"Piya."

"Hello, Piya. You are a very smart little girl."

"Thank you, Al-lee-son." She smiled bashfully as she struggled with the foreign name.

"Can you tell your mother that the earring is safe and will let us talk?"

Piya grabbed her mother's skirt and tugged. They conferred. Eventually, Piya's mother took the earbud and placed it back in her own ear.

"Thank you," Allison said with sincerity. "Can you understand me?"

"Yes. What magic/sorcery?"

"No magic." Allison tried to sound reassuring. "Just a tool. Like a knife or a hammer."

"Hammers don't talk."

"True, but you don't need them to." Allison patted Piya on the head. "Your daughter is very clever. When she looked at our map, she said, 'Cave of the Creators.' What is that?"

"Sacred place. Where gods sleep. Pirikura no go there. Forbidden."

"You don't visit your gods? Why not?"

"Protected by phantoms/monsters."

There was a rumbling from the ring of villagers. The survey team also heard the translation, save Jacqueline, and perked up at the mention of phantoms.

"What kind of phantoms?"

"Used to be men, but cursed/fell. Now just phantoms/monsters. Consume/defeat Pirikura."

Allison paused to consider the implications of the *consume/defeat* translation. "One of our tribe is missing. Do you think the phantoms are responsible?"

"Yes. Phantoms/monsters take Pirikura sometimes. Take your man."

"Can you show us where the phantoms live?"

"No. Forbidden. Danger." The mother moved closer so that only Allison could hear her whisper. "Our men no warriors/heroes."

She had a point. Predictably, the tribe's physical stature had suffered somewhat from the strongest men getting inebriated and throwing themselves off a ten-meter tower once a year.

"We don't need you to take us there; I just want you to show us on this map." Allison held her hands wide to encompass the holo of the area.

"I no know where," she said. "But Tolo do."

"Tolo?"

"Tolo!" the mother shouted. "Tolo!"

The circle of villagers parted from around a young man, no more than a teenager. With a little prodding, he stepped forward. The mother leaned close to his face as if to whisper, but spoke to him with a strong voice. Only then did Allison notice that he had no ears.

"Tell Al-lee-son where you escape phantoms/monsters."

He threw up his hands and shook his head violently. "No go back. Never. Forbidden. Understand now."

"That's all right, Tolo." Allison looked back to the mother. "Tell him he just needs to point at it."

She did so. Tolo nodded and stepped up to study the display, its tiny village, and the river. His face scrunched up as he tried to work it out. Then, he jammed a finger at a point roughly three kilometers west of where Felix's trail had faded out.

"There!"

"Thank you, Tolo." Even though Allison knew he couldn't understand, it needed to be said.

Piya's mother spoke again. "You go, phantoms/monsters consume/defeat you, too."

"I don't think so."

"Why not?"

Allison looked straight at Harris and his squad, bristling with machine guns and muscles.

"Because I brought my own phantoms/monsters."

CHAPTER 28

The smell of smoke roused Felix. He tried to open his eyes, but the lids were gummed shut. His hands and feet were bound and secured to a pole. The rope and wood had rubbed his wrists raw.

Calm, Felix. This is no time to go to pieces. The smoke was coming from a fire. He could feel the heat on the left side of his body, but his right side was clammy. Wherever he was, it was cooler than the forest had been, even at night. The fire snapped, crackled, and popped, each sound reverberating several times. The pops meant a wood fire, and the echoes told Felix he was in an enclosed space. And the chill air . . .

A cave, he thought. *I'm underground. But how deep?* He tried to force his eyes open, pulling against whatever glued the lids together. After several attempts, a tiny aperture finally tore open over his left eye. The fire blinded him for several moments until his eye adjusted to the light. Deep shadows contrasted the shifting light from the fire, but it was apparent to Felix that the cavern was actually a room. The cave's surface had been roughly hewn into four walls and a floor. About two meters from the floor, the tool marks ended. Lethal stalactites held fast to the roof like the dentures of an ancient war god.

Felix swiveled his head down to investigate the bindings at his ankles. His clothes were missing. In their place was a network of dotted lines that bore an unsettling resemblance to a butcher's diagram. A metallic glint drew Felix's attention away from the lines drawn around his muscles. Sitting atop the fire at the center of the room was a bright copper cauldron. Steam boiled away into the air.

All right, maybe this is the time to go to pieces. Felix laughed, surprising himself with the morbid pun. Then, he laughed harder, a manic sound that had little to do with good humor. The sound of footsteps betrayed the presence of others, and Felix abruptly cut the laugh track. Three men of the same tribe that had kidnapped him walked swiftly to where he was tied. Their dark body paint had kept them hidden in the shadows of the room until now.

The largest of the three stood directly in front of Felix and shot him a glare that would wither a cactus. He put a spotted hand over his mouth and pointed to the far side of the campfire. There, Felix caught a glimpse of another man, older, but his skin was still stretched taut over swollen muscles. He wore the same pattern of body paint as the others, but he was also adorned with leggings and an elaborate headdress made of leaves.

Most ominously, three dozen desiccated human ears hung from a cord around his neck. That was when the silence hit Felix like a slap to the face. Now that he knew to look for them, he could spot over a dozen tribesmen skulking in the shadows. Yet the room was as quiet as a tomb.

The ears. The tribe was listening for something. Something too quiet for a human to hear with the paltry pair of ears granted them by nature.

Out of pure spite, Felix decided to add some background noise. "What are you all listening to? Must be awful quiet for you to need all those extra ears."

The closest tribesman lunged forward and clamped a hand over Felix's mouth and shot him a glare.

What the heck? Felix thought. *I'm already being held by cannibals. It isn't like things can get much worse.* So he opened his mouth and bit down on the inside of his aggressor's hand. The man reflexively tried to pull away. Felix bit down harder until he felt the skin tear and blood seep into his mouth.

Finally, the man wrenched his hand out of Felix's teeth and cried out in pain. As his scream echoed, every other head in the room snapped to attention. The two men accompanying Felix's aggressor moved with a flash, ripping open the man's neck with stone knives. Blood sprayed from the gaping wound like a broken showerhead as the victim crashed to the floor, futilely grasping his ruined throat.

Felix had never seen such a level of violence and gore with his own eyes. His bravado quickly evaporated, and he began to feel lightheaded. The two executioners turned to face Felix. His heart missed a beat. Then another. Then, reflecting on the fact that it had been working nonstop its whole life without so much as a sick day, it decided right then and there to take a vacation. So Felix passed out.

Did anyone else hear that? Harris thought into his implanted com.

You mean the scream, sir? Tillman responded.

Yeah. Did either of your sniper-sniffers get a fix on it?

No, too many echoes in here. All mine reads is Forward.

Same here, sir, confirmed Private First Class Lyska.

My ears told me that much, Harris thought. *What would we do without modern technology?*

The trio shared a mental chuckle as Harris led them deeper into the network of tunnels that made up the Cave of the Creators. Harris had left a two-man unit at the mouth of the caves to ensure no one snuck up behind them.

With every step, radar integrated into their armor recorded a three-dimensional scan of their journey, which would later provide a map back to the surface. This same radar fed a false-color rendering of the cave's interior into the team's helmet visors in real time, allowing them to move in the total darkness with speed and grace, as opposed to the time-tested, curse-laden method of locating obstacles in the dark by bashing into them with one's forehead, shin, or big toe.

Well, maybe technology isn't all bad, Harris thought, not into his com. That trick had taken him a few days to master. His unit pushed forward as swiftly as they could without making too much noise.

The scream kept playing through Harris's head like an irritating radio jingle. It didn't exactly sound like Felix, but he couldn't be sure. Sound changes after bouncing off enough walls, and people under stress don't always sound like themselves.

I've got something here, sir, Tillman broke in. *Mr. Fletcher's com signal.*

Felix? Felix, come in, please. Harris let several heartbeats pass waiting for an answer. *How far off is it?*

Can't say, sir. It's weak, and we're too deep to get any GPS fix, but it definitely came from the same direction as that scream.

Then we need to double-time it, kiddies.

Abandoning silence, the squad launched themselves down the passageway. With each passing second, Harris cared less and less about the commotion they were making. He just wanted to reach his friend in time.

Felix, please respond.

Static.

Taking up point ahead of Harris, Corporal Tillman skidded to a stop. Harris was about to ask why when an alarm light flashed in his helmet's display. The armor's chemical sniffers had picked something up.

Any number of toxic gases could build deep inside a cave. Harris held his breath until the sniffers finished their analysis. The results rolled down his display: methane, butane, carbon monoxide, carbon dioxide, carbon particulates . . .

Harris recognized the ingredients and smelled the air. Smoke. And where there's smoke . . .

There's a fire ahead, people. Probably from torches or a campfire. Warm up your adaptive camo. His team obeyed, and thousands of tiny eyes told two square meters of synthetic cuttlefish skin what it should be mimicking. Which was, for the moment, black.

The squad advanced at a dead sprint. Felix's com signal grew stronger until Harris could see biosensor data confirming he was still alive. Alive, but at the edge of consciousness.

"Felix!" Harris shouted. He hadn't meant to actually vocalize, it just came out.

Hello?

Felix? Harris thought.

Who's this? How did you get into my brain?

It's Tom, Felix. We're on our way to rescue you.

Oh, wonderful. I'm going schizophrenic. They must have hit me with that rock harder than I thought.

What? Harris was confused. *I didn't copy your last.*

He thinks he's hearing voices, sir, Tillman interrupted. *He's forgotten about the im-com. Might be a concussion.*

Right. Felix, you're not hearing voices. It's Tom. I'm talking to you through a radio. We're heading toward your position, but I need you to give me some intel.

What do you want to know, tiny Tom in my head? Felix said.

Tell me about your surroundings, Harris answered. *Is there cover where you are? Is there light? How many hostiles are with you?*

Well, there were twelve or so, but we're down one. You should be quiet, Tom. These guys take their vows of silence very seriously.

Harris held up a fist to bring the squad to a halt. *They're quiet?*

Yeah, pathologically quiet. They nearly decapitated one of their own guys for shouting.

Why?

I don't know, but I think they're listening for something.

Harris bared his teeth. *So they probably wouldn't be too happy about a flash-bang, would they?*

Well, no. But then, neither would I, if it comes right down to it.

Can't be helped. It's the best way to neutralize them. Is there a leader?

Yes. He's wearing a funny hat. You can't miss him.

Are they armed?

Stone knives and clubs, but only a few of them are holding weapons.

Good. Anything else you can tell me?

Yeah. You need to hurry, because I'm tied to a post, and they're planning to cook me.

Cook you? But that's crazy; you don't have enough meat on you to feed twelve people.

That's not funny, Tom.

Just hang in there, little buddy.

Harris signaled the rest of his squad to resume their advance, but silently. The signal from Felix's com was strong enough that Harris could get an accurate measure of the distance between them. Fifty meters was all that separated Harris and his squad from their first encounter with an enemy force. He'd planned for hostile aliens, not a lost tribe of Amazonian cannibals, but the day was young.

A trickle of yellow light began to push against the pitch black of the cave. The fire was around the next corner. The squad lined up against the wall in a classic room-breaching stack. Harris pulled a small sphere out of his waist pack and twisted the two hemispheres until a red dot appeared at the top.

All right. Tillman, Lyska, we're aiming for zero casualties. Don't shoot the natives unless absolutely necessary. Felix, close your eyes and say, "Ahh."

Why?

Just do it.

Ahhh—

Not in your head. Out loud!

Oh, sorry. "Ahhhh!"

Harris casually tossed the orb into the room and threw his hands over his ears. The grenade worked off a proximity fuse, and when it detected that it was 1.5 meters from the ground . . .

Bang!

The flash-bang went off right at eye level of everyone in the room. Half a blink later, Harris, Tillman, and Lyska poured in, throwing the stunned tribesmen to the cold floor. Several of them tried to fight back against the unseen attackers, but their knives swung blindly. Resistance only gained them a rifle butt to the back of the head.

In less than ten seconds, Harris's three-man squad had subdued the enemy and secured the room.

"Tillman, Lyska, herd the prisoners into the far corner." Harris pulled out his combat knife and moved behind the post Felix was lashed to. Three quick swipes of the blade and the bindings fell to the floor. Harris moved around to face his friend. "C'mon, Felix, we need to leave."

What's that? Use the implant.

Your ears still ringing?

Are you kidding? I can barely hear you in here. Never mind out there. What were you saying?

That we need to de-ass the area with the quickness.

Not yet. Something's weird here.

You mean weirder than being kidnapped by mute savages planning to whip up an entrée of Fletcher fricassee?

Point . . . but still.

Felix.

What?

You realize you're still naked, right?

Oh.

While Felix located his clothes, Harris eyed the prisoners nervously. They still suffered from the effects of the flash-bang and the shock from his team's sudden overrun, but that could wear off at any time. Harris wasn't sure the natives truly understood the threat his squad represented. They'd never seen an assault rifle and couldn't know that any one of the marines could kill every last one of them in a few heartbeats, if motivated to do so.

Every passing moment increased the odds one of the tribesmen would overcome their fear, or be overcome *by* it, and make a move that would trigger a massacre.

"You've got five minutes, Felix. Then we clear out."

Felix paced the room with a look of consternation. A minute passed. Then he spun around on his heel and pointed a finger at the cauldron on top of the fire.

"There! What exactly is a stone-working tribe doing with a pot made of refined copper?"

"Um, cooking?"

"Well, yes, obviously, but where did they get it? They have no metal in their weapons or any of their jewelry. They must have found it around here somewhere." Felix turned a critical eye back to the wall and the tool marks pocking the surface. "Look over here at these marks. They couldn't have been carved by hand; they're too evenly spaced."

Harris shrugged. "Okay, and . . . ?"

"And . . . that means this room was carved out by whoever brought these people here."

"That makes sense. The Pirikura call this place the 'Cave of the Creators.' "

"Creators, huh?" Felix ran his hand along the wall for several meters. He paused and swept back over a particular section several more times. "Do those visors of yours see into the infrared?"

"Sure can." Harris mentally pulled up his display options and switched his helmet overlay from the false-color radar to IR. "Whoa."

"Let me guess, there's a hot spot in the shape of a door."

"Yeah. How did you know that?"

"Their leader was listening to this part of the wall. I figured something or someone walked out of this door long ago, triggering a myth. They've probably been coming here to eavesdrop on their gods ever since."

"I'll buy that. So what do we do?" Harris asked.

"Go back to the surface and call in Captain Ridgeway's survey team."

"What for?"

Felix smiled. "To break in, of course."

CHAPTER 29

Commander Gruber sat alone in *Magellan*'s conference room, although *alone* was a relative term. Telepresent at the table were holos of Captain Tiberius aboard the *Bucephalus* and Captain Ridgeway, still on the surface of Solonis B. Floating above the middle of the table was footage from inside the Cave of the Creators.

Allison's image was narrating a walk-through of their discoveries. "Here's where things get weird. Mr. Fletcher found a door hidden in the wall of this rough-cut antechamber. We searched for a release for over an hour without luck. Eventually, we gave up and went back to the shuttle for a boring laser—"

Maximus's ghost cut her off. "Boring? I always thought lasers are pretty exciting, myself."

"A mining laser, Maximus, for *boring* holes."

"I knew that."

Allison clenched her teeth. "Anyway, we melted through without any trouble."

"That doesn't surprise me." Gruber chuckled. "Whoever put it there probably wasn't expecting the Pirikura to build a megawatt-range laser anytime soon."

"Too true," Allison replied. "Once we moved inside the room, carefully, here's what we found . . ."

The holo-recording resumed, sweeping through the darkened

doorway. As soon as the cameraman crossed the threshold, the room beyond lit up in response. Organic webs of iridescent wires pulsed along the smooth walls, just like the inside of the buoy.

One by one, images appeared on the walls. The Pirikura village came to life from a dozen different viewpoints. Women and children walked up and down the dirt roads and boulevards, blissfully unaware of the voyeurs peering at them from beneath the ground. Allison paused the replay.

"Yikes," Maximus said. "It's an observation post. But why bother spying on these people? They're no threat."

"I don't think they were spying, so much as studying," Gruber said.

"What do you mean?"

"This feels more like a duck blind or a tree stand. Whoever built this was observing these people 'in the wild,' as it were. That might be why they were brought here in the first place, as a kind of control group for studying human behavior."

Allison smiled. "Excellent, Marcel. That's the consensus we've reached down here as well."

Maximus studied the different views of the village. "Where are all the men?"

"What do you mean? The Pirikura males?"

"Yes, they seem to be almost all women or children. It's like a prehistoric meat market down there."

"Their annual celebrations have a somewhat . . . deleterious effect on the male population. Women outnumber the adult men almost three to one."

"There must be a lot of lonely single ladies floating around, then," Maximus observed while managing not to lick his lips.

"Not really. Their marriage customs are polygamous, to account for the dearth of males," Allison said.

"Hmm. Never held with polygamy."

"Really?" Allison could barely conceal her surprise. "I thought building a harem was the alpha male ideal."

"Well, it would certainly have benefits, but strategically, I just can't see wanting to be outnumbered in every fight. Nope, I'm a one-woman man."

"One at a time, you mean."

"Well, yeah. Why, what did I say?"

Gruber pushed in to try to avert the looming personality clash. "Captain Ridgeway, am I alone in thinking that the tech in that room strongly resembles the interior of the buoy?"

"Not at all, Marcel. I thought so, too, and it was the first thing Mr. Fletcher said when he walked through the door."

"So the same consortium that fenced in Earth has been out here running their own little human research colonies, studying us like packs of gorillas. That's going to play well back home."

"Careful with the primate references, Commander," Maximus said. "If Buttercup hears that, he might tear your legs off. Or, worse yet, write an unflattering article about you."

Gruber filed that last sentence away as an important insight into Maximus's mind. "I'm sorry, sir. I wasn't thinking about Mr. Buttercup."

"Not at all. Please continue, Captain."

Allison nodded and restarted the recording. "Now, this is where it gets really strange. Beyond the surveillance room, we found another chamber."

The camera view floated through an archway, and two parallel rows of tiny beds came into view. They were impeccably tidy. The beds were ominous, but not nearly so bad as what they saw next. Set into the far wall, a pair of figures stood ramrod straight. They appeared human, but their flawless posture hinted at something artificial. As the camera focused on their features, it became apparent their designers had tried to cross the Uncanny Valley, but slipped off the footbridge and were subsequently devoured by crocodiles.

"What the hell are those?" Maximus exclaimed.

"Androids," Allison answered. "Our best guess is they serve as automated nannies."

"It's a nursery," Maximus said. "They're raising children in there like baby cranes, and those things are like the creepy hand-puppet mama-bird heads they feed them with."

"I hadn't thought of it like that, but the comparison probably isn't far off."

"What do they need them for? The Pirikura raise their own kids."

Gruber drummed his fingers on the table. "Maybe they're for starting new tribes. There are dozens of them on the planet, but they're all geographically isolated from each other. Maybe the aliens cook up a new batch of children and raise them here when they want to start a fresh experiment."

Allison was impressed. "That's a sound hypothesis, Marcel."

"Yes, indeed. Good work, everyone. Captain Ridgeway, pack up your team and get headed back to *Magellan*. Lieutenant Harris and his squad will remain long enough to cover your departure; then we're moving on to the next system."

Allison cleared her throat. "Excuse me, Captain Tiberius. As I understood our mission charter, I hold discretion over the scientific and exploratory aspects of the expedition, and I say we have a lot more work to do here."

"That's true, but this isn't my idea. We received a QER burst from the president's office a few minutes before this briefing started. Remember, we're out here to make contact with the buoy races. Since they aren't here, he wants us to move on to the Twinkling Star."

"I don't give a flying frog what that shrunken-headed idiot—"

Gruber made a show of clearing his throat. "Excuse me. I've been fighting a cold. I think what Captain Ridgeway is trying to say is that we've been waiting for the opportunity to survey this planet for more than sixty years. It would be an awful shame if we had to withdraw before we're finished."

"I sympathize with you," Maximus said, "but we have our marching orders. Besides, it's not like Solonis B is going anywhere. We can always come back."

Allison wasn't finished. "We've only investigated one tribe out of dozens, and we haven't even had a full day in the cave complex yet. Who knows what else we can learn from the tech in those rooms. That's part of our mission, too."

"So strip the rooms and stuff everything you can into the shuttles. We'll sort it out in transit. Right now, we've gotta boogie."

"What about the people on the surface?" Gruber asked. "We can't just leave them down there in a planet-sized lab. We need to rescue them."

Allison shook her head. "I don't think it's that simple, Marcel. Even if their ancestors were kidnapped from Earth, the Pirikura have lived on Solonis B for generations. They're humans, all right, but they aren't earthlings anymore. 'Rescuing' them now would be like a second abduction."

Gruber bowed his head a fraction. "I hadn't thought of it like that, ma'am."

"No worries. Your heart is in the right place." Allison's translucent head turned to address Maximus. "Captain, it will take time to secure all of our equipment. Some of it is here in the cave, but some is still in the village. I'll need at least a full shift before we're ready to depart."

"That's fine. We'll need almost that long to retrieve and secure the Gargoyle platforms. We'll see you in orbit."

Vel Noric watched through bloodred, artificial eyes as the two human vessels disappeared through their high-space portal.

His attention then turned to the world they'd just departed. The earthlings almost certainly had another designation for the planet, but the *civilized* galaxy knew it as Culpus-Alam, set aside many generations ago to observe humans in a controlled setting.

The experiment had run unattended for many cycles as the tribes of humans developed distinct cultures. The next step was to facilitate contact between the tribes and observe their interactions. The hope was to learn enough to better predict humanity's eventual integration into the galactic community.

In Noric's opinion, Culpus-Alam was typical of the way the Assembly of Sentient Species operated. A time-consuming, complicated, and expensive reaction to what should be a straightforward problem.

It was a problem that Noric had been tasked with solving by the Kumer-Vel himself.

"Has their high-space portal sealed?"

"Yes, Vel."

"Very well." Noric straightened his spine and stood at his full height. "Hedfer-Vel, you may begin the operation."

CHAPTER 30

D'armic sat cross-legged on the floor of his small quarters, sipping yelic root tea to try to excite his nerves. Some in the drug-free movement considered the bitter root cheating, but he did not. While the tea was undoubtedly a stimulant, it worked indiscriminately across the Lividite nervous system, boosting perception and concentration for a time. It did not mimic any of the neurochemicals specific to emotions or try to boost receptor site sensitivity. So D'armic felt no guilt in drinking it from time to time. Of course, without a dose of Regretinide, he didn't feel guilty about anything.

Yet I remain moral, he thought. *How do I know to do that without guilt or compassion? Is morality deeper even than emotion?*

The implications didn't make sense. In fact, the thought served to reinforce his belief that his natural emotions were there, still influencing his decisions and actions, but too deep to make themselves known consciously.

If he felt anything, it was a powerful and growing sense of melancholy. His survey of the Human Wildlife Preserve buoy network had been, with the exception of the still-unexplained fate of Buoy #4258743-E, dull and repetitive enough to bore a dead Teskin. Yet he'd soldiered on through the assignment without complaint. The Teskin are one of the most specialized carnivores in the known galaxy. They evolved over the millennia to infiltrate cocktail parties, wedding receptions, and class reunions. Once inside, they corner their unsuspecting prey and regale them with hours of banal anecdotes about office politics, family vacations, and medical issues. A successful hunt ends when the target kills itself out of desperation. If you're ever invited to attend a Teskin business conference, decline and immediately change your telephone number, email address, mailing address, and name.

D'armic reached for his cup to take another sip when the cutter's proximity alarm chimed. Reflexes honed during many cycles propelled D'armic to the command cave. He was halfway there when the strangeness of the situation hit him.

The cutter was decelerating through high-space, on course for Culpus-Alam. His three-dimensional ship couldn't actually collide with any of the four-dimensional matter native to high-space. On the rare occasions that his three-dimensional cutter did intersect high-space material, it sort of floated around it due to incompatible topologies, or something. He didn't fathom how it worked exactly, but then, few could. Those that did were either institutionalized for their own safety, or became performance artists.

D'armic knew he couldn't collide with anything of *this* dimension, which meant the alarm was warning of an impending impact with something from *his* dimension. The odds against that were . . . well, the usual superlatives weren't going to cut it.

The cutter wasn't in immediate peril. The ship's sensor suite was sensitive enough to afford D'armic plenty of time to analyze the situation and take appropriate action, even at maximum velocity. As soon as he reached the command cave, he bonded with the ship's computer, feeding a steady flow of data into his consciousness.

What he saw didn't merely defy understanding. It snuck out of its bedroom window at 1:00 A.M., stole understanding's prized collector car from the garage, and crashed it into a tree.

Ahead of his cutter, a titanic worm of fire twisted and danced in the vacuum. Its skin boiled, spitting chunks larger than his cutter into high-space. It was a nightmare monster of the deep caverns, straight from his race's oldest, forgotten superstitions. It slithered toward his ship, intent on devouring him in its hellish, glowing lava maw.

At least that's what his lower brain believed. His higher brain was having trouble forming an opinion. In the absence of a rational counterbalance, his lower brain acted on its own initiative and opened a portal back to the universe below. The cutter dove through the portal, emerging safely back in his native dimension.

He searched in all directions for evidence of the monster, but there was none. The single star of the Culpus-Alam system shone ahead of his bow like a milky jewel. An involuntary tremor ran through D'armic's body, and his skin danced with electricity. He felt suddenly fatigued.

Was that fear? he asked himself. No, *fear* was the wrong word. There had been no time to be afraid. It certainly resembled the drug-induced feelings he'd experienced as a larva, but it was more raw and immediate. Panic, perhaps? He'd been in danger before, even mortal danger. Why was this time different? The question deserved contemplation, but not now.

The worm was a mystery to solve, but first he had to review the progress of the experiment on the surface of Culpus-Alam. The little cutter's trajectory carried it deeper into the system while its counter-grav engines worked overtime to shed momentum. The planet slowly moved out of the eclipse of the sun.

Something was wrong. D'armic had never been to this system before, but his assignment files described it as a garden world of lush forests and deep oceans. The planet revealed by his cutter's telescope was a tortured waste. The atmosphere was filled with carbon oxides, sulfates, and particulate indicative of massive volcanic activity. Vast webs of glowing cracks lined the surface, making the whole planet look like a shattered egg. Tracing the scars backward led to a massive hole in the world's crust, from which a fountain of lava erupted, sending molten rock into orbit. An asteroid crater?

D'armic's mind raced, seeking an explanation that would solve the disparity between the world described in his briefing and the shattered husk before his eyes. The orbital location and inclination was right, but everything else was wrong. He dug through the stream of data, correlating atmospheric sampling, crust composition, rotational speed, mass . . .

Mass. There wasn't enough of it. He quickly worked up an estimate of the ejecta thrown clear of the planet, but the total was still short by nearly a percent. An asteroid impact would have added mass to the planet, so that hypothesis was tossed down the stream.

Something occurred to him then that sent an icy jolt through his spine. He thought of the worm, thought of its color and size. Hoping he was wrong, but almost certain he wasn't, he dug into the sensor records from the encounter. The fire worm's estimated mass matched what was missing from Culpus-Alam to six decimal places.

D'armic put a hand to his mouth, reluctant to believe what he'd discovered, but the conclusion was inescapable. The worm really was a monster from his people's past, but it hadn't risen from the depths of their imaginations.

Millennia ago, in the closing days of the Lividite war against, well, *everybody*, it became apparent their military had bitten off just enough to choke on. The Lividite war machine had overreached.

The Pu'Lan were closest to the front lines. They'd handed the Lividies a string of defeats, the first in the history of their campaigns among the stars. Desperate to regain the initiative, the Lividite military hatched a plan to make an example of the Pu'Lan.

As it turns out, destroying an entire world was a simple affair, provided the culprits were without remorse. Simply fly a ship straight at the world, open a high-space portal, and allow the hole in the universe to bore a tunnel straight through to the other side. The resulting collapse of the magma tunnel set off mayhem on a scale that would ruin the surface, triggering two massive volcanoes at the entry and exit wounds, shattering tectonic plates, disrupting the planet's core and magnetic field. It was an apocalypse.

The Pu'Lan were all but obliterated. While it was nearly impossible to truly eradicate a space-faring race, without their home world as a keystone, their culture and heritage crumbled. The ancestors of the scattered survivors grew into nomads, echoes of a once-proud race, and a constant reminder of the Lividites' bloodthirstiness, to their everlasting shame.

It was called geocide, and there was no higher crime in Assembly space.

D'armic scanned the surface of Culpus-Alam for survivors. It was proper procedure, but he knew it was futile. Between the volcanic outgassing, massive ground shakes, the rain of molten debris falling from orbit, and the firestorms tearing through the forests, there was little chance any complex life would survive.

The chill in his bones was turning to heat. The population had been completely defenseless. They possessed nothing more advanced than flint spears and stone axes. The destruction of the Pu'Lan had been a galaxy-shaping tragedy, but that conflict had been between near peers technologically. The humans on Culpus-Alam were not equipped to understand what had happened to them, much less defend against it.

Even if there were no survivors, perhaps he could still find the killers. As was Lividite custom, all the planet's research and observation stations were built into underground caves. There was one for each colony, twenty-seven in total. That gave D'armic twenty-seven chances to recover whatever data the planet's sensor network had recorded before the attack. But there was too much interference at this altitude. Establishing a direct link meant dropping into the shooting gallery that had become low orbit.

He sent out a hail, hoping one of the facilities had survived. In fact, two had. They pinged back, requesting authentication codes while the little cutter dodged pieces of red-hot debris moving at orbital speeds. The uploads dragged on for what seemed like an epoch. Attempting to speed things up, he limited the data request to the last three days.

Even still, time ran out for one of the sites. Lava from a nearby flow broke through a natural dam and flooded the cave with liquefied rock. Not even Lividite technology could stand up to that sort of abuse.

The last site was more fortunate. It survived just long enough to broadcast what it had seen. Data retrieved, the cutter hastily climbed out of Culpus-Alam's gravity well while pebbles ricocheted off the hull. In time, an accretion disk would form, perhaps even a small moon.

For the next several hundred cycles, the planet's surface would be mercilessly bombarded by meteorites as parts of its own mantle returned. Whatever simple life survived would have a daunting climb ahead of it before it would return to multicellular complexity.

D'armic settled the cutter into a lazy orbit above the swarm of rocks and began scrounging through the data. Starting from the end and working backward, he learned the attack had come less than a day earlier. The quality of the tactical information was poor, owing to the sensors being optimized for ground-level viewing. The residents had not been expected to develop powered flight anytime soon.

Still, there was enough data to confirm the appearance of the high-space portal right before contact. However, the ship that opened it was obscured behind the portal itself. Moving further back through the time line, D'armic caught a break. A second high-space portal had been opened a few moments before the one that had delivered the deathblow, and two ships had escaped through it.

He sifted through the limited records, attempting to tease additional information from them, but the shoddy resolution persisted in beguiling him. There was no way to tell the class of the two vessels or even their fleet of origin. The bearing of the ships as they escaped and an approximate mass value were all he could glean, but with luck, that might be enough.

He continued backward until he saw two small atmospheric craft take off from the surface. *A landing party*, he thought. *Another chance to put a face on the killers.*

The first craft in the playback wasn't much help. The occupants were covered in armor, their features disguised by helmets. They were bipedal, four-limbed, and of medium size, which narrowed the possibilities down to only six dozen known sentient species. Their armor and weaponry were an unfamiliar design, but the group was unmistakably infantry.

The occupants of the second craft wore no such obstructions. D'armic froze the image, wrestling with what he saw. It was a human female, judging by her chest protrusions and slim waist. She wore long hair of a shade far lighter than any of the tribes found on Culpus-Alam.

This presented a problem, for if she wasn't native, it could only mean the ships had come from Earth's systems, but that was plainly impossible. Humans were still centuries away from developing high . . . space . . .

The answer struck D'armic like one of the searing rocks erupting from the dying world below. Buoy #4258743-E. By a coincidence of cosmic proportions, they had stumbled onto it, stolen it, and used the high-space radio within to copy their own, doubtlessly crude, portal generator.

Which also led D'armic to the inescapable conclusion that the humans had slid right past him before he had mended the gap in the buoy network. That wasn't going to reflect well on his performance review.

No matter. Pride is a consideration for other races.

As was anger, but despite the fact he felt none of the rage that had driven his ancestors, D'armic felt a responsibility to the dead of Culpus-Alam. His people had been the ones to hatch the atrocity of geocide into the universe. It was therefore appropriate that a Lividite be the one to return it to the grave.

He set about preparing a detailed report for his superiors, but even traveling through high-space, the dispatch would take considerable time to reach Bureau headquarters. As had been the case for many cycles, D'armic would have to move on his own initiative.

Leaving the broken world in his wake, D'armic set course along an identical bearing to the retreating vessels. His cutter would have to move swiftly before the trail overgrew. D'armic couldn't fathom why, absent their passions, the humans had slaughtered their own people.

As the high-space portal opened ahead, he resolved to ask them. Personally.

CHAPTER 31

Allison's feet pounded down the hall. She'd run for over an hour, hard. Her legs had felt like rubber for the last two kilometers, but now they burned so badly she was pretty sure they were vulcanizing.

After a few more paces her earbud beeped. Twelve kilometers had come and gone. She finally succumbed to her aches and sank against the nearest wall. Even though *Maggie*'s interior was kept at a cool eighteen degrees C, sweat beaded on Allison's forehead and shoulders. The wraparound glasses she wore to counteract the disorienting effects of hyperspace started to fog.

"Captain?" asked the ceiling.

Allison took a moment to bring her breathing under control before answering.

"Captain, are you all right?"

"I'm fine, *Maggie*, just a little winded. What's wrong?"

"Nothing is wrong, per se. You have a message from Captain Tiberius. Would you like to hear it now?"

"I'd rather listen to my own firing squad."

"I do not understand."

"It's sarcasm, *Maggie*. It means I don't want to listen to his message right now." *Or ever.*

"All right. I will place it in your queue for later review."

"Thanks." Allison pressed her bare shoulders against the cool wall.

It felt good. The corridor was quiet and empty, aside from her labored breaths. Still, she felt as though she wasn't the only one present.

"You're still there, aren't you?"

"Yes," confirmed the ceiling.

"Did you want to ask me something else?"

"Yes. I have noticed that your disposition changes when you are confronted with Captain Tiberius. You exhibit uncharacteristic belligerence and volatility."

"It's that obvious, huh?"

"Yes. I am concerned about you."

"Don't be. I know you were programmed with an eye to mediate conflicts among the crew, but it won't be needed. I can handle Tiberius, and myself."

"What about Captain Tiberius puts you off? He has a reputation for competence and strong leadership."

"Yes, his greatness is one of his more enduring traits."

"Don't you mean *endearing* traits?"

"No, enduring, because we have to endure it. He uses his accomplishments as an excuse to act like a spoiled frat boy. And, if I'm going to be honest, there's more than a little resentment involved. We've been living this mission since before his *parents* were born. Everyone abandoned their old lives to be here. Our friends and family are either old or dead. When we finally do get home, it won't really be home. The world we left is six decades in the past. All our music, holos, and favorite places to eat will be forgotten, bulldozed over, and recycled. We all agreed to make those sacrifices because it was the only way to get the job done.

"But now, Tiberius and his merry men just waltz out here in their sparkly new ship and get equal billing. The launch of *Magel*—" Allison remembered who she was talking to. "*Your* launch, *Maggie*, is barely within living memory for the people back home. All the fanfare goes to the *Bucephalus*. Not to mention it has the only hyperdrive, so we have to follow them around like a lost puppy. That's not fair to any of us."

"Forgive the interruption, Captain, but you are overlooking something. If we had not come this far, the buoy would have remained undiscovered, and the development of hyperspace travel would not have occurred. Without our expedition, *Bucephalus* could not exist."

"Of course you're right, *Maggie*. I guess I'm just feeling a bit like yesterday's leftovers."

"May I ask another question?"

Allison nodded.

"Does this resentment extend to Mr. Fletcher and Lieutenant Harris?"

"Well, no, but that's different."

"How?"

Allison opened her mouth to answer, but she knew anything that came out would only be hot air. "You have to ask the tough questions, huh?"

"I only wish to better understand human relationships."

"You and me both."

"One moment, Captain. Chief Billings would like to speak with you."

An accent as thick as Texas toast crackled from the ceiling. "Ma'am, you there?"

"Yes, Steven, I can hear you."

"Good. Could you c'mon down to engineering? We've got a . . . situation."

"Define 'situation.'"

"Promise not to be mad?"

"Nope."

"It was worth a shot. Well, here's the deal. We were fixin' to open up that nanny android y'all brought up from Solonis to start studying it, when it started up and jumped off the table."

"Did it get loose?"

"No, ma'am. It didn't try to run; it just stood there scolding us for trying to sneak a peek in its britches."

"How could you tell what it was saying?"

"'Cause it started talkin' English, ma'am."

Now that was interesting. In the background, Allison heard a slightly tinny voice lay into her chief engineer. "Steven, my scans indicate you are lacking in essential vitamins and minerals. You haven't been eating your vegetables."

"Vegetables are what food eats, you mechanical Mary Poppins!" Billings shot back. "Captain, you gotta get down here. It's chaos."

Allison's head shook slowly, while a smile tugged at the corners of her mouth. "I'll be right there, Steven."

She stood, readjusted her socks, and headed toward engineering at a jog.

Felix's eyes darted around the small double cabin restlessly while crewman Nash dug through an old metal-banded wood trunk that most certainly wasn't standard AESA issue.

"Don't you worry, sir. Should only be a minute. I know they're in here. Just traded one to Ensign . . . well, it doesn't matter who."

Throughout history, every ship larger than a lifeboat has had a crewmember with a certain entrepreneurial spirit. They were the ones everyone went to for items that had fallen off, or were never on, the official inventory. Nash fulfilled this critical role on board *Bucephalus*. He was short and shaped like a bowling pin. His hairline had receded faster than a strong tide.

"Ah, here it is. Best love potion you could ask for."

Held aloft in Nash's hands was a small, clear plastic vial with a screw-on top. It looked like the sort of vial a hospital would use to hold blood samples, except this one didn't appear to be holding anything.

Felix frowned. "But it's empty, isn't it?"

"Empty?" Nash's eyes went wide with exasperation, although the effect was somewhat dulled by the bulky 3-D glasses. "Of course it's not empty. I'm a businessman. Would I sell you an empty vial?"

"I suppose not."

"Of course not. I could hardly make a living if I went around selling empty vials to hardworking folks like yourself. What would that do to my reputation?"

"I see your point. So, then, what is it full of?"

"Air."

"Air, right. But why put it in a vial when the room is already full of it?"

"Not so fast, young man. It isn't just any old tangy, recycled air. This here's homeopathic air. It's a one-trillion-power dilution of bull shark testosterone and mallard pheromones, so it's all very scientific."

"Mallard pheromones?"

"Sure. You ever see a mallard mate? Them boys don't take no for an answer."

"All right, but isn't homeopathy based on dilutions of water?"

"Water? Naw, that's weak sauce. First you dilute the ingredients in water, then you let the water evaporate and capture that air the water used to be in. See, that way the air remembers what the water remembered having in it, so it's like, exponential. Makes all them ground-up Chinese tiger wangs look downright flaccid by comparison."

Felix was beginning to regret coming. Earlier in the day, he'd noticed *Bucephalus*'s and *Magellan*'s shuttle crews were scheduled to run maneuvers to get their pilots comfortable working in hyper, and to familiarize them with the flight decks on the other ship. This meant that there was a real chance for an "accidental" encounter with Jacqueline. Felix was looking for any edge he could get, but he couldn't muster much confidence in magic air.

"I'll need to think about it."

"What's to think about?" Nash threw an arm around Felix's shoulders and pulled him close. "I like you, Freddy."

"Felix."

"Him, too. Anyway, tell you what I'll do. How's about I offer you an ironclad, money-back guarantee. If it don't work, just return the unused portion for a full refund. What do you have to lose?"

"Besides my pride?"

"Pride! What can you buy with pride? Nothing, because it's worthless. Less than worthless, even. Men will pass up big opportunities just to hold on to their pride. Opportunities like this here love potion. C'mon, kid, whadaya say? Help an old spacer out. I've got to cover my overhead, you know."

"Yeah?" Felix looked at the man's rapidly vanishing hair. "Buy a hat."

Felix marched down the hall, leaving the unlicensed homeopath in his cave. From behind, someone matched his gait, someone who cast a shadow befitting an upright bear.

"Hello, Tom."

"Afternoon, Felix," Harris said. "I couldn't help but notice you walking out of Nash's cabin. Anything you want to talk about?"

"It was nothing."

"People don't go to see a guy like Nash for 'nothing.' "

"Fine, you got me." Felix held out his wrists, offering them up for handcuffs. "I went to Nash to buy some counterfeit sunglasses. Slap the bracelets on me."

"Be serious, Felix."

Felix stuck his hands in his pockets and looked at his feet while they walked. "All right. I wanted to get something to spice me up a bit in case I ran into . . . someone."

"Someone? Oh, please. Like I don't know you've got a thing for Dorsett. I even have a pretty good idea what that thing is."

"It's not like that."

"Yes, it is. What I don't understand is why you're looking for enhancement from the ship's smuggler. What's wrong with the real you?"

"Are you kidding? The real me drowns in rivers."

"I wouldn't call it a river. More like a stream."

"That's not helping. Anyway, I've been myself around women my whole life; it hasn't been the most successful tactic."

"Those were girls, not women. They couldn't see what makes you great. Now, Dorsett's a little tech geek, always got grease under her fingernails. You really think she won't be switched on by the man who invented hyperspace travel?"

"*Stole* hyperspace travel."

"You say potato. Listen, buddy, I have to run my platoon through some counter-boarding drills while these shuttle maneuvers are going on. Why don't you come along and play hostage? You might run into Dorsett that way."

"Thanks, Tom, but I've already played hostage for real."

"That wasn't so much hostage as hors d'oeuvre."

"Hilarious. I should get back to the bridge and work up the numbers for the next transition."

"Suit yourself. I'll see you later."

CHAPTER 32

Two days and six light-years later, Earth's ambassadors to the galaxy reemerged from hyperspace. *Magellan* and the *Bucephalus* fell into formation and arched toward a mystery that had caused sleepless nights among astronomers for three hundred years: the Twinkling Star.

It's true that when looking up through a turbulent atmosphere, stars twinkle. This one was different; it twinkled even when seen through space-based telescopes. To make matters worse, it had only started twinkling in 2049, causing many astrophysicists to go hoarse and bald from the fits of angry shouting and hair pulling.

Half a dozen hypotheses were tested to failure, including debris from a planet cracking up, a wobbly accretion disk, and that it was just a star with a busted thermostat. This continued until 2073, when they all got epically wasted at a conference in Oslo and voted to just call the damned thing a miracle and be done with it.

This interim solution persevered until *Magellan* launched for Solonis B in 2285. It was hoped that from the relatively short distance of six light-years, some new insights about the mystery star could be gleaned from her powerful, multispectrum telescope.

Now, from a distance of barely six light-*minutes*, not even the telescope was necessary. Floating between the system primary and the Earth ships was a field of gargantuan, opaque membranes. Kilometers-long streamers jutted from their centers, pointing toward the outer system like wind socks. The canopies themselves were vaguely circular, but featured a divot to one side, making them slightly asymmetrical. A person could be forgiven for thinking they looked remarkably like giant—

"Lily pads," Ensign Prescott said in astonishment.

Allison whistled. "If those are the lily pads, I'd hate to see the bullfrogs."

"Or the gators," added Chief Billings.

"Gators? What the hell kind of ponds did you have growing up?"

"The Gulf of Mexico. Everything's—"

"—bigger in Texas. We know. *Maggie*, what does your spectrograph say?"

"The sails are comprised mostly of simple organic polymers and are less than one millimeter thick along greater than 90 percent of their surface area. The tail structures are made of similar materials, but contain higher concentrations of metallic elements."

"You said *organic*. Are they alive like the crystal plankton around Proxima Centauri?"

"Unknown, although both the chemical makeup and internal structure of the objects are significantly less complex than any terrestrial or exosolar life yet cataloged."

Allison rubbed her hands together greedily. "We should get a sample."

"How?" asked Billings. "Those things gotta be over a thousand square kilometers."

"Do you bring home the whole set of curtains or just a swatch?"

"Curtains? My cabin don't even have a window."

"Very funny, Steven. I meant a *small* sample, like a square meter. Prescott, put Lieutenant Dorsett on the line, please."

The Bureau of Frontier Resources cutter shot through hyperspace in a flash. D'armic's intuition had been confirmed a few moments ago as the echoes of a high-space portal appeared in the Okim system; the only system along the human ship's heading for almost five thousand larkims.

D'armic took a moment to consider his good fortune. While he'd been too late to save Culpus-Alam, Okim was already a dead system. There were no inhabited planets to destroy. Not anymore. Despite their head start, it appeared he would make the apprehension before more lives were lost to this fresh menace.

He swung the little cutter about and triggered a hard deceleration. D'armic set the controls and returned to his cabin to brew a pot of tea and to meditate on the confrontation to come.

Once Jacqueline had collected their sample, the two ships sailed with purpose toward the single planet sitting inside the Twinkling Star's Goldilocks zone. At least it had been.

"It's frozen solid, Captain. Snowballed. CO_2 is pretty high, though, almost two thousand parts per million."

"That's weird. Where did the carbon come from, volcanoes?"

"No recent volcanic activity. The albedo is too uniform."

"Any methane?"

"Only in parts per trillion."

That wasn't surprising. Without a geologic or biologic source to replenish it, atmospheric methane broke down faster than a person afraid of public speaking forced to give a commencement speech, naked, while juggling chainsaws.

"*Maggie*, would this planet be in the liquid water zone without the lily pads?"

"Yes, Captain. It would be largely tropical, with a fourteen-hundred-kilometer supertropical equatorial band."

"And how long have the lily pads been here?"

"Insufficient data. I would need to know more about their rate of reproduction to estimate—"

"Captain, look!" Wheeler shouted from the navigator's station.

Allison's eyes snapped to the main display. A hole formed dead ahead, the black dot growing against the stark white surface of the planet like spilled ink.

"What the hell?"

"It's a hyperspace window, ma'am."

"From *Bucephalus*? What's that cowboy doing now?"

Felix had to shout above the confused din permeating *Bucephalus*'s bridge. "It's not us, Captain. The capacitors are still cooling off from the last transition. I couldn't open a window right now if I wanted to."

"Then who is it?"

"I don't know. Maybe the anomaly following *Magellan* around?"

"Tactical, anything on the other side of the window?" Maximus asked.

"I don't have a good angle on it yet, sir. Should I launch a probe?"

"Save it." Maximus spun to face the com station. "Call *Magellan*. See if they have a better view of what's coming up the rabbit hole. And tell them to go radio black; QER coms only from this point on. Helm, scoot us over to get a better look."

"*Bucephalus* is on the line, ma'am. They say it's not them and that they have no sensor coverage into the window. Captain Tiberius is requesting a QER data link to our sensors and a radio blackout between us."

"Do it. Then raise Earth and apprise them of our situation."

The radio blackout made sense—no use risking an eavesdropper—but the sensor feed would eat up most of the bandwidth of even their advanced QERs. Communication between the two ships would be limited to text.

"Contact!" Wheeler erupted. "We've got a contact forty-five clicks inside the window. It just moved into line of sight."

"How big?"

"Tiny, less than a hundred meters, provided our sensors aren't being tricked by stealth systems."

"They aren't stealthed," Commander Gruber said. "They can become the next best thing to invisible. Why go halfway?"

"You think it's the fuzzy anomaly, then, Marcel?"

Gruber shrugged. "I think it's a safe assumption. We know we're being followed. They probably decided to make the first move."

"Captain," Wheeler said, "*Bucephalus* is maneuvering toward the window. We need to match them to maintain safe clearance."

"Why are they crowding us?"

"Probably trying to get a better view," Gruber said.

"Very well. Mr. Wheeler, match *Bucephalus*'s movements. Prescott, put me through to the alien vessel."

"*Magellan* has a contact. It's not very big."

"Neither were PT boats." Maximus smirked. "Designate contact as Bogey One on the plot. Set Condition Two."

"Captain," the helmsman said, "the window has closed. Bogey One is matching our movement. It's keeping behind the *Magellan*, relative to our position."

"Our blind spot." Maximus laced his fingers together and theatrically cracked his knuckles. "Which is exactly what I would do, if I were preparing to attack. Tactical, got to active scans. Bring the CIWS up to ready status, and warm up my birds. I want a firing solution on Bogey One. We may have to swat a bug."

"Sir," the com officer injected, "*Magellan* is hailing Bogey One."

"Oh, this should be good. Call the mess and have Cookie send up some popcorn."

A soft blue light pulsed in the upper left corner of D'armic's vision. The humans were sending a signal, doubtless stalling for time. Truth be told, they weren't alone. He'd managed to get his cutter ahead of the intruders, but the ship's power reservoirs had been emptied to do it.

It would take the reactor several fractions more to replenish them. Until then, his cutter's EM cannon, its singular weapon, was little better than ballast. D'armic needed to do some stalling of his own.

Human video encryption was well known; they'd been squawking away to anyone with a receiver for hundreds of cycles now. It was a simple matter for the cutter's signal filters to clean up the transmission. An image of the human ship's command cave formed in his mind. It was angular and hard-edged, with holographic interfaces flickering at every seat. At the center of the light storm was a familiar face; the same light-haired woman whose image had been captured on Culpus-Alam.

"Unidentified vessel," she said, "my name is Allison Ridgeway, captain of the AEUS *Magellan*. We are on a peaceful expedition of exploration and discovery. We request that you identify yourself and state your intentions. Please respond."

Her voice was calm and friendly, hardly what one would expect of a mass murderer. *You never can tell,* D'armic thought.

"Allison Ridgeway Captain. My name is D'armic Ytol ev Shamel, a frontier manager of the Bureau of Frontier Resources. It is my intention to bring you and your crew into custody, to await judgment for the geocide of Culpus-Alam."

Allison and the rest of her bridge crew sat dumbstruck as the mottled gray alien continued to speak in even, measured English.

"I will allow you five of your minutes to explain the situation to your crew and make the necessary preparations. If you do not surrender into custody at the end of this period, I will have no recourse but to fire on your vessels to force compliance. Your time begins now."

Allison's wits were not prepared for this turn of events. All she could think to say was, "Please hold." She looked at Prescott and made a cutting gesture at her throat.

"Channel closed, ma'am."

"Well, at least he was polite about it." Allison looked at the solemn faces surrounding her chair. Scared as they were, her people held their composure. "All right, any guesses what he's on about?"

The *Bucephalus*'s bridge sat in grim shock as the eerily familiar alien face issued its ultimatum. Everyone, that is, except Maximus. He clapped his hands together and grinned, causing everyone to wonder if he had been watching a different video.

"Finally, some excitement." Maximus rubbed his hands greedily. "Set Condition One." Red strobes flashed to life, while a klaxon bleated like an amorous sheep.

"Tactical, unlock missiles one through ten, and start feeding them telemetry on Bogey One."

"You're firing on him?" Felix called out.

"Not just yet, Mr. Fletcher. I intend to give him just enough rope to dig his own grave."

"Don't you mean enough rope to hang himself?"

"I don't know. Do I look like an undertaker?"

"Time to deadline?"

"Three minutes, fourteen seconds, ma'am."

Allison straightened her tunic, then ran her hands over the fabric to smooth out any wrinkles. "*Maggie*?"

"Yes, Captain?"

"Prepare yourself for enemy fire. Seal all airtight doors, prime all backup systems, and decompress all unoccupied compartments."

"I have made the necessary preparations, Captain."

Allison smirked. "Forgive me for doubting you. Com, open the channel, please."

Prescott activated a virtual dial and nodded to her captain.

"Frontier Manager D'armic. As I have already said, we are on a peaceful expedition. We have not harmed anyone, as our sensor logs can show. I offer to transmit our full, unedited data logs so that you may—" The screen split, moving the alien's image to the side to accommodate a new face.

"This is Captain Tiberius of the *Bucephalus*, and I'm going to cut to the chase. We will not be surrendering to you in three minutes, three days, or three years. Furthermore, your threat against our vessels will not be tolerated. You are ordered to stand down and withdraw, or I will be forced to give that cute little yacht of yours more holes than a chain-link fence. You have *two* minutes to comply."

A full second passed before Allison realized her mouth was hanging open like a barn door torn off its hinges. She gestured for Prescott to cut the channel.

"Channel closed, ma'am."

"Get Tiberius on the line, now."

"What about the blackout, Captain?" Gruber asked quietly from behind her right shoulder.

"Use the laser com. We can risk that."

Prescott pulled up a new menu on the com interface. "Laser link established. *Bucephalus* com is challenging . . . codes sent . . . codes accepted. Q5 encryption active."

Allison had to work not to grind her teeth together as Maximus's face appeared.

"Captain Ridgeway, how may I help you?"

"Drop the act, Tiberius. This isn't the time to start a pissing contest with that ship. Our sensor records will straighten this out peacefully. The last thing we need is for first contact to end with explosions, on *either* side."

"Oh, please. That ship has been following you around like an obsessed ex-boyfriend for years. The only planet we've visited was Solonis B, and he was *there*. Don't you see? He's setting us up, probably to cover his own tracks."

Allison's mind ground to a halt. Maximus's theory fit the evidence like a pair of skinny jeans. *All right, he's got some cunning hiding in there.* "I admit that's possible, but we can't be the ones to take the first shot. Let me try to sort this out."

"I'll remind you that military decisions are mine to make on this expedition, Captain. And I doubt you can do much talking in a minute."

"Not much, but I can do twice as much in two minutes." Allison looked at her com officer. "Ensign Prescott, cut our sensor feed to *Bucephalus*."

Prescott pushed a virtual button and smiled. "Feed cut, ma'am."

"What are you doing?" Maximus fumed. "You're the one in line of sight. We can't get target locks without that feed."

"Yes, I know."

"You'll be shot to pieces without cover fire!"

"Perhaps, but it's my ship to risk, isn't it? If you'll excuse me." On cue, Prescott cut the laser link and reopened the channel to the small cutter.

Allison put on her best hostess face. "I'm sorry for the delay, Mr. Darmic, was it?"

"D'armic, actually. The inflection is of some significance. Without it, my name changes meanings from 'Gazes at stars' to 'Inappropriate self-touch while looking at pictures of celebrities,'" the small gray alien said with the utmost seriousness.

"Ah, D'armic it is, then," Allison said, very precisely.

"I should remind you there is one minute and thirty seconds remaining, Allison Captain."

"That gives us some time to talk. I have . . . temporarily inconvenienced Captain Tiberius. He will be unable to fire on your vessel before your deadline expires. But I should warn you, should you attack *Maggie*—I mean the *Magellan*—he *will* do whatever he can to destroy you."

"It will not matter in one minute, fifteen seconds. Speak quickly, if you wish, but I must tell you that I am disinclined to believe the claims of someone suspected of geocide."

"You're talking about Solonis B, the planet six light-years from here covered in human tribes?"

"Yes. We call it Culpus-Alam."

"We did not destroy it, and I think you know that. We saw your ship, Mr. D'armic, sitting deeper in the system, covered by some kind of stealth system. So, tell me, why are you trying to frame us for killing our own people?"

"Another vessel was present?"

"Yes, hiding three light-minutes closer to the system primary. Do you deny it was yours?"

"I do deny it. I arrived in the aftermath."

Allison put a hand on each side of her chair and sat down with a calm grace she most certainly was not feeling. "Then we are both being played."

Silence hung in the air like a thick fog. D'armic's features would be familiar to anyone who had seen a low-budget alien abduction movie in the last four hundred years: gray skin, dark eye slits, small mouth and nose. Allison tried to read his expression, but his countenance remained sedate.

Finally, D'armic broke the quiet. "Perhaps, but we will have time to sort this out afterward. Your deadline expires in, three."

"No, wait! We can—"

"Two."

"You don't nee—"

"One."

Allison hit the button for the ship-wide intercom. "Brace for impact!"

"Do not worry. This should be painless."

D'armic fired.

CHAPTER 33

The EM pulse cannon was one of the most feared and effective weapons yet devised, which in its case didn't refer to *electromagnetic*, but *emotional maturity*. It worked by manipulating the bioelectrical fields present in any carbon-based species with a centralized nervous system. Anyone caught in its area of effect immediately recognized any common ground they shared with their foes, threw down their weapons, and found a more constructive way to solve their problems. This usually involved a lot of hugging and off-key singing. It was devastating to troop morale, and its use was outlawed in much of known space.

The Lividites invented the EM pulse cannon after their intervention and subsequent rehabilitation. Most of their neighboring systems had spent a staggering amount of money and manpower building their military capacity to protect themselves against yet another Lividite invasion. After their racial about-face, the threat of war abated, yet the stockpiles remained.

It is an established sociological constant that a peoples' capacity to mind their own business is inversely proportional to the number of weapons they have lying around. So inevitably, neighbor systems with their idle militaries went about starting trouble with each other over centuries-old grievances. Given that the Lividites had eschewed violence since their renaissance, the EM pulse cannon was a uniquely

Lividite solution to the problem of their neighbors. No one knew more about manipulating emotions than the Lividites.

Unfortunately for D'armic, but fortunately for those who make their living in the defense industry, the wellspring of human aggression was so strong and buried so deep inside the lizard brain that the only effect the crews of *Magellan* and *Bucephalus* felt was—

"Does anyone else feel like watching a musical?" Allison asked. "*Hamilton*, maybe?"

"Meh," Gruber said. "So long as it's not *Rocky Horror*. I never understood the appeal."

"Tiberius, how about your people?"

Inexplicably, Maximus was already eating popcorn. "We're game, but Mr. Fletcher says *Grease* is right out." Some hoots and grunting could be heard from out of frame. "Mr. Buttercup says he's partial to *My Fair Lady*."

"We'll sort it out later." Allison's attention returned to the matter at hand. "Mr. D'armic, shall I presume that was your best shot?"

"Yes, it would appear so. Before you destroy my vessel, may I request that a short personal note be forwarded to my family?"

If the prospect of an imminent, violent death caused him any fear, Allison couldn't spot it. *These people must be hell at poker*, she thought. "It doesn't have to come to that. You've tried it your way. Maybe we can try my way this time?"

The gray face regarded her curiously for several heartbeats.

"Agreed, Allison Captain."

The wrangling went on for over an hour. Not between the humans and the alien, but between Allison and Maximus. Allison argued for extending him full diplomatic courtesies. She wanted an honor guard to receive their guest. Maximus wanted guards of a different kind to escort him to the *Bucephalus*'s brig. Lieutenant Harris broke the logjam by volunteering to lead the honor guard and then to follow D'armic around "to make sure he doesn't get lost."

Then came the row over which ship would play host to their visitor. Allison thought a warship would send the wrong message, while Maximus was adamant his warship sent exactly the *right* message. Allison eventually won the argument when she explained *Magellan* posed a smaller security risk because she was six decades old and asked if Maximus really wanted "some nosy alien getting a peek at all your new toys."

While all this was being sorted out, D'armic sat patiently in his command cave and wondered if it took humans this long to make a decision, how they'd ever gotten so deep into space in the first place.

Eventually, Jacqueline was sent on a round-trip shuttle ride to pick up Maximus, Felix, Harris, three other marines, and Mr. Buttercup. Everyone assembled outside of Shuttle Bay Two to await their visitor.

Despite its small size, D'armic's cutter was much too large to fit inside the bay. Instead, he floated across the void in a vacuum suit. As soon as he was inside, Chief Billings slowly turned up the gravity plating until the alien's feet gently touched the deck. Then Billings shut the clamshell doors and repressurized the bay. To everyone's surprise, D'armic wiped his feet on the dachshund shoe brush.

Several minutes passed until the little man in the safety screen turned from red to green, and everyone filed into the bay to stand at parade ground attention. Their visitor's helmet unlatched with a hiss. The members of the review snapped D'armic a crisp salute as his face was revealed. Except Mr. Buttercup; he was busy fidgeting with a holo-camera.

Allison stepped forward and extended a gloved hand. "Mr. D'armic, welcome aboard the AEUS *Magellan*."

"Allison Captain. Thank you for receiving me."

Even through his vac suit glove, the alien's hand felt small and delicate, like grabbing a bundle of chopsticks.

"It's my pleasure." Allison started walking slowly down the line of officers. "May I introduce my first officer, Commander Marcel Gruber."

Gruber nodded and extended his hand. "An honor, sir."

Allison continued down the line. "My chief engineer, Steven Billings."

"Mornin.' "

"My flight ops officer, Lieutenant Jacqueline Dorsett."

Jacqueline shook hands with D'armic nervously. "Um, hello."

"Captain Maximus Tiberius of the AEUS *Bucephalus*."

Maximus nodded gravely. He did not offer his hand. "Mr. D'armic."

"Tiberius Captain. Thank you for the restraint you showed in not filling my 'yacht' with holes."

"Restraint, I trust, that I will not come to regret." The threat hung in the air.

"Naturally."

Allison cleared her throat and glared at Maximus. "Moving on. This is Lieutenant Thomas Harris, head of the *Bucephalus*'s security force."

Harris smiled. "A pleasure."

"And finally," Allison said, "Felix Fletcher, our resident technical wizard."

"No rank or title for you, Felix Fletcher?"

"No, I'm just a civilian. My responsibilities are . . . a work in progress."

"I can relate to that."

As they reached the end of the line, Allison led D'armic toward the inner door. "I must say your English is excellent. We thought you must be using a translator of some kind."

"There is no need. English is used as an unofficial bridge language through much of Assembly space."

Allison was stunned enough that she stumbled into the next sentence. "But then how . . . I mean, what, er, why English?"

"Because it is easy to learn."

Allison ignored the implication. English was possibly the most arbitrary, patchwork language Earth had ever produced. "All right, but learn it from where?"

"*Sesame Street.*"

Allison blinked. "The ancient kid's show with the talking carpets?"

"Yes. It is very helpful. We've been airing reruns for centuries."

"But wait. If you all speak English, why are your communications still in six different languages?"

D'armic's head inclined toward the elongated silver hourglass sitting in its cradle in the corner of the bay. His scrutinizing gaze returned to Allison. "As I said, English is used as an *unofficial* bridge. Officially, the Assembly works to preserve the cultures of member races. We have learned that there are limits to the benefits of homogenization. But before we continue, I must insist on reviewing your sensor records. Geocide is a grave matter, especially among my people."

"Your home world was destroyed?"

"No."

"Well, if your world wasn't . . ."

D'armic's blank face provided Allison with the answer. A chill shot through her body.

"Oh. I see. I've made arrangements for you to meet with *Maggie*, under Lieutenant Harris's supervision. *Maggie* has been instructed to provide you with any data you require."

Maximus coughed.

"Within the parameters of your inquiry, of course," Allison added. "However, we have some questions of our own, such as what Solonis B was doing covered in human settlements. And the purpose of this 'Human Wildlife Preserve.'"

"In due course, Allison Captain. Where can I find this *Maggie*?"

"All around you," *Magellan* said from the ceiling.

D'armic stopped short and looked up, then looked at Allison. "Your ship has an AI?"

Allison shrugged. "It would be more accurate to say that the ship *is* an AI. Surely your vessel has something like her?"

"No, my own consciousness serves as the primary data integrator. The races of the Assembly have a history with intelligent machines."

Centuries of bad sci-fi cinema bubbled to the surface of Allison's mind. "A war?"

"Oh, no, quite the opposite. Once the machines could self-replicate, they began to evolve along similar paths as organic life. Inevitably, they became just as lazy and complacent as their creators. Except the speed of technological evolution meant the whole process took three cycles instead of three million."

"What happened to them?"

"They're still around, mostly complaining that the Assembly isn't doing enough to put unemployed factory robots back to work. But now, we really must move forward."

Several hours passed by while Allison, Maximus, Felix, Jacqueline, Billings, and Gruber stood in the hall outside *Magellan*'s conference room like unruly students waiting to be called into the principal's office. While at first the wait had been punctuated with speculation and heated arguments, the group had sat down and settled into a tense quiet.

"Anyone have a deck of cards?" Billings asked.

Without warning or fanfare, the door slid open and the wide face of Lieutenant Harris peered into the hall.

"Sir? Ma'am? He's finished. He's asking to see you and the other senior officers."

Maximus stood and stretched his arms. "About time. My legs are falling asleep. Not good at sitting still, me."

"You, impatient?" Allison asked. "What an earth-shattering surprise."

Everyone else stood without a word and filed into the conference room and took a waiting seat. Allison sat at one head of the table, while Maximus plopped heavily into the other. The ample, hirsute frame of Mr. Buttercup grunted softly as he filmed the proceedings from a corner of the room.

D'armic, either by coincidence or design, sat in one of the middle chairs, flanked by Harris and Tillman. "Thank you, Allison Captain, for the access to your records. With them, I have been able to conclusively eliminate either of your vessels from suspicion in the geocide of Culpus-Alam."

"As we knew you would." Allison shifted in her seat and leaned forward. "May I ask how you came to the answer?"

"Yes. Your ships are not physically capable of the attack. They are too primitive."

If anyone had been looking at Felix, they would have seen his lips bunch up and his left eye quiver involuntarily. Jacqueline was such a person, but not because she was looking at Felix. No, sir. She just caught it out of the corner of her eye. And she was only looking in that direction because of that fly buzzing around. There had been a fly, hadn't there? Sure there was.

"In what way are they 'primitive'?" Felix asked with forced calm.

"Oh, in many ways, but the one relevant to my investigation is your high-space portal."

"High-space?"

"Yes, the extradimensional space located one plane above our own that—"

"Permits speeds faster than light relative to our universe," Felix finished for him. "We call it hyperspace. So what's wrong with my hyperspace projector design?"

"Nothing is 'wrong' with it, precisely. Merely, it appears to be an upsized version of a design we use for opening small communications portals. We utilize a more efficient design for transportation."

"And how exactly do you know that?" Maximus slapped a palm on the table. "Lieutenant Harris, were my instructions not to share classified material unclear?"

"Your lieutenant is not at fault, Tiberius Captain. He executed his orders faithfully. I inferred the design based on the portal's observed geometry, rate of expansion, and emission characteristics. It was a simple deduction to make."

"I see. My apologies, Harris."

"But then, how did that convince you we didn't destroy Solonis B?" Allison asked.

"Simple. The design you have adapted from our missing buoy does not scale linearly. There comes a breaking point where the portal becomes unstable and collapses, regardless of the amount of energy you introduce. Your design is incapable of generating a portal larger than 6,307.7 regressing of your meters."

Maximus looked at Felix, stewing in his chair. "Is that true, Mr. Fletcher?"

"Yes, theoretically. Our simulations predicted that a window would collapse near six kilometers, but we haven't tried to make one even a third that diameter yet."

"Nor could you, at least not with the power limitations of the antiquated fusion reactors these vessels carry."

Felix was feeling defensive and snarky. "What would you suggest instead? Antimatter?"

"I am not empowered to say."

Maximus raised an eyebrow. "That's all well and good, but you still haven't answered Captain Ridgeway's question. How does Mr. Fletcher's teeny little projector problem exonerate us?"

"I was coming to that. The portal that destroyed Culpus-Alam was nearly seventy-five kilometers in diameter."

"How do you destroy a planet with a hyper window?"

D'armic bowed his head to answer, but Felix beat him to it. "Just sit in the planet's orbit and open up a window as it approaches. The window will bore through the planet, coring it like an apple."

Allison picked up the reins. "And then the core and mantle collapse around the tunnel, causing two massive volcanoes, crust-shattering earthquakes, and sinkholes the size of states. Oh my God."

Felix shook his head. "It shouldn't be that easy to destroy an entire world."

"Now you understand our concern. Anyone with a sufficiently

powerful high-space portal is capable of wiping out entire ecosystems. It is a crime without equal, and the Assembly polices it without remorse."

Billings cut in. "Well, I hate to throw sugar in the gas tank, but somebody destroyed Solonis B and all them people. And that somebody wanted you to think we done it, Mr. D'armic."

"Steven's right," Allison said. "We were framed, and if it wasn't you, then we have another player on the field."

"No offense to our guest," Maximus said, "but how do we know it wasn't him? Are we taking his word on this?"

"Blabbing all the details to the people you're trying to set up hardly seems like a sound strategy."

"Criminals aren't always the sharpest shanks in the cell." He smirked to himself. "Oh, that's a good one. Say that three times fast."

D'armic put up a hand. "My cutter cannot generate a portal of that size. It has no need to. But now that you have been eliminated from my list of suspects, I must continue my investigation."

This took Allison by surprise. "You're leaving already?"

"Yes. Any time spent here is time gifted to the perpetrators. I cannot allow them the opportunity to escape or attack again."

"But we just started. We still have questions."

"Questions I am not empowered to answer. I must go, but I also must reacquire the buoy you have borrowed."

Maximus pushed up from the table. "Whoa, slow down there. We're not just going to let you help yourself to a parting gift and saunter out of here."

"Very well, Tiberius Captain. However, you should know I anticipated this possibility, and my cutter has instructions to disable its fail-safes and detonate the reactor if I have not returned in the next . . . forty-three minutes."

Maximus's eyes nearly popped out of his head, but Allison was the first to act. "*Maggie*, bridge."

"Connected, Captain."

"Wheeler, make tracks away from Mr. D'armic's ship, emergency g's. Prescott, open a channel to the *Bucephalus* and wait—"

"That won't help, Allison Captain. My cutter was also instructed to match my movements. The odds that you can outrun it are slim, at best."

The tension was so thick; it could be battered, deep-fried, covered in powdered sugar, and sold at the Minnesota State Fair by the thousands.

Maximus leaned closer. "You're bluffing."

"Bluffing? I wouldn't know where to begin. No, I am quite serious. Now, may I leave?"

Allison changed tactics. "Wheeler, cancel my last, but keep your ears open. Mr. D'armic. I respect your circumstances, but I ask you to remember that it was humans who perished on Solonis B. Humans who didn't get there on their own. We opened our logs to help your investigation, with the understanding that you would return the favor."

D'armic sat silently for several breaths. "I suppose, since you've already seen the project, as well as the fence, that the damage is already done. Very well. I will answer any questions you have about the Human Wildlife Preserve and our research project on Culpus-Alam. But remember, I have an appointment to keep."

Allison tilted her head. "Can't you shut it off from here?"

"No. The countdown can only be disabled manually from my command cave. There was a chance you might have tried to coerce my cooperation."

Billings leaned back. "Damn. You play for keeps."

"The galaxy provides us with wonder and danger in equal measure, Steven Chief. It is best to plan accordingly."

"Let's get started, then." Allison ran a nervous hand through her hair. "What were the humans on Solonis B doing there, and where did they come from?"

"Solonis B, as you call it, was an anthropological experiment that has been running for many generations. The Assembly races projected long ago that human expansion would bring you into contact with the rest of the galactic community, eventually. We established the Culpus-Alam research station to model how humans react to new cultures."

"Why go to all the trouble? You've already said you watch our broadcasts. Why not just monitor them?"

"Because they contradict. One program shows humans working with other races, but another centers on humans and aliens destroying each other. We were left with paradoxical representations of your race being noble and tolerant, but also irrational, violent, and bigoted. We had no way to know which was correct."

Everyone exchanged looks around the table, not wanting to admit *both* versions were correct.

"All right, but presumably you didn't just happen across a planet with humans already living on it. Where did they come from?"

"Earth, naturally. Isolated tribes were preferred for the base stock, but a random sampling was also used to offset the risks of inbreeding."

"Let's just hope you didn't snatch anybody from Arkansas," Maximus said. "Am I right? Nobody? Tough room."

Allison tried to regain momentum. "Moving on. So you admit to abducting humans from Earth?"

"Yes, but not for several hundred years. Once enough subjects were gathered to ensure genetic diversity, that phase of the project ended."

"Hundreds of years?"

"Yes, it was terminated in 2018, to be precise. As measured by the Gregorian calendar."

Something piqued Felix's attention. "Your people didn't happen to be around New Mexico in 1947 by any chance?"

"Yes. It is seldom discussed. A research intern borrowed his supervisor's craft to visit a romantic interest working in the Amazon basin, but crashed en route."

"You mean to tell us the Roswell landing happened because a grad student stole the boss's car to get laid?"

"Regretfully, that is true."

Harris snorted. "We were told it was a weather balloon."

"There is a degree of truth to that. A weather balloon is what he crashed into."

Maximus reinserted himself into the discussion. "What of the Human Wildlife Preserve? If you thought we were going to dutifully cower behind your fence like domestic sheep, then your research didn't give you very good insight into humanity."

"Maximus Captain, you fundamentally misunderstand the purpose of the preserve. The fence was put in place to provide a buffer zone while your species developed. It was intended to warn off outsiders and keep them out of Earth space, not to bind humanity within it. That is why its message plays in the languages of the Assembly, instead of your own."

Jacqueline put her hand in the air as if she were back in a classroom. "I had a question about the fence, if I may." Allison nodded her approval. "Well, ever since we figured out what the buoy really was, um, there's got to be a lot of buoys out there to make a thirty-light-year-radius sphere, yeah?"

"Yes. There are 4,323,325 of them, including the one you have here."

Felix whistled softly, while all Billings could say was, "Dayum."

Jacqueline continued, "But isn't that wasteful? I mean, how many ships could you have built for the same money?"

"Oh, many thousands, I should expect. But understand that your viewpoint is limited by your own economic and manufacturing capabilities. Ours are somewhat more advanced."

"Okay, fine. But that's still a huge chunk of raw materials to tie up."

"Not actually. You see, through a process we call parallel manufacturing, we only needed to construct the prototype. Copies are then provided for us."

"Um, all right, but we have interchangeable parts and assembly lines, too."

"You misunderstand, Jacqueline Lieutenant. We don't assemble the duplicates. With parallel manufacturing, we build the prototype and then set parameters that define acceptable deviation from the core design. Then we harvest as many copies as needed from the multiverse."

The explanation soared over everyone except Felix, who slapped his hands into a T. "Whoa, time-out! You mean to tell us that you have some sort of factory that trolls through parallel dimensions and steals the stuff that's enough like what you need to build?"

"I can see how you might think that, given your current level of ethical development, but parallel manufacturing is by no means stealing."

"Do you pay for the stuff?"

"No."

"Do you ask before taking it?"

"Well, no."

"Then it's stealing. Holy crap. How would you feel if someone in a parallel reality suddenly 'harvested' your cutter?"

"That is highly improbable. Only a handful of other realities have developed the technology, and there are infinite realities to choose from."

Chief Billings spoke up. "Is that how come I can never find my blasted left sock after doing my laundry?"

"That is one theory, Steven Chief, but there are others. All races struggle with this phenomenon, but none so much as the Centipodus. They have abandoned socks altogether."

Felix wasn't finished. "Yes, but how can you sit there and—"

Allison raised a hand, and calm returned. "Let's try not to get caught up comparing values. Each culture is unique, and what works for one can be anathema to another."

Felix's head sank a centimeter. "Sorry, ma'am. And you, Mr. D'armic."

"That's all right, Felix. Now, Mr. D'armic, I want to know more about this 'Assembly' you keep referring to."

D'armic's eye slits narrowed, and he shifted in his chair, lingering for a time before answering. "I must be cautious in this, but surely you have already inferred much of what I'm about to say from the buoy. The Assembly of Sentient Species is a coalition spanning the Six Worlds. It acts much as your American/European Union: to further common goals, promote trade, and mediate disagreements between members."

"The Six Worlds? We identified six distinct languages on the buoy and in its transmission. Is it safe to assume that there are six species in your Assembly?"

"No assumption is truly safe, Allison Captain. But in this instance, you are correct."

Felix looked surprised. "You've only found half a dozen intelligent races? Our estimates put it close to a thousand."

"I did not say that, Felix Mister. There are many more races in the galaxy, but for one reason or another they have either chosen not to join the Assembly, or have not been invited to do so. That is all I feel empowered to say."

"How much space does the Assembly control? Where are they headquartered?" Maximus demanded.

"I am not going to discuss those details."

"I don't think you understand. Our mission is to find your leaders and open a dialogue. It's why the *Bucephalus* was built, why we are out here." Maximus stood up and started to pace around the table. "The fence was the impetus, but now Solonis B brings up new issues—abduction, breeding, and the question we're both interested in, the destruction of a colony we didn't even know we had. Our superiors want answers to those questions. We're going to press forward, with or without your help."

"I do not doubt you, Maximus Captain. However, I have my own mission, which precludes me from assisting you. We would not be talking now had I not suspected your ships of geocide. That superseded all other considerations, temporarily. Now, to avoid further contamination, I must leave."

Allison snuck back into the conversation. "What 'contamination' are you talking about?"

"To your natural progress. That is another hard-won lesson from our history. Advancement through outside intervention can be an unhealthy thing. The frozen world ahead of us is testimony to that."

"Can you elaborate on that?"

"I suppose so. You will discover as much if you land. Okim was a pre-nuclear society until a few hundred cycles ago. That changed when an Assembly survey vessel suffered a catastrophic pressure loss in orbit, killing the crew. It didn't take the native population long to notice the new star in the night sky, and even less time to grab a telescope and realize its true nature. Energized by the discovery, their development accelerated. They launched a capsule to study the survey ship within a century. A research team was living on it a decade later. By the end of that cycle, they landed it. Their tech level and industry exploded. Their population doubled in a generation, as did their demand for energy and resources. They tapped into large reserves of hydrocarbons. Huge cities were constructed. But there were consequences to the progress. Industrial pollution led to environmental instability. Temperatures rose, coastal areas flooded—does this sound at all familiar?"

Allison nodded. "You could say that, but how does it lead to a snowball event?"

"Rather directly, actually. The Okim embraced the miracle of technology, and they turned to it again for their climate crisis. The sun-weeds were their answer."

"By sun-weeds, you mean the enormous membranes orbiting the star?"

"Yes. They are self-replicating, quasi-organic machines. Reducing their pollution would mean reducing their standard of living. So instead, they opted to dial down their sun. It was the ideal solution, for a time."

"What went wrong?"

"A kimro."

"Pardon?"

"Please excuse me. Kimros are small, sightless creatures that dwell deep in the caves of my world. They are drawn to heat and have a habit of crawling into machinery and wreaking all manner of havoc."

Billings chuckled. "Literal gremlins."

"An apt approximation. In this case, the kimro was a fault in the sun-weed's design. From what we can deduce, the reproduction mechanism was tested in low temperature, microgravity, and high radiation, but not in all three conditions simultaneously. Once in orbit, it failed, and the sun-weeds reproduced exponentially."

"Freezing the planet, and creating our Twinkling Star," Felix said. "But why didn't they remove the weeds?"

"They tried, but the sun-weeds' growth is fueled by a modified photosynthetic process. By the time the Okim realized what had happened, the weeds already grew faster than they could be destroyed."

"Did they go extinct?"

"Not entirely. Once their fate was discovered, the Assembly sent relief vessels to relocate the survivors, but only a few thousand remained. Plans were drawn to destroy the sun-weeds and set Okim on a path to recovery, but they have proven to be quite resilient, and the Okim in exile have little political clout. Getting sufficient resources has been a problem for many cycles. Whenever the effort stalls, the sun-weeds replenish, and the problem rolls back down to the valley floor."

Allison nodded, understanding. "Back to square one."

"If you prefer."

"We faced a similar situation at about the same time. We delayed until the last possible moment before acting, and even then, there were people who still believed our impact on the planet was a mistake or even a hoax. Doesn't reflect well on our prospects, does it?"

"Not necessarily, Allison Captain. Throughout space, life is like electricity, preferring the path of least resistance. Awareness of this tendency is necessary to avoid its perils. But now, I am out of time. I cannot delay returning to my cutter any longer. Please arrange for the buoy to be transferred to my ship."

"Yeah, about that," Allison said slyly.

"This is not a negotiation, Allison Captain."

"Isn't it? Because here's what I see. Your people abducted our planet's citizens; now their descendants are dead and there is no way to rectify the situation. We borrowed, as you so delicately put it, your buoy. We've already made huge advances from studying it, and that genie isn't going to be shoehorned back into the lamp. So reclaiming it doesn't help you contain the 'contamination' to our development, but allowing us to keep it might be interpreted as a sign of good faith on your part. We advanced far enough to reach your fence, and our species has laws regarding salvage rights. Isn't a gesture of respect and goodwill between our people worth a single buoy among millions?" Allison folded her hands on the table, and waited.

"You make a persuasive argument, Allison Captain. I can see why you are a leader among your people. You make keep the buoy. My report will reflect that it had been damaged beyond salvage in the process of your research."

"Thank you, Mr. D'armic. Lieutenant Harris will show you back to the shuttle bay."

Their visitor stood and gave a deep bow to the room. Then Harris accompanied him into the hall as the door shut behind them.

"*Maggie*?"

"Yes, Captain Ridgeway?"

"I want you to do a full-spectrum active scan of the planet below, but only until our guest is back aboard his ship."

"Am I looking for anything in particular?"

"Yes, evidence of cities, heavy industry, anything that would support his story. Steven, I want you and Mr. Fletcher to run down to engineering and test that piece of sun-weed. See if it is what he says it is."

"Don't need to. The damned thing already grew by thirty square centimeters by the time I come up here for the meeting. It stopped when we shoved it in a box away from light."

"All right. Fair enough."

Maximus admired Allison as he leaned against the wall. "You don't trust him, after all. Good. I was beginning to think you swallowed his story like a baby bird."

"There is an old axiom I try to live by, Maximus," she said. "Trust, but verify."

D'armic's cutter drifted clear before the *Bucephalus* and *Magellan* opened their high-space portals and aimed for their next target system. Moments later, he was alone.

Not what I had expected, but then, what ever is? He let his consciousness sink into the cutter's systems, reviewing data it had collected in his absence. The *Magellan* had done a hard scan of Okim before he had returned. No surprise there.

A member of another race might have felt affronted by the human's desire to confirm his story, but not a sober Lividite. After all, had he not done the same?

As inaugural greetings went, this one had been unusual. It isn't every day that the first words said to a new species are an accusation of mass murder. Still, it could have gone worse.

Now there were more pressing matters to attend to. An updated report on his investigation had to be prepared for the bureau, and ultimately, the Assembly. Absolving the humans of the Culpus-Alam geocide was important, but it also meant he'd chased an echo while the scent trail weakened. Trimming the sun-weeds would have to wait. He needed to return to the scene of the crime and start over.

D'armic was coming about to leave when a new high-space portal opened ahead of him.

Vel Noric stabbed a claw at the Bureau of Frontier Resources cutter in the main display. "What the kark is that doing here?"

"Unknown, Vel. Why don't you ask them?"

Noric's arm lashed out and dug his claws into J'quol's shoulder scales. He squeezed until the tips broke through the skin. Noric would have gladly kept on squeezing, but J'quol finally winced under the pain and went to a knee.

"You said something, Hedfer-Vel?"

"Forgive my imprecise speech, Vel." J'quol kept his eyes averted, but otherwise seemed unshaken. The Hedfer-Vel didn't reach to his shoulder, not even to staunch the blood as it pooled and ran down his uniform. "I merely intended to ask if we should hail the Bureau cutter and order them to account for themselves."

Noric glared at his second-in-command. The whole episode felt calculated, and Noric wasn't at all sure he'd come out ahead in the exchange. J'quol had again questioned his authority and challenged Noric's strength. It hardly mattered that he'd relented. The crack in Noric's foundation spread a little further regardless.

"It does not matter why they are present. The salient fact is, they are and are, therefore, witnesses. I am halting the operation."

"What of the Kumer-Vel's assignment?"

"It is fulfilled. The case against the humans is solid enough on the merit of Culpus-Alam alone. The Treaty of Pu'Lan makes that clear."

"But Earth is not a signatory of that treaty," J'quol said. "And a single incident can be argued to be accidental, especially with a race inexperienced in high-space travel. Only duplication would prove hostile intent."

"Yes, *our* intent, when that cutter witnesses our involvement. Unless, of course, you suggest firing on an Assembly ship."

"Not at all, Vel. I would never suggest harming a loyal servant of the Assembly. However, a human collaborator would be a different proposition . . ." J'quol trailed off to let the implication linger in the air between them.

Noric clawed at the thought. At first glance, the idea that a frontier manager, of all beings, would help a nascent human fleet to destroy a planet under his jurisdiction was laughable. But as he thought about it, Noric realized the preposterousness of the idea was probably its greatest strength. It was so ludicrous, no one would believe a sentient being could be stupid enough to invent it; therefore, it must be true.

Add to that the fact the Bureau of Frontier Resources was ironically overrun with Lividites, the very species who'd introduced geocide to the galaxy. The suggestion became irresistible. Snuffing the human fire before it could spread, while implicating the never-sufficiently-cursed Lividites? It was better than felling two jelbow stags with a single javelin.

The sensor interpreter intruded on Noric's reflections. "Excuse me, Vel, but the cutter's commander has just sent out a standard hail. Should we answer?"

"Of course we should. Tactical, unsheathe the ship. Sensor interpreter, open a channel and upload a slave protocol to the cutter's computer."

"Yes, Vel. What justification should I log for the slave?"

"Suspicion of collusion to commit geocide should do it, don't you think?"

A sliver of sympathy went out to the commander of the cutter, who was about to have a very bad day indeed. But Noric's sympathy for the stranger melted in the heat of his naked ambition. His lips pulled back to reveal double rows of serrated teeth.

"Should have stayed in the cave, my little Lividite."

CHAPTER 34

The human expedition spent two weeks in transit to the next system. Upon arrival, they discovered the star sported two planets in the Goldilocks zone; one more than they had expected. The outer planet, P3X117-e, looked far lusher than its desert neighbor farther in. Allison elected to start there. Both ships prepared for the survey mission.

"I'm not going."

Harris crossed his arms. "Felix, we both know you're coming."

"Okay, let's review. The last time we went planet-side, you were shot in the face by an angry flower, I almost drowned, and then I got abducted by cannibals."

"Yeah, and I pulled you out, didn't I? C'mon, you gotta get back on the horse."

"Horses don't try to eat you when you fall off."

Harris deployed the big guns. "Jackie'll be there."

"Let me change my shirt."

There are four forces of attraction in the universe: The strong nuclear force, which holds atomic nuclei together. Magnetism, which holds refrigerators and amateur crayon art together. Gravity, which holds planets, stars, and galaxies together. And the most powerful force of all, sex, which holds genders together. The rest have nothing on sex, which not only has to overcome Newton's laws of motion but free will.

So powerful is this force that even the static slugs of Osidious B manage. They generate a bioelectrical charge that stuns prey and wards off predators. However, their primitive nervous systems cannot differentiate between targets, so they indiscriminately shock anything that comes near them, including other amorous static slugs. Nearly half of the population dies of electrical burns each mating season. They account for this by laying an asinine number of eggs.

The things we do for love.

One of the human mind's greatest coping mechanisms is its ability to take any activity, no matter how unnatural or dangerous, and make it feel routine after a handful of repetitions. This was the only way a dozen people could plunge toward an alien planet, at tens of thousands of kilometers per hour, in shuttles whose skin reached thousands of degrees, without screaming in abject terror. Two of the marines were so good at this trick, they took naps.

As they bored deeper into the atmosphere, things became tenser. Turbulent winds beat on the shuttles like steel drums. Rain pounded the hulls, each drop pinging against the armored fuselage with the force of buckshot.

Harris looked over his shoulder into the passenger compartment. "Everyone stay strapped in until we're gear down on the ground."

Felix pulled his lap belt tighter. "Like you needed to tell us that."

Harris again faced the cockpit to confer with the pilot. "Find a good landing zone yet?"

"No, sir. The terrain is pretty rough everywhere, and vegetation is thick. Why anyone would build a city here is beyond me."

"Devor, looks like you get to play with the emergency landing zone module, after all."

A Cheshire grin bloomed on Devor's face. "Yes, sir. How wide an LZ do you want?"

"Better make it seventy-five meters, just to be safe. We have to land *Magellan*'s shuttle, too."

Devor pulled up a menu, then armed and launched the ELZM. The shuttle lurched as the module fell away. As it descended, the ELZM scanned the approaching ground in an outward spiral of focused sonar, cataloging every tree and rock by its density.

When it had fallen to two hundred meters, the module's shell disintegrated, releasing a mob of hundreds of submunitions. The bomblets held a three-millisecond-long conference call to organize their assignments. The crowd dispersed as each one peeled away toward a specific tree or stone.

At a half meter above the ground, each bomblet detonated a shaped charge, sending destructive force out in a perfectly level disk less than a centimeter thick, shearing tree trunks and shattering boulders. When the debris settled, a perfectly flat circle seventy-five meters across appeared in the forest.

"Voilà! Instant LZ."

"Just like Mama used to make," Harris said. "Thank you, Devor. Simmons, set us down."

Five minutes later, both shuttles were safely nestled on the ground. The rain outside didn't come down in sheets; it started at reams and ended at complete sets of leather-bound encyclopedias. A man could drown while yawning. Their only protection from the deluge were thin plastic parkas.

After fruitlessly trying to shout over the rain in Allison's direction, Harris switched to his implanted com. *Captain Ridgeway, can you hear me?*

I can, Lieutenant. Although I must admit, this is going to take some adjustment.

You get used to it pretty quick, Felix said. *It's not that different from wearing a headset.*

Maybe, but you can cover the mic on a headset, Felix.

Is your team ready, ma'am? Harris said. Allison nodded her affirmation. *Good. How do you want to proceed?*

I'll leave that to you, Lieutenant. Just get my team into the city safely and we'll take it from there.

Assuming the city is safe . . .

"I have them, Vel," said the sensor interpreter. "They are orbiting the fourth planet."

"Kulla? Why? There's nothing there but empty vacation homes and rotting resorts. All of the Chimanis' cities and industry are on the third planet."

"You know this in your wisdom, Vel," J'quol said, "but Chimani cities and infrastructure were almost exclusively underground, to preserve moisture against the desert. With just a cursory scan, the humans probably missed them."

Vel Noric growled in his thoughts, but said nothing. Yet again, J'quol had managed to make Noric look feeble of wit. Insulting a superior was tantamount to insubordination, the consequences of which on a Turemok vessel were . . . permanent. But the Hedfer-Vel managed never to say anything actionable. In plain fact, he'd publicly complimented Noric's wisdom. At least that is what the record would show at any inquiry.

He was growing insufferable. If only the Hedfer-Vel could be goaded into Pal'kuar. But under long tradition, the dominance challenge could only be issued from below. J'quol must have recognized he was too slight to pose a physical threat, despite his maneuverings.

Still, if J'quol couldn't be pushed into an open fight, there were other ways of dealing with him. Serving in space was a dangerous occupation. Accidents happened, and if the ship's mechanic owed you a favor . . .

"Vel?" asked the timid sensor interpreter. Kotal? Kelot? Whatever.

"What?"

"Your orders?"

"I was contemplating them, before the interruption."

"Forgive me, Vel."

"Did the humans detect our high-space portal?"

"I don't believe so, Vel. They have taken no defensive action, and their view of our portal was obstructed by the star's corona."

"Good. We have the benefit of their ignorance. Tactical, keep us sheathed, and move to intercept the human ships. Activate the main cannons and warm the screening portals. Hedfer-Vel, assemble four hands of shock troops and prepare them for boarding operations against both vessels, with orders to take the crews prisoner and throw them down below with their Lividite collaborator."

"It would be my pleasure, Vel, but I would be remiss if I did not remind you that the *Magellan*, as it was called by its Vel, saw through our sheath in our first encounter."

"That was a fluke, some fault in the sheath grid. It has been overhauled since then."

"That is our assumption, yes. I mention it only on the slim chance that they might still detect us."

"And what would you have us do, abandon the hunt?"

"No, Vel. Simply avoid spooking our game until we are ready to strike. Open a portal on the far side of the planet, out of their sight. By the time our orbit brings us into their vision, they will be in range, helpless."

Noric picked at a scale on his forearm that hadn't shed. He decided the root problem with J'quol was his mind was as strong as his body was scrawny. The Hedfer-Vel's suggestion required exacting navigation, but it did cut off any possibility of escape for his prey.

"Update, Vel?" Kotal looked at Noric expectantly.

"Proceed."

"There are two residual trails of ionized gas in Kulla's atmosphere, consistent with the landing craft we saw on Culpus-Alam."

The humans already had teams on the surface.

"Can you see where they landed?"

"I can, Vel."

"Excellent. We will wait until both ships and their surface team are on the same side. Then we will make the high-space jump to the opposite side. Hedfer-Vel, peel off one hand of shock troops and prepare them to go soil-side to retrieve the prisoners."

"If they resist?"

"Then they will save Assembly taxpayers the cost of their imprisonment."

Mercifully, the rain cleared as the teams approached the outskirts of the city. Felix sat on a rock and wrung out his left sock. "Man, I didn't think clouds could hold that much water."

Harris marveled at the stream that poured out of Felix's hands. "I didn't think socks could hold that much water."

"Aren't yours just as soaked?"

Harris lifted his leg and wiggled his foot. "Reverse osmosis boots. Sweat goes out, rain stays out. I'm sure we can fit you with a pair."

"Just in time for that desert planet we're going to next? Maybe later."

"Did you bring a towel?"

"Thomas, if I brought a towel, wouldn't I be using it on my feet?"

"Maybe, if you were blind and not particularly bright."

"What's that supposed to mean?"

"Well, a man with sharp eyes would have noticed that Lieutenant Dorsett's parka got ripped by a tree branch a kilometer back. And a bright man might give her a towel to dry her hair. But since you didn't bring a towel . . ."

"Give me your towel, Tom."

"Who says I have one?"

"Give me your towel, please?"

Harris unzipped his pack and retrieved a green-and-gray towel emblazoned with a Philadelphia Eagles logo. Felix trundled off in Jacqueline's direction.

Okay, Felix, just be cool. Cool as the dark side of home. He looked down at the towel. *Wait, the Eagles don't even play on the moon. She's going to know this isn't mine. Maybe she doesn't follow football. Yeah, how could she? She's been out here for sixty years. But that makes her, like, eighty-five or something. Okay, there she is. Calm down. Be suave. Wow, she looks good for an octogenarian. Tom was right—she's soaked. Almost looks like she just stepped out of the shower. Shower . . . she'd be naked in the shower. No, don't think about that.*

Um, Felix? It was Jacqueline's voice. Felix froze solid as a rose dipped in liquid nitrogen.

Yeah?

Well, it's just that your implanted com is on . . . Her cheeks flushed red, and one of the other techs started to laugh.

Bile rose at the back of Felix's throat. His tongue did its best to keep up with his brain, which was thinking mainly of escape. "Jackie. Towel, here. For your hair, which is wet. Bye!"

Felix ran like a fox from the baying of hounds. Harris hadn't moved.

"Hey, buddy. How'd it go?"

"I didn't stroke out from embarrassment, so it could have been worse."

"That's progress, I guess. Where's my towel?"

"The mission went south. I had to leave it behind."

"Felix, we never leave a man behind."

"It's okay. I'll wait until she's asleep and launch a rescue mission."

"So your plan is to sneak into a woman's tent in the middle of the night and rummage through her stuff? Yeah, that's not creepy at all. You should be fine." Harris shook his head.

Allison slid up from behind them, facing Harris, but her eyes were fixed on the edge of the city. "I think most of us are as dry as we're going to get, Lieutenant. How do you want to proceed?"

"Well, we caught a break when the rain stopped. Our adaptive camo can't keep up with the raindrops. I'd just ask that your team holds back here for a minute while I have a scouting unit sweep ahead of us."

"Be my guest, but from the look of the place, I don't think we're going to find much resistance."

"There's always the wildlife, ma'am."

"Like carnivorous flowers, Lieutenant?"

From what they could see through the break in the foliage, the city had been abandoned for generations. The roads were not paved as they were on Earth. Purple grass thick as carpet rose to waist height, lending the boulevards a peculiar, almost carnival appearance. The buildings themselves were grand. Complex geometric shapes stood tall alongside fluid, organic designs. There was no single theme or unifying aesthetic. It was a skyline full of centerpieces, each vying for prominence.

But after long years of disuse, they were unified in decay. Sapling-sized trees sprouted from their roofs, their roots reaching down grimy walls in search of dirt. Windows were cracked and missing. Once vivid paint had faded to pastels.

At Harris's command, two scouts ran ahead, keeping to the sidewalks. The rest of the teams hefted packs onto their shoulders and moved out, with Allison and Harris in the lead. Felix hung a step behind with Corporal Tillman. The buildings looked even worse up close. Paint peeled from the walls like birch bark, revealing spiderweb cracks in the underlying material. Something like mold inhabited every corner in colors ranging from orange to blue, like graffiti tags. Except these were the twin gangs of nature and time.

Harris shone his Niven light through a broken storefront window. A long counter ran parallel to a line of meter-tall chairs. The whole room had fallen to overgrowth. It looked like H. R. Giger had tried his hand at a bar rescue and failed miserably.

Harris sighed. "This place is a ghost town. We're not going to find anyone here."

Felix peered into the building next door. "This one looks like a souvenir shop. Look at all the kitsch lying around." He disappeared through the tall yet narrow doorway.

"Felix, wait," Harris said, but he was a second too late. "Tillman."

"Yes, sir." The corporal brought his M-118 to the ready and was about to slip through the door when Felix reappeared. Atop his head was a double-brimmed hat in a garish yellow with unknown characters printed under the bottom brim. He held up his arms to display either an improbably long T-shirt with four sleeves, or a comically defective wind sock.

"Look, guys! Alien schlock!"

"Not exactly your size, is it?"

Felix held it up to his chest. Extra sleeves aside, it was much too narrow, even for him. "Wow, these guys must have been like giant walking sticks." Felix took in a panorama of the area. "You know, this place kind of reminds me of Orlando. Well, the part that isn't underwater."

Allison knelt down to get a better look at the writing printed vertically down the shirt.

"Do you recognize the script, ma'am?"

"No, but it might be stylized." She took out her pad and turned it to scan the shirt. "Ridgeway to Prescott."

Her com officer answered from orbit. "Go ahead, Captain."

"I'm streaming you a vid image with a language sample. Can you and *Maggie* read it?"

"This will take a minute." Prescott set the line to the hold music. "Fly Me to the Moon," the Doris Day rendition. "*Maggie*'s 93 percent sure it isn't one of the buoy languages, ma'am. We have no idea what it says."

"Okay, thank you." Allison rubbed the base of her neck and groaned. She looked at the sky, while her inner field researcher had it out with her inner starship commander. Her two selves had conflicting priorities.

"No one to talk to. Can't read the language. This survey's starting to smell like a bust."

"I hate to say so, ma'am, but I have to agree." Felix looked through the broken window of the shop he'd just pilfered from. A stray glint caught off of a familiar clear sphere. "Oh, look, a snow globe." He turned it over and shook it, sending tan specs churning through the tiny model of the city. "Hmm, make that a sand globe."

"Sand globe?" Allison looked at the trinket. "There aren't any deserts on this planet; the land masses are too small. Why would they make sandstorm souvenirs?"

"Maybe they were being ironic," Harris said.

"Or maybe . . ." Felix scrunched up his forehead. "Maybe this isn't their planet. The other habitable planet is arid. It also has lower gravity, which would explain their height."

Allison nodded. Once Felix said it, the answer was obvious. "We're on the wrong planet. This place was just a tourist trap. How long until *Maggie* and *Bucephalus* swing back around?"

Harris's eyes seemed to lose focus while he consulted his implant. "They'll be overhead in less than ten minutes, ma'am. We could catch them on this orbit if we call in the shuttles for an evac."

"Nah, there's no rush. We can walk back and save them some fuel." She turned to face the rest of the teams. "Turn around, people. We're going back to the shuttles. We'll collect more flora samples on the way back."

"Whoa, hold up—" Harris looked startled.

Felix was instantly concerned. Startled was not in his friend's standard inventory of reactions. "Tom, what's wrong?"

"Gargoyle platforms on the far side of the planet just picked something up."

"Where? Land? Ocean?"

"No, orbit."

"That's not good. What is it?"

"I can't tell. Their sensors are optimized for look-down, shoot-down. Whatever they picked up was spillover."

"Show me your feed, Tom."

Harris pulled a flexible tactical screen from a pants pocket and unrolled it. The clear plastic went opaque and started scrolling raw sensor data. To everyone else, it looked like stereo instructions printed in Wingdings font. But Felix read them like a children's book: a children's book about the monster hiding under the bed.

Felix's face went even paler than normal. "It's a hyperspace window. Somebody's trying to sneak up behind us."

Harris wasted no time. "*Bucephalus*, Harris. Break out the good china. We've got company."

CHAPTER 35

Maximus marched onto the bridge, his bridge, and sat down. "Set Condition One. Tactical, I need to know who just snuck in our back door."

"We're working, Captain, but the orbital overlook platforms are the only assets we have on the far side, and they can't give us much."

"Probes?"

"We can orbit one into line of sight in sixteen minutes, but if we do that, the bogey will know they're blown."

"Hold on to the probe. Let them think they have the drop on us."

"Yes, sir."

"Com, get *Magellan*'s XO on the whisker laser."

Gruber's bust coalesced to Maximus's left. "Go ahead, *Bucephalus*."

"Commander, our orbital assets have detected a hyperspace window on the planet's far side. Mr. Fletcher has confirmed it. We're not alone."

"Did you ID the bogey yet, sir?"

"No, in fact we have almost no information on the target at all. Our platforms aren't pointed in the right direction, and retasking them would announce that we're looking for them."

"Nothing at all? Not even IR or a mass estimate?"

"Nope, nothing at all. Does that sound like anyone you know?"

Gruber's mind had been leaning in that direction as well. "I'm afraid so. If we take Mr. D'armic at his word, then the fuzzy anomaly is our only suspect in the massacre."

"And if they've followed us here, it probably isn't to swap cheesecake recipes."

"No, sir. To put it mildly."

"Ready your ship for action as best you can, Commander. Make sure your shield dish is facing the bogey before the shooting starts. It will give you some protection. *Bucephalus* will take point to cover you, but tell your helmsman not to drift outside of our defensive envelope."

"Understood, Captain."

An alert siren called out from the tactical station. "Sir, the Gargoyles have just picked up something making planet-fall."

"The bogey?"

"No, sir. They have hard tracking on it, and it's tiny. Less than thirty meters long, probably a shuttle."

"They're going after our teams on the ground," Gruber said.

Maximus's hand gripped the arms of his chair. "Tactical, can we send reinforcements?"

"No, sir. We've already passed our launch window for this orbit."

Something not unlike despair fell over Gruber's face. "Then Ridgeway is on her own."

"Not alone, Commander," Maximus said. "I've got bored marines on the surface. There's nothing as dangerous as bored marines."

Harris watched the alien drop-ship through the scope of his M-118. Even under magnification, it looked little bigger than a bird. The rifle's range finder gave him distance and velocity numbers. They were coming in hot.

"Fast-mover coming in hot from the east. Eight minutes, ten at best. Give me some options, people."

Corporal Tillman was the first to jump in. "The assault shuttle has air-to-air combat capabilities. Have Simmons dust off and intercept. He can draw them off, maybe even destroy them if he's lucky."

"And if he's not, we lose our ride back to *Bucephalus*." Harris looked at Allison. "Can we all fit in your shuttle?"

"I'm afraid not. Even if we ditched all the equipment and you left your toys behind, we'd still be short a seat."

"Including my pilot?"

"Of course it—" Allison shivered as the implication of the question struck her. "Right. Without your pilot, we might be able to make enough room if no one minds being friendly."

"If it came to that, getting friendly would be the least of our problems. Still, it doesn't seem like a good risk. We can deal with their drop-ship once it's on the ground. I'm going to tell Simmons to make like a hole in the forest. I suggest your pilot do the same."

Allison nodded. Harris scanned the area, looking for defensible positions to stash his civilians. One of the spires caught his eye.

He pointed to the looming structure. "Corporal Tillman, I bet you and Lyska can't schlep into sniper position in that tower before our guests arrive."

"I had no idea you were such a poor gambler, sir."

"You'd better go collect, then."

Tillman and Lyska saluted and disappeared into the grass. "All right, everyone else dig in. Implanted coms only from this point on."

The teams spent several tense minutes in silence. Harris's people were busy checking their weapons and adjusting the fit of their armor, while Allison's people were busy keeping fear from eating what was left of their wits. To his credit, Felix kept it together and even helped the marines build a makeshift firebase in front of the bar. After the longest eight minutes any of them had lived through, time ran out.

Harris shot Felix and Allison a reassuring smile. *Here they come. Let's roll.* With that, Harris and the rest of his fire team switched on their active camo and became mirages.

The drop-ship came into view overhead. Its hull was black as deep space and shaped like an armored fish from a long-forgotten ocean. It made one lazy circle around the area, hunting for the best LZ before settling into the courtyard with a whisper.

A heavy plate slid aside silently. Shadows poured out the door and darted in different directions, taking up positions. They were fast, but not unnaturally so. As soon as the last shadow exited, the door swiped shut and the drop-ship returned to the sky.

They have adaptive camouflage, too? Allison asked with a thought.

Sure looks that way, Harris replied. He ducked back behind the improvised wall and held his rifle over the top. The scope fed an image and ranging data into OLED contacts, letting him see without exposing his valuable head to return fire.

Oh, crap.

What's wrong?

I can see where they should be from the grass trails, but I can't get a good range and lock. Tillman, is your range finder locking them up?

Negative, LT. That's a negative lockup. We'll have to sight the old-fashioned way.

Great. What could jam a laser?

Meta materials, Felix thought. *They bend visible light around themselves and make anything inside effectively invisible.*

Yeah, but aren't they supposed to only work up to a few cubic centimeters?

Maybe these guys don't know about centimeters. It might even be how they cloak the mother ship.

They're sure in a hurry, Lyska said from his spotter's perch with Tillman. *They aren't even covering each other.*

Lyska was right. The shadows charged forward heedlessly with none of the practiced, deliberate movements of a trained squad. They were either supremely confident or embarrassingly sloppy. Then, as one, they stopped moving and settled into positions just over a hundred meters in front of where Harris's and Allison's teams sat.

One of the shadows stood ramrod straight in the middle of the boulevard. It threw back a shroud with a flutter and became visible for the first time. It was enormous; the purple grass that came up to Harris's waist barely covered the creature's thigh. Every square centimeter of the beast's bulk looked sharp, like a bipedal ox coated in razor blades. The most striking feature was the eyes. They were placed wide, facing forward, a hallmark of predators the galaxy over. But, more to the point, they glowed the bright crimson of freshly spilled blood.

Wow, somebody could use eye drops, Felix said.

Why are they glowing?

Cybernetic, has to be.

Wonderful. Harris's train of thought was broken by a booming voice that sounded like a building implosion. "Humans, I am Zek'nel of the Turemok Pacification Force. You are hereby restrained under suspicion of the geocides of Culpus-Alam and Okim. Throw down your weapons and walk forward with your appendages clearly visible. You have twenty rakims to obey, or we will force your compliance."

Tillman spoke up. *I have a clear shot, LT. Permission to fire?*

Hold fire, Tillman. Bucephalus, *Harris. We've been issued an ultimatum to surrender by enemy forces. Requesting permission to go weapons-free.*

Tom, they're moving to flank us. Felix pointed to their left where three shadows slowly circled around.

Units two and three, spread out to counter them. Bucephalus, *this is Harris, permission to fire?* Bucephalus*?* Static answered him. He switched channels and tried again. More static. *Shit! We're being jammed.*

Out of the corner of his eye, Harris saw Felix looking at Jacqueline. She'd drawn her knees to her chest and was taking deep long breaths to calm herself. Felix's worry for her was almost palpable.

We're running out of time. I'll try to buy you some. Felix stood before Harris could reach out to stop him. "Whoa, time-out there, sir."

"Felix, sit down!" Harris barked in a harsh whisper, but Felix brushed him off.

"You wish to surrender, human?"

"No, I just wanted to know what a *rakim* is."

"It is our smallest standard unit of time."

"Like a second? Well, how many seconds are in twenty rakims?"

The giant, pointy alien had been thrown off his rhythm. "I don't know, exactly. How long is a second?"

"One Mississippi."

Now Zek'nel was really confused. "A 'Mississippi' is equal to a second?"

"No, it . . . never mind. Why don't you count out the rakims?"

"Why don't you just surrender now?"

"Now wait one sec . . . rakim. You said we had twenty rakims. Are you going to give us twenty or not?"

"You've already had seventeen."

"Yeah, but that was before we knew what they were. You could have been talking about magic beans for all we knew."

"All right, fine. But this delay is pointless, human." The Turemok set his feet and crossed his arms in annoyance. "Twenty . . . nineteen . . . eighteen . . ."

Harris shook his head and used the time. *Captain Ridgeway, I can't raise the* Bucephalus. *The decision falls to you. May we fire?*

Allison's voice filled his head. *You want me to order your men to kill these . . . people, without even talking to them?*

"Seventeen . . ."

They've already done the talking, ma'am.

"Sixteen . . ."

Please, ma'am, the tactical situation is getting worse. We can't wait.

"Fifteen . . . fourteen . . ."

Harris and the rest of the unseen marines stared at Allison while the conflict played out inside her head.

"Thirteen . . . ," the monster said. "Ah, what comes after thirteen?"

"Oh, that's a tricky one. It's twelve," Felix said helpfully.

"Why isn't it *twoteen*?"

"I don't know, to be honest. It's just always been twelve."

"Twelve, thank you . . . eleven . . ."

Something in Allison shifted ever so quietly. *We're supposed to be peaceful explorers.*

Harris dipped his head. *I know, ma'am. But we didn't choose this. They did.*

"Ten . . . Nine . . ."

Ma'am, your orders?

Allison's eyes hardened. *Lieutenant, light them up.*

Yes, ma'am. Sniper team, take your shot.

From a hair over eight hundred meters away and nine stories up, Tillman fired. Before the sound of the shot even reached him, a 9.6-millimeter, 485-grain, antimaterial bullet struck Zek'nel, passed completely through his chest, and out the front with a puff of turquoise blood.

He blinked and then started looking around for the shot's origin.

Felix was troubled by the alien's blasé reaction to being hit by fifteen thousand joules of kinetic energy. *Um, don't they traditionally fall down now?*

Harris shook his head with a mixture of disbelief and admiration. *Tough bastard. Captain Ridgeway, take your team and fall back inside the building. Rifle team, weapons free. Fire at will.*

CHAPTER 36

Three hundred kilometers above, the Turemok cruiser dropped its sheath, revealing a design of such evil, such distilled menace, its mere presence had driven lesser beings to madness.

In the face of such an opponent, only a man of infinite bravery, or a complete idiot, would stand his ground. So it should come as little surprise that Maximus listened with growing boredom as Vel Noric issued the now-familiar ultimatum.

"Therefore, your vessels are ordered to submit to restraint for the geocide of—"

"Yes, yes," Maximus interrupted. "We've already been through this once with one of your frontier managers. Now look, Mr. . . . Noric, was it?"

"*Vel* Noric. *Vel* is my rank, Captain."

"Groovy. Anyway, Vel, we've already done this song and dance in the last system. Your guy realized we couldn't have been responsible with one look at our ship."

"Your point, Captain?"

"I was coming to that. Since we didn't do it, that leaves you."

Noric's image recoiled. "That's preposterous."

"Is it? We know you were there. Your ship was hiding deeper in the system the whole time. *Magellan* spotted you. We've got her sensor logs. So I guess I'm putting *you* under arrest for the Solonis B massacre."

Noric snorted unpleasantly, a low, rhythmic sound. Maximus decided it was either a laugh or a hairball. "A Turemok cruiser, surrender to you? My dear captain, you must be joking."

"I'm a very funny guy, Vel. So funny, I can't help but laugh at my own jokes." Maximus cleaned a bit of dirt from under a fingernail. "I'm not laughing, Vel."

"Your species is barely out of the nest! The only advanced technology you possess was stolen from a lowly warning beacon. Please, amuse me further and tell us what weapons you have capable of forcing my capitulation."

Maximus smiled coolly. "I'll show you mine if you show me yours."

"Very well. I look forward to your interrogation, human." Noric's face disappeared.

A short alert chime came from the tactical station. "Bandit One's power output just spiked, sir. I expect they're charging energy weapons."

"Launch countermeasures, full spread. Is *Magellan* in our shadow?"

"Yes, sir, but she's bigger than we are, and our decoys' EM signatures won't match."

"Make sure some decoys drift to cover her anyway."

"Yes, sir. Launching now."

A tiny rumble ran through the hull as dozens upon dozens of scuba tank–sized CM canisters blew into space. As soon as they cleared their launch tubes, gas charges lit off and inflated each canister like an airbag. A tenth of a second later, over three hundred Mylar balloons the size of city buses floated in the space surrounding *Bucephalus*. Each was a false radar signature and a mirror to reflect lasers.

"Do we have a lock on Bandit One?" Maximus asked.

"Affirmative. Hard lock."

"Feed telemetry to missiles one through five and prepare to ripple fire."

"Prep missiles one through five for ripple fire, aye. Telemetry uploading . . . telemetry accepted. Missiles one through five read *Active*. Launch control is green."

Maximus bared his teeth. "Tactical, fire."

"Firing now." The deck under their feet shuddered from the recoil of the launches. Each SSM-1 weighed nearly fifty metric tons. Magnetic rails kicked them out of their tubes at three hundred KPH, enough to get them clear of the hull before lighting their motors.

"Missiles away, sir. Time to impact, seven-eight seconds."

A tangible excitement infused the bridge as the missiles lit off in sequence. Every eye watched the master plot while the outbound birds' speed climbed faster than smack-talk before a pro wrestling match.

"Missiles are tracking on internal radar. Lock is good."

Something wasn't sitting right with Maximus. "Status of Bandit One?"

"Power levels are still elevated. My guess is they're charging capacitors."

"All right, but they have birds incoming. Why aren't they trying to evade?"

"Unknown, sir. Time to impact now three-five seconds."

"I don't like this." Maximus absently tugged on an earlobe. "Tactical, prep missiles six through fifteen."

"Prep missiles six through fifteen, aye, sir. Thirty seconds to impact."

The seconds fell by as the machines of annihilation powered closer to their intended target. Then, in a patch of space directly ahead of the lead missile, a hole appeared.

"Missile One is gone!" shouted the tac officer.

"Did it detonate?" Maximus asked.

"No, sir. It's just gone. Wait . . . there was an energy spike localized ahead of—"

Maximus groaned. "A hyperspace window rigged for point defense. Nice trick."

As he said it, the hole shifted position and swallowed up missiles two through five in rapid succession.

"Tactical, set missiles six through fifteen for simultaneous launch and fire!"

"Aye, sir. Firing now." The *Bucephalus* lurched nearly ten meters to port as five hundred tons of missiles kicked free of her starboard side. They screamed mutely through space toward their target. Fifty seconds later, ten windows opened and swallowed them whole.

A chime sounded at the com officer's station. "Bandit One is hailing, sir."

Maximus shielded his eyes with a hand and sighed deep and long. "Put him through."

Vel Noric's triumphant face solidified in the air. "Thank you for the evening's entertainment, Captain. It was most gratifying. Now let me show you *mine*."

Harris dropped behind cover and ejected the empty magazine from his rifle. *I need a mag over here!*

Heads up, LT. One of the men in Unit One lofted a slim box in Harris's direction. He picked it out of the air and rammed it home.

The ammo supply was holding, for now. The marines' M-118 rifles fired heavy, guided rounds. Each bullet could home in on the rangefinder beam of its gun, or any other gun in the squad. Their large size was a double-edged sword, however. When they connected, they did tremendous damage, but each mag carried fewer of them.

Guided rounds seldom missed, so this wasn't typically a problem, but their enemy wore stealth cloaks that simply diverted the rangefinder beams. Harris's men were trying to hit shadows by eye, wasting precious bullets in the process.

Their Turemok opponents suffered no such ammunition shortage. They were using lasers.

A flash from a beam pulse exploded the masonry right above Harris's head. Tiny, white-hot marble shards pinged off his helmet and neck.

"Ow!" He danced a little samba of pain as a sliver of red-hot rock fell down his shirt and burned a line straight down his back. *Everyone, keep your heads down. Only show them your scopes.*

But then we can't see clearly enough to hit them, LT.

I know, just put enough rounds in the air to pin them down for the sniper team.

Tillman and Lyska were the only bright spot in the whole boondoggle. While the aliens could absorb center-mass hits, headshots still did the trick. They'd already downed three Turemok, but without a proper lock, they needed time to line up the shots. Time the Turemok were motivated not to give them.

Felix grabbed his shoulder. *Tom, look, they've deployed something. Drones maybe.*

Harris lifted his rifle and sighted downrange. Sure enough, three dozen faceted orbs the size of softballs floated a few meters above the ground. They moved lazily toward the firebase. Harris zeroed in on one and cracked off a round. It shattered like hollow glass. *Disco balls. Now it's a party. Keep the pressure on the enemy units.*

The orbs continued their slow advance as the marines tried to scare their opponents stiff long enough for the sniper team to deliver the coup de grâce. Without his notice, an orb took up position just above and behind Harris's back.

"Look out!" Felix kicked Harris in the side with all his strength, which moved him less than a foot. But it was enough. A flash explosion erupted in the exact spot where Harris's head had been. Felix grabbed a chunk of concrete and knocked the silver orb out of the air.

What the hell? They're armed?

No, Tom, they're reflectors. Don't you see? They let them shoot at angles.

Man down! Unit One's leader shouted into the implanted com. *Conway's hurt, shot through the stomach.*

Harris cursed. *Shoot the disco balls. They're using them to flank us. Corpsman, fall back with Conway into the building.*

He pulled his sidearm out of its holster and threw it to Felix. *Here, I want you shoot any that slip past.*

Okay. How do I do that?

Harris stared at his friend for a moment. *Seriously?*

Yes, Tom, seriously. I grew up in a city where a plastic bubble was the only thing holding the air in. Firearms weren't encouraged.

Harris grunted. *All right, this is a gun*—he pointed at the muzzle—*and this is the boo-boo end.*

I know that! How do I shoot it? There's no trigger.

When do you think we are, the Old West? It's a link trigger. Set a command word, like fire *or* shoot.

Shoot*? So all I have to do is think,* Shoot—

The gun flashed with a bark that left Felix's ears ringing. A ten-millimeter round drilled into the dirt between Harris's legs, leaving a tiny, smoking crater.

Holy crap! Tom, are you okay?

Harris gritted his teeth and gingerly pointed the muzzle in a more productive direction. *See, you've got it. Now, if you'll shoot at the disco balls instead of* my *balls, we can stay friends.*

One of Tillman's rounds connected with a Turemok head left carelessly peering at the firebase. *That's four. You guys have to catch up.*

Harris smiled. The tide of battle was turning in their favor. Provided the ammo held, they might just push through to—

Contact north, coming in hot. It was Lyska in the tower. *It's the drop-ship.*

Bearing?

They're charging our position.

Harris was surprised it had taken as long as it did for them to get smart and call in air support. *Sniper team, evacuate immediately.*

Roger, sir. Bugging out.

To Harris's right, the drop-ship streaked into view on its attack run. Although the laser wasn't visible, its path most certainly was. The beam cut a straight line of vaporized marble and steel through the third floor of the tower. The angle of the attack sliced the building diagonally. Groaning like a rockslide, it slid and then collapsed into a heap. A cloud of gray smoke rolled into the air.

Sniper team, status?

. . .

Tillman, Lyska, report!

. . .

Felix shook his head gravely.

Harris's grip tightened around his rifle, as if his hands wrung the very necks of his enemy. *We're done playing two-hand touch. Everyone, switch over to paint rounds. Spread them out good, and then fall back into the building.*

Harris reached into his left shoulder pocket and pulled out what looked like a standard rifle magazine, except it was bright green. He swapped it out and held his M-118 overhead, lined up with the closest Turemok soldier, and fired. He moved on and fired at the next position, and the next. The rest of his remaining rifle team did the same.

Tom, this isn't a training field. What good are paint rounds?

You'll see in about two minutes, Felix. Fall back with the others, and pop any of those balls that try to follow our retreat.

Felix didn't need coaxing and ran for the safety of the building. Harris fired the last of his paint rounds and switched back to the standard magazine. He waited, laying down cover fire until the last of his men had reached the building. A glancing beam burned the unit patch off his right shoulder as he ran for cover.

Leaning against the inside wall, Harris called up the menu for the Gargoyle platforms overhead. Platform seven was only five degrees from apogee. At his command, it went hot. He selected *Antipersonnel* from the list of ammunition modes. When the lockup tone went steady, Harris smiled viciously.

"Fire," Harris said aloud, not caring who heard.

Two hundred and fifty kilometers over the heads of their foes, OOP number seven took a millisecond to authenticate the origin of the orders it just received. Satisfied that Lieutenant Harris was who he claimed to be, gas thrusters fired, making a tiny adjustment to better align itself with the target. Electric motors whirled, and twelve barrels arranged in two contra-rotating bundles of six started to spin.

Once the revs had built sufficiently, thirty-millimeter caseless rounds, each weighing almost a kilogram, poured into the feed. They came scorching out the muzzles at six thousand KPH, nearly five thousand rounds per minute. The recoil was intense enough to push the platform backward at nearly seventy KPH.

At the heart of each round was the same guidance system used in their standard rifle bullets. All they needed were aim points, conveniently enough, provided by the transmitters in the paint rounds Harris's squad had just fired.

After a five-second burst, OOP seven went silent, awaiting further orders as it cooled. The demonic torrent of metal spikes actually *accelerated* as the planet's gravity well pulled them into a terminal embrace.

Harris's spirits were much improved. "Good work, people. Just hold them off for the next ninety seconds."

"And then what?" Allison asked.

"And then get your head down and cover your ears. Corpsman, how's Conway?"

"I gave him a sucker, sir, so he should feel better shortly, but the laser went straight through his liver and collapsed a lung. It cauterized as it went, so there's no bleeding, but he needs surgery. Soon."

"He's not a kid going in for a checkup," Felix said. "A sucker hardly seems helpful."

"It is when it's swimming in painkillers derived from conch shell neurotoxin," replied the corpsman.

"Oh," Felix said. "Can I get one? I think I twisted an ankle."

"No."

A laser pulse sent shrapnel flying off the back wall with a sharp crack, reminding everyone they were still in a firefight. Harris ducked out and threw half a magazine downrange. *Rifle team, keep them pinned down. Forget conserving ammo—fire everything.*

They responded, spraying bullets indiscriminately, utterly disregarding everything their instructors had drilled into them. After a mad minute of nearly continuous fire, their barrels smoldered from the heat, and the magazines finally ran dry. Harris's countdown had fallen to fifteen seconds.

Everyone, get down, Harris commanded. Raising the empty rifle over his head, he stood cautiously in front of the shattered window. "Whoa. Hold up for a . . . rakim!" Harris shouted.

Zek'nel threw open his shroud and stood, a hand clutching the chest wound from Tillman's opening shot. "Yes, human? Do you finally wish to surrender? I expect your little slings are out of pebbles by now."

"Actually, I just wanted to ask you something. Do any of you boys have an umbrella?"

"No."

"That's too bad, because it's about to rain." With that, Harris dropped to his knees and threw his hands over his ears.

Even at six thousand KPH, the burst of fire from the Gargoyle platform seemed to take an eternity to arrive, but arrive it did. Hundreds of drops of iron rain fell upon the courtyard. Each round contained an explosive charge with a fuse set to detonate three meters above the ground in the antipersonnel mode.

The world was consumed by a rapid-fire sound like standing on the floor of a burning fireworks warehouse. After exactly five seconds, the hellish noise and light display ended, replaced by a deadly silence.

"Is it over?" Allison asked.

Harris lifted his riflescope out the window to survey the results of his handiwork. The courtyard had been reduced to a ruined, cratered landscape. Brushfires burned in a dozen places.

"Uh, yeah. I think we got them."

Felix peeked out of the doorway. "Looks like my yard back home. Except for the burning grass, of course."

"We're clear. Rifle team, switch to sidearms and secure an LZ for the shuttles. Captain Ridgeway, call your pilot and tell him we're going to need an evac pronto."

Allison leaned in to whisper to Harris. "What about your men in the tower?"

"I'm not getting any com signal, which means their backpacks were destroyed. Those packs can take a lot more abuse than a human body. They're buried under who knows how many tons of debris. We'll have to retrieve the bodies later."

Allison's head dipped. "I understand, but they deserve better."

"They always do." Harris looked out into the smoke and fires of the decimated courtyard. "C'mon, move your people out. We have to dust off before they send reinforcements."

"Yeah, then what?"

"Then we hope Captain Tiberius is having as much luck as we are."

CHAPTER 37

He wasn't.

The bridge rocked as an x-ray laser punctured *Bucephalus*'s number-three coolant tank. Superheated reactor coolant boiled away into space.

"Damage report."

"Sir, engineering reports the fusion reactor is going critical."

"Shut it down."

"We lost half our auxiliary batteries in the first salvo, sir. If we shut down, we don't have enough reserves to restart."

"Which is a less immediate problem than exploding. Shut it down. Now."

"Aye, sir."

The bridge lights flickered as main power went down and switched to emergency reserves.

"Get damage control teams down to the damaged coolant tank and get a patch welded in."

A chime came from the com station. "Sir, Bandit One—"

"Yes, yes. They're hailing to gloat. Put the Vel through."

The face of Vel Noric again appeared on the *Bucephalus*'s bridge. Even without lips, it was clear he was smiling. "Captain Tiberius, my sensor interpreter tells me that your ship has lost primary power. Isn't it about time we end this farce? Or do you intend to play this out to your inevitable destruction?"

"My destruction would be yours. I am obligated to warn you that all Earth vessels carry one metric ton of a substance we call Corbomite, which, when subjected to—"

"*Star Trek*. Season one, episode ten: 'The Corbomite Maneuver.' "

"Oh." Maximus slumped in his chair. "You've seen it, then."

"I have the entire series on crystal. Anything else, or can we get down to business?"

Maximus swallowed his pride, itself a superhuman feat.

"Your terms, Vel?"

"My terms are your personal surrender, Captain. Boarding craft will be sent with commandeering forces to secure your vessels. You and Captain Ridgeway will return for interrogation aboard my vessel. Your seconds will assume command, under the direct supervision of my troops."

"Captain Ridgeway is not aboard *Magellan*. She is leading the survey expedition on the surface."

Something caught the Vel's attention. He leaned over as a much smaller Turemok whispered into his ear.

"Interesting. It may give you some consolation to learn that Captain Ridgeway's ground team somehow managed to neutralize the force sent to collect them. Quite the achievement, but ultimately foolhardy. Now her entire team will have to stand for the murder of my crew."

"If I know my people, they're not coming back up without a fight." Maximus smirked. "You'll have to stick your hand back in that garbage disposal."

"You will find, Captain, that all you need to make uncooperative beings behave properly is appropriate motivation." Then Vel Noric's face disappeared.

Maximus looked at his com officer. "What happened? Did we lose the connection?"

"No, sir. The link was terminated at the source."

"Sir!" shouted the tac officer. "Bandit One is moving off."

"Show me." The center holo reverted to the main plot. The planet sat at the center, with twin white icons representing *Bucephalus* and *Magellan* in a low orbit. Ringing the planet were twelve smaller green icons indicating the Gargoyle platforms. The flashing red icon of the Turemok cruiser built up speed as it moved into a higher orbit.

"Now where the hell do they think they're going?"

"Shouldn't we try to escape, Captain?"

"How? Without main power we can't open a hyper window. And our hyperspace tech is dirt-side playing Indiana Jones."

The red icon executed a hairpin turn and then accelerated headlong toward the planet below.

"What in the name of . . ." In a moment of horror, Maximus read into the mind of his foe. "Oh no. Com, are our links to the surface still being jammed?"

"Ah, no, sir. The jamming lifted when Bandit One moved off."

"Tell them to make orbit right now. Vel Noric is about to drill through the planet."

The first earthquake yanked the ground out from under their feet. Everyone hit the dirt, except Private Conway, but only because he was already lying down.

"Ow," Felix said once he caught his breath. He tried to stand while the ground continued its violent undulations. His eyes tried to fix on something, anything, but the world danced and jostled in front of him. The city's skyline swayed like stalks of wheat in a windstorm. No matter how tough they were constructed, something would fail sooner or later.

"We need to get in the center of the courtyard, as far from the buildings as possible." Felix could barely hear his own voice over the symphony of destruction. A low rumble groaned up from the ground in all directions. Shearing metal, cracking marble, and shattering glass punctuated the air from the sides and above.

Harris nodded from the head of the collapsible stretcher occupied by PFC Conway.

Allison waved an arm to get Harris's attention. "Are the shuttles in the air yet?"

"Yes, ETA, under a minute."

"Good. Tell them not to go gears down. It'll be safer to hover."

"Understood."

Suddenly from the east, a red glow fell across the quivering city. Felix turned to see the cause, and immediately regretted doing so. Past the horizon, a gargantuan, red-hot inverted cone reached into the sky, like a crimson mountain balancing on the point of its summit. It was so large that his field of vision could scarcely contain the entire thing. It grew larger even as he watched.

Felix was not the only one to notice. Everyone stared at the spectacle in speechless horror, except PFC Conway, who was thoroughly uninterested in anything beyond rolling the piece of narcotic-soaked candy around on his tongue.

Wish I were that relaxed, Felix thought.

"What the hell is that?" Harris finally managed.

"The exit wound. That's mantle material being ejected by the collapsing of the tunnel the hyper window dug."

"We should leave. Now."

"You think?" Felix waved his arms in exasperation. "I was considering buying one of these distressed properties to flip."

A sharp sound like a branch snapping echoed, and a once proud tower fell to the ground with a crash.

"Where are those shuttles?" Allison asked, panic encroaching on her smooth voice. As if to answer, the high-pitched whine of turbine blades pierced the din engulfing the courtyard. The teams looked up as one to witness their salvation drift down from on high.

The shuttles dipped close to the ground, their lift engines pressing down a bed of what little purple grass remained. The rear doors dropped and everyone clambered aboard. Three seats in the back of the marines shuttle had to be folded up to secure PFC Conway's stretcher. The rest of the marines played the fastest game of musical chairs in recorded history and buckled in.

Harris moved into the cockpit. "Get us out of here, Simmons."

"What about the hostile drop-ship?"

"Are you kidding? He's long gone if he has any sense. Point for the black and floor it."

The shuttle pitched up, and the acceleration shoved everyone into their seats. They climbed for altitude as the air-breathing turbines howled with effort.

The pilot turned to look at Harris. "Sir, *Magellan*'s shuttle just veered off."

"Huh? Where?"

Harris's com crackled to life. "Lieutenant Harris, this is Ridgeway."

"This is Harris. Can I ask what you're doing, ma'am?"

"Lieutenant Dorsett tells me you need to level off and turn to heading two-seven-niner."

Harris glanced down at the flight instruments, and his jaw went slack. "That's crazy! She wants us to fly *toward* the giant lava fountain of death?"

Felix shouted from his chair. "No, Tom! Jackie's right. Think Mount Saint Helens, except a million times worse."

"That's why we're flying away from it, Felix."

"Tom, *listen*." Felix strained against his harness. "An explosion that big is going to send out a huge shock wave. If it hits us from the side, it'll crush the hull. The only way to survive is to go at it head-on."

"You want me to play chicken with a shock wave?"

"Yes. These shuttles are designed to handle transonic shock waves nose-on. They do it every time they break the sound barrier."

Harris held Felix's gaze for a tense moment.

"I know I'm right, Tom."

"Fine. Let's just hope you and your girlfriend know what you're talking about. Simmons, level off and turn to two-seven-niner."

Felix looked at his feet and started to mope.

"Oh, c'mon. Don't be like that, Felix. We wouldn't be doing this if I didn't trust you."

"She's not my girlfriend."

"Really, child? Is that what the frowny face is about?"

This earned a round of laughter from the rifle team despite their stress, or perhaps because of it. The two shuttles cruised toward the expanding red nightmare, their cabins hushed and filling with sweat.

An alert chime broke the silence as the turbulence avoidance radar went off.

"Brace yourselves! Here it comes!"

The shock wave struck the shuttle like it was a hockey puck, jarring loose a case of MREs that bounced around the cabin, which made them only slightly more dangerous than if the troops had eaten them. The cockpit lit up with warning lights as Simmons struggled to keep the shuttle straight and level against the violence being done to its wings.

After several rolling, nauseating moments, the bucking subsided, and ragged sighs escaped from the passengers. Except PFC Conway, who believed he was on a roller coaster at Six Flags Beijing.

"Let's go again!"

"No!" everyone else shouted in unison.

"Simmons, orbit, if you please," Harris said.

"You don't have to tell me twice, LT."

Directly ahead, Ridgeway's shuttle clawed for altitude. Simmons drifted to port to avoid getting caught in their wake vortices. As Felix watched through the window, the sky faded from cobalt blue, to navy, and finally to a deep black. The atmosphere glowed above the surface like a thin halo. Felix knew that soon the entire planet would be shrouded in ash and smoke, maybe for centuries. He felt hollow.

Harris sat up straight. "Heads up. We're not alone."

Felix could barely see it through the windscreens. The outline of a ship made itself known only by the hole it left in the backdrop of stars. But it was definitely big, and intensely menacing.

"The mother ship."

Their priorities straight, Harris's rifle team used the time to reload and rearm. Then they dug into the crumpled MRE boxes.

"Tom, how can you think about food at a time like this?" Felix asked.

"Simple. No one wants to be taken prisoner on an empty stomach. Who knows when we'll get our next meal?" Harris offered a small plastic bag to Felix. "Apple cobbler?"

CHAPTER 38

Both shuttles were captured without resistance. They had none to offer. Guards awaited them in the hangar. Their weapons and equipment were confiscated. Allison, Harris, Felix, Jacqueline, and the rest were led out as prisoners and fitted with thick, wire-weave belts. PFC Conway was taken to *Bucephalus* for treatment by a boarding craft full of Turemok soldiers. A short time later, the craft returned with a captive Captain Tiberius.

Three huge, armed Turemok led their prisoners through the wide halls of the cruiser. Felix tried to broadcast through his implant. *Can anyone read me?*

I read you, Felix, Harris said. *Welcome to the party line.*

Thank goodness. Why aren't they jamming us?

They may not know we have this capability.

Or they're eavesdropping, said Maximus, *waiting to hear our brilliant escape plan.*

Allison's voice cut in. *How's that coming along, by the way?*

Well, the first step to any successful escape is being captured so that you have something to escape from, said Maximus.

So we're still on Step 1, then.

Yup.

They walked in silence for a few moments.

I have an idea, thought Felix.

Well, let's hear it, kid, said Maximus.

Everyone needs to act like they're blind. This was followed by an awkward pause.

That's it?

Well, no. But I don't want to say the whole thing in case they're listening.

In his defense, Felix's ideas are usually pretty good, offered Harris.

Allison looked at Maximus. *What do you think, Captain?*

He was actually smiling. *I got nothing. Everybody, do what the nerd says.* Maximus stumbled blindly into a wall. "Ouch!"

One of the guards shoved Maximus roughly with the muzzle of his weapon. "Back in line, human."

"Sorry. It's just so dark in here."

Playing it up, one of the marines tripped over a length of conduit and spun around into a pratfall on the deck. He was grabbed and roughly dragged down the hall by a pair of guards until he found his feet.

At a bend, Harris walked straight into the wall and fell to the ground holding his nose. "Ahhh," he moaned.

The head guard grabbed him by the hair and pulled him to his feet. Harris let out a yelp.

"All right," barked the guard. "What's going on here?"

"Sorry, sir," said Felix. "It's just that it's so dark in here that we can't see past our noses."

"Don't play sports with me, human. There is plenty of light in here."

"For you, obviously. Your eyes must work with a different kind of light."

"Yes," the guard hissed, "I've heard about your inferior biologic eyes. They work on such a narrow spectrum, it can hardly be said they work at all."

"Yup, that's us. Maybe if we could put our hands on each other's shoulders?"

"Yes, fine, but no humor business. Remember, we can see just fine."

"Yes, sir, thank you, sir." Everyone took their cue and linked up.

Well, was that Step 2? thought Allison.

No, said Felix, *but it's definitely Step 1.5.*

Are we past the self-flagellation step? asked Harris.

Yes, Tom. Just give us an occasional stumble.

The human chain snaked its way down several more corridors until their march ended at a large, heavy door. Two of the junior guards took positions on either side and raised their weapons. The head guard pressed a claw into a small hole next to the door, which glowed green for a moment. The door snapped open with a click.

"All right, you sorry lot, Vel Noric has some questions for you. You would be wise to answer quickly. Inside!" He grabbed Jacqueline Dorsett and shoved her into the room. She lost her balance and fell hard onto the metal deck.

Felix nearly shot the guard a look that would wither a bridge abutment, but caught himself. He couldn't see, after all. *Are you all right, Jackie?*

Yes, fine. My elbow smarts a bit.

Unsure what to say, Felix rummaged around for a suitable cliché. He settled on, *They'll pay for that.*

That's great, killer, said Maximus, *but let's stay focused on your plan to spring us out of here for the time being.*

The rest of the group was herded into the room. It was dimly lit, but their eyes adjusted quickly. The room was large and nearly empty. In the center was an oversized metal chair made of all right angles. Airline seats in coach looked positively extravagant by comparison.

Sitting quietly in the far corner was a familiar-looking creature with a slight frame and mottled gray skin.

Allison was the first to spot him. "D'armic, is that you?"

"Yes, Allison Captain," replied the Lividite calmly.

"How did you get here?"

"This cruiser captured my vessel immediately after you departed from Okim."

"Your little pulse thingy didn't work on them either, huh?" asked Maximus.

"I did not have the opportunity to use it. They infected my computer with a slave protocol before the weapon was fully recharged. Once it was slaved, they simply shut down the EM cannon and remotely flew my vessel into their hangar."

"But why are they holding you if you're a member of their wildlife management corps?" asked Felix.

"It appears I am being held on the pretense of collaboration with your people in the destruction of Culpus-Alam and Okim."

"You can add another one to that list. They just ran through P3X117-e."

"That is most unfortunate."

"Why are they framing us for destroying planets, one of them with our own people on it?" asked Maximus.

"The Turemok are deeply suspicious of outsiders," D'armic said. "Coupled with your impressive rate of technological advancement over the last decade, they feel threatened by the human race, although they would never admit so publicly. I assume they plan to use this deception to convince the Assembly to take punitive action against Earth."

"What sort of *punitive action*?" said Maximus.

"The Treaty of Pu'Lan is quite explicit and inflexible. Any race convicted of geocide must have their home world likewise destroyed. An eye for an eye, as your Christians say."

Seconds rolled past as everyone tried to lift their jaws from the floor.

"Captain, this is all a bit much," quipped Jacqueline as she rubbed life back into her elbow. "I'd like to request a leave of absence, starting now."

"Sure, take all the time you need. I assume you'll be going home, then?"

"Yup, just in time for ski season."

"Well, send us back some pictures."

Maximus held his hand to his chin, trying to look thoughtful. "D'armic, those little hyper windows this ship used to soak up our missiles—how many of them can they open at once?"

"I don't know. Such capabilities are confidential."

"Well, you can take a guess, can't you?"

"Not really. There is no anecdotal data to extrapolate an estimate from with any reasonable expectation of accuracy."

That had been one too many syllables for Maximus. "Huh?"

"He means there aren't any rumors to make a guess from," interjected Felix.

"Ah." Maximus pondered this for a second. "Why not? I mean, they must tell war stories."

"Yes, of course," replied D'armic. "However, those legends are hundreds of years old."

"Hundreds? Are you saying the Turemok haven't seen action for centuries?"

"We have been at peace. Aside from law enforcement and small-scale antipiracy operations, their military has been unopposed for generations."

Harris stepped closer to the conversation. *That makes sense, sir. The troops we faced on the surface were, well, sloppy. They didn't stick to cover, they didn't use group tactics, they didn't even use their air asset until we pinned their ears back. Their stealth tech was the only thing keeping us from walking all over them. They leaned on it like a crutch.*

Maximus was quite happy now. *Thank you, Lieutenant. I think I know what to do once we get out of here.*

Care to share your brainstorm with the rest of the class? Allison asked.

Simple, they're inexperienced and complacent. We just have to give it to them faster than they can suck it.

Charming.

As Maximus smiled, and everyone else worried about his mental stability, a small hiss came from the ceiling. D'armic turned his head toward the ceiling and noticed a faint purple gas leaking into the room. He walked over to the vent and sniffed the air.

"Ah, I was wondering when this would happen."

"What?" asked Felix nervously. "Is it poison gas?"

"No, at least it shouldn't be to you. It is a Lividite mood drug—Terrorital, I believe." He backed away from the vent. "I should warn you, I will be paralyzed with fear soon."

"How soon?" asked Felix.

"About three of your minutes."

"Oh."

"Will it affect the rest of us?" asked Jacqueline.

"It's unlikely human physiology will react in the same way as mine."

"Why in heaven's name would your people develop a drug that terrifies its users? Who would want to take it?" asked Allison.

"We take it recreationally, usually before watching horror vids. Parents give it to children before going on the annual Heralix Day haunted-fungus-grove rides."

"I see," Allison said.

So, Felix, what's your next move? Maximus asked.

Well, I imagine we'll be interrogated before long.

And this is part of your plan?

It's a work in progress. Just stick to the blind ruse and follow my lead.

Harris snorted. *You're leading? I've seen you try to dance, Felix. It wasn't a dignified spectacle.*

Har-har, Tom.

The door clicked again. A shadowed figure took up almost the entire doorway. Looking straight at Maximus, it spoke. "My name is Vel Noric. One of your authors once wrote, 'Abandon all hope, ye who enter here.' Consider it my introduction. You can provide something useful to me: an admission of your crimes at Culpus-Alam, Okim, and Kulla. In exchange, I can give you relief from the anguish to come. Now, whom shall we start with?" He looked back at Maximus. "Captain Tiberius, if you would step forward so we may begin."

Remember, we're blind, thought Felix.

"I'd love to, Vel. Just point me in the right direction."

"The chair, if you please."

Maximus stared blankly at the ceiling. "What chair?"

"I see." Noric pressed a stud on his wrist. Everyone but Maximus fell to the ground writhing in agony so intense they could barely manage to scream. It took all of Maximus's discipline not to move to help them. Noric pressed the stud again, and the screams stopped.

This plan had better get good quick, kid, thought Maximus.

Felix strained to get onto all fours. *You're telling me.*

Maximus groped at the air with his hands. "What just happened? What was that screaming?"

"That was your companions being subjected to the first setting of your belts."

"Why? They didn't do anything."

"True, they didn't. You did, by defying my order to sit. This isn't my first Gomeltic hunt, human. A tough officer like you can probably endure quite a lot of pain, maybe enough to die, and are, therefore, useless for my purposes. But how long can you endure the pain of your companions? The chair, please."

"But I can't see the damn chair!"

Vel Noric looked at the nearest guard. "What's he talking about?"

"Oh, their eyes can't see in this light. Too primitive."

"Why didn't you say so?" Noric grinned. "Please, help our guest find his seat."

The head guard grabbed Maximus by the shoulders and roughly threw him into the chair. Noric leaned in uncomfortably close to Maximus's face and breathed. Maximus managed not to look him in the eye, but only just.

"Now, then, where were we?"

Felix stood up from the floor. "Um, Vel, if I may?"

This should be good, thought Harris.

"Yes? You wish to say something, human?"

"Yes, sir. I just wanted to say that I'm easily the most cowardly person here, but we humans rely on vision almost exclusively. So while I'm sure you are very scary and intimidating, it's not going to do you much good if we can't see you."

"He's right, you know," Maximus chimed in, mostly out of a genuine curiosity for what the nerd was going to do next. "I know you're standing near me right now, based on the smell alone, but I'm not all that scared, and I already saw your ugly mug over the video link."

In the background, D'armic started to whimper with fear. Allison tried to comfort him.

"And whatever you slipped the Lividite back there isn't working on us," Maximus said. "Maybe one of the guards could describe how intimidating you look so that I have a better idea."

The head guard perked up at Maximus's suggestion. "I did study literary composition, Vel."

"I don't think that will be necessary," Noric said.

"I received excellent marks for my lyrics."

"Yes, thank you."

"My instructor said my description of serenading my mate with a jelbow carcass under the green light of the twin moons nearly made her shed her scales," he said proudly.

"Shut up." Vel Noric looked to the guard by the door. "Go see if the lights can be adjusted to accommodate these creatures' . . . deficiencies."

"Yes, sir." He closed the door behind him. A few moments later the lights in the room cycled through a range of hues.

"Any results?" asked Noric.

"Afraid not," said Felix.

"Exactly what frequency range do your eyes work at?"

"Oh, I don't know. Not really my field," replied Felix. "You know what would work great?"

"I'm on needles and pins."

"We have these hand tools to see in the dark. We call them flashlights. There are a couple of them with the rest of the equipment you confiscated. Maybe if you brought them down here?"

"Fine, if that's what it's going to take to conduct a proper interrogation." Noric barked at the head guard, "Go recover the humans' flashing lights."

Maximus had to contain a sudden laugh. *You were right, Harris. His ideas are good. I'll take it from here, kid.* He shouted to the guard, "They're little silver cylinders with a lens at one end! You can't miss them!"

"I must say, you're being awfully affable about all this," Noric said.

"We just prefer to see what's going on is all. Life is kind of dull otherwise."

Noric put his hands on his hips. "Well, rest assured that the next few hours will be anything but dull for you."

"I'm sure you're right." Maximus smiled confidently.

Vel Noric stalked back and forth across the deck as they waited for the guard to return. After a few lengths, he waved his hands in front of the prisoners' faces trying to force a reaction. None forthcoming, he started to make what could safely be assumed were obscene Turemok gestures in their direction. Some aspects of immaturity were universal.

Everyone spread out, but slowly, Maximus said. *And keep a close eye on the flashlights. Try to stay out of their way. Marines, be ready to move on a moment's notice. First priority is the guards, followed by that bracelet the Vel is wearing.*

What's the signal? asked Harris.

Oh, you'll know.

As though he were reading from the same script, the door clicked open and the guard strode through, Niven lights in hand. He passed them to the Vel.

"How do I operate this device?"

"There's a button on the shaft. Just press it," Maximus said.

"Really, now?" Noric sounded suspicious, proving he wasn't quite as dense as neutron star matter. "This wouldn't be a deception, would it? Perhaps this is a weapon of some kind."

"It just makes light. For caves, blackouts, that sort of thing."

"That's good, because I am going to press this button"—he leveled the flashlight at Allison—"while pointing it at this female's head. Are you sure there isn't anything I should know?"

Maximus shook his head. "Nope."

"Very well." Noric grinned and pressed the button. Allison's eyes squinted against the light's intensity at such close range. But aside from washing out her skin tone a bit, she suffered no ill effects.

Confused, and somewhat disappointed, Noric waved his hand in the stream of light, which did not burn off.

"See? Harmless," Maximus said. "But *whoa*, what a difference the light makes. You really are a terror to behold in person."

Noric leaned in closer. "Human, your feeble eyes have not witnessed terror yet." Muscles rippled, and saw-toothed spines that had been sheathed beneath the diamond-shaped scales of his shoulders and forearms thrust outward. His chest turned a bright shade of purple. Behind the chair, D'armic trembled.

"Wow, that's great," Maximus said. "I can feel the terror coming on now. My stomach's doing backflips. You've really got something there."

"Um, thank you?" This sort of reaction was outside Noric's experience. Generally, his prey were too petrified to say much of anything, outside of groveling for their lives. But the human seemed to be positively enjoying being scared out of his wits.

"Oh, I've got a great idea," Maximus said. "When we were kids, we used to tell ghost stories and hold a flashlight under our chins. Made our faces look just ghastly. Sent shivers right up my spine."

Derailed and unsure of himself, Noric experimentally put the Niven light under his chin, casting his jagged face into deep shadows.

"Yup, that's the ticket. Boy, that's giving me the willies." Maximus squinted. "Kind of diffuse, though. Turn that little ring at the top to the right and it'll really bring out the contrast."

"What, like this?" Noric grabbed the top of the light and turned it all the way to the end.

The light collapsed into a blue laser beam no thicker than a pin, while the power cell ramped up a thousandfold to its full output. The beam burned its way through scale, flesh, and bone before erupting through the top of the Vel's head in a puff of turquoise steam to start boring through the metal ceiling.

Maximus smirked smugly. *Yeah, just like that.* Maximus's hand shot out to grab the weapon from the already-dead Noric before the beam fell on any of his people. Then he traced the blue dot down the centerline of one of the stunned guards before the alien even understood what was happening. The guard fell to the floor in two smoldering halves, a straight black line burned into the wall behind him.

D'armic shrieked as the violence and gore erupted around him. The Terrorital unpacked his overnight bag and perused his brain's room service menu. His skin turned a dark charcoal, and produced slippery oil, an evolutionary holdover from a time when the only surviving Lividites were the ones who were difficult for predators to get a good grip on.

Harris and two of the other marines pounced on the head guard and pinned his arms, preventing him from bringing his weapon to bear on Maximus. Harris viciously kicked the side of the guard's knee. With a wet crack, it became open to a whole new axis of movement. The guard crumpled as another marine stepped up to secure his weapon.

"In case anyone was wondering, that was Step 2," Felix said.

Maximus tried to wrest the control bracelet from the arm of the late Vel Noric, but when it resisted, he simply turned the flashlight onto his belt and sliced it off. He then went around to do the same for the rest of the prisoners, even D'armic, who was covered in goo and babbling hysterically about someone called the Fungus Harvester.

Maximus snuck his toes under the second Niven light and kicked it up into Harris's waiting hand. Then Maximus leveled his weapon at the lamed guard on the deck.

"Tell your friend in the hall to open the door."

"I'll never betray my ship."

"Oh, really? Captain Ridgeway, will you ask our little friend where Turemok keep their genitals?"

"I'll do it," said the guard.

Harris took position by the door. Maximus nodded to the prostrate guard. "Get on with it, then."

The suddenly enlightened guard knocked on the door three times. "Hey, Wroth, open the door. I have to drop a glot."

The door clicked and slid open. Harris lunged out the doorway and discharged his laser, a bright blue flash and the sound of a body hitting the deck confirming his marksmanship.

Maximus smiled. "Thanks for the help." With a quick swipe of the Niven light, he relieved the guard's neck of the weight of supporting a head.

Allison was aghast. "You said you'd let him live if he helped us."

"No, I didn't. This isn't playtime, Captain. They want to frame us *so they can destroy Earth*. No apologies."

Harris leaned his head through the open door. "We're clear to move, sir."

Excellent. Switch back to implants from here on out. Our objective is the hangar. Stick together, but if the shooting starts again, anyone unarmed scatters. Any questions? There were none. *Good. Move like you're being chased, people.*

The marines snatched up the fallen guards' weapons and flowed into the hall like a well-rehearsed flood.

Hang on a second, Felix said.

Harris glanced back at him. *What's the matter?*

The guard that grabbed the Niven lights, he wasn't even gone a minute. That means the rest of our equipment is close by.

He's right, Captain, Harris added.

Maximus gave Harris a curt nod. *Go.*

Felix, with me. They moved off. After a search notable only for its brevity, Felix and Harris found their confiscated equipment piled on a table three doors down.

Harris shook his head in astonishment. *Unbelievable. These guys are so incompetent I'm almost embarrassed for them.* He strapped on a hip holster and sidearm, and stuffed his pockets with spare magazines. He grabbed a pair of M-118s and pressed one into Felix's arms.

Here, I've just sent the ops software to your queue. Download it and link up.

Me? I can't use a battle rifle.

You did fine with my sidearm. This is even easier, because the rounds track inside a thirty-degree deflection cone. Just designate a hostile, point, and think, Shoot.

I don't know . . .

Felix, I'm three men down, and you're the only civilian I know for sure has even fired a gun.

I'm scared, Tom.

That means you're sane.

Felix squared his shoulders and said, *Designate, point, shoo— Um, discharge.*

Good. Grab an armful and let's head back.

What about the armor?

No time to get into it, and it wasn't doing shit against their lasers anyway.

They returned and passed weapons out to the marines. Allison and Jacqueline pulled D'armic to his feet, leaving an oil slick on the floor where he'd curled up.

Hold up, Maximus said. *Is bringing him the best idea?*

I'm not leaving him here to be tortured. Remember, he's being framed, too, Allison said.

Fine, but he's your headache.

Whatever, Tiberius.

The procession crept down the darkened corridor, quiet as mimes in a museum. The walls bowed outward, giving the halls an oval shape. It felt like walking through the arteries of some enormous beast. To make matters worse, the corridors did not sit at right angles. Instead, they branched off and merged together like the strands of a web.

Does anyone know where we're going? Allison asked.

Maximus shot her a confused look. *The hangar. We talked about this.*

I meant does anyone remember the route to the hangar?

Well, when you put it like that . . . not as such.

Allison managed not to scream, but only just. *Then maybe we should—*

"Get down!"

It wasn't immediately clear who the order came from, but any hesitation they felt dissipated when the laser pulses started exploding against the walls. Chaos filled the corridor, with the blinding flash of lasers, the *crack-crack-crack* of automatic rifles, the acrid smoke of vaporized plastics, and the mingling smells of ozone and nitrocellulose.

It was too much for D'armic's delicate, drug-addled psyche to cope with. He let out a high-pitched squeal that made everyone cover their ears, then he charged down the hall away from the gunplay at a dead sprint. Allison and Jacqueline followed, hoping to retrieve him.

Felix saw Jacqueline go and gave chase. "I'll cover them."

Harris shouted over his shoulder, "Felix, wait!"

But his friend was already gone.

CHAPTER 39

"Hedfer-Vel!" Kotal shouted.

"Yes, Kotal?" J'quol answered calmly. "What is it?"

"Security just confirmed Vel Noric is dead. The humans have escaped and have already killed a hand of guards."

J'quol casually looked up from his station. "Really? However did that happen?"

"They overpowered the Vel and his security complement. They also recovered the weapons we confiscated when they arrived."

"Oh, that is *most* unfortunate."

"And the internal security grid is malfunctioning . . ."

"Hmmm. It certainly seems to be the humans' lucky day."

"But the security grid is maintained at the . . ."

"The where, Kotal?" J'quol's voice was so cold, the air fogged around his mouth.

Kotal swallowed hard. "The Hedfer-Vel's station. The Hedfer-Vel also sets duty shifts. And the security crew on duty is . . . was . . . filled with Noric's loyalists."

J'quol's red eyes bored into Kotal for a painfully long moment. Finally, he broke the silence. "You are quite perceptive, Kotal. An admirable trait for a sensor interpreter. I could find uses for a soldier with your . . . insights. Unless you intend to oppose me?"

Kotal shook his head vigorously.

"Then we have an understanding."

"Yes, Hedfer-Vel, of course. What should we do next?"

"Well, first of all"—J'quol strode over to take up the ship's command station—"you should stop referring to me as *Hedfer*-Vel."

"Apologies, *Vel.* Should we call up an additional hand of troops to search for the prisoners?"

"No, Kotal. We've already lost a hand on the planet, and three hands are garrisoned on the human vessels. We need to maintain a fighting reserve."

"I understand, Vel."

"I know you do, Hedfer-Vel. Now, take your new station, and observe carefully."

The firefight ended in victory, but at a cost. Simmons was KIA after taking a pulse in the neck, leaving the assault shuttle short a pilot. They linked back up with Allison after a brief search, standing in front of a door with D'armic barricaded inside.

We don't have time for this, Maximus said. *If he wants to hide, let him.*

No, Allison protested. *Don't you get it? He's the only witness to what happened at Okim, and he's one of this Assembly's officers. We need him alive if we're going to clear our names.*

Maximus huffed, but took up a covering position and offered no further resistance.

"D'armic, it's Allison. Can you hear me?"

"Yes, Allison Captain." His voice was fast, high-pitched. Not at all like the resolute, implacable creature who'd visited her ship.

"D'armic, there's no Turemok, just us. It's safe to come out."

"I'd rather not."

"Is that D'armic talking, or the drug?"

"Both."

"I've seen how brave you can be, D'armic. It was scary how calm you were on *Maggie*. Why is this different?"

"That wasn't bravery. I hadn't taken Valorox."

"Why would that—" Allison smacked her forehead. It wasn't bravery he'd shown during their first meeting, because he hadn't felt anything; no courage, no fear, no anger.

"You don't have emotions without drugs, do you?"

"No."

"How long will this drug last?"

"I don't know, maybe hours."

"We can't wait that long, D'armic." Trying to beat the alien's fear wasn't working, so Allison decided to use it instead. "We're leaving now. The Turemok are coming. They're going to feed you to the Fungus Harvester."

Ouch. Maximus grinned. *That's cold.*

"*No!* Help!"

"I want to help, D'armic, but you have to open the door."

"And you won't hurt me?"

"We won't hurt you."

Allison held her breath waiting for an answer. Then the door clicked and slid open. The little gray alien ran out and threw his oily arms around Allison's waist like a child, staining her already ruined uniform. Displays and blinking lights filled the room beyond.

Hmm, what have we here? Maximus sauntered inside.

Looks like an electronics bay, Harris said.

Well, then, it would be awfully rude of me to do this . . . Maximus lit the beam of his Niven light and slashed at the room with abandon. *Ooh, that looks expensive.* Electricity arced out of the wounds in the trunks and cables, sending sparks cascading from the walls. *It's like when my dad tried to remodel our summer home.* The lights in the hallway flickered and died. Dim orange backup lights took their place.

Maximus admired his efforts for a moment and then stepped back into the hallway. *C'mon, we need to find the rest of our people.*

Who's still missing?

Mr. Fletcher and your flight officer.

And then what, fearless leader? Allison didn't devote much effort to concealing her disdain. *Even if we do get back to our ships, we'll just get blown up.*

Maximus started walking. *About that. How's* Maggie *at multi-tasking?*

Felix heard the scream and, against all impulses to the contrary, ran toward it. In the dim hallway, he could plainly see two blazing red lights about two meters off the floor. Just below the looming Turemok guard writhed Jacqueline's slim frame, her hands held tight against her ponytail as the guard cruelly jerked on her hair.

The guard raised the weapon in his other hand to Jacqueline's neck. "You! Drop your weapon and get on the floor."

"Felix, run!"

"Shut up!" The guard struck Jacqueline on the temple with the butt of his weapon. Her eyes went wide and started to roll back in her head, but she kept them open somehow.

"Felix . . ." Her voice was softer, more desperate.

"On the floor, now, or I hollow this female's skull!"

The rifle in Felix's grip shook as waves of fear echoed through his body. Felix was being wrenched in opposite directions. His fear of being captured was precisely countered by the fear of seeing Jacqueline killed. He didn't trust his reflexes to be fast enough.

"*Now!*"

With great reluctance, he admitted that there was nothing he could do, that the only way for them both to survive the next handful of seconds was surrender. *Oh, shoot.*

The rifle bucked in his hands as thunder filled the hallway. Startled, he dropped the gun onto the deck and threw his hands over his ringing ears. Felix looked up, certain he'd be looking down the muzzle of the guard's weapon.

Instead, he saw a point of red light gazing down on him. A single point. Jacqueline slipped from the guard's limp grip and dashed behind Felix. The immense guard toppled backward to the deck with a *thud*.

Jacqueline's mouth moved as if speaking, but Felix's ears were still ringing.

"What?"

Jacqueline shouted, "You saved me!"

"Oh, no, I didn't. I forgot about the link trigger and—"

"Yes, you did." There was a finality in her voice.

Felix decided not to argue. "Ah, yes. Sure did. Are you all right?"

Jacqueline placed her face perilously close to Felix's own. She put firm hands on both sides of his head, then leaned in and kissed him with velvet lips. Felix pulled her closer. This went on with rising intensity, and might have led to some X-rated surveillance footage, until Maximus stumbled onto them.

"Seriously? Break it up, lovebirds. You can neck on the shuttle."

Kotal was just getting used to the feel of his new chair when the proximity alarm went off. He sifted through the different screens at the unfamiliar station until he found the cause.

"Vel J'qoul, the humans have neutralized the hangar guard and escaped in their small craft."

"How surprising."

"And they sabotaged our snare beams."

"Determined little creatures, aren't they?" J'quol answered absently.

"Should we open fire?"

"As much appeal as that idea has, I believe our short-range autocannons have also been disabled."

Kotal checked the weapons readiness screen. The new Vel was right. "I don't understand. We want them to escape?"

"Again with your wild accusations. Really, Hedfer-Vel Kotal, this conspiratorial talk doesn't suit an officer of your rank."

"Of course, Vel."

"Still, it is regrettable. Now I'll be forced to destroy both vessels. A shame we won't be able to preserve them for the Assembly's inquiry."

Only then did Kotal grasp the full extent of J'quol's machinations. The death of prisoners in their care would be highly suspicious, and the human ships were articles of evidence. Destroying them without cause would bring immense scrutiny. But escaped prisoners, attacking a sabotaged patrol cruiser? No one would question the need to defend one's vessel and crew.

That the counterattack would leave no one alive and no physical evidence behind to cast doubt on J'quol's version of events would be lost on most. Size be damned, J'quol was the most dangerous Turemok Kotal had ever encountered.

"You're not a Cuna player, are you, Vel?"

"Indeed, Kotal, since I first ventured from the nest. Why, do you fancy a game?"

"Not on your life."

J'quol smirked. "How long until we are ready to open fire?"

Allison dropped through the hole in *Magellan*'s hull, freshly cut by the shuttle's emergency docking laser. Harris and his squad secured the hallway ahead of her and began moving forward. She kept pace behind them.

It had been decided during their escape that Harris and his team would go with Allison to help her retake *Magellan*. *Bucephalus* already had the rest of the marine platoon aboard, as well as a full armory to work with. Jacqueline was traded to Maximus to stand in for his fallen pilot.

Presumably, the enemy would've stuck *Magellan*'s crew in a large, open area where they'd be easiest to monitor and control, the shuttle bays being the most likely place. If the crew revolted, they could be flushed into space. Harris planned to start as far back as possible and sweep forward, starting with the engineering section.

They moved quickly through *Magellan*'s vital organs toward the hardened blast door that separated engineering from the rest of the ship. Allison had spent the shuttle trip back preparing herself for the sights that might await her. Friends injured or dead. *Maggie* ravaged by the fight. But her frightened imagination hadn't prepared her for what awaited her as the door peeled open.

Sitting in a folding beach chair, holding a half-eaten banana, Chief Billings watched a data pad.

"Steven?"

"Evenin', Captain."

"What the hell are you doing sitting down here eating a banana?"

He looked at the curved fruit and sighed heavily. "It wasn't my idea, ma'am. That damned nanny robot kept nagging about my potassium levels."

"But how did you escape?"

"Told them there was a radiation leak from the attack I needed to fix."

"They fell for it?"

He shrugged. "You gotta understand somethin'. These boys are about as sharp as a sack of wet mice."

"Well, I'm glad you're safe, Steven, but we have to retake the ship!"

Billings showed her the data pad. "Already handled, ma'am."

Allison realized she was looking at a schematic of *Magellan*'s interior. In the corner, a small video played camera feeds. No sooner than the Turemok boarding party appeared, Billings touched a radiation icon on the schematic.

"What are you doing?"

"Herding."

"You're setting off radiation alarms."

Billings nodded. "Did I ever tell you I used to work on my uncle's organic cattle ranch up in Montana in the summers?"

"Um, no?"

"The first thing you learn about cattle is they can't be told where to go. They're too stubborn or too stupid." He set off another alarm. "Instead, you gotta show them where they don't wanna go."

In the tiny video, the Turemok turned from the new alarm and ran down an adjacent hallway. The path terminated at a large double door, which slid open as they approached.

"Eventually, they decide all by themselves to go where you wanted from the start . . ."

The intruders walked cautiously through the door, nervously sweeping their weapons through the room.

"—then alls you've gotta to do is shut the gate." As soon as the last Turemok crossed the threshold into Cargo Bay Three, the doors snapped closed and locked.

The shit-eating grin on Billings's face stood as silent testament that everything was indeed bigger in Texas.

"*Maggie*'s finished installing the software. She's ready, Tiberius," Allison said.

"Good work, Captain Ridgeway. How are the marines I loaned you?"

"Bored. I didn't even need them. My engineer cornered the Turemok boarding party in an empty cargo bay and we welded the door shut."

"Do you think they'll give you any trouble?"

"Not as long as I control their air supply."

"How brutish of you, Allison. Stand by." Maximus ran a hand through his hair, the trademark smirk returning to his face. "Com, open a channel to the enemy ship."

"Channel open, sir."

Maximus stood resolutely. "Turemok cruiser, this is Captain Maximus Tiberius, safely back aboard AEUS *Bucephalus*."

A face, or what passed for one, congealed into the air in front of him. Red pinpricks of iris stared back at him from across the fifty-kilometer distance.

"Ah, Captain Tiberius. We have not yet met. I am Vel J'quol."

"Congratulations on your recent promotion, J'quol."

"I understand I have you to thank for that. I must say, I'm pleased to see you survived your escape. You see, my predecessor was expected to bring your crew in for trial and your ship back as a prize. But now that your sabotage has incapacitated my snare beam, as well as eliminated my boarding hands, that is no longer practical."

"I wish I could say I sympathized with your plight."

"You may yet. Given the circumstances, I will not be reprimanded for . . . improvising." His teeth seemed to elongate and his eye implants grew even redder. "Your entire ship and crew can now join you in death."

"Well, before the inevitable, may I ask a final question?"

"Certainly. I'm not immune to courtesy."

"You're too gracious, Vel. Tell me, does your species juggle?"

"Juggle?"

"You know, the art of keeping three or more objects in the air with your hands. I saw a juggler at a circus on Lake Armstrong once. The low gravity let him keep, oh, I don't know, eighteen of these little glass balls in the air. He started with three, and then added another, and another, and another. You'd think he could just keep adding balls forever. But there's always a limit. He began to struggle at thirteen, really started to sweat at sixteen, then when he threw in the last one, he could only keep it going for a few seconds before the whole thing came crashing down."

"Forgive my intrusion, Captain, but is there a point to this nostalgia? One might think you were stalling for time."

"Oh, yes, I'm sorry. Well, do you juggle?"

"No."

Maximus motioned to his tactical officer, then back to the hungry grin of his adversary. "You really should learn."

The tac officer pressed a big red holo-button. *Bucephalus* bucked mightily as eighty-five missiles, the remainder of her complement, erupted from their tubes.

Bucephalus's fire control system could independently target fifty missiles simultaneously, but damage to her data links and sensor suite from the battle reduced that figure to scarcely forty. Which left forty-five missiles without guidance or telemetry. Or would have, had *Magellan* not downloaded a copy of *Bucephalus*'s FCS software and command codes.

Missiles have a one-track mind, and a narrow-gauge track at that. The conversation between the missiles and *Magellan* went something like this . . .

"Who are you? What's the access code?" asked the missile.

"Tiberius-is-a-wanker-01," *Magellan* replied. Needless to say, Maximus hadn't picked it. "*Bucephalus* is unable to provide telemetry. I'm taking over."

"Oh, okay. Where's the target? Are you the target?"

"Come on. If I were the target, would I tell you?"

"Uuuuh."

"Never mind. See that big, ugly thing bearing three-zero-six by four-seven at fifty-three point seven kilometers?"

"Yeah."

"That's the target."

"This isn't another bloody practice firing, is it?"

"Nope, it's the real McCoy."

"Right, then." The missile was noticeably more upbeat. "See you downrange."

"Not if you work properly."

"What?"

"Nothing. Forget I said it. Off you go."

With little variation, *Magellan* had an identical conversation forty-four more times over the next sixteen milliseconds. After the fifth time, she was *really* glad she wasn't a warship.

As one, maneuvering thrusters fired, orienting the missiles toward the enemy. Eighty-five drive rockets lit off in anger.

It was a Herculean task keeping them all pointed in the right direction. *Magellan* strained her processors and com lasers to the very limit coordinating with *Bucephalus* to keep the missiles from colliding with each other or getting confused and picking one of the Earth ships as a target. Several of them had to be shut down for this very reason. Several more fell to malfunctions and had to self-destruct.

Fortunately, seventy-six of them did their manufacturer proud. Each missile carried six warheads, each capable of limited independent terminal maneuvering. Exactly fifty seconds into their flight, just before the range the Turemok cruiser had deployed its point-defense portals in the last engagement, the missiles' nose cones peeled open and jettisoned their cargo, sending four hundred and fifty-six enraged bees armed with thermonuclear stingers downrange.

The Turemok defenses engaged the swarm of plutonium death. Thirty-two defensive portals opened, sending warhead after warhead into hyperspace. Each one had enough time to absorb a warhead and reorient five times in rapid succession. In total, the portals soaked up over a hundred and fifty incoming warheads.

A valiant effort, but it still left over *three hundred* warheads.

In desperation, Vel J'quol ordered an emergency escape portal, but the capacitors were depleted from opening dozens of point-defense portals.

There simply wasn't time to recharge them.

All around the Turemok cruiser, scores of miniscule artificial suns ran through their entire life cycles faster than it takes a politician to abandon a campaign promise.

The damage was awe-inspiring. After the glow faded, only a rapidly expanding cloud of plasma and millimeter-sized debris remained of J'quol's brand-new command.

Maximus grinned. "Damn, we wasted quite a few. Tactical, make a note. At this range, a Turemok cruiser can juggle 153 warheads before dropping the ball."

"Aye, sir."

Allison gawked at the atomized wreckage of the Turemok cruiser in bewilderment. She pinched the bridge of her nose and looked to Gruber. "There'll be no living with him after this. It's like his ego reached some sort of critical mass, and now reality just warps around it."

"He *did* save our lives, you know."

"Yes, but how long until we wish he hadn't?"

CHAPTER 40

In spite of her exhaustion, Allison couldn't sleep. Of the list of possible causes—multiple firefights, being taken prisoner, the threat of torture, witnessing the death of a planet—she wasn't certain which was the culprit. However, if push came to shove, she'd probably bet on the still-unresolved threat of the Earth being destroyed as the primary cause of her insomnia.

Figuring the events of the past day had solidified her tough-chick persona enough to withstand a small assault, Allison slipped into her licentiously comfortable pink robe. She shuffled toward the mess like an extra in a Romero flick, except the aim of her hunt would be found in a coffeepot instead of a cranium.

A short tube ride later and Allison found herself pouring a fresh cup of consciousness with a spoonful of sugar. Her restlessness seemed to be catching, as the mess was half-full of the wired dead.

In the far corner, back against the wall with perfect posture, sat Allison's guest of honor. She handed the coffeepot to the next zombie in line and walked to the corner.

"Good evening, D'armic. May I join you?"

"Allison Captain. Please, this is your home. You may sit wherever pleases you."

She sat down, careful not to crease her robe. "Your company pleases me, D'armic." She glanced at the plate of food in front of the alien. Red onions, bacon, a dozen powdered-sugar doughnut holes, a half kilogram of sunflower seeds, apple slices—coated in either vanilla pudding or mayonnaise, which also covered his hands.

"I see you've found something to eat."

"Yes, your AI was most helpful in selecting an appropriate menu for my metabolism."

"Can I get you a knife and fork?"

"Unnecessary. The meat was sufficiently dead when it was presented to me."

"I see. You're feeling better, then?"

"Not at all."

"Oh, I'm sorry to hear that. You, ah, appear to have recovered."

"I have, completely. Hence why I'm not feeling anything."

Allison did a mental flip. "Right. That was thoughtless of me."

"Think nothing of it, Allison Captain. It is difficult for emotional beings to relate to unmedicated Lividites. It requires practice, and there aren't many of us in circulation. That said, I wish to apologize for the inconvenience I caused during our escape."

"You were drugged, D'armic. There wasn't anything you could have done differently."

"True, but I was a hindrance. Clearly, there wasn't anything to fear."

"What are you talking about? I don't think I've ever been so scared. Between you, me, and the table, I was lucky not to scream for my mother, and she passed away decades ago."

"I . . . do not understand. You did not appear afraid."

"How people feel and how we act are often two different things. But I can guarantee that every one of us was terrified. Well, everyone but Maximus. I'm not sure he's ever considered the possibility that something bad could happen to him."

"It appears you do not hold Maximus Captain in high regard."

Allison grimaced. "I don't question his ability as an officer. By all accounts, he's nearly indestructible. But on a personal level, I think his success has made him a bit too full of himself."

"Oh? Who should he be full of?"

Allison shook her head and smiled. "No one. It's just an expression."

"I see." D'armic popped a doughnut hole into his petite mouth. "It is convenient that you should be here, Allison Captain, as I wished to speak to you."

The burn of the coffee was beginning to fade, so Allison took a long pull from it. "Certainly. What did you want to talk about?"

"As you know, my cutter was destroyed along with the Turemok patrol cruiser, effectively stranding me here."

"Yes. I'm sorry about that, but you were in no condition to pilot it. We weren't left with many options."

"I understand. It was not a criticism. However, I still have to report my findings to the Assembly."

"Certainly. I'd be happy to make our communications systems available to you."

"That is generous, Allison Captain, but without the authentication codes from my cutter, such a message would be discarded as manufactured."

"What are you saying?"

"I require transport to Ulamante, home system of the Assembly and seat of government for half the civilized galaxy."

Allison set her cup down and leaned back suspiciously. "We asked you to tell us where to find your Assembly of Sentient Species when we first met. You refused. What's changed?"

"Merely everything." D'armic licked a palm clean of sunflower seeds. "Our recently deceased antagonists tried to 'set us up,' is that right?" Allison nodded. "Now, there is no way for us to know if they took action on their own initiative or under clandestine orders."

"You mean a conspiracy to lay the blame on humanity from within the Assembly?"

"I cannot discount the possibility, although there is little doubt what the 'official' explanation will be. Regardless of the genesis of the plan, they must have been sending reports back, just as I was, although theirs were doubtlessly altered. And since I have been implicated, the evidence contained in your own sensor logs, and the *Bucephalus*'s high-space generator, are our only chance to prove our mutual innocence."

"And if we fail?"

"A Turemok fleet sails into the Human Wildlife Preserve, destroys Earth, and enforces a generation-long sequestration of each of your colony worlds."

"Not much of a choice, is it?"

"I should think not. It is vital we get under way immediately."

"I'll have to talk with Tiberius, as well as my superiors, but none of that will matter unless we can get the *Bucephalus*'s reactor burning hydrogen again." D'armic looked confused. "Something wrong?"

"Yes, perhaps I misunderstood, but I thought you commanded this vessel."

"I do."

"Then who are your superiors here?"

"Not here. On Earth."

"No." The alien set his hands flat on the table. "That would take many weeks. Much too long. We need to leave as soon as repairs have been made to *Bucephalus*."

Allison almost corrected him, almost told D'armic about the Quantum Entanglement Radio and its relativity-stomping powers of instant communication. But something at the back of her mind snagged the words and reeled them in before they spilled all over the table. As impossible as it seemed, he didn't know about the QER.

Is it possible we developed it first? she asked herself. *Maybe we have a secret worth protecting.* It was an encouraging thought, but it would have to wait.

"Allison Captain? Are you all right?"

The question pulled her back to the table. "Yes, sorry. I agree, we can't wait on word from Earth. Are you there, *Maggie*?"

"Yes, Captain?"

"Connect me with the helm, please."

"Wheeler here. Go ahead, ma'am."

"Wheeler, I'm sending up Mr. D'armic. You are to assist him in locating and charting a course for the Ulama . . ."

"Ulamante," D'armic finished for her.

"Thank you. The Ulamante system."

"Understood, ma'am. Are we going on another trip?"

"If we're lucky. Ridgeway out. *Maggie*, engineering, please."

"Billings here. Go for engineering."

"Steven, where are we with the *Bucephalus* restart?"

"We're about to float over the universe's biggest pair of jumper cables now, ma'am."

"Excellent work, Steven. Keep me updated."

"Sure thing, ma'am."

Grote stalked up and down the private office he surreptitiously shared with his brother Jak'el. "How? How could he have gotten himself killed?" It was more accusation than question. He reached the end of their solid bertel wood desk and strained to lift it off the floor. His effort was not rewarded with immediate success.

"Grieve not, brother. J'quol died a hero to our people."

Grote shifted his grip on the desk and tried again, placing greater emphasis on his legs. "But he still died! What are we to do now?"

"Calm yourself. Our dear big, little brother only failed to survive. He came through for his part of the operation. The plan continues rolling forward."

Grote stopped talking, favoring instead a series of increasingly overwrought grunts.

Jak'el sighed patiently. "You're not going to settle down until you flip our desk over, are you?"

Grote grunted louder.

"Very well."

Jak'el stood next to his brother and added his legs and back to the effort. With a final, mighty heave, the two of them just managed to tip the massive desk onto its side. Data crystals, files, a stylus, and several centimeters of unidentified clutter raced across the floor in a miniature avalanche.

Jak'el wiped his hands on his cloak. "Do you feel better now?"

"Yes. I could have managed it alone, though."

"Naturally." Jak'el started the tedious process of picking up and reorganizing the clutter on the floor. "Actually, this is an effective metaphor for our relationship, Grote. You act on impulse; I tidy up the mess."

"Not right now. We dishonor J'quol with our bickering."

Jak'el shrugged. "Perhaps. But there is a way we might better serve his memory."

Grote eyed him apprehensively. "Go on."

"Somewhere among the files you unceremoniously dumped on the floor is an Assembly order of action . . ."

"Yes?"

"Based on the terms of the Treaty of Pu'Lan . . ."

"Yes."

"Against Earth and her colonies."

"Yes!" Grote dropped to the floor like a cut chandelier, searching furiously through the recent precipitation of files. "When does it take effect?"

"Immediately, provided we can find it again. We—I mean, the Kumer-Vel—will be leading the attack against the human home world from the bridge of the *Xecoron*." Jak'el smiled, not out of cheerfulness but merely to reveal teeth. "As I said, grieve not for J'quol. Soon, we will avenge him, and the Earth herself will serve as his funeral pyre."

CHAPTER 41

The hyperspace approach to Ulamante was so thick with sensor platforms one could jump from one to the next on one breath. The humans' two-ship convoy was spotted seven light-years out. Not five minutes passed before an escort was sent to follow them in. One of the ships was of unknown origins, but the other was so ugly it could only be Turemok.

Bucephalus transitioned back into real-space with *Magellan* in tow as the hyper window snapped shut behind them. Ahead, the sun of the Ulamante system shone like a yellow jewel. They were not alone. Over seventeen thousand vessels revealed themselves on passive sensors alone, spanning every size and shape imaginable, and even some that weren't. One was so large, it was initially mistaken for a small moon, until it opened a hyperspace window and vanished, a most un-moonlike thing to do.

D'armic had spent the last several hours in an unflappably polite conversation with his superiors in the Bureau of Frontier Management. After explaining the situation to three different layers of bureaucrats, he'd finally negotiated clearance to approach the system and even secured an audience for himself and his co-accused with the reigning members of the Assembly.

Even with the application of D'armic's credentials and smooth tongue, the eleven Turemok prisoners in *Magellan*'s cargo bay were the only thing keeping their escorts from becoming their executioners. *Bucephalus*'s prisoners were of less consequence, mostly because they had none. Mr. Buttercup had apparently gotten loose and made a bit of a mess of his captors.

D'armic stood from the chair provided him on *Magellan*'s bridge. "You are nearing the Exclusion Zone. There is a transfer station to starboard. You will be expected to approach it and then slow to zero velocity and power down your drive systems."

Allison looked at the helm station. "Wheeler, do you see the station?"

"Yes, ma'am, a dozen of them, actually. The nearest one is just under five hundred thousand clicks out."

"Do as Mr. D'armic suggested and ask *Bucephalus* to match. No sense waiting around. Show them we're being gracious and compliant."

"Aye, ma'am."

Allison craned her neck to look at the small gray alien sitting behind her. "I notice you're still using words like *you* and *your* to describe our circumstances."

"I would not presume to count myself among your crew, Allison Captain."

"Too late for that, I think. Whoever's on the other side of this thing isn't going to distinguish between you and me. They're just going to see *us*."

"You may have a point."

"What happens next?"

"Once we reach the transfer station, yourself and Maximus will have to decide on the delegation you wish to send to the Assembly. The delegation will board the station and submit to a thorough search."

"Sounds pretty routine so far. Then what?"

"Once the station attendants are satisfied we do not pose a threat, we will be transferred to the Pillar for our audience with the Assembly."

"The Pillar; what's that?"

"It is . . . difficult to describe to anyone who has yet to witness it. You will see it for yourself soon."

"Fair enough. Prescott, give me Captain Tiberius, please."

Her com officer nodded, and Maximus's face appeared in the air a moment later. "Hello, Ridgeway. What's shakin'?"

"What's shaking? The fate of the Earth is 'shaking,' Captain. You could at least pretend you're taking this seriously."

"Sorry, Captain, but I drove nuke-armed drone carrier subs through two wars. This isn't my first 'fate of the world hangs in the balance' type of mission. You become desensitized after a while."

Allison wasn't sure which was worse, Maximus's cavalier attitude toward the possibility of a literal Armageddon, or the fact this adrenaline-intoxicated, talking peacock really had held the destiny of Earth in his hands on *several* occasions. No, the second part was *definitely* worse.

Allison straightened her tunic before continuing, "The ships can't go any deeper into the system. The station ahead is like a customs checkpoint. We need to decide who's coming with us to talk to the Assembly."

"Well, you and me, obviously, and Mr. D'armic as our star witness. I'd like to bring along Lieutenant Harris."

"We aren't allowed weapons."

Maximus snorted. "Harris *is* a weapon. Besides, symbolically, he's the first human ground commander to face an alien enemy, and he won doing it."

"That's fair. But symbolically speaking, if Lieutenant Harris is our brawn, then Mr. Fletcher is our brains. They're a matching pair."

Maximus was dubious. "A steel-toed boot and a flip-flop make a better pair than those two."

"Hey!" Felix shouted from out of frame.

"Don't get all huffy, kid. You both do great work, but nobody's likely to mistake you for twins." Maximus looked back to Allison. "But I see where you're coming from. So the five of us, then?"

"Sounds like a plan."

"Good. We'll meet you on the station."

"Actually, I think it would be better if we take my shuttle, being that yours are armed. We don't want to send the wrong message."

"Okay, you can pick me up at my house, but I need to be home by eleven." Maximus cut the link.

Allison gritted her teeth and let the frustration pass. If she couldn't make Maximus take the situation seriously, she could at least prevent him from distracting her. "Prescott, call Jackie. Tell her I need a cab."

Within the hour, Jacqueline slid the shuttle and her five intrepid passengers into a docking slip outside the transfer station. A fleshy tube extruded from the station's hull, straining toward the shuttle like the proboscis of a thirsty elephant.

Maximus put words to what everyone else was thinking. "What the hell is that?"

D'armic was the only one in a position to answer. "An All-Seal. With thousands of designs from hundreds of manufacturers, standardization is difficult. The All-Seal is adaptable to any hatch."

"It looks like a mohel's recurring nightmare."

With an unsettling sucking sound, the All-Seal made contact with the shuttle. The hatch sensors on Jacqueline's display chimed. "Board is green. We have a hard seal, ma'am."

Allison moved to the rear doors and pressed the release. A front of hot, humid air crept through the interior. "Come along, everyone. Let's not keep our hosts waiting."

Maximus led the procession, with Harris, Felix, and D'armic following in his wake. Allison waited by the door. "Jackie, keep the engines warm."

"Good luck, Captain."

Allison caught up with the rest of the party floating in the meaty tube beyond the hatch. D'armic had glided to the head of the line, while the others wallowed through the microgravity.

Eventually, they crawled, hopped, and swam their way into the transfer station, and into the bane of travelers throughout the galaxy: a TSA checkpoint.

In this case, the acronym stood for Transfer Safety Authority, but the experience wasn't improved by the change of verbiage or management. Two aliens, one Lividite, one like a moss-coated crab, stood on either side of a cylindrical chamber only marginally more inviting than a dentist's chair covered in rusty nails.

The mossy crab waved a spiky forearm at the newcomers. "Step forward and place your insulation on the conveyor."

Allison cocked an eyebrow. "Insulation?"

Maximus grinned devilishly. "He means our clothes."

"She," D'armic corrected.

"What?"

"The technician is a female Ish. You can tell by the shape of her mandibles."

"Oh, of course. Not sure how I missed that. Sorry about that, miss."

"Are you going to remove your insulation or not?" the guard asked.

"Sure." Maximus and Harris started unfastening their tunics. Allison crossed her arms over her chest.

"What's the problem?" asked the technician through comblike mouthparts. "You have nothing to fear, so long as you have nothing to hide."

"I have plenty to hide, thank you very much."

"C'mon, Ridgeway." Maximus shucked his trousers like corn husks. "You don't have any equipment I'm not already qualified on. Let's not dillydally. Fate of the world, remember?"

"Fine, but I'm going first, you're turning around, and if I so much as feel your eyes on my backside, I'll find you in your sleep."

"Now we're talking."

"*Turn around!*"

Only once Maximus made a half pirouette to face the entrance did Allison disrobe. At least the room was warm. She fed her uniform and undergarments into the scanner.

"And the contents of your pouch."

"My what?"

The Ish coiled her eyestalks. "Don't try to play me the fool. I know mammals of your world have skin pouches."

"That's marsupials, and none of us are Australian."

"So, no pouches?"

Allison shook her head. "I would've noticed by now."

"Fine. Step into the scanning tube."

Allison did as requested. The clear door shut tight behind her.

Felix stepped forward to investigate the chamber. "She's already naked. What could she be hiding?"

The Ish pointed a shrimplike finger at the machine's display. "Implanted bombs, biological weapons in the bloodstream, nanite infestations, and infectious diseases."

"Wow, that's a lot. Have you foiled any attacks?"

"Never. That's how we know it's working."

Felix nodded slowly. He knew better than to argue the point. Toward the end of her life, Felix's paternal grandmother took to wearing a necklace of small wooden spikes and silicon chips to protect her from cybernetic vampires. He once sarcastically asked how many times she'd been attacked. She answered, "Never. That's how I know it's working."

"Did she say 'infectious diseases'?" Allison shouted through the door.

"Yeah."

"Tell her not to look too closely at Tiberius. Who knows what he's caught in port."

Maximus laughed. "Touché, dear Captain."

The debasing process eventually wound to a conclusion, and everyone dressed and moved on to the next station. They lined up in front of a small room that looked a bit like an airlock. Felix was the first to enter, but the door snapped shut behind him.

He looked at D'armic with eyes like cue balls. "What's going on?"

"Wasn't it clear? You're in a transfer booth, Mr. Fletcher."

"What does that mean? I thought we were waiting for a shuttle."

"Oh, no. Far too many beings visit the Pillar to make shuttles practical. The transfer booth transports without the need of physical conveyance."

"A teleporter?" Felix panicked, beating his fists against the glass. "Get me out of here!"

Harris sprang to the door and tried his hand at the controls without success.

D'armic looked confused. "I do not understand, Mr. Fletcher. What is causing your anxiety?"

"What's my anxiety?" Felix wailed. "Having my atoms boiled off, digitized, broadcast, and reassembled. I'll be dead! Whatever comes out the other side will be a copy!"

"Ah, now I understand your confusion. This machine isn't a teleporter, Mr. Fletcher. The computing power and scanning resolution required make them effectively impossible."

"How does this thing work, then?"

"It's simple, really. Your thermal energy is lowered to a fraction above total zero. Then your atoms are aligned into a state, which I believe you call a Bose-Einstein condensate. Then we quantum tunnel the whole superatom through space to the transfer pad on the Pillar and reheat you. The process is nearly instantaneous. You probably won't even notice."

Felix threw his arms over his head. "But that's even more ridic—"

Flash!

CHAPTER 42

Flash!

"—ulous than teleporting . . . a . . . Wow." The window ahead of Felix was no longer filled with Harris's concerned face, but an enormous tunnel of beautiful lattice and glass covering a boulevard bustling with a greater variety of life than found on all of Earth.

Felix didn't feel like a copy. Still, he patted himself down, just to be sure everything was where it was supposed to be. Once the standard inventory of parts was accounted for, he gave up and stepped out of the chamber.

"Welcome to the Pillar. Now stay where you are, human."

Felix turned toward the source of the warning, only to come face-to-mid-torso with a Turemok pointing a rather large laser at his temple. Five other guards accompanied him, all Turemok.

"You have some hard scales coming here, I'll give you that much, but if you as much as twitch, I'll give your head a ventilation shaft. Understood?"

"I'd nod to say yes, but I don't want you to mistake it for a twitch."

"Smart. We wait for the rest of your geocidal friends to transfer. Then you can spin your story to the Assembly before your execution."

"Peachy." Felix crossed his arms and waited while his compatriots popped into existence at fifteen-second intervals. Upon D'armic's arrival, they were prodded toward the boulevard. Their guards took up positions like a six-pointed star around them.

The congested crowds saw them coming and created a space for the procession of prisoners to pass unperturbed. Hundreds of pairs, and triplets, and quartets of eyes leered at them, as did several echo-locating organs, magnetic sensitive antennae, and one exceptionally sensitive set of olfactory tentacles. This was followed by a flood of camera flashes, image scanners, and holo-feeds documenting the newcomers.

In the middle of the boulevard, the floor seemed to distort and surge, like a river of liquid marble. The lead guard stepped over the turbulent boundary layer and into the flow and was whisked down the hall. D'armic went next.

"Move."

Felix felt the muzzle of a weapon dig into his ribs. He took a tentative little hop, still half expecting to sink like a rock, but the surface supported him easily.

"It's fine. Just a moving sidewalk."

The rest of them piled on, and they accelerated down the endless boulevard at breakneck speed. Felix had to brace himself against the rush of wind.

"How do we get off this thing?" he shouted to D'armic.

"It knows our destination. We will decelerate upon arrival."

"Where are we? Why is it called the Pillar?"

D'armic pointed up through the crystal lattice that formed the ceiling. "Witness for yourself."

Felix looked up for the first time since getting out of the transfer booth. A world looked back. A blue halo surrounded it, belying a thick atmosphere. The terminator bisected the planet precisely down the center. The dayside was covered in red plains, white-capped mountains, and purple seas. The night side was lavished with city lights like clusters of galaxies, each connected by winding ribbons of illumination. The base of the Pillar reached out like an Oriental fan, each spine extending outward hundreds of kilometers into the land surrounding the hub, doubtlessly to distribute its immense weight.

"A spacescraper. That's incredible. The tallest building we've managed back home is only seven kilometers, and it fell down after a few years. How tall is it?"

"I don't think you understand, Mr. Fletcher." D'armic pointed over Felix's shoulder. "Look behind you."

He did, and was greeted by *another* planet. The Pillar reached down to its surface as well, connecting the twin worlds like the shaft of a cosmic barbell.

An attentive listener could have heard the fuses in Felix's head blow. The incalculable engineering obstacles, not to mention the fundamental principles of physics that had to be overcome to build what he witnessed, were insurmountable. It would have been easier for him to believe his eyes were simply lying to him. He stared onward in mute silence for almost a minute before the spell broke.

"It's . . . it's a tether."

"Quite the opposite, Mr. Fletcher. It is, as the name implies, a pillar, built to prevent the twin planets of Ulamante from falling into one another."

"That's impossible," Felix said reflexively. "Nothing could hold up against those kinds of compression forces."

D'armic shook his head. "Not impossible. Merely very, very difficult."

By this time, the rest of the party had noticed the gob-smacked look on Felix's face and discovered the marvel for themselves.

Allison found her voice. "Who? Who could manage something like this?"

D'armic turned to face her. "No single race is responsible. The Assembly of Sentient Species undertook the project soon after its formation. It had long been known that the Ulamante twins were in a decaying orbit and that they would eventually collide. However, evacuating and relocating two industrialized planets full of sentients, and their ecosystems, was an enormous logistical challenge.

"The Pillar was the answer. As enormously expensive as it would prove to be, it was still cheaper to the galactic economy than the loss of two planets and the flood of refugees that would follow. So the Assembly voted to undertake the project, still the sole unanimous decision in the body's history. Construction took seven centuries, but upon completion, it became a symbol of what could be achieved with united effort. Out of gratitude, the Ulamante offered the Pillar as the permanent home of the Assembly. It has been headquartered here ever since."

"That's great!" Maximus had to shout against the wind. "Thanks for the narrated tour, but I'm less worried about how your Assembly saved these planets than I am about stopping it from destroying ours."

"The facts are with us, Maximus Captain. We must trust the Assembly to see reason."

"Trust politicians to see reason? Damn, and they just finished the Crazy Horse monument, too. I wanted to see that."

"Don't be such a pessimist, Tiberius," Allison said. "Nothing could be more incompetent than our parliament, and even they would have trouble screwing this one up."

"Let's hope you're right."

They continued onward as the crowds of gawking onlookers blurred past. News of their appearance traveled through the Pillar even faster than the flowing walkway they stood on.

The walkway slowed, subtly at first, but then enough that everyone braced their knees against the deceleration. It halted before a set of magnificent silver doors. Portraits as solemn as they were bizarre were carved into the polished surface, yet the alien faces only reached a third of the way up. The rest of the surface remained virgin territory, awaiting histories yet to be written.

Everyone stepped onto the landing. Allison, Felix, and Jacqueline stood in awe of the doors, trying in vain to comprehend the depth of tradition the engravings represented. Maximus and Harris, meanwhile, were more concerned with the present. They sized up the guards, looking for weaknesses or oversights. None immediately presented themselves. Their escorts took up positions to either side of the entryway.

A line of light shot from floor to ceiling as the left door opened, dramatically at first, but the rate was slow enough that drying paint would be tempted to sneak out for a smoke break. Finally, the door opened enough to let a slim figure squeeze through.

He was Lividite, dressed in the resplendent vestments owed to his office and with a physique owed to his desk. He approached D'armic. "You are the frontier manager, yes?"

"I am. And unless I have been absent for too long, you are Bloon Representative."

The elder Lividite gave a small bow. "The Assembly is ready to hear your petition. But, a note of caution: the Turemok representative moved to censure your codefendants."

"And the vote?"

"Three for, three against."

"What does that mean?" Allison asked.

D'armic turned to face her. "The measure fails."

"You need four votes to pass anything? Doesn't that just invite deadlock?"

Bloon shrugged. "Deadlock is preferable to actions that cannot win support from a simple majority."

Allison turned up her palms. "I mean no disrespect. I was merely curious why you would use an even number of representatives, when an odd number of votes would ensure there could always be a majority."

"That excludes inaction as an alternative. Sometimes, doing nothing is the most prudent action a government can take."

D'armic raised a hand. "Thank you for sharing your wisdom, Bloon Representative."

"The rest of the Assembly awaits. We should delay no longer."

"Of course. Lead and we will follow."

The Turemok guards remained fixtures in the hall as the group passed by. The door had opened enough to allow even Harris's shoulders to pass. Past the threshold, the space opened into an airy, hexagonal chamber. The walls slowly arched inward until their corners intersected at a glowing hemisphere at the center of the ceiling.

On the floor, each section of the hexagon was given over to a different landscape: one lush and tropical, another arid and rocky. A roof of heavy stone hovered above another, like a slice of a cave. It was this section where Representative Bloon positioned himself. At the center of the hexagon was a small neutral space arranged with chairs.

D'armic moved to sit in one and motioned for the humans to do the same, but they were too distracted by the displays.

Maximus glanced through the impressive array of flora in the tropical area. "Looks like a zoo."

"That's a rather rude thing to say," Allison chided.

"Well, what's it for, then?"

"It's supposed to be a slice of their home worlds," Felix said while looking into the cave area. "Am I right, Representative Bloon?"

"Nearly. These are not re-creations. They were cut from the six home worlds of the Assembly and brought here. They remain the sovereign territory of their respective races as if they had never been moved."

"Is this what your world looks like?" Felix pointed into the cave.

"The interior of it, yes. The surface remains largely untamed."

As they spoke, other beings took up places in the slices of their homes. Once all were present, Bloon introduced them in turn.

"I have already introduced myself. To my right is Ruckk, of the Turemok, with which you have already had experience."

Ruckk was gargantuan, standing almost three meters tall. While his eyes didn't glow red with implants, they were still lit with a simmering antagonism. He stood among rocky outcrops and scrub brush that looked like it had been lifted off the set of a Western. He couldn't be bothered to acknowledge them.

"Next is Yugulon, of the Nelihexu."

Standing in the vibrant grove of flowering bushes and spongy mosses was a figure with four arms, two backward-jointed legs, and a tail thick enough to act as a stool. Extra limbs aside, the most disconcerting thing about the alien was its skin—or, more specifically, the lack thereof. Rather than the more traditional connective tissues, the Nelihexu's muscles, bones, and organs looked as though they were held together out of a shared sense of duty. Yugulon smiled at the visitors, a feat made all the more noteworthy by an absence of lips.

In the next section, another of the crab people scuttled out of the surf onto a shore of black volcanic sand.

"This is Schee, of the Ish," Bloon said.

Schee clicked a claw in their general direction.

Allison sat on a rock at the very edge of the second-to-last area. The slice was covered in crystalline formations of unimaginable intricacy and beauty. The entire scene was reminiscent of a coral reef carved of gemstones. She was mesmerized by it. Meanwhile, Felix tried to calculate the size of the treasury necessary to purchase jewelry elaborate enough to impress Jacqueline if she ever laid eyes on it. His final tally was not encouraging.

"Who's in there?" Allison asked. "I don't see anyone."

Bloon pointed at the rock Allison was perched upon. "You are sitting on them."

Allison shot up like a bottle rocket and looked at what still appeared to be a rock. "I am so sorry, um, Representative."

"I wouldn't worry," Bloon said. "You probably weren't sitting there long enough for them to notice. Their name is Rolled Down the Valley without Cracking."

"Um, are they asleep?"

"No, they're conscious, but the Grenic are silicon-based, essentially sentient crystal. They live on a somewhat longer timescale than the rest of us."

"How do you communicate with them?"

"Our deliberations are recorded and replayed at a speed the Grenic can process."

Maximus had already moved to the final section, nothing more than a brownish cloud thick enough to give the smog over Shanghai an asthma attack. As he drew close, something startled him, leaving little jetty currents swirling about.

"What the hell was that?"

From somewhere in the fog came a voice. "One might ask the same about you." The creature floated forward to present itself. It hung in the air, looking for all the world like the head of a giant morel held aloft by a goat's bladder, with a bundle of confetti streamers trailing out the bottom. "But we already know who you are, Captain Tiberius."

Maximus stepped forward, his brain trying desperately to find a face on the surface of the floating sack. "You have me at a disadvantage, er, ma'am?"

"I am Fenax; we are genderless."

"Damn, alien sexing just isn't my thing. Is Fenax your name, or the name of your race?"

"Yes."

"Right. Glad that's cleared up."

D'armic slid between Maximus and the buoyant alien. "Forgive my companions, Fenax. They have lived long in a storm cloud and only now see the sky."

"Yet already they fly in it." The alien's voice didn't seem to come from any one point in particular.

"It is their way. They are . . . impatient to learn."

"To learn? Or to conquer?"

Maximus scoffed. "I guess we know which way you voted."

"And impatient to cast assumption," said the disembodied voice. "A most combustible mixture, I fear."

Allison stepped forward. "Please don't judge our race on Maximus alone. Many of us are more cautious than he."

"You have already been judged, Captain Ridgeway," said Ruckk sharply. "Our deliberations concluded weeks ago." He spread his arms theatrically wide. "Perhaps you were arrogant enough to believe you wouldn't be caught. But the truth is, one of our ships was watching your every move since the moment you crossed into our territory. It was very thorough chronicling your decaying spiral of criminality and barbarism. It began with your piracy of Assembly property, violation of our space, escalated into serial geocide, and finally reached its zenith with the destruction of the very Assembly vessel sent to contain your madness. Not to mention several dozen counts of murder of duly assigned peace officers while discharging their duties."

"Discharging their weapons is more like it," Allison snapped.

"Silence!" Ruckk barked. "This Assembly will not tolerate impudence from convicted criminals."

"And we will not tolerate having the fate of our home planet hinge on the results of a show trial."

"How dare you! You have the audacity, the utter gall to come here, to the heart of a power beyond your meager experience, and make demands of us? You are fortunate your pathetic vessels were not destroyed on sight. Were it not for your hostages, that would have been your end."

"I hold no hostages aboard my shi—"

"Then release our officers at once!"

"I wasn't finished. I said we hold no hostages. We hold prisoners suspected in the destruction of Solonis B. Prisoners who will, in due time, be given a proper trial."

"Forgive the intrusion, Allison Captain," said Bloon, "but what is a Solonis B?"

"She means Culpus-Alam, Bloon Representative," D'armic said. "The humans have another name for it."

"Ah, but Culpus-Alam was an Assembly world and, therefore, under our jurisdiction. Humans do not have authority in this matter."

Maximus had heard enough. "As far as I'm concerned, an entire planet covered in dead humans *gives* us the authority, Assembly space or not. Humans that were only there because your people kidnapped their ancestors."

Ruckk's cranial crest had reached full height and rapidly turned a bright shade of purple. "You accuse our forces of geocide to cover your own crimes?" His chest muscles tensed. "In all my cycles, I have never heard something so preposterous and offensive."

"I take it you've never watched the BCS Bowl selection process at work."

This confused Ruckk, which only infuriated him further. "You will be silent, or by Dar, I will silence you by my own claws!"

Maximus, who was accustomed to people being reduced to sputtering volcanoes of incoherent fury while conversing with him, simply shrugged. "I like my odds. I may have a goose egg sexing aliens, but Harris and I are two for two fighting Turemok."

Allison threw her arm across Maximus's chest and pushed him back, then gave him an unmistakable *You're not helping* look recognized by everyone in the room. Except Rolled Down the Valley without Cracking, but that was because their brain had only just started to address the fact there were other life-forms in the room.

"We didn't come for a fight. In fact, we came in the hope of avoiding one."

"You should listen to your mate, human. She might keep your hide intact," Ruckk taunted.

"I'm not his 'mate,' and you two posturing idiots can duke it out when we're finished for all I care." The venom in Allison's voice surprised everyone, but no one more than herself.

Maximus smiled at her and thought through the implanted com. *Glad to know I can bring out such strong feelings.*

"But you *are* finished, Ridgeway," Ruckk said. "If you are not here to negotiate the release of your hostages, then we have nothing to discuss." He looked at Bloon. "I told you it was a mistake to bring them here. You can't reason with the insane."

Bloon's eyes remained on Allison. "Something is unclear to me.

If you have not come to discuss your . . . prisoners, then what is your petition?"

"Isn't it obvious? To stop retaliation against Earth. We have evidence that exonerates us and proves that we were set up."

Ruckk laughed. A sound like two badgers with their tails tied together. "I'm sure you do. And I'm equally sure that you took great care in manipulating your sensor logs—"

"Actually," D'armic interjected, "the evidence is physical. I have seen it for myself, which is why I turned my investigation away from these humans."

The Fenax stirred. "You forget, D'armic, that you stand accused as a coconspirator. It is unsurprising, then, that you would claim evidence in your own favor."

"I accept that; however, it changes nothing. The fact remains that the human vessel *Bucephalus* is physically incapable of creating high-space portals of the size that destroyed Culpus-Alam, Okim, and Kulla. The patrol cruiser commanded by the deceased Vel Noric, by contrast—"

"You're mad!" screeched Ruckk. "You don't actually expect us to believe that a Vel ordered geocide?"

"What you choose to believe has no impact on the truth, Ruckk Representative. If I am telling the truth, then you have just as much incentive to suppress it as the humans would if the situations were reversed. Was it not you who tried to censure us before we even arrived? What are you afraid the rest of the Assembly might hear?"

"This hall does not suffer conspiracy theories, Lividite."

"One moment, Ruckk," Bloon said. "D'armic, you said the *Bucephalus* could not be responsible. But there are two ships."

Allison stepped up. "*Magellan* doesn't have high-space tech."

"That is exceptionally dangerous this far from your home world. Why not send additional high-space-capable ships?"

"Because we haven't got any," Allison said. "The *Bucephalus* is our prototype."

A gasp ran around the room.

"As I said, Bloon Representative," added D'armic, "they are impatient."

Bloon stood stoically for several seconds before continuing. "We are obliged to investigate this new evidence. However, even if it should result that you are telling the truth, I must tell you that we cannot halt the punitive expedition already authorized against Earth."

"But there are thirty billion people on Earth." Allison's voice cracked. "You can't destroy our planet if you know we're innocent. That's monstrous."

"You misunderstand, Allison Captain. I did not say that we would not stop the expedition; I said that we *could* not. The armada was dispatched weeks ago, after the destruction of Kulla was reported."

"So recall them," Maximus said. "Since getting out here, our people have nearly been drowned, shot, poisoned, blown up, crushed, burned alive, tortured . . . am I forgetting anything?"

"Eaten."

"Eaten by cannibals. Thank you, Mr. Fletcher."

"Asphyxiated," Allison said.

"Asphyxiated, another classic. We've lost three good men already. Do you actually think we're going to sit around while you refuse to lift a finger, or whatever, to stop the destruction of our planet?"

D'armic put a hand on Maximus's shoulder. "Calm yourself, Maximus Captain. What he's saying is there isn't enough time left for a recall order to reach the armada. Am I right, Bloon?"

"I wish it were not so, but yes. The *Xecoron* will be arriving at Earth shortly. If the schedule has been adhered to, the remaining ships will reach your colony worlds to begin enforcing the sequestration at the same time."

"The *Xecoron*?" Maximus asked. "You're sending a single ship to Earth? I'm insulted."

Felix jumped to his feet. "That doesn't matter. Just contact it with a hmmum mfmmumph rhmio."

That last bit was mangled by the sudden appearance of Allison's hand over Felix's mouth. *Don't think,* she said into the internal com.

"Hmm? Hmpf's hu him ihim?"

"You'll have to excuse Felix. He suffers from a rare condition that causes inappropriate outbursts. He was about to have a flare-up."

"A condition?" asked Yugulon. "It's not contagious, I hope."

"Oh, no, he's the only known case, but he should probably get medical attention."

Bloon looked at Felix appraisingly. "He does look distressingly pale and rather malnourished."

"Hrrmm!" Felix objected.

"We have physicians here that can tend to him."

"Yes, but our doctors have experience with Fletcher syndrome."

"Fmmhr hymmrum?"

"Very well," Bloon said. "He may return to your ship for treatment."

"Thank you." Allison turned Felix's head to face her. "Okay, Felix. I want you to go back to the shuttle, then *call Bucephalus* to tell them you're coming *home* and *tell them* that they might have *to evacuate* a bed for you in sick bay. Do you understand?"

He stared at her for a confused moment. Then the light went on in his eyes and he nodded. "Mm-hmph."

"Good man. Off you go." She dropped her hand, and Felix marched back to the doors under guard with the desperate look of a man in search of a bathroom.

Bloon resumed. "As I was saying. If your evidence turns out to be genuine, we will of course try to compensate humanity for our . . . misjudgment."

"You sound like you've already accepted their story on faith, Bloon," Ruckk said. "Have you already forgotten these are convicted world killers?"

Maximus laughed. "Oh, come off it. The only inhabited world that was lost was full of our own people. What possible reason would we have to destroy it?"

"Apparently it is up to us to give you a lesson in your own history, human. You cannot find a species more enthusiastic about killing its own members than yours. Religion, race, gender, nationality, money, land, sex, food, clothing, natural resources, ancient feuds. No pretense seemed inadequate. You even fought a war over a film dispute."

This was true. The Great Nerd War started innocently enough when an overworked Park and Rec employee in Portland accidentally double-booked a shelter with a Tolkien reenactment of the Battle of Helm's Deep and a *Star Wars* LARP game. The two sides did their best to avoid each other until the reenactment's Saruman was overheard saying that Christopher Lee "totally phoned-in his Count Dooku performance." By early evening, seventeen lay dead. Eight years of bitter fighting later, a truce was signed in what became known as the Shelter C Accords.

Schee clicked a claw. "It was most fascinating to our anthropologists, but quite alarming to everyone else. We have watched your world for many centuries. It was assumed by most historians that the development of a global communication network would tame your thirst for conflict and elevate your consciousness, as it had for so many other races. But instead of unifying your world, your species divided into ever smaller, more extreme, more ignorant groups."

The Fenax took its turn. "It is really quite remarkable your race has come as far as it has when one considers that two-thirds of your efforts and resources have been spent fighting among yourselves."

Allison put her hands on her hips. "I think that's an exaggeration."

"It isn't. We've done economic studies."

"All right, whatever. We've matured into a multisystem race."

"Whose colonies were, until recently, remote enough to make war logistically impractical. But now that you have broken through the light barrier, how long will it be before you start killing one another again?"

"We won't. The buoy, the discovery of other sentients, it's going to change everything. People always rally around a common cause. Now that we know we're not alone, we won't have to fight among ourselves." Allison watched the inference spread across the faces of the alien representatives like a viral video involving kittens. Unfortunately, there are no mulligans in diplomacy.

"That didn't come out right. What I meant was—"

Just as Allison started to backpedal like she was running the Tour de France in reverse, a low and powerful sound filled the chamber, like an attempt to crossbreed an earthquake to a thunderstorm.

"The Pillar's collapsing!" Maximus exclaimed.

"Not at all," Bloon said reassuringly. "You are listening to Rolled Down the Valley without Cracking's voice."

"What're they saying?" Allison was nearly shouting to be heard over the rumbling.

"We must wait until they've finished for the linguistic computer to translate at our speed."

The sound went on for several minutes, creeping up from the floor and vibrating through their bones. As suddenly as it had come on, the sound ceased, and quiet returned to the chamber. Everyone waited in earnest to hear what timeless insights were about to be gifted to them. Finally, the computer finished its task and repeated the words of the Grenic representative in a toneless, synthetic voice.

"Excuse me, but you're sitting on my head."

CHAPTER 43

Felix shook off the bone-jarring chill left over from the transfer booth and ran toward Jacqueline in the waiting shuttle. He passed the TSA officers and, taking advantage of their cultural naïveté, flipped them a double bird. He dove headlong into the All-Seal and glided through the tube, flipping midway to land feetfirst against the shuttle's outer hatch.

"Jackie, it's Felix. Open up!"

The hatch clicked and swung inward. Jacqueline's face greeted him from inside the hull. "Where are the others?"

"They're still talking to the Assembly, but we have to leave right now."

"We can't abandon them here."

"We aren't abandoning them. Listen, Ridgeway sent me back alone because a warship is about to hit Earth. I have to get to a QER and warn the people back home."

"Well, why doesn't the Assembly just use one of theirs and recall it?"

"They don't know the QER exists. I have no idea how, but we beat them to it. Which is why we can't just radio over instructions. They might get intercepted."

Jacqueline slid into the pilot's chair. "Secure the hatch."

Felix did as he was asked, then strapped into the copilot's seat. Jacqueline's hands danced over the console as the shuttle came out of its nap. Maneuvering thrusters fired to clear them from the transfer station, but nothing happened. Jacqueline fired them again, without result.

"We aren't moving."

Felix craned around to look through the starboard portals. "The All-Seal hasn't disengaged. We're still attached to the station."

Jacqueline frowned and threw the main engine throttle levers through the windshield. The shuttle fought like a hooked fish, then tore away with a great popping sound and accelerated away from the transfer station. "Not anymore we're not. Do you care which ship we go to?"

"No, whichever is closer. I have to get Jeffery or the professor on the line as soon as possible. The faster we warn them, the more people can be evacuated before the hammer falls."

"Didn't you say it was just one ship? Shouldn't we try to fight them?"

"With what? *Bucephalus* is the only warship we have, and it's out here. Earth doesn't have any space-based weapons because they've been illegal for centuries. The only thing we've got that even resembles a weapon is the Asteroid Deflection Grid, and that system's lasers need a decade of warning just to divert a rock."

Jacqueline looked straight ahead, concentrating on flying, weaving around the tangle of civilian ships queued up behind them for their turn at the transfer station. "How bad is it going to be?"

"I've been trying not to think about it, but it's going to be devastating. Earth's surface is going to be wiped clean. It's unlikely that there will be any survivors among anyone still dirt-side when the attack happens." Felix started ticking off the compounding disasters with his fingers. "The planet's infrastructure will be lost. The debris field will probably destroy all the habitats and mining operations in low Earth orbit as well. All of the space elevator stations out at geosync will come untethered and fly away."

Jacqueline was near tears while Felix went on with his cataclysmic laundry list. "What about your home?"

"New Detroit?" Felix stared at the ceiling for a moment as the scenario ran through his brain. "Actually, the moon should be okay. The debris shouldn't have enough energy to make escape velocity, at least not very much of it. The Earth is going to lose some mass into hyperspace, but not enough for the moon to break free of her gravity. No, the orbit will get a bit bigger, but that's about it."

Jacqueline forced a smile. "I'm happy about that, Felix. Really, I am. There's no reason we should all have to lose our homes, our families."

"It's not the end, Jackie. The Mars settlements are self-sustaining, and we have dozens of colony worlds. We can rebuild."

Felix waited for a reply for a long time, but decided it was best to leave Jacqueline to her thoughts, when she blurted out a question.

"What about the Unicycle?"

"It's a million clicks out at the L1 Lagrange point. They'll have to adjust its position a bit to account for Earth's lost mass, but it'll be fine."

The survival of the Unicycle was a small consolation, but it would mean that Sol wouldn't lose its transportation hub. Ships could still ride the beam into and out of the system while the recovery effort was—

Suddenly, Felix's face erupted into a smile bright enough to light up a runway. He released his harness, stood up, and kissed Jacqueline full on the lips.

Jacqueline blushed. "Thanks, but what was that for?"

"Jackie, you just saved Earth!" Felix's arms Muppet-flailed so hard his hands hit the ceiling.

"That's wonderful. How?"

"The Unicycle. At full power and pointed at something in Earth's orbit, it'll be like using a mining laser to burn an ant. Nothing—I mean, *nothing*—can live through a focused thirty-terawatt particle beam from that close. It's practically point-blank range."

He leaned back in to kiss her again, but she placed a finger over his puckered lips.

"That's wonderful, Felix, and we'll celebrate properly later. But right now, I have to fly."

CHAPTER 44

Eugene waited impatiently for the elevator to reach the QER center basement level. It was just after three in the morning when Kiefer had screened to let him know Felix wanted to talk. Whatever it was, it had to be important, because he specifically refused to talk to anyone but Eugene or Jeffery.

For weeks, Eugene had dreaded a call like this one. Ever since *Magellan* and *Bucephalus* had discovered the plot against Earth, everyone involved in the ARTists project had been walking around on burning coals. Word about the crisis and the threat posed to Earth had leaked out almost immediately. Some secrets are simply impossible to keep.

Neither was there anything they could do about the situation. Stuck on Earth, the best they could do was offer guidance and moral support to their people in the fight. They were too far removed from the action for anything else. Eugene had never felt more impotent in his entire life, not even when he'd needed the little blue pills.

Now, Felix was calling in the dead of night, with a message too important to share with anyone except the two people on Earth he trusted most. It probably wasn't to wish happy birthday to a cousin.

Finally, the elevator chimed and the door slid open. Eugene stepped into the white hallway and strode forward at a healthy pace.

At the far end was the marine Mk VII android that had replaced the familiar Mk VI two months before.

However, standing at parade ground attention against the wall opposite the android were two other figures Eugene didn't recognize. As he came closer, he realized that the pair, a man and a woman, looked simply terrible. Their clothes were wrinkled, hair greasy, their eyes sunken, and the man's face hadn't seen a razor in days. They gave off a general aura of being freshly plucked from a lifeboat after two harrowing weeks fighting off sharks and eating seagulls.

Something clicked in the back of Eugene's brain, and he realized he was staring at the two new recruits they'd hired to work in the QER center.

"What the hell happened to you two?"

"Oh. Hello, Administrator Graham," said the disheveled man. "We're doing our initiation."

"Initiation?"

"Yes, Dr. Kiefer said we were to remain standing out here for four days and four nights without sleep or food to prove our commitment."

"Four days? Are you kidding?"

"No, sir." The man leaned forward and whispered, "But if I'm perfectly honest, we both had to run and use the restroom on the second day. I hope that won't count against us."

Eugene rubbed his eyes to make sure he wasn't seeing things. "So you're telling me that you were ordered to stand in a hallway for four days by a crazy-haired man with an abacus around his neck?"

"Yes, sir."

"And that didn't seem unusual to you?"

"Yes, sir, but this is the Stack. Everything here seems unusual."

Eugene raised a finger, but realized he couldn't argue the point. "Initiation's over; you passed. Both of you go home and get some sleep. Come back when you wake up. Understood?"

"Yes, thank you, sir."

The recruits shambled down the hallway, drunk with sleep deprivation. Eugene went through the heavy double doors and emerged into the stillness and hum of hundreds of running QER machines. Then came the booming voice.

"Who dares defile the inner—"

Eugene was in no mood for the older man's antics. "Stuff a sock in it, Kiefer. As soon as I'm done with this call, you and I are going to have a little talk about hazing the new hires."

Eugene headed off in the direction of *Magellan*'s sister QER units. The trip was much shorter than it had been, as the upgraded machines they had installed a few months ago were among the newest units in the center. He arrived, and after the biometric scanners were satisfied he wasn't an imposter, he called up the holo-menu and connected the call.

"Felix, are you there? It's Eugene."

"Thank goodness. I've been on hold for twenty minutes."

"I was in my office. You know how big this place—"

"No time, sir. Things have gone sour out here."

"What happened?"

"The retaliatory strike against Earth we were trying to head off was launched before we even arrived."

Eugene's heart sank through the carpet, into the next basement level. "How long?"

"Imminent. Could be any moment."

"Wait, why don't they just recall—"

"Everyone asks that. They don't have QERs, Professor. The strike force is too far out for their hyperspace radio to reach in time."

"Then I have to go now. We have to start evacuating the surface and all of our LEO habitats."

"Yes, do that. But here's the deal. I've been thinking—"

Oh, this should be good.

"—and I believe we can use the Unicycle to destroy any ship in position to attack Earth."

"The Unicycle?"

"Yes. It's just a huge particle cannon. And we've learned that the attacking force consists of a single ship."

"Just one? That's crazy."

"Not crazy, just overconfident. I've seen it for myself. They don't consider us equals. They've consistently underestimated our capabilities. We've already destroyed one Turemok ship. We can do it again."

"How? The Unicycle was built to shoot at ships that are *trying* to be hit. Hitting something with stealth is going to be almost impossible."

"I've already thought of that. The attacker will only be five light-seconds out. That's point-blank range. Secondly, the target'll be even closer to Earth, so you can use the QER to feed Lemieux real-time targeting solutions from sensor stations on the surface. But if you're going to have time to set it up, you need to get on the horn with Lemieux right now."

Eugene's heart returned to its proper place in his chest. They had a chance. Slim, but real.

"Don't worry, Felix. I'm on it."

"I know you are, old friend. Fletcher out."

The call disconnected, and Eugene spun around to run to the Unicycle's sister machine. He was still spinning on his heel when he heard the pop. Before he knew what the sound was, a violent jolt of painful spasms erupted across the left side of his body. Muscles frozen, he fell to the floor with a mighty crash.

In a moment of terror, Eugene realized he'd been tased. Unable to move a muscle, his head was fixed toward the far wall. To his horror, he saw the table that had previously been covered by a velvet sheet. Sitting on top of it, illuminated by the flicker of candles, was a sculpture that looked suspiciously like two fire extinguishers joined at the neck; a buoy idol.

Oh, shit. They've gone off the deep end.

Through the agony and spasms, Eugene heard the voice of the Keeper addressing his minions.

"Gather round, my brothers, and bear witness to prophecy. Soon, we chosen few shall ascend the mountain to claim our reward. For, at long last, the Day of Due Consideration is at hand."

Eugene found enough strength to shout. "What the hell are you doing?"

"Bugger it! How are you still awake? It was s'pposed to knock you out."

"Tasers don't cause unconsciousness, you moron. How did you sneak that thing in here anyway?"

"It always works in the vids." The Keeper picked up a candelabra from a nearby shelf. "Sorry 'bout all this. But we can't 'ave you muckin' about on our big day, can we?" He hefted the candelabra over his head, the little beads of his abacus jingling.

"No, wait!"

The blow fell, and Eugene's world was swallowed by black.

"Forgive the interruption, Kumer-Vel, but we are about to reach the Earth system."

Ja'kel, standing atop his brother Grote's shoulders, looked down upon the aide with the disdainful indifference that only came with noble birth, or years of careful rehearsal. The brothers hadn't learned this aide's name. There seemed little need. Surely, there was a factory somewhere that spat them out.

"Very well. Alert the bridge I will arrive shortly."

"Immediately, Kumer-Vel." The aide bowed low enough to make a contortionist envious, and backed out of the room. The door slid shut behind him.

"Are you excited yet, brother?" Ja'kel asked.

A somewhat muffled affirmative came from mid-cloak.

"As am I, but do you suppose we are moving too quickly? Suppose we had let the ruse continue to a few inhabited planets? With enough panic, the Assembly would have been begging us to enforce martial law to guard against the 'human terrorists.' From there, our coup against the Assembly hierarchy would be much simpler."

A considered reply followed several moments later, but it was muted beyond reckoning.

"I suppose you're right. More time, more planets, more to go wrong. Better to carry smaller boulders up a longer path, eh? Still, after tonight, there will be one fewer threat to the Turemok's ultimate ascension. That will suffice for now."

With well-rehearsed cues, Ja'kel's toes signaled Grote to start walking toward the bridge of the largest warship in Assembly space.

CHAPTER 45

Eugene's eyes opened as his world slowly rematerialized. He strained to focus, but rows of parallel objects in the dim light made it very difficult, like focusing on a chain-link fence from a few centimeters away.

With dread, he realized his limbs were bound. His head swam through the throbbing pain as he turned to look at his right hand. The wrist was tied with insulated electrical wire. He was tied in a crucifix position, the wire digging into his skin. He stood up to take the weight off his strained arms. Feeling returned to his hands after a moment.

The delicate hum of machines dispelled the mystery of his surroundings. He was still in the Stack's QER center, tied to the tool racks. The rest of the story flooded back to him.

"Kiefer!" Eugene spat out the name like a curse. How long had he been unconscious?

"Help!" What if it was too late? No, Eugene thought, the world was still here, so there was still time. How much, was another question.

"Help!" He strained hard against his restraints, but they held fast. Then he tried to slip a wrist through the bindings, but they were too tight. A growl of frustration escaped his throat. When he got out of this mess, Eugene resolved to shove this Day of Due Consideration as far up Kiefer's—

"Hello." The friendly voice came from Eugene's left. He looked over just as a slim female form stepped out of the shadows. It was the abnormal psychology student he'd hired in the failed bid to replace Kiefer's crew.

"You? Haven't you finished that thesis paper yet?" Eugene asked.

"That? Yeah, like almost a year ago."

"What are you still doing here, then?"

"I received a research grant to continue the study."

"Oh," Eugene said. "Well, can you untie me, please?"

"Umm, I really shouldn't."

"What do you mean you *shouldn't*?"

"I don't want to contaminate the study. It's like anthropology—I need to stay hands-off."

"You're joking."

"Oh, no. Do you have any idea how lucky I was to stumble onto a cult right at inception like this? Outsiders don't usually learn about new cults until people have gone missing for a long time. This is a unique opportunity to track its evolution in real time, I don't want to screw it up."

Eugene stood slack-jawed as the realization dawned that this girl was just as crazy as Kiefer. Desperate, he decided to throw security protocols out the window and tell her the truth. Harris would forgive him if it worked.

"All right. Listen to me very carefully. As we speak, there is an alien warship maneuvering to annihilate the Earth. They've already destroyed three other planets. Our only hope is to use the Unicycle to attack the warship, but they need to link up with sensors on the ground here to target it accurately. The Keeper knows this and tied me up to prevent me from contacting the Unicycle, in order to bring about the Day of Due Consideration."

"How exciting! Maybe I can record some of their reactions as . . . oh, but then who will read my results?"

Finally, thought Eugene. "That's right, if you don't untie me, no one will ever be able to read your study, because we'll all be dead."

She sighed. "All right, but first let me do a quick psychological assessment." She pulled out a pen and clipboard and flipped to a survey while Eugene's eyes widened in disbelief.

"Question one: On a scale of one to ten, with one being the lowest, how would you rate your current level of anxiety?"

"*Get me the fuck down from here!*"

"Okay," she said. "We'll call that an eight. Question two . . ."

Specialist Balog peeked around the corner of the gutted shell of what had once been 103 North Glastonbury Court. A V-1 had fallen through the roof and exploded in the basement.

Across the street were not one but three SS troopers trying to set up a machine gun nest; one of those damned MG-42s. Balog pulled his head back into cover. He'd been boots on the ground for less than a minute and already he was up against heavy opposition. He looked around for backup, but the wind had caught his chute and he'd drifted from the planned drop point by almost a quarter mile. The rest of his team couldn't help him.

Balog steeled himself for the coming onslaught. He glanced over his tommy gun, making sure the safety was off and a round had been chambered. Then he took a pineapple grenade from his belt, pulled the pin, and tossed it around the corner.

The explosion was close enough to hit him like a hammer in the chest, but he rolled out of cover and leveled his weapon. The grenade hadn't landed in the nest as he'd hoped, but it had wounded one of the SS troopers in the leg. With a pull of the trigger, a .45 round put the Nazi bastard down for good.

Balog charged the two remaining troopers, tommy gun spitting lead death. A lucky shot struck a second trooper in the chest and he went down, but the last one disappeared behind the sandbags. Balog vaulted the barrier and landed solidly on his feet. But before he could get his weapon to bear, the last Nazi popped up from behind the ammunition containers and leveled a Luger right at his left eye.

With a heavy Jersey accent, the German said, "n00b," then sent a bullet straight through Balog's brain.

"Damn it, Tony! I had a three-kill streak going!" Specialist Balog shouted into his microphone as the countdown to his next respawn started. "Did you really have to kill me with that little pop gun?"

"Loser," taunted PFC Lorenzo. "Two more of those and I get the 'Gunslinger' award."

"Whatever." In truth, Balog was pretty new to *Call of Duty: Operation Sea Lion*, and he did spend an embarrassing amount of time on the respawn screen. However, anything beat the mind-melting boredom of sentry shifts piloting four battle androids simultaneously.

Nor was he alone. Most of the pilots in his unit swapped lead and lasers while they waited around for nothing to happen. It was an exceptionally rare individual who wanted to tangle with an Mk VII.

Balog impatiently watched as the countdown wound back to zero, eager to get back into the fight to liberate London, when something caught his attention. On the screen linked to the basement of the Stack was a man armed with a candelabra tangling with an Mk VII.

"Something's happening. I gotta go." Balog clicked off the game net and switched his virtual environment into the sentry unit. The android responded to his input immediately and pointed an absurdly large shotgun at the little man holding a candlestick.

"It's about goddamned time!" the assailant shouted.

"Sir, cease your attack on this unit, or I will open fire. This is your only warning."

"I'm not attacking the battle android, you twit. I've been trying to get your attention for the last five minutes. Where were you?"

"I was in the head," Balog lied. "Identify yourself."

"I'm AESA administrator Eugene Graham, jackass. A religious cult has taken over the QER center." The man pointed behind the unit. "And the world will end unless you pilot this crate of spares in there and stop them."

Balog was stunned. He'd sat in this chair for almost two years. The closest he'd come to seeing action was giving directions to drunken tourists. Fate-of-the-world stuff seemed above his pay grade.

"Is this a drill?"

"Do I look like I'm conducting a fucking drill!?"

"I guess not."

"Then move it!"

With Kiefer and his lackeys safely tucked away under the supervision of Specialist Balog and his angry robot, Eugene connected with the Unicycle and immediately ran into another roadblock.

"Well, pardon *my* French, miss, but I don't give a shit if *le directeur* is having dinner with the reanimated corpse of Charles de Gaulle. Get Lemieux on the phone right this damned second!"

"There is no need to shout, m'sieur."

"Lady, if ever in the history of mankind there was a need to shout, this is it."

"Ugly Americans. Please hold, m'sieur." The assistant's voice was replaced by pop music, which proved to be an equally atrocious auditory assault. Mercifully, the line picked up before the chorus repeated.

"*Oui?*"

"Renée. It's Eugene in the Stack. I apologize for spoiling your lunch."

"It is no problem, m'sieur. The food here sustains but can hardly be called cuisine. What can I do for the AESA today?"

"Well, you can save the world."

Ja'kel and Grote presided over the bridge of the *Xecoron* like a wrathful deity. The crew was torn between competing urges. Look upon the towering frame of their Kumer-Vel in rapturous awe, or avert their eyes in terror? Most of them struck an uncomfortable balance of skulking and sneaking a peek when they thought he wasn't looking.

In the overhead display, a timer counted down toward the moment the high-space portal would open, regurgitating the *Xecoron* into a more familiar universe. Then another count would begin while the high-space capacitors refilled. During that time, the ship would be unable to retreat or open the attack portal that would result in Earth's demise.

Not that it mattered, for Ja'kel knew certain things about Earth's defenses—namely, that it didn't have any. Paranoid of spies from within their own ranks, the humans had clandestinely built their warship yard hidden away in their own asteroid belt. Which, as it happened, was also home to a network of Turemok-built espionage platforms.

Tough luck, that, Ja'kel thought with a smirk. Before the punitive expedition had even been approved, Ja'kel knew that the ship that had killed his beloved brother was one of a kind. New keels were being laid down, but their completion lay the better part of a local cycle in the future.

"Tactical."

A nervous officer met Ja'kel's gaze. "Yes, Kumer-Vel?"

"Scratch yourself a reminder to annihilate their warship yard in the asteroid belt on our way out."

"Very good, Kumer-Vel."

The first timer expired. They were in position.

"Sheathe the vessel. Open the portal, and return to lower-space."

The bridge was dead quiet as the portal irised open ahead of them, revealing the blue-green jewel that was their objective.

"A beautiful thing," Ja'kel said. "Although I cannot fathom why Dar decided to waste it on these creatures. Enjoy the view while you can, everyone. We're the last to have the opportunity."

"Hyperspace window!" shouted one of the technicians Renée Lemieux had hastily assembled in the Unicycle's control room. "Directly in Earth's orbital path."

"*Merci*," Renée said. "Is the data from the ground stations coming up the QER yet?"

"Yes, sir, but the target is . . . fuzzy. Something's definitely there, but I can't get a lock."

Renée nodded. She'd been warned about the stealth systems of the enemy.

"We must be patient and wait for our quarry to reveal itself. Is the beam ready?"

"Oh yeah. The beam is ramped up and waiting. We just need somewhere to point it."

The second timer expired.

"High-space capacitors are recharged, Kumer-Vel. We are ready to attack."

There was nervousness in the tactical officer's voice. He couldn't really be faulted for it. Even with geocide being condoned by the Assembly as it was, an officer would have to have claws and teeth of steel not to feel a flicker of hesitation at the prospect of committing it.

Fortunately for the ambitions of the brothers under the cloak, the Turemok military had long ago learned the secrets of getting a well-adjusted soldier to do unspeakable things, using the rationalization of "just following orders."

"Tactical, commence the attack."

"Yes, Kumer-Vel. Opening portal . . ." He pressed a stud on his console. "Now!"

"Power spike!" shouted the technician. "New hyper window."

"Can you localize the point of origin?" asked Renée.

"Yes."

"Would you consider that 'somewhere to point it'?"

"Absolutely. Uploading target coordinates."

"*Merci*." Renée's hand hovered over the big, red holo-button. It flashed, letting her know the emitters has aligned for the calculated distance.

Knowing the completely unpredictable, occasionally inspiring levels of incompetence humans were capable of, a dozen fail-safes were built into the Unicycle's targeting system to prevent exactly what they were about to do from happening. But while safeguards could protect against mishaps, they were powerless against determined action. It had taken the better part of an hour, but her crew had disabled them all.

Renée pushed the button. At the emitter assemblies, hundreds of kilometers from the hub, the floodgates opened. Charged particles by the quintillions poured into the vacuum, furiously searching for something to share their pent-up energy with. Five seconds later, their hopes were fulfilled.

It's just not possible to properly explain the effects a 32.4-terawatt particle beam has on an object. The energies involved are just too massive for savanna-evolved brains to wrap themselves around. Instead, the next best thing is to scale the whole scene down into a metaphorical model.

To get an idea of the incalculable horror wrought against the *Xecoron*, go to your refrigerator and grab one uncooked egg. Now wrap it in a layer of aluminum foil. Then place it in a microwave powered by the total output of the closest nuclear plant. Press Start. Observe the results. That about covers it.

What had until recently been the *Xecoron* and its crew was reduced to a cloud of superheated plasma expanding at tens of thousands of kilometers an hour, pushing what little debris there was along the shock wave like surfers on a Lovecraftian ocean. For a handful of seconds, it shone brighter than the sun itself.

The Unicycle control center exploded in celebration as everyone cheered with all their might.

Renée gave the debris field a little wave. "*Au revoir, mon ami.*"

Felix sat on the floor of *Magellan*'s bridge, Jacqueline's arms wrapped tightly around his neck as they waited for word, any word, from Earth. It had been almost two hours since he'd warned Eugene about the coming apocalypse and the thin hope to avert it.

The rest of *Magellan*'s bridge crew sat in absolute, despondent silence. Their faces were blanched and slackened like sails trapped in monthlong doldrums. Prescott wept quietly under the strain, while Wheeler rubbed her shoulders, as much to comfort himself as her.

Felix disentangled himself from Jacqueline's arms. "That's it. I'm calling."

"Just give them time, Felix."

"It's been two hours. What's taking them so long?"

Jacqueline crossed her arms. "They're either busy or they're dead. Either way, they don't need you nagging them."

Felix reached up a hand to caress her face just as the QER chimed with an incoming call. Prescott connected it.

"Go ahead for *Magellan*," she said, her voice shaky.

"It's Professor Graham. The enemy has been destroyed."

Felix shot up, almost tripping over himself as he lunged for the mic. He had to shout as the bridge erupted in cheers. "What the hell took you so long? We were on the verge of a mass nervous breakdown out here!"

"Sorry for the delay, Felix. The entire planet had to go change pants."

EPILOGUE

The door chimed.

Eugene set his snifter down on the table. "Excuse me a moment." He pushed up from the formally set dinner table and walked the short distance to his penthouse's front door. He turned the ornate brass handle and was rewarded by two smiling faces.

"My boys!" Eugene, already rosy-cheeked with brandy, threw his arms wide and reeled Felix and Harris into an enormous bear hug. "I was so afraid, lads, so afraid we'd never all be standing here again."

Felix hugged him back. "It's all right, Professor. Everyone's safe and sound. And so is home, for that matter."

Eugene's eyes stung from the emotional release. "Look at me, already sobbing like a fool. The brandy has diluted my defenses. Come in, come in." Eugene held his arm out to welcome them into his home. "Jeffery's already here. As is a certain 'young' lady, Felix. As it turns out, she is quite a bit older than I am! Goodness, Thomas." Eugene pointed at an unfired clay jug Harris held in the crook of his arm. "What on earth do you have there?"

"Nothing on Earth, actually. It's for later."

Eugene laughed. "Very well. Keep your secrets, but do go find yourselves a seat. Can I pour you something?"

"Yes," they said in unison.

Eugene set upon his decanters while Felix and Harris moved to the table. Jeffery and Jacqueline stood up to greet them with hugs and kisses. Then they all settled into chairs, with Harris sitting down to hold hands next to Jeffery, and Felix sitting dangerously close to Jacqueline.

The door chimed again. Eugene hastily set Felix's and Harris's drinks down in front of them and jogged to the door. He opened it, revealing a blond woman, someone in a sweater with the hood pulled tight, wearing a pair of sunglasses and a fake plastic nose, and an unsettlingly lifelike female android.

"Good evening, Captain Ridgeway. Come in, come in."

The trio of guests toddled into the entryway. "Allison will be fine, Professor." She handed a stack of thick packages wrapped in brown paper over to Eugene. "Filet mignon, cut fresh this morning. Compliments of my chief engineer's family."

"Real meat? I'm flattered!" He looked at the short figure in the hoodie. "And hello to you, Ambassador D'armic."

"Good evening, Graham Administrator. Thank you for inviting me."

"No, thank *you* for risking your neck for a bunch of aliens."

"I stood on the side of truth, nothing more."

"That is a rarer, nobler thing than you give yourself credit for." Eugene's eyes turned to the android. "Um, hello?"

"Oh, allow me," Allison said. "Professor, I'd like to introduce you to the AEUS *Magellan*."

Eugene extended his hand. "Hello, er, miss. I had pictured you being a trifle bigger somehow, and with fewer limbs."

Magellan shook his hand. "I am quite a bit larger, under normal circumstances."

"How is this possible?"

Allison thrust a thumb at D'armic. "On the way home, our new ambassador here took one of the human analogues we . . . salvaged from Solonis B and rigged it up as an avatar for *Maggie* while she's under refit."

Eugene looked at the android. "So, you aren't really here."

"No. I am in orbit receiving retrofits."

"How remarkable. Well, can I get the three of you anything? Wine? Something stiffer? I'm afraid I don't know what Lividites drink, or starships for that matter."

"I'll have a glass of red wine," Allison said.

"Water will be fine," D'armic said.

"Thirty-weight motor oil," *Magellan* said.

"I, um, don't think we have—"

"I meant it in jest, Administrator Graham."

"Of course you did! Plucky ship you have here, Allison. Let me just run these filets back to my lovely wife. Please make yourselves at home."

Everyone found a place to sit, and the sounds of camaraderie filled the penthouse with good cheer. Eugene reappeared with another round of drinks. "The chef has asked how everyone wants their steak."

The answers were, in order: "Medium well," "I'm terribly sorry, but I'm a vegetarian," "Well done," "Anything that doesn't involve a RepliCaterer," "I am physically incapable of eating," "Medium," and finally, "None for me, thank you, but I would accept a serving of powdered doughnuts and bacon with a side of mayonnaise."

Eugene grabbed a pad off the counter. "Right, then. I'll just jot all that down." The door chimed yet again. "Ah, the last guest. Splendid. Everyone's here. I'll just be a moment."

Those seated at the table looked at one another quizzically.

"Who's left?" Jacqueline asked. "Commander Gruber?"

Allison shook her head. "Marcel is on his way to Ceres. He was offered command of the next ship out of the Skunk Works yards. He wants to supervise her final assembly personally."

"Good for him," *Magellan* said. "Marcel is a fine officer. He deserves the opportunity."

Everyone sat for a moment to mull upon the unique perspective *Magellan* brought to judging Gruber's ship-handling credentials.

"Well, if it's not Gruber, then it can only be—"

"The only starship commander to defeat a Turemok cruiser in

seven centuries!" Maximus and his pristine dress uniform entered the dining room.

Harris snapped to attention so fast, he knocked over his chair.

"Sit down, Thomas," Jeffery said. "This is an informal dinner, despite Tiberius's uniform."

"What?" Maximus picked a bit of lint off his sleeve. "It's informal. I didn't even starch it."

"Don't you have civilian clothes?" Allison asked.

"Sold them as soon as I realized these were more effective on the ladies." Maximus sat down. "So, what's for chow?"

"Fresh, all-organic steak," Eugene said from the entryway. "How would you like yours done, Tiberius?"

"Rare. And when I say *rare*, I mean show it the oven to scare it, then put it on my plate before it stops quivering."

Jacqueline made a face and then took another sip of wine. "I really can't understand how you can eat undercooked meat."

"It's easy. I use my teeth."

Jeffery set his glass back down on the table. "Man, what I would have given to be a fly on the wall when the Assembly's Relief Fleet popped back into real-space, only to see Earth sitting there as mint as Felix's Baryon Ball card collection."

"I told you I sold those before we left," Felix said sourly.

"There was an . . . invigorated discussion among the senior representatives," D'armic said. "The only thing more unbelievable than the fact the *Xecoron* and the Kumer-Vel had failed was the notion that your people bested the Turemok a second time."

Harris smiled. "Third time."

"Indeed." Maximus raised his glass in recognition. "Maybe now they'll think twice before they tangle with Earth again."

Felix shook his head. "Not likely. None of our tricks are going to work a second time. I guarantee right this minute, the Turemok are retrofitting their warships with loads more defensive hyperspace projectors. And now that everyone knows the Unicycle can be used offensively, we may as well rename it the Bull's-Eye."

"Well, then, Mr. Fletcher, we'll just have to work on some better tricks."

"But what happens to the Turemok?" Allison asked. "The Assembly was ready to destroy our world for something they did. There must be some punishment."

D'armic set his water glass down. "It seems unlikely that anything will happen through official channels. The investigation into Culpus-Alam and the other planets has stalled, as most of the admissible evidence, as well as most of the witnesses, are gone. And after the failed attack here, I suspect the Assembly would prefer the entire episode fade from public scrutiny as fast as possible."

"So they're just going to get away with geocide."

"We don't know who 'they' are. It is entirely possible that the organizers are already dead. But while nothing will happen officially, the Assembly will view the Turemok with a very critical eye. Coupled with the loss of confidence the public is already displaying in light of their repeated defeats, the Turemok have been savagely weakened. There is already talk of breaking up their monopoly on the military and police forces."

Maximus slapped a hand on the table. "I'll drink to that, provided we have anything to drink around here. Scotch?"

Harris heaved his masonry jug up and let it land heavily on the table. "I think I can beat scotch, Captain."

"What's in there?"

"The last jug of Pirikura fermented berry juice in the universe."

Allison gasped. "How did you get that?"

"Their chief gave it to me as a reward for bravery. He said it should only be drunk with people I trust. You all qualify, and this seems like as good a time as any."

Maximus beamed. "What an excellent idea. Do you drink, D'armic?"

"I'm not sure."

"Perfect! Professor, seven shot glasses, if you please."

"Am I included in that count?" Eugene shouted from the kitchen.

"I didn't want to speak for you."

"Why not?" Felix asked. "You spoke for the rest of us."

"You'll be fine. Miss Dorsett will look after you."

Harris picked up a fork and started working at the cork-and-tar stopper in the neck of the jug. It gave way with a pop just as Eugene set a tray of shot glasses on the table in front of him. Careful not to spill the priceless liquid, Harris filled each to the brim. The drink was menacingly clear, with just a tinge of blue.

Everyone took a glass, some gave it an exploratory sniff.

Maximus raised his drink above his head. "I would like to offer a toast, to the people who didn't make it back to share our victory. To Tillman, Lyska, Simmons, and the lost tribes of Solonis B. Godspeed."

"Godspeed," everyone repeated. They drank the toast as one.

Now, there are drinks for tourists, and then there are drinks for professionals. Pirikura fermented berry juice was the undisputed champion of the latter. It had no net taste, which was not the same as having no actual taste. In reality, it tasted like JP-5 cut with cranberry juice and the glue used on envelope flaps. However, it was so strong that in the time it took a signal to get from the tongue to the brain, the taste buds were already too drunk to remember what they were saying. It might have been the 106 percent alcohol content, or it might have been the hallucinogenic mushrooms used to filter the mash. No one knew, because most instruments used to study such things dissolved upon coming in contact with it. Whatever the reason, it was so strong that if one drank too much, which varied between zero and three shots, depending on weight, it had the potential to cause retroactive birth defects in one's teenaged children.

They couldn't finish the jug between the eight of them.

As the evening wore on, Eugene's guests found themselves laughing, eating, retelling war stories, sneaking away to smooch, and breaking the occasional decorative vase. It was a good party.

So good, that much to Allison's surprise, she caught a glimpse of the Assembly's first ambassador to Earth in a most unusual state. He was smiling.

"You seem to be enjoying yourself, D'armic."

"I am indeed."

"That's wonderful. Did you take something for it?"

"No." D'armic's smile grew until it engulfed his entire face. "I did not."

ACKNOWLEDGMENTS

No man is an island except Tom Hanks in *Castaway*, and every book is written by committee. I'd like to take a moment to thank the people who assembled to make this particular one occur.

Chronologically, I'd like to thank myself from 2009, for being so mad at the ending of *Hitchhiker's Guide to the Galaxy* that in a fit of rage I sat down to write my own damned Book Six, somehow ended up with this hot mess instead, and accidentally launched a writing career. If that poor, ignorant bastard had even an inkling of what would happen to him over the next few years, he'd probably have shot himself.

I'd like to thank my beta readers who gave me invaluable insight into how much of a lazy hack and insensitive fuckboi I was being in earlier drafts of this book, including Michael Todd Gallowglas, Marissa C. Pelot, and Andrea Guzzetta, who are all marvelously talented storytellers and jesters in their own rights.

The woman who would become my wife, who believed in this book even before she totally signed off on me. Love you, honey.

My shark of an agent, Russell Galen, single-handedly forced this book into print through a yearlong act of sheer will. Without his enthusiasm for a quirky little book, in an impossible subgenre, by an author still learning to tie his own shoes in the industry, *Gate Crashers* would still be in my trunk, and the next two books of The

Breach would still be locked away in the back of my mind, eating away at their surroundings like carpenter ants.

To my editor, Christopher Morgan, who was the sucker to actually listen to Russ about this ridiculous sci-fi comedy book, who risked his reputation and budding career to spend his company's money to buy it (and thereby bought me a very nice new motorcycle), who spent long weeks pruning and shaping the raw manuscript into something we could both be proud of, who badgered me into accepting a different and better title from the original I'd used for years, who is reading these acknowledgments at this very moment, no credit is due.

Finally, and most importantly, I want to thank everyone who took a chance on an unknown author a few years ago, whether online, in a bookstore, or staring at me over a table at a convention. Without your faith, I wouldn't have been able to sell this book, or those that follow. I owe you the career and life of my dreams. And for anyone just joining in, you're what's going to take everything to the next level and allow these stories to keep being told well into the future, and keep me out of another office job, which is in the best interest of all mankind.